TOO
LONG
GONE

DAVE SIVERS

ISBN: 978-1-9997397-1-3

DAVE SIVERS

Dave Sivers grew up in West London and left school aged sixteen to embark on a civil service career that took him to exotic places including Rhode Island, USA, Cyprus, Brussels, Northern Norway and Sutton Coldfield. Along the way, he moonlighted variously as a nightclub bouncer, bookie's clerk and freelance writer. He also picked up a first-class honours degree from the Open University.

Writing has always been his passion and, since giving up his day job, he has launched a second career as a novelist. He is the author of the popular Archer and Baines series of crime novels set in Aylesbury Vale. His other writing includes the Lowmar Dashiel crime fantasy novels, short fiction (published and prize winning), articles and columns in magazines and newspapers, and material for the amateur stage.

Dave has appeared at numerous literary events and is a regular speaker at libraries, WIs and other groups. He is a founder of the BeaconLit literary festival, a member of the Crime Writers Association and a past Chairman of Chiltern Writers.

Dave lives in Buckinghamshire, England, with his wife, Chris.

www.davesivers.co.uk
Twitter: @DaveSivers

For Alan
1953-2002

Still miss you, mate.

1

Warren Carter jabbed furiously at the button that was meant to be calling the lift for him and was, so far, steadfastly refusing to cooperate. The button should have been lit up with a reassuring blue glow, the display above the stainless steel door giving some indication of which floor the lift was currently sat on. But there were no lights anywhere.

"Bloody thing!"

It was the third time this month it had been out of order. Warren knew he could do the stairs to his third-floor flat, but he was a big man, hardly at the peak of his fitness and, frankly, pissed.

A Saturday afternoon down the pub with his mates, watching live sport on the big screen and downing pints had left him uncoordinated, fuddled and dying for a pee. He should have known better. Before things went wrong, before the divorce, he and Gail would have found better things to do at the weekend. But she'd fallen out of love with him, or so she'd said, and his four-room box in this tired so-called (by the letting agents) apartment block was all he could afford after his now ex-wife and the lawyers had taken their share.

He knew it could be much worse. It was in Spencer Street, in an okay part at the north end of Aylesbury, and most of the neighbours seemed nice enough. Even some young professionals. But the damned lift and the lights on the stairs and landings kept failing – pretty appalling in a building not much more than a decade old. Plus he was lonely and too often at a loose end. Too easy for the lads to rope him into their second-Saturday-of-the-month binge afternoon.

Sighing, he shoved his way through the door into the stairwell and surveyed the climb like a mountaineer about to embark on some epic ascent. Well, the prospect felt pretty epic to him, but, unless he grew wings, there was nothing else for it. Once indoors, he could nuke himself a microwave curry and settle down in front of the telly with some strong black coffee.

By the time the first two flights of stairs were behind him, his breathing was already laboured. With leaden feet, he managed the last thirteen steps and then wove his way along the corridor to his front door: number thirty-five, third on the left. He rummaged in his pocket for his key, half fumbled it out, lost his grip, found it again, only to drop it on the floor.

"For Christ's sake!" He bent down, snatched them up, and straightened too soon. The world spun. Warren wobbled until he felt stable enough, then he threaded the key into the keyhole at the fourth attempt and swayed before crossing the threshold.

What the fuck was that smell? He knew he wasn't the world's best when it came to chucking out the rubbish, but surely nothing could have gone off so badly since he went out? Christ, it smelt like rotten eggs.

Even with his senses so drink-impaired, he worked out pretty quickly that it was coming from the kitchen. Something was ticking away at the back of his brain: it was a smell he recognised.

The kitchen was on the darkest side of the building, and the light was fading in there. He wouldn't be able to see a thing. His hand went to the light switch.

Even as he flicked it, Warren realised what that smell was.

"No!" he gasped, as if he could somehow take the action back.

And then the explosion swept him away.

2

Showered, shampooed and changed into fresh clothes, Detective Constable Joanne 'Joan' Collins breezed out of the front entrance of her Aylesbury apartment block, a great evening in prospect. The sky was overcast, there was a hint of drizzle in the air, and what warmth this March day had held was giving way to the cool of the evening. None of this could dampen her mood. She had to admit that, since she'd been seeing Charlie, she'd been aware of a decided spring in her step and a smile never far from her face. And it had been noticed. Her colleague and friend, DC Jason Bell, the only person she'd even told that she was finally dating again, had teased her more than once, asking her who she was, and what she'd done with the real Joan Collins.

Not that Collins had entirely changed, she acknowledged, as she walked across the small car park to her Ford Fiesta. Her first floor apartment in Whitehead Way was less than a mile's walk from Aylesbury Police Station. Even though she hadn't drawn the short straw for weekend duty, and despite there not being too much on at the moment, it was always too tempting for the conscientious Collins to drop in on a Saturday to get her paperwork up to date. At least she'd walked out mid-afternoon without a twinge of conscience.

Yes, Collins thought as she started her car, tonight was going to be perfect: pick up Charlie, see a film, a bite to eat, then back to Charlie's flat. Collins would be staying over, and the thought gave her goosebumps. She switched on the sound system and Beyoncé featuring Jay-Z: 'Crazy in Love' flowed from the speakers, as she pulled out into the Aylesbury traffic. It suited her mood.

Driving the short distance across town, headed north towards Spencer Street and Charlie's home, she couldn't help playing over in her mind their first meeting: they'd literally bumped into one another on their way out of the town's court building, where Charlie had been representing a client and Collins giving evidence in another case. Both had been checking their phones, neither watching where they were going.

Charlie had come off worse, bundles of papers flying. Collins had helped pick them up, both of them apologising. Eyes had met, hands had touched, and Collins was still convinced she'd felt the sort of jolt that was only supposed to happen in fiction.

"I'm on a break," Charlie had said. "I don't suppose you fancy a coffee?"

By the time Collins had returned to the station, they'd arranged their first date. That had been a month ago and, right from the start, nothing had ever felt so right to Collins.

Crossing the busy heart of the town, she was jolted out of the memory by a loud *boom!*, like a giant trapdoor being slammed. Her first thought was that it must be some kind of explosion; her second, that there had been a terrorist attack. But where?

As if in answer, a column of smoke began rising into the sky, dead ahead. Collins cut the music off, calling it in on the hands-free as she coaxed more speed from the Fiesta, anxious to find out what had happened. To see if she could help.

"No idea," she said as she turned right onto Coldharbour Way, "but it was definitely an explosion. Get emergency services on standby and I'll call again when I know exactly where it was."

But now her scalp was already tingling, a thought, heavy with dread, insinuating itself into her mind.

"No," she whispered, *"please, God, no."*

Yet the closer she came to the dark smoke, already casting a dark cloud over this corner of Buckinghamshire's county town, the more certain she was that something terrible had happened in Spencer Street. Moments later, she was drawing up across the road from Charlie's block, her worst fears realised.

The road was a mix of styles and ages of property. A row of older buildings, including one of the few remaining independent petrol stations in the area, had been demolished a decade or so ago, as Collins recalled. Spencer Court had replaced them, a four-storey block - nothing swanky, but decent enough modern flats for rent. Now half the third floor was gone, as though a huge hand had simply ripped it away, leaving a gap on the right-hand-side, belching smoke and flames. The smoke parted like a curtain for a moment to reveal part of one of the top floor flats, above the space where the seat of the explosion must have been, still there and jutting out precariously, nothing supporting it. Much of the lower part of that side of the building had collapsed, dust rising from a pile of rubble.

People were already emerging from the building's entrance: first the panickers, running; then the shocked, shambling; some were visibly dusty.

The pavement was strewn with glittering glass, bricks and other debris. A man sat on the kerb, blood running down his face from a head wound. He seemed to be the only passer-by to have been hurt. A miracle, of sorts. Others stood gaping, stunned.

Her gaze returned to the collapsed side of the building. Collins knew Charlie's flat was on that side, on the second floor. All her instincts shrieked at her to run inside, to get up there. Only her professional training held her back, the knowledge that, until the emergency services arrived, she was the only person on the scene with any authority.

And now some of the emerging residents were turning to look at the wreckage. Bystanders were starting to move forward. Guessing their intent, Collins pulled out her warrant card and moved to meet them.

"Police," she said. "You have to keep back. It's dangerous."

"But there are people in there," protested a man with a shaven head and heavily tattooed neck. "We need to help them."

"Fire and ambulance are on their way," she said. "You need to let them do their job. Some more could come down. A bunch of people charging in there could even help bring it down. If people can get out, they'll make their own way. If they can't, we don't want to be part of the problem."

There was a murmuring amongst the people surrounding her, and it didn't sound like assent.

"But there's fire," Tattoos persisted.

"I know. All the more reason for no heroics." *Charlie!*

There were more grumblings from some of the would-be rescuers. Collins locked eyes with the tattooed man. "Something you guys *can* do is see if any of these people need help. Get them as far away from the building as you can. If there's another explosion, all sorts could come flying this way." She looked at the man, still sitting on the pavement, blood still streaming down his face. "And does anyone here have medical training?"

One woman, in her fifties, raised a hand. "I'm a nurse."

"What's your name?"

"Lynne."

"Lynne, can you see how that injured guy is? A couple of people go with her? Ideally he should be moved to safety." Now the walking wounded were coming out of the building, some assisted, some not. A couple were hobbling. Here and there, she saw blood. "You need to check these people too. Just until the ambulances arrive."

Even as she spoke, she could hear the first distant sirens. She'd been scanning every emerging face, desperate to see Charlie's, but there was no sign. She realised she didn't know how many flats there were in the block. Four to a floor? Five? She started calculating how many people might have been in the flats when the explosion happened, then stopped. It was Saturday night. Anybody's guess. People could be out, away, who knew what?

Smoke drifted across the road, getting in her eyes and irritating them. The would-be helpers were already moving amongst the survivors. The nurse, Lynne, was crouched down, talking to the injured man. Collins realised she should have issued instructions for everyone to be assembled across the road, together, so they could be asked what they knew about who might still be inside.

Like Charlie.

"Joan?" A voice beside her. She turned to see the face she'd been praying to see.

"Oh, Christ, Charlie, I thought you were still in there."

Charlie held up a Tesco bag. There was a Metro, five minutes' walk away.

"Sorry. I nipped out for wine, and there was a queue."

For a moment, Collins' professionalism went out the window as she threw her arms around this woman who'd made everything make sense to her, reveling in the feel of her, the smell of her hair, the scent of her perfume. She held her at arm's length, drinking in the face she was falling in love with, china blue eyes and fine features, framed by short blonde hair.

Collins had only finally admitted her sexuality to herself when she'd met Charlie. Even Jason Bell had no idea she was seeing a woman. But right now, she didn't care who saw.

"I thought I was going to have to go all Lara Croft and go in there looking for you."

Charlie gestured to the building. "What... what happened?"

"I don't know yet." *Stupid.* "Well, some sort of explosion, obviously."

Before Collins could say more, a gasp went up from a section of the little crowd of survivors and helpers, whose own common sense had placed them exactly where she would have directed them. She followed their collective gaze to the top floor flat, the one suspended above the hole in the side of the building, The flat was now ablaze and her stomach flipped as she registered that a window had been opened and a figure was leaning out. A man, bearded. She thought he was shouting something, but the roar of flames, together with the wail of approaching sirens, drowned him out.

Collins sprinted as close to the building as she dared, cupped her mouth. "Stay there! Help's on its way." She bellowed as loudly as she could, knowing he could no more hear her than she could hear him.

But would that help arrive in time? The flat, which Collins would have sworn wasn't even on fire when she arrived – surely only a matter of minutes ago – was fast becoming an inferno. She burned with frustration, knowing there was nothing she could do for the man. He started climbing onto the window ledge.

"No!" she bawled. "Stay there, if you can!"

For an instant, she thought he looked back inside. Maybe he'd heard after all? Then a tongue of flame lapped around him and he was falling, arms windmilling, as if he could somehow defy the pull of gravity. Charlie buried her face in Collins' shoulder.

Collins didn't hear the thud as his body impacted on the pavement. She was deafened by the sirens, as the first fire engine finally arrived.

3

Four days later.

Aylesbury Vale was never entirely crime-free but, up to the weekend, it had been ticking over nicely, with no big cases placing demands on the CID team. Detective Sergeant Dan Baines imagined that coppers from the metropolises thought it was always that way; that places like the Vale, with its mixture of market towns and rural villages, offered a comparatively cushy number. Certainly his boss, Detective Inspector Lizzie Archer, had imagined so when she'd transferred in from the Met a few years ago. A notion she'd soon amended. There was often plenty of crime to go around, and even some nasty bastards of the organised crime variety had moved in a while back.

In any event, the lull was over and Aylesbury nick had been back to its usual hive of activity since Saturday night, when an explosion had wrecked a block of flats in Spencer Street. Four days ago now. In all probability, the disaster had been a tragic accident – the experts were already saying it was most likely that the cause had been a gas explosion - but the site had to be treated as a crime scene until that was confirmed.

The business of establishing what had happened was painstakingly slow. Whilst experts, supported by Crime Scene Investigators, sifted through the wreckage, trying to piece together what exactly had occurred, everyone at the nick with any time to spare was talking to anyone and everyone who might have seen or heard anything.

Twenty flats, thirty occupants. About a dozen passers by, and a few dozen more who had hurried to Spencer Street when they'd heard the explosion – either to see if they could help, or just to rubberneck and take mobile phone footage. At least two films of one poor devil by the name of Lee Wren, plunging 40 feet from the top floor, had already gone viral on the Internet.

Baines detested the ghoulishness of it but, at the same time, such footage could often be useful in piecing together what had happened. So far the response to an appeal for people to come forward had been good, if sluggish in some cases. People didn't think, or didn't realise, they might have valuable evidence, or they didn't see the news and missed the appeal. Today was Wednesday, and people were still trickling in.

Baines had just thanked a witness for coming forward, and he yawned as he watched a uniformed officer escort her off the premises. Thirsty, he headed for the small kitchenette that served this part of the building to grab a coffee.

Saturday's incident could have been so much worse, Baines reflected as he waited for hot water to boil. Everyone who had been in the flats when the explosion happened had been accounted for, one way or another, and there had only been three confirmed fatalities so far. That could still change. Five other victims were in Stoke Mandeville Hospital in critical condition, including Lee Wren. It was a miracle he had survived at all.

One of Baines's DCs, Joan Collins, had been first to the scene and had witnessed Wren's fall – or leap, it was impossible to say which, no matter how many times you watched the footage. By sheer good fortune, she had been visiting a friend in the block and had called the explosion in, and the prompt arrival of the emergency services was partly down to her. Firefighters had got to grips with the blaze before it had got completely out of hand, and paramedics had treated the injured, including the unfortunate Lee Wren. As it was, he was touch and go. A slower response, and the guy might already be amongst the fatalities.

The Crime Scene Manager in charge, Phil Gordon, had opined that one of the dead, Warren Carter, had most likely been at the centre of the explosion, at flat 3C. He'd been swiftly identified by his dental records, as what was left of him wasn't recognisable. His neighbour, an elderly lady called Irene Allen, had been in less of a mess and had simply had the misfortune to have been near to the adjoining wall to Carter's kitchen, where the dead man had been found. The blast had taken out the wall, and Irene with it. The third fatality was twenty-year-old Ollie

Hall in the flat below, crushed when 3C's floor had collapsed on top of him.

Spencer Court would be uninhabitable for the foreseeable future, and it was far too soon to tell if the building was in any way salvageable. Baines doubted that it would be. Meanwhile, the surviving inhabitants who were not in hospital were staying with family or friends, or in hastily arranged emergency accommodation. The local community had rallied round admirably to provide clothes, food and other essentials to people suddenly made homeless in just the clothing they stood up in. Collins' friend was thankfully okay and staying with Collins for the time being.

Coffee brewed, Baines returned to the large open office that housed DI Archer and her team. He stood in the doorway for a moment, watching his colleagues hammering away on keyboards, talking animatedly on phones, chattering to each other. DC Jason Bell stood by DC Will Tyler's desk, jabbing his finger at something in a document he was holding. Tyler was nodding, scribbling notes. It was getting on for lunchtime. Soon, someone would volunteer to do the sandwich run and start taking orders.

The buzz in the air was at odds with the slightly musty smell that pervaded the office these days. The building was feeling a little tired to Baines, and the furniture was overdue an upgrade. Resources had been tight for years, and there was never enough for all the division's crime fighting needs, let alone improving the working environment. But no one ever complained.

He felt a surge of pride in his team.

"No work of your own, Detective Sergeant?" said a voice behind him, almost making him jump and spill his coffee.

He turned to face DI Archer.

"Making do with watching everyone else's work?" she added. But her blue eyes were twinkling.

"Something like that." Feeling unaccountably mawkish, he moved into the office, heading for his desk. Archer followed him. He sat. She perched.

"How was your witness?" she asked.

"Same as the rest, really. Heard the explosion, dashed round the corner, saw the side of the block sliding down, Took a few pictures on her mobile and stood gawking and snapping for a while. She went away for a couple of days on Sunday morning, but spotted the appeal for witnesses on social media, so when she got back she thought she might as well come in. Some of the photos might be vaguely useful, but I doubt it."

She nodded. "It's really a waste of a DS's time, you doing these interviews, but we need to get through them…"

"Sure," he said. "I get it."

In all likelihood, what they were doing was largely going through the motions anyway. Phil Gordon's money was not only on a gas explosion, but specifically on either a leaky pipe or some fool forgetting to turn a gas tap off – in all probability the late Warren Carter. Quite a picture was already emerging of a sad man who was half-drunk half of the time; several sheets to the wind on a Saturday evening, after a session in the pub watching football with his buddies.

If Gordon was right, then not much detecting would be required. But meanwhile, Baines would rather be interviewing witnesses than doing dreary paperwork.

"Okay, then," Archer said, apparently satisfied. "Joan will write it up?" Collins had accompanied Baines for the interview.

"Of course. She'll make a better job of it than me."

"How is she?" Archer's eyes softened with concern. "Saturday must have been traumatic, even for a copper. I know she keeps saying she's fine…"

"I think she really is. Made of tough stuff, our Joan."

"And has she said how her friend is? The one who lived in the block?"

"Okay, I think. You know Joan has taken her in?"

Archer smiled as she nodded, her mouth lopsided, the result of nerve damage she'd suffered in a bottle attack a year or so before her transfer from the Met. Her makeup, and the carefully cut blonde hair she tried hard to keep in place, concealed a crescent-shaped scar that Baines knew she remained self-conscious about.

"At least we know Joan's got a friend," Archer remarked. "Her social life has been a bit of a closed book to me."

"Me too. And I've known her since she was in uniform."

He felt suddenly bad about this. Collins was a private person. She had a great sense of humour, but she was very much the person most likely to be first in the office and one of the last to leave. Did she have a boyfriend? A gang of mates? He was supposed to be her line manager, yet in many ways he hardly knew her.

"I'll leave you to it, then," Archer said, making no move to do so. "By the way, how are the arrangements for the big day going? I'm still honing my speech to perfection."

Baines was getting married in less than a fortnight, to Karen Smart, the woman who shared his life and his home in the village of Little Aston – and the identical twin sister of Baines's first wife, Louise, who had died well over a decade ago.

After Karen, Archer was the person Baines trusted the most in the world, so he had decided to go for broke on strangeness by asking her to be his best man.

Hence the reference to a speech.

He made a show of grimacing. "I suppose you'll be putting plenty of embarrassing stuff in it?"

Archer winked. "Was Pontius a pilot?"

Before she could bait him further, her phone rang. She moved away as she answered it, and he started checking his email. A few minutes later, she was back.

"That was Phil Gordon, calling from Spencer Court."

"Oh? Any wiser on what happened?"

"He didn't say. But there's another body. You're driving."

He arched an eyebrow. "Really? It doesn't take a detective to work out what killed them."

"Actually," she said, "it does. Well, that and the pathologist."

"I don't understand."

She was already walking towards the door. "Trouble with *this* body is that it was already dead before the explosion."

"How do we know?"

"I'll fill you in on the way."

4

Scaffolding had been erected at Spencer Court, and emergency crews had made tremendous, if painstaking, progress with clearing the site, which was still cordoned off. A few onlookers still hung around, and the pile of flowers and other tributes beyond the cordon continued to grow. The sky was a grey dishrag, pregnant with rain, as if it was barely containing its tears for what had happened here.

Baines parked his Ford Mondeo, and he and Archer made for the large crime scene tent that had been hastily erected at the base of the damaged building. One of the uniformed officers responsible for controlling access lifted the blue and white tape as they approached.

Inside, the pathologist, Dr Barbara Carlisle, stood thigh-deep in a hole in the ground in what was just about recognisable as what was left of someone's ground floor flat. Phil Gordon stood outside the hole, hands in the pockets of his crime scene suit.

"Blimey, Phil," Archer commented, "all you need is a shovel to lean on."

"I love work," the Geordie said with a grin. "Me, I could watch it all day long."

"So glad you two are enjoying yourselves," Carlisle said, straightening up.

"Any idea what we've got here, Barbara?" Baines asked. Archer had told him what she knew so far, but that wasn't a great deal.

"Give a girl a chance," the pathologist said. "The short answer to your question, Dan, is 'a skeleton', but I'm guessing you'd like more. That will take a lot more time. But there's one thing I can tell you right away."

"Go on."

"As you'll see when you get closer, this poor devil was buried in concrete."

"Between the floor of this ground-floor flat and the foundations," Gordon added. "The floor broke up when the explosion happened and half this side of the block fell down. It'll take a while to get all the remains out, but we've cleared most of the skull, and half the torso, as you can see."

Baines moved closer to the hole, giving himself a better view of the macabre sight. The skull, minus a few teeth, seemed even in death to be howling with pain; this, together with rib bones, some visibly fractured, seemed to be emerging from the concrete as if the skeleton was making a bid for freedom. Four white, skeletal fingers protruded from the concrete, a foot or so from the skull. They looked as if they were stretching yearningly towards something out of reach.

"And what are the bones telling you, Barbara?" Archer wanted to know.

"I've seen enough already to conclude that the victim had been the victim of a sustained and savage physical attack, probably a fatal one. The skull's fractured and indented in several places."

"No chance the damage was sustained when the building fell down?" Baines wondered.

"No. It's not recent damage." Carlisle looked grimly from Archer to Baines. "You know I don't do speculation. But my initial reading of what I'm seeing is that this person was beaten or kicked to death. Probably both."

The detectives digested this.

"Gender?" Baines asked.

Carlisle shook her head. "You know I can't answer that yet. I need to see the pelvis."

Baines understood. The female pelvis is adapted for child-bearing and is distinctively different from its male counterpart.

"No ID, I suppose?" Archer asked

"Not so far," Gordon replied. "No clothes, wallet or jewellery. I'm not holding my breath, either. Even so, I'm betting it's been here as long as the building."

"Tell us again how you came across it," Archer prompted.

"Well, the crews were removing the rubble and they were down to floor level here. The collapse had ruptured the concrete floor, down to the foundation." He fiddled with his camera, moved towards the detectives, and showed them a photograph on the rear screen. "This is what they saw first."

Only the whitened fingers were visible.

"We had some luck," Gordon admitted. "The concrete the body was encased in was pretty crumbly. Whoever put our victim here either didn't really know what they were doing or, more likely, they mixed it in haste. But it'll make it easier to clear it without making a complete mess of the scene."

Baines dredged around in his memory. "I vaguely recall these flats being built. They're where the old petrol station was. Ten years ago, give or take."

"Eleven," Gordon corrected.

"So we're looking for someone who went missing around then." Archer nodded.

"That's my thinking." Gordon stroked his chin. "Or, I suppose, at some point in the past decade someone could have taken the floor up and laid a new one."

"Fair point." Archer turned to Carlisle. "DNA?"

"The lime in the concrete has stripped the body down to bare bones, as you can see. In theory, the bones could hold DNA for years, but we don't know what condition they'll be in. If they're badly deteriorated, we might only get mitochondrial DNA."

"That would give us the mother line?"

"Yes. But that's of limited use."

"Because?" Baines pressed.

"Because," Gordon said, "it can't be loaded to the national database, or the missing persons database, for a random search."

"The missing persons database does do one-off searches, though," Archer said. "Right?"

"True. But then we'd most likely get quite a number of inconclusive hits."

"Still, something to work with," Baines mused.

"Age?" Archer asked, turning back to Carlisle. "Race?"

"I'd really need to work with a forensic anthropologist to get a decent picture," Carlisle said. "Someone a bit more specialised than me. And I certainly can't make much of a judgement here. Once I get these bones up on my slab, I might be able to form some initial impressions. Adult, though, I'd say. Look at the teeth."

Baines leaned over, careful not to overbalance. "What are we looking at?"

"It looks like all the adult teeth have come through. What I can say with reasonable confidence is we're looking at someone who was probably over twenty one at the point of death. Beyond that, we need an expert."

"An anthropologist, you say?"

"Yep. It's a specialised area of forensic science, far better than I am at analysing human remains with a view to establishing identity and investigating suspicious deaths. They're often called upon to help identify victims of major disasters, or in mass graves. It all gets increasingly complex as the body passes through different phases of decomposition."

"I don't suppose you know one?" Archer asked.

Carlisle smiled. "I do, as it happens. I'll see if I can persuade her to come down."

"Down?"

"From Liverpool."

"Time frame?"

Carlisle arched an eyebrow. "I've no idea how busy she is, or whether she's even in the country. If she is, I'll try to twist her arm."

"Okay." Archer looked unhappy. "Meanwhile, if you can do all you can to start narrowing down the victim's profile, we'll check out exactly when this building went up and who's been on the missing persons database since then."

"We need to talk to the site owners at the time and the builders, too," Baines said.

"Yes. Someone put this poor sod in here, and you don't just slip a corpse into the wet foundations while everyone's on their tea break. We need to know who was working on the site and who had access, and we'll need to talk to every one of them."

"Good luck with that, after all this time." Gordon commented. "You know what the building trade's like…"

"I don't care what it takes," Archer said. "This was someone's child. Maybe someone's spouse or lover. Maybe a parent. Somebody's been missing them for far too long. So we're going to find out who he or she is. We're going to find out who did this. They think they got away with it. We're going to prove them wrong."

5

Back at the office, Archer had hastily called her team together. Now she moved to the front of the briefing room, standing in front of an almost bare board. All that currently occupied the space were photographs of the collapsed Spencer Court block, and of the victim's skeleton, half exposed, half encased in concrete; and a floor plan of the block..

Outside, the threatened rain had materialised, and Archer spared a thought for the team working at the site, whose job had just been made that little bit harder. But this room seemed immune to the vagaries of the weather. It was always airless and stuffy, all year round.

She scanned the faces of her core team - Baines, Collins, Bell, Tyler - and several other officers likely to have roles to play. Her boss, Detective Chief Inspector Paul Gillingham, sat at the back, as was his way, leaving her to run the show, but keeping himself up to speed. DI Steve Ashby sat beside him.

Ashby didn't have a team of his own, but claimed to have a wide network of sources and contacts that he worked. For years, Archer had been sceptical about how much actual work he actually did, but she had to admit he pulled some invaluable rabbits out of the hat and, recently, he'd been proactive in using his ears and eyes on the streets to support colleagues' investigations. He seemed to drift into briefings when he thought he could contribute.

"Okay," she said, when she had everyone's attention. "Most of you probably know this already but, just so everyone's on the same page, a skeleton has been discovered underneath one of the ground floor flats at Spencer Court. Flat 1C to be precise."

She briefly ran through what little was known so far, using the images on the board to illustrate her points.

"So all we know right now," she said, "is that the body has, in all probability, been there undisturbed for over a decade. Even that isn't certain yet, but we can take it as read that our mythical 'golden hours' immediately after the crime have long since passed. We already know there's unlikely to be any useful evidence on the body, and any other worthwhile information may also be harder to come by. That might make it tempting to assume that this investigation is less urgent than it would be for a more recent murder."

There were a few nods and murmurs. With a recent crime, positive action in the period immediately after the crime was reported could maximise the chance of securing material that would be admissible in court. Memories fresh in witnesses' minds, documents and CCTV recordings were more likely to be readily available. The greater the passage of time, the more material could be lost to the investigation.

"But we have one advantage over the killer, or killers," Archer continued. "We know the body's been discovered. They don't. For years they must have been imagining they were safe. Have they been sleeping soundly? Or having nightmares? Have they been fearing this day will come? What will they do when the news breaks?"

"Maybe they'll turn themselves in," Ashby suggested, deadpan.

"That'd be nice, Steve." Archer allowed herself a grim smile. "If they do, job done. Meanwhile, we can't keep it to ourselves for long, but let's use the next few hours to know all we can know about this case."

"First step's to ID the victim, surely?" Gillingham spoke up from the back. "Once we know that, people who knew the person could be questioned. Maybe a picture could be built up of their last movements."

Archer nodded. "I agree, Sir, but the last time I spoke to Phil Gordon, they were still getting the remains out of the concrete. It's a painstaking job and we want Dr Carlisle's forensic anthropologist to have as much as possible to go on. Once we have an idea of gender, height, age, anything distinguishing about the bones, we can start looking through missing persons files from the time. I've asked Will to make a start on pulling those together."

"I've already put in a request," Tyler said.

"Good, thanks, Will. Meanwhile," Archer continued, "we might be missing a lot of detail – exactly how our victim died, where they died, why they might have been killed. But we do know where they ended up. We need to know who built the block, and they need a visit. I doubt anyone just casually wandered onto the site while work was in progress and tossed a body into that concrete. It must have been done out of hours, and in a way that wouldn't elicit suspicion. We need to know who had out of hours access. Also what the security arrangements were. So, Joan..." She turned her gaze upon Collins. "Can you chase up the company and someone senior who can actually answer some questions? Then set up a meeting with them for DS Baines and myself."

"On it, guv." Collins was already making a note.

Archer turned to Bell. "Jason, can you liaise with Phil Gordon and Dr Carlisle, please? Don't hassle them unduly, but I want to know when they've recovered the remains and when there's likely to be a post mortem."

"Of course." The red-headed Scot seemed to finally be managing his propensity for blushing when attention was on him. Only the slightest pink tinge rose to his cheeks.

"And see if you can find out who's occupied that flat since it was built. We can't rule out the floor having been taken up later and then replaced with the body underneath it."

"I'll check it out," Bell said.

Archer looked around the room. It all felt so inadequate, yet they had to start somewhere. "Any other thoughts?"

"I can ask around," Ashby said. "See if there were any whispers on the streets around the time those flats were built. I mean, a body in foundations? It all sounds a bit gangland, doesn't it?"

"Gangland?" Gillingham scoffed. "I know the Connolly family's got its fingers in a lot of pies these days – not that we can prove a thing – but they're still a fairly new kid on the block. We're talking ten, eleven years ago?"

"You're right, Sir, up to a point," Baines chimed in. "We didn't have the sort of serious organised crime we do now, and it wasn't as sophisticated. But there's always been bad boys in the Vale, and by no means all of them have been above a bit of violence. Someone with a body on their hands knows someone in the building trade..."

"Good way of getting rid of a corpse, too," added Collins. "Bury it and scavengers might dig it up. Weight it and chuck it in the canal or the river, then some fisherman snags it..." She shrugged. "If it hadn't been for that explosion, our body was gone forever."

"And without a body, it can be hard to be certain there's even been a crime," Baines said.

"All good points," Archer said. "Thanks, Steve, that would be great."

Privately, she doubted that Ashby's 'asking around' would yield much, but she wasn't about to turn down help from him. It was only in the past year or so that their working relationship had turned from hostile to somewhere between civil and cordial.

She checked her watch. "Okay, let's reconvene at 7 o'clock and see where we're up to."

6

On her way back to the office, her head full of the case, Archer almost collided with Superintendent Andrea Lambert. She started to apologise, but the other woman waved it away.

"No harm done," Lambert said, "and I'm glad to nearly bump into you. I was planning on giving you a call today."

"Oh?"

The Super always managed to make Archer feel shabby in her presence. Lambert's uniform was as immaculate as ever, as if it had just come out of the dry cleaner's bag. Her buttons gleamed, and even the crown insignia on her shoulders seemed to glint under the fluorescent lighting. Not a light brown hair was out of place.

"Can you spare me a mo?" Lambert asked. "My office? There's some coffee on the go."

The Superintendent's office was as pristine and business-like as its incumbent. Some senior women would soften their domain, perhaps with some plants, some pastel prints. Little feminine touches. Not Andrea Lambert. The wall held only framed certificates and a photograph taken at what must have been her passing out parade. Papers on her desk were neatly stacked. The only clue to the gender of this room's occupant was the electric-blue dress hanging in a polythene bag behind the door.

A coffee maker was gurgling on the bookcase by the window, and Lambert poured Archer a black one with no sugar, remembering exactly how she liked it. It was one of the little touches Archer appreciated about the Divisional Commander. In her first week in the job, Lambert had made a point of holding one to one meetings with each of her senior officers, and Archer had been impressed with how much the new arrival knew about her.

"I've read your file," she'd said simply. "I like to know who I'm working with. It seems you were quite the rising star up until your accident. You might even be sitting in my seat by now."

Archer knew it was true. That broken bottle had ruined more than just her looks. It had shattered her self-esteem and her self-confidence, and she'd also lost a man she'd hoped to share her future with. She'd transferred to the Vale looking for a fresh start, but it had been hard to start with.

"I'm also pleased to hear that you're getting back on track here," Lambert had said. "We can't have enough women in the upper echelons. Women in the force might have come a long way in recent years, but we still have to work twice as hard to get anywhere. So if I can do anything to help you get on, I'll do it. Just as long as you earn it."

Now Lambert handed the mug to Archer and gestured to the guest chair opposite her own seat before pouring her own drink. Archer sat down, cradling the mug, enjoying the aroma.

"So," Lambert began, once she had settled behind her desk, and selected a pen from a pot on her desk, "I hear the Spencer Court blast has unearthed something nasty. DCI Gillingham gave me the headlines earlier, but can you fill me in on the details?"

Archer told her what little was known and what action was being taken to identify the body and try to get a handle on how it had come to rest under a ground floor flat in Aylesbury. The Super listened attentively, only interrupting to ask the occasional question.

"That all sounds good, Lizzie," she said finally. "You're on top of it, by the sound of it. Identifying the victim will be key, assuming that's possible."

"If you can think of anything else we should be doing about that –"

"No. I'm sure Dr Carlisle's bone expert will be worth waiting for." She paused. "You know, we never get a proper chance to chat. Maybe we can get a drink, or a bite to eat after work one evening?"

Archer blinked, taken by surprise.

"Only if you're comfortable with it," Lambert added. "To be honest, there's something I'd like to sound you out on."

Archer found herself hesitating. She didn't want it to get around that she was friendly with the Super outside work, and maybe currying favour. On the other hand, if it was just a drink and a chat...

"That would be good," she said. "Thank you."

"Not tonight," Lambert said. "I've got some boring function to go to. One of the downsides of this job. Hence the dress." She pointed to the back of the door. "How about tomorrow, though? Say about 7?"

Archer didn't suppose that the Spencer Court body would demand that she worked especially late tomorrow.

"Sounds good," she said.

She walked back to the office feeling both good and uneasy at the same time. She still had a slight disquiet about socialising with Aylesbury Vale's top copper, but at the same time she was curious about what Lambert wanted to discuss with her.

Interestingly, when the news had broken last year that Lambert, not yet 40 and reckoned to be a high flyer, was to be the new Divisional Commander, DCI Gillingham had had nothing good to say about her. They had some history, hadn't seen eye to eye, and Gillingham had expected to be forced out in no time. But he was still here, and Archer had often wondered what the bad blood was about. When they'd worked together before, Gillingham had been Lambert's boss. Maybe he was just put out to be working for someone who'd once taken orders from him.

From Archer's viewpoint, keeping on the right side of Lambert was no bad thing. She had no real regrets about forsaking London for the Vale, but she didn't want to remain a DI forever, and she already felt her chances of fulfilling the potential she'd once had were dwindling. She hated brown nosers, and certainly had no intention of becoming one. But Lambert seemed to have an eye on her future and a willingness to encourage her. Archer liked her, and could see why her rise had been meteoric.

The nearest thing she'd ever had to a mentor before had been DCI Nick Gibson, her old boss at the Met. She'd missed that - having someone approachable she could talk to about difficult decisions. It was a role Gillingham had never attempted to play.

So, if someone like Andrea Lambert was prepared to be that person, that was fine by Archer.

She headed back to the office in cheerful mood, but that wasn't to last. She'd barely reached her desk than Will Tyler hurried over.

"Something on my screen you need to see, guv."

She rose from her chair, sighing inwardly, and followed him to his desk, The website of the *Aylesbury Echo*, one of the Vale's local papers, was open on his computer screen, and she found herself staring at an article bearing the by line of Claire King, its chief reporter:

Disturbing Find in Gas Blast Block?

The story underneath was all speculation. It was obvious that either King herself had been sniffing around the site, spotted the crime scene tent, and made some assumptions, or some well-meaning member of the public had done so and decided to tip the *Echo* off. But for all that the article was substance-light, one passage especially made Archer's heart sink:

'We contacted the Aylesbury Police enquiries desk, but they have no comment to make at this time. It is not clear what they are keeping the public in the dark about. Do they have evidence that the explosion was not accidental? Or has the blast uncovered some dark secret from the past? It wouldn't be the first time a cache of ill-gotten gains, or even a dead body, has been concealed in a building, perhaps even buried in the foundations.'

"It's obviously a fishing expedition, guv," Tyler remarked.

"Obviously. But she's close enough to the truth to tip off whoever put that poor guy there in the first place. Will, can you find out who she spoke to here, and bollock them for not letting us know? But the damage is done now." She shook her head in annoyance. "So much for keeping it under wraps."

7

Joan Collins had been as efficient as ever. Within less than twenty minutes of Archer returning to the office, she was checking whether a 4pm meeting with a building firm called Howard and Burns would work for her and Baines.

"Never heard of them," Archer commented

"No, they're not Premier League. One of the larger local firms though. And they built Spencer Court. Managing director's a Mrs Sophie Savage. Her father was the Howard in the partnership, but he died. She's happy to meet with you. They're based in Princes Risborough."

"Tell her we're on our way," Archer said.

On the route of the pre-Roman Upper Icknield Way, Princes Risborough nestled between the Vale of Aylesbury and the western slope of the Chiltern Hills. It had originally been known simply as Risborough, had been a royal manor held by King Harold before the Norman conquest, and had afterwards formed part of William the Conqueror's lands. In due course, Risborough had been gifted by Edward III to his son the Prince of Wales, later known as the Black Prince – and hence became known as Princes Risborough.

These days it was a bustling little town with a pretty high street and an attractive market square, complete with a market house with a bell turret. Its proximity to Chequers, the Prime Minister's country residence, meant that famous faces were often seen to be visiting the town – but it always spoke to Archer of a quintessential Englishness that was comfortable in its own skin, without a trace of smugness.

For a small town, it boasted numerous listed buildings, but the dull, square building housing Howard and Burn's offices - just a stone's throw from the High Street – was not one of them.

Sophie Savage's office was modern and tastefully decorated. The walls were adorned with black and white prints of some of the firm's projects, but she had managed to balance it out with some feminine touches: a hint of peach in the wall colouring, flowers on the meeting table she now sat at with Archer and Baines, and a subtle floral pattern to the sofa in the corner.

Savage herself was probably in her late forties, petite, with dark-brown hair in an elfin cut and sharp brown eyes.

"First of all," Archer said, "thanks for seeing us at such short notice."

"I understand it's about the explosion at Spencer Street." Savage shook her head, her mouth a grim line. "Terrible. You obviously know we built those flats?"

"That's why we're here."

"Of course. But I thought it was a gas leak or something. Our engineers have always been well-qualified. I can't think it's our fault."

"Maybe. Maybe not. Those enquiries are ongoing, but that's not what we're here about."

"Then what..."

Archer raised a palm, forestalling further interruption. "Look, we'd appreciate it if you kept this to yourself for now." She ignored the fact that the *Echo* already had a sniff of the story. "The explosion and subsequent collapse of part of the building tore up part of the concrete floor at ground level. It exposed a dead body in the foundations of flat 1C."

Savage stared at her. "You're joking."

"Hardly. So what do you know about it?"

"Me?" The woman's glanced at Baines, then back at Archer. "But you can't think..."

"One possibility - a probability, in fact - is that the body was put there when the flats were going up. Someone on your firm must know about it."

"That was over ten years ago. Even if - and I say *if* - anyone from here was involved..." She shrugged. "It was a long time ago, and in this trade, the workforce comes and goes. Some would have been from Eastern Europe and some may have long since returned home."

"But you can check out who worked on the project, yes? Your personnel records?"

"We'll do all we can to help, of course. But how can you be sure someone didn't have the floor up later?"

"We can't." Baines spoke up for the first time. "But we'll have a better idea about that when we know whose remains they are. Meanwhile, who'd be best placed to know what went on at that site?"

"Well, the site manager, of course. I can check who that was."

"How quickly?" Archer pressed her.

"Shouldn't be that difficult. Just a sec." Savage rose and stepped out of the office. Archer could hear her in conversation. Then she returned. "My PA's going to pull up the file and get those details."

"Thanks. How long have you been the boss?"

"About three years, since Dad died. I'm his only child."

"Sorry for your loss." The cliché was out before Archer remembered how she hated its hollowness. "So were you involved in the Spencer Street project? Or should we speak to someone else?"

"As I said, it was a long time ago, but I didn't tend to get involved in the actual construction. I was more on the admin side back then. To be honest, I can't remember that much about it."

As if on cue, Savage's PA, whom Archer and Baines had met when they'd arrived, came in with handful of papers. She handed them to her boss.

"Let me know if you need anything else," she said as she headed for the door.

"Thanks, Donna," Savage said.

"That was quick," Archer observed.

"You're lucky. My dad was a bit of a stick in the mud. Accepted technology grudgingly and insisted on paper files right up to his retirement. Damn good filing system, too. I ought to chuck them out and go completely paperless, but I don't quite have the heart."

She flicked through the papers. The detectives waited patiently.

"Okay," she said finally. "So the site manager was Barry Prince. He retired four years ago." She scribbled on a pad, tore the page off, and slid it across the table to Archer.

"Those are all the contact details we have for him. For all we know, he's moved by now."

Archer glanced at it. A Wendover address.

"Pension records?" Archer asked. "If he's no longer there, I mean."

"Yep, I'm sure we could track him down if need be."

"What else have you got there?"

"The pages of the project plan that set out how the site would have been secured. Pretty standard. Eight foot fencing, good lighting, an alarm system that would have alerted an on-call security guard. CCTV. Bottom line is, no one could have easily got in there after the workforce packed up for the day. Take a dead body in and - what? Bury it in concrete? And we don't notice? I can't see it."

"And yet it happened," Baines observed drily. "It rather reinforces the idea that one of your people - someone with out of hours access to the site - was involved in some way."

Her face clouded. "Jesus."

"You must have employed some dodgy customers over the years," Baines suggested. "With the best will in the world, they can't all have been whiter than white."

Savage's eyes flashed. "Let's get this straight, Sergeant."

"Detective Sergeant."

"Whatever. We don't employ too many people with criminal records. That's not to say we'd never give a second chance to someone genuinely trying to go straight, with some decent character references. But one step out of line, and they're gone. Same goes for any employee who forfeits our trust. We think a lot of our reputation."

"So would your personnel records show if anyone, shall we say, let you down, who worked on Spencer Street?" Archer probed.

"Maybe, maybe not. Probably not," Savage amended. "What with data laws and all the litigation around these days, we'd be reluctant to put on record too baldly that we'd fired someone for dishonesty or for losing our trust. Unless we'd pressed charges and they'd been convicted, of course."

"And has that happened?"

"Not in my memory. We'd urge them to resign quietly rather than be sacked or prosecuted. We prefer it that way, to be honest, and I'd imagine the workers would too. Still, I'll check it out, but Barry Prince is your best bet. He'd have known the workforce."

"And he was trustworthy?"

"I'd say so, yes." But was that a hint of a hesitation? If so, was Sophie Savage hiding something, or just being cautious?

Archer suppressed a sigh. Identifying the remains was one hurdle. Finding out who hid a body at Spencer Court could be a much bigger one. Unless they got lucky and the victim's identity pointed to any obvious suspects.

"Meanwhile, I'll need whatever details you do have of who worked on the site."

"I'll see what we can do. We try to keep good personnel records, but they're not perfect. Anyone in the industry who claims theirs are is deluded. If you give me an email address, we'll send you what we have."

Archer drew a card from her wallet and placed it in front of Savage. "If anything else occurs to you, give me a call."

"What did you make of her?" Archer asked Baines on the way back to the car.

He frowned. "Honestly? She seemed pretty straight to me, but whether she'd be entirely open if she felt the firm, or its reputation, were at risk…"

"You think she might cover something up?"

"I think she's got a loyalty to her dad – you could see that in what she said about the paper files. But, chances are, the people at the top knew nothing about the body. This Barry Prince should have had more of a finger on the pulse."

Archer checked her watch. "Fifteen – twenty minutes to Wendover? Shall we see if he's home?"

8

Barry Prince's home was on the Aylesbury Road, a mile or so from World's End garden centre, where Baines happened to know Archer had once bought bedding plants for her pocket handkerchief of a garden. A demanding case had broken immediately, and her neighbour, Dominic Newman, had taken pity on her and offered to plant them up. Archer insisted there was nothing more between her and the man next door than a good friendship, but both Baines and Karen lived in hope that there was more to it than that. They always seemed so comfortable together, and Dominic was clearly good for Archer.

The house was on the right, and Baines had to wait for a gap in the stream of rush hour traffic before he could turn into the drive. The house itself was an unassuming semi, not especially new, but hardly ancient. The front garden suggested that either Barry Prince had been taking a pride in it since his retirement, or it was Mrs Prince – if there was one – who made regular trips to World's End. A Ford Fiesta, four years old, sat in the drive, gleaming. There was just enough room for Baines to tuck his Mondeo in behind it.

"You do the talking," Archer said as they got out. "A chat between two blokes who know all about bricklaying and the like."

"But I don't," Baines protested.

"He doesn't know that. I'll act the dumb blonde and ask stupid but telling questions."

Baines grinned. "I'd like to see that."

The man who answered the door was on the short side, wiry, and with his head shaved, perhaps to mask advancing baldness. He blinked when they showed him their warrant cards and introduced themselves.

"Yeah, I'm Barry Prince," he confirmed. "Guilty as charged. How can I help?"

"Perhaps we could come in?" Baines suggested.

"Of course." He led the way inside and Baines closed the door behind them. The lounge was possibly over-furnished, and Baines recognised many of the items as Ikea or similar. He spotted a framed photograph on a low sideboard. Unmistakably Barry Prince in a hard hat.

"Are you stopping?" Prince asked, gesturing to a blocky grey sofa. "I can get tea. Paula!" he called without waiting for a response. "We've got company!"

"I thought I heard the bell." The voice was followed by footsteps coming down the stairs. A second or two later, a woman with black hair and grey roots showing put her head in.

"These are the police, love," Prince told her.

"You finally caught up with him?" Her eyes danced as she looked from Archer to Baines and back again. "Just a joke."

"Just a few things we thought Mr Prince could help us with," Baines said.

"Could you rustle up some teas and coffees?" Prince suggested.

"We really don't – " Archer began.

"Of course," Paula said brightly. "What can I get you?"

Perhaps sensing this would go more quickly if she just accepted, Archer requested coffee. Baines opted for tea and the woman left them. Barry Prince eased himself into a chair that matched the sofa.

"So," he said, looking Baines in the eye. "Spencer Street?"

"You guessed." It wasn't so surprising.

"I wondered if you'd be wanting to question me. You spoke to Howard and Burns?"

"We did,"

"Well, I do remember that project, and I can tell you straight off, we had good lads on that job, and the gas fitters were our best team, in my opinion."

Defensive? Baines watched his eyes for signs of shiftiness. For what it was worth, he saw none.

Baines told him about the grim discovery made in the aftermath of the blast, again watching him carefully. Prince appeared to be honestly shocked.

"Are you sure?" he whispered.

"We'd not be here if there was any doubt." Baines resisted the temptation to roll his eyes.

Prince puffed out his cheeks. "Bloody hell." A cloud passed across his face. "A body? And I'm guessing you want to know if it could have been put there when the block was going up?" Archer nodded again. "Well, the short answer is, not during the day it couldn't. And our out of hours security wasn't bad at all."

"Still, it would obviously have been outside working hours, if it had been done during the build?" Baines checked.

"For sure. But even that's not so simple."

"How so?"

"Okay, quick lesson in house building. We'd have prepared all the floors and put in things like skirting protections, then pumped gallons of concrete into the house, while guys in big wellies ran in and out of all the rooms, and smoothed it all out. I think, if your body had been buried before that stage, we'd have noticed."

"Fair point," Baines acknowledged.

"Well, similarly, if the body was put there after the cement was laid, you'd have to hack the cement open in one room and then cement over the body."

"And?"

"Apart from the noise and effort, the cement would be wet and a much darker colour for days afterwards. Unless, of course, someone got in and did it when the concrete was still drying out. I suppose if it was done at the weekend, and done well, they could get away with it, especially as we were always under time pressures. If it looked okay, no one's going to examine it that closely."

"But that'd point to someone knowing the state of the concrete." Baines pondered. "A slice of luck, but possible."

"I suppose. But, more likely, one of the occupants did it after we released that flat."

DAVE SIVERS

"Perhaps," Baines acknowledged. "But we'd like to focus on the out of hours possibility for now. Who would have had access after everyone knocked off?"

"Well, me of course. A few other guys, but I can't remember them all now. It was a long time ago, and I've worked a lot of sites."

"Try," Archer urged, abandoning her dumb blonde role already.

"I'd have to have a think and get back to you. But probably Sunny Garfield. He worked a lot of jobs with me, and he was always an early starter. That was why he tended to have a key. Dennis Ryan often went in at weekends. So did Peter..." He snapped his fingers as if trying to conjure something up. "Peter... Peter... Hay? Haigh? Christ, my memory. There might have been a couple of others."

"But those three," Baines said. "You're pretty sure they were at Spencer Street?"

"These days, I'm not sure what I had for elevenses, half the time. Sorry." He looked awkward. "Look, I might be better than this later. If any other names come to me, I'll give you a bell."

Paula Prince came in with a mug in each hand and put them down in front of Archer and Baines.

"I've got some homemade cake, if you'd like."

Baines's stomach rumbled.

"Thanks," Archer said, "but no thanks."

Baines glowered at her.

"Your loss," Barry said as his wife departed.

"And the men you mentioned." Baines returned to the matter in hand. Checked his notes. "Garfield, Ryan and either Hay or Haigh. Where can we find them?"

"I still see Sunny. I can get you his address. Dennis, I think retired to the coast somewhere. I'm fairly sure we still send him a Christmas card. I'll ask Paula."

"And Haigh?"

"Haynes." Prince snapped his fingers again, triumph in his eyes. "Peter Haynes." He smiled a sad smile. "But the last time I was with him was Chilterns Crematorium. I wouldn't know what they did with his ashes."

"All right," Archer said, departing from the script as Baines had known she would. "Let's try a different tack. Can you think of anyone on that site, or that you worked with around that time, who might have got in any trouble? Or maybe been capable of murder?"

"Half the lads were capable of murder after a skinful," he told her. "But seriously? Well, not Sunny or Peter. Straight as dyes. Dennis?" He frowned.

Baines thought he might be considering keeping something back. "Remember, this is a murder enquiry."

"I know." Barry Prince sighed. "All right, then. He was a nice guy, most of the time, but he had a high maintenance wife – still does, so far as I know – never enough money, and a temper on him if you pressed the wrong buttons. Everyone was surprised when he retired. He went a bit early, and one of the guys had a holiday wherever the hell it is he lives now. Bumped into him on the sea front, and Dennis invited him and the missus home for lunch. By all accounts, the house was pretty tasty, and he was driving a Merc. We reckoned he must have come into some money, but maybe he got it somewhere else. Know what I mean?"

Baines glanced at Archer, who lifted an eyebrow.

"Can you check that Christmas card list?" he said.

"Sure. I'll ask Paula now. Not that I can really imagine Dennis, nor any of the others, come to that, lugging a body in there and burying it in concrete."

"And there was a security guard, wasn't there?" Archer interjected. "He'd have had out of hours access."

"Well, it was a security firm."

"Oh." Baines made a face. "That wasn't made clear to us."

"Really?" Prince shrugged. "Not deliberate, I'm sure. When you're in the business, you assume people will know."

"Do you remember which company it was?"

"Hopper's, most likely. We used them a lot for a while. I think one of their guys would pop over during the night to see everything was secure. At least they were supposed to. Lazy bunch of buggers, in my experience. People employed to sleep!"

"You said you used them 'for a while'," Archer said. "Did you get a better price? Or was it because you weren't satisfied with them?"

He brushed something off his trousers. "Like I say, they were a lazy lot, and I wasn't the only one to tell the bosses I thought they were falling down on the job. And things were going missing from other sites they were supposed to be guarding. The word gets around. Their contract wasn't renewed."

Archer took a sip of her coffee. "When you say things went missing...?"

"Nothing from Spencer Court," he said. "Not that I remember, anyway. And I don't mean the Hopper's guys were nicking them. Not themselves. There was suspicion they were leaving gates unlocked." His eyes widened. "Oh, but you can't think…" He shook his head, "No, I can't see it. They might have been bent, but we're talking about murder."

"Can you remember who they had looking after Spencer Court?"

"Not right now, no. It might come back to me."

A thought crossed Baines's mind. "Tell me," he said, keeping his tone casual, "did you ever have anyone walk off the site one day and just not come back?"

"All the time. We mostly got good workers, but you can always get the odd unreliable one. We had the odd drug user. You get so you can tell. You must know what I mean, your line of work?"

Baines and Archer said nothing.

"Well, anyway. So long as they showed up and did their jobs, that was fine. They could even let us down once. Second time, unless they were permanent staff, it was goodbye. But as I said, nothing went missing from Spencer Court."

"And no*body*?" pressed Baines.

He looked troubled. "I'd have to rack my brains. Like I say, it was a long time ago. But you've been to the office. They'll have records."

"I gather they may not be perfect. Ideally, we'd like descriptions. Heights, that sort of thing."

"Well, I've not been much use, have I?"

"Everything's useful," Archer said. She and Baines handed him cards. "If anything at all comes back to you, however trivial, give one of us a ring. And we'll need those addresses before we go."

He stood on the doorstep and watched them get back in the car.

"Well," Archer said as Baines drove away, "not all useless. We need to look into Dennis Ryan and Hopper Security."

"I'd like to probe Prince's background, too. Nothing he said raised my suspicions, but you never know. He had access too, and pointing us in other directions could be a damn good smokescreen."

"Agreed. But all that'll keep until tomorrow. We need a catch up with the team."

"Who knows?" he said. "maybe someone's at the station, confessing, even as we speak."

Archer sighed. "If only it was that simple."

9

There was a buzz around the briefing room when the team reassembled at 7pm. It was often the way at the start of an investigation. Kicking off, Archer asked Bell if he had any more information on the crime scene or the post mortem.

"Some good news, guv," he replied. "It seems they've got the skeleton out of the concrete and it's been safely transported to Dr Carlisle's mortuary. She's seen enough to confirm that the victim's a male, but that's as far as she's prepared to go without a post mortem. Which is tomorrow at 9am, by the way, if that suits?"

"Fine by me." She glanced Baines's way. "You'd better come too, Dan."

"Wouldn't miss it." His faux enthusiasm couldn't quite disguise his dislike of mortuaries. Not that many coppers were exactly fans.

"So does that mean she's got her bone expert on board?"

"Yep. A…" He checked his notes. "Professor Belinda Kennewell. I did an Internet search. She sounds pretty awesome. Mass graves in war zones. Victims of natural disasters too. Fellow of the Royal Anthropological Institute –"

"Maybe you should go instead of me, Jason," Baines suggested. "You sound a bit smitten."

Bell coloured.

"We get it, Jason," Archer said. "She knows her stuff. Which is good to know. Let's hope she can help narrow down what we know about the victim." She turned to Tyler. "Speaking of which, Will – how are you getting on with missing persons?"

"Well, I'm glad we're only looking in the Vale for starters," Tyler said. "I did a bit of digging and it seems between 250,000 and 300,000 people go missing in the United Kingdom every year. That said, around ninety one per cent of those cases get solved within forty eight hours, with the person either being found or simply returning home. And ninety nine per cent of all missing persons cases are solved within a year. That still leaves around 3,000 people nationwide who are still missing a year after they're reported. Three quarters of those reported tend to be aged over twenty four, and three quarters are likely to be male. Over eighty per cent of persons reported missing were white."

"And here?" Archer probed, already feeling daunted.

"Okay. So I've got details for the whole of Thames Valley. Oxfordshire has the highest incidence of missing persons in Thames Valley – that's those unaccounted for. About 2,300. On average around twenty people a day are being actively sought in the county. That's before you start on Bucks and Berks. But still, I've managed to whittle it down to those reported missing in 2004 to 2005, when Spencer Court was going up."

"Let's hear it, then."

"For Thames Valley as a whole, as far as I can make out, there are as many as 81 people who went missing in those years who are still unaccounted for. 61 are male. In Bucks, you're talking – hang on, I've got it here…" He rustled papers on his lap. "Yeah, 17 males. I've gone through them and there are just three who went missing from the Vale. I can give you their details."

"Let's save that for now," Archer said, "but that's terrific work, Will. Let's hope our man's one of those three. If so, identifying him mightn't be the nightmare I feared it would be. Even if we have to look at the full Thames Valley list, it mightn't be too bad if Jason's professor is as wonderful as he thinks she is."

She finished making notes on the board behind her.

"All right. So DS Baines and I have been trying to find out how the body might have got where we found it. Would you sum up, Dan?"

Baines recounted the visits to Howard and Burns and to the former site manager, Barry Prince.

"So it's a trip to the seaside to see this Dennis Ryan, and someone else needs to speak to Sunny Garfield. And there's Hopper's Security to talk to. I want to know more about this security guard. Meanwhile, Jason?"

"Yes, guv?" There was a note of caution in his voice, Archer thought. Perhaps he feared he was about to be teased again about his enthusiasm for Professor Kennewell.

"Did you find out who's lived in that flat since it was built?"

"I did," he replied. "Fortunately, there's only been two: The first residents in flat 1C were Richard and Sharon White. They were there seven years and, since then, it's been Thomas Evans and Amber Kane."

"Do we know where they are?"

"Thomas and Amber have been put up in the Travelodge by their insurers. The Whites moved to Furzton, in west Milton Keynes. I've got an address."

"Excellent. I'll divide up the jobs at the end. Anything else?" She checked her list of action points, then her gaze found Steve Ashby, next to Gillingham at the back of the room. "Oh, yes, Steve. Did you ask around your contacts for…" She tailed off, not entirely sure what he'd had in mind.

"I made a start," he said, "but it's a big fat blank so far. I'll do some more tomorrow. Maybe if we can start to narrow down who this guy was, or even ID him…"

"Okay," Archer said. "I think we've made a decent start, everyone. So DS Baines and I will attend the post mortem tomorrow. Joan, Jason, can you follow up the present and past occupants while we're doing that? Then we'll regroup just before lunchtime." She scanned the room. "Good. Let's go home and get some rest."

* * *

Baines found that the case hung heavily on his mind as he drove home. He'd tried not to let it show, but Archer's comment that someone had been missing the person buried at Spencer Court for too long had struck a nerve with him.

Some four years before the flats had even been built, a serial killer known as the Invisible Man had claimed Baines's wife –

42

and Karen's twin - Louise, as his last victim. Baines's son, Jack, had disappeared at the same time and, some 15 years later, no trace of him had ever been found. Only Karen, Archer, and his counsellor, Dr Tracey Walsh, knew that the years of grief and not knowing his son's fate had brought Baines close to a breakdown two years ago.

Jack had been two years old when he disappeared, yet every time Baines heard of an unidentified body turning up, he wondered if this was the day he would learn the truth. Logic told him that Jack had probably died soon after his abduction, but that didn't stop Baines hoping he might still be alive somewhere. For a while, he'd even been haunted by dreams and waking visions of the teenager Jack may have become.

He knew the Spencer Court bones couldn't possibly be Jack's. They'd been too long under the flats, Jack would still have been a child when they'd been put there. But that reality didn't stop him praying they had a name for the victim soon.

He tried to focus on positive thoughts as he drove into the Buckinghamshire village of Little Aston, close to the Bedfordshire and Hertfordshire borders. The small house he and Louise had purchased, what seemed like a lifetime ago, had never been intended as a long term home, but a stepping stone to something bigger. It was the house Louise had died in, and the house he'd hung onto ever since, entertaining an irrational hope that Jack would be coming home to it one day. The home that had been filled with love and optimism for the future had ensnared him with ghosts from the past, even though love also lived there again now. When he and Karen had got engaged, they'd agreed that it was time to let the place go. When they returned from honeymoon, it was going on the market.

As he drove along the street to his house, passing other homes with lights in the windows, all kinds of lives and events going on behind the closed curtains, he practised the smile he'd have on his face as he walked through the door. The last thing Karen needed this close to the wedding was a gloomy fiancé.

"Hiya!" he called as he stepped over the threshold, heaving cheeriness into his voice. There was no answering call. Just for a moment, he was transported back to that terrible night when he'd arrived home to find the place in darkness. He hadn't immediately thought something might be wrong then; that this was the start of the worse night of his life.

"Karen?" he called. For a moment, silence seemed to mock him. Then he heard movement upstairs. He started up the stairs, past pictures Louise had loved, mingled with some Karen had chosen, and saw Karen emerging from the bedroom.

"Sorry," she said. "I..." Her voice tailed off. She raised her hands half-heartedly, then let them fall by her sides. By now he was on the landing with her. He could see she'd been crying.

He put his arms around her and she nestled into his shoulder.

"Hey," he whispered. "What's up?"

Her voice was small. "What's ever up? I rang my parents."

His heart sank. "Oh, Karen..."

"I rang them again to ask them to rethink. I mean, it's their daughter getting married. The one they're supposed to love. To their son-in-law, who they professed to love like a son when he was married to my sister. The father of their beloved grandson."

She was crying again.

"Shh," he soothed. "What did they say?"

She pushed herself away from him and wiped her eyes with the heels of her hands. "I spoke to Dad. He was all pompous, the way only Dad can be. Said they'd made their position perfectly clear. As far as they're concerned, what we're doing is defiling Lou's memory. He said it was like spitting on her grave."

Anger surged in Baines then. "He said that? Right..."

He'd slipped off his suit jacket as he'd walked through the front door. He'd draped it over a bannister post to comfort Karen. Now he started to put it on again.

"Where... what are you doing?" Karen sobbed.

"He can't talk to you like that."

"Please, please. Leave it. Just... leave it." Her face was a mask of misery. "If they don't want to come, there's nothing we can do. Don't drive them even further away."

Baines didn't see how that was even possible. His in-laws were refusing to come to their daughter's wedding because they thought her relationship with her brother-in-law was somehow sick. They – or rather Karen's dad – had actually told her Baines was 'settling' for her as a substitute for Louise. They'd declared that, if 'this travesty of a wedding' went ahead, they didn't want to see Karen or Baines again. How much further away could anything drive them?

He knew she was right, though. However slim the chances that her parents would come around, him turning up on their doorstep to confront them with angry words was hardly going to make it more likely.

He put the jacket back and opened his arms again. She stepped into his embrace.

"Maybe they're right," she sniffled. "Maybe what we're doing *is* wrong."

"You no more think that than I do. This is right. Louise would be happy for us."

"Would she, though?"

He held her at arm's length, looking into her eyes. "You were even closer to her than I was. You know she would."

She looked back at him, their gazes locked, for a small eternity. Then she nodded.

"Of course, you're right. She'd give Dad and Mum a right telling off. Anyway," she shook herself, "I made a chicken casserole. When you texted you were on your way home, I decided to wait for you. It'll be nice to eat together."

Far too often, the demands of the job saw Baines arriving home late to see what Karen had left in the fridge for him. It often made him feel guilty. Despite the threat of redundancy, which had hung over her for ages now, Karen still worked full time herself. The thought of her coming home from a gruelling day to prepare a meal, and then sit eating her share alone, made him feel like a rubbish partner, even though he knew she understood.

He'd never quite understood what Louise had seen in him. That Karen also loved him made him feel doubly lucky.

While Karen blasted the casserole in the microwave, Baines busied himself laying the kitchen table and pouring them each a glass of white wine.

"So," she said, waiting for the microwave to ping, "you're busy again. You said the quiet spell wouldn't last."

"It never does." He put the wine bottle back in the fridge.

"Is it something they found in the block of flats that exploded?"

He looked at her. "I didn't know you studied the *Echo*'s website."

"I don't, it was on the BBC local news."

It shouldn't have surprised him. A few years ago, the Little Aston community column in the *Echo* had carried a snippet about motion-activated radios that had been installed at the local allotments to scare deer away. The animals occasionally strayed from nearby Ashridge Forest, and had been known to find their way onto the plots and decimate holders' crops. The radios were tuned to BBC Radio 4, and the 'Today' programme had been so delighted at the prospect of John Humphrys' dulcet tones frightening the wildlife that they'd given the story a mention. Presumably, whatever system they had for trawling local news had found Claire King's half-baked online speculation.

"I don't think they could have contacted the press office," he said. "We'd have heard. What did they say?"

"Oh, I can't really remember. Something about speculation that human remains may have been revealed by a blast at a block of flats in Aylesbury. An unnamed source had noticed a lot of police activity." The microwave pinged and she slipped on oven gloves and removed the casserole dish. "So is there a body?"

He sighed. "Yeah. And Claire bloody King's been sniffing around the site." Had King actually seen a body bag coming out and being loaded into a van? "It doesn't really matter, I suppose. We wanted to start questioning a few people before the news broke, that's all."

"Do you know who it is yet?" She started to dish the food up into large bowls: a spoonful for him, a spoonful for her, and repeat. It was exactly the way Louise used to serve up.

He shook his head. "We're approaching it from two ends: trying to identify the deceased and trying to narrow down who could have put him there. Hopefully, we'll find a connection.

Maybe a motive or two. The remains have been there for years – it's just bones. We've got an expert attending the post mortem, who we're hoping can tell us all about our victim."

Karen placed a steaming bowl in his usual place at the table. "I take it we're talking murder?"

"Yes, and an old one."

"Makes everything harder, surely?"

"In some ways, yes. In most ways, actually. Evidence is lost, memories aren't so fresh. But it's not all doom and gloom. Do you remember me talking about Mac – DS Duncan McNeill?"

"The one who jacked it in after…" She grimaced. "… after Lou was killed?"

"Yes. The job had been grinding him down for ages, and the Invisible Man, what happened to Lou and Jack, and the way the case just dried up after the killings ended, put the cap on things for him."

McNeill had taken his pension and returned to his native Scotland, Aberdeen to be precise, where he'd met and married a widow with a young son. He and Baines had vaguely kept in touch for the first few years, then the contact had petered out.

"Anyhow," Baines continued, "Mac found some work with his local force, working cold cases as a civilian. I remember us chatting on the phone about it, and he reckoned the whole passage of time could work both ways. New forensic techniques are coming online all the time, that might not have been available to the original investigation. And people's stories can change."

Karen frowned. "Really? Don't their memories fade, though?"

"Sure. But, for example, a loyal partner may have provided an alibi or backed up a suspect's story, believing them to be innocent and wanting to spare them the pain of a lot of police scrutiny. Fast forward a few years. Now the partner's been playing away and that loyalty has evaporated. The wronged woman – or man, I suppose – might even want to punish them by admitting their recollection might have been faulty."

He took a sip of his wine.

"People can also recollect something years on that they'd forgotten at the time," he continued. So maybe we'll have some luck after all."

"So, now you've got a murder case," she said, not looking at him, "might we have to cancel the wedding? Or at least the honeymoon?"

He stared at her. "What? No, of course not. The leave's been booked for ages."

"It's hardly unusual for leave to be cancelled at short notice." She regarded him gravely.

Where was this coming from? "Yeah, but a wedding… Lizzie wouldn't even consider doing that to me."

"So we'll tie the knot okay, but we should postpone the honeymoon to be on the safe side? As we might have to rush our vows before you dash off to interview some suspect. I suppose I should just be thankful if you don't leave me standing at the altar."

Knowing the wedding was a sensitive subject already, thanks to her parents, he reined in his irritation with the direction this conversation was taking.

"Look," he said, putting down his cutlery, "in the first place, Aylesbury Register Office doesn't have an actual altar, to the best of my knowledge. And secondly –"

A huge grin split her face. She licked an index finger, marked up an imaginary point with it, then pointed it at Baines.

"Gotcha!"

He rolled his eyes. "Well, that was hilarious."

"It was. You should have seen your face." She sipped wine. "I know you won't jilt me for the job, Dan."

"Well, I should think so," he said, trying – but failing – to appear upset.

"You'd better not, or the next body that gets dug up might just be yours."

10

Even the strong, chemical smell of antiseptic couldn't altogether mask the reek of death that hung over every mortuary Baines had ever visited. Barbara Carlisle's lair at Stoke Mandeville Hospital was no exception.

On the occasions when Baines was forced to come here, afterwards he would strip off in the garage before going into the house. He kept an old tracksuit in there to change into, and a hanger on which he'd leave his suit to air. His shirt and underwear would go straight into the washing machine, and then he'd make a beeline for the shower. Anything to keep that stench - real or imagined - out of his living space.

In theory, at least, today's post mortem should be less gruesome than most. No flesh to slice through, no organs to weigh, no stomach contents to empty out for analysis. Even so, looking at those white bones stretched out on Carlisle's spotless stainless steel table made him uneasy. He didn't need to be a pathologist to see the damage that those bones had suffered: breaks, fractures and compressions. Those remains, and the dead person's identity, might be shrouded in mystery, but one thing was entirely clear.

They had died hard.

Today, Carlisle was accompanied as usual by her assistant, Bruce Davenport, ever a man of few words, but also by a woman Baines hadn't seen before. Carlisle confirmed that this was the Professor Belinda Kennewell that Jason Bell had so enthused about. Baines wondered if the professor's smiling grey eyes, and the dark hair escaping from her scrubs cap, would have lived up to the Scot's imagination.

"She's one of the world's foremost forensic anthropologists," Carlisle said, "and she's come down from

49

Liverpool to help us today. We're lucky she was able to come – she's much in demand all around the world."

Kennewell held up her gloved hands in protest. "Don't build me up too much, or they'll be expecting miracles." She might be based in Liverpool, but Baines detected no hint of a scouse accent. Home Counties, he thought. "Besides," she added with a wink to Baines, "you did bribe me with a case of champagne."

"I might chuck in a bottle of Prosecco myself, if we can get closer to identifying this poor soul," Archer said.

"In that case, we'd better get down to business."

Kennewell and Carlisle moved closer to the table.

"Well," the professor said, "the first thing I can tell you is that we seem to have pretty much a complete skeleton here, and I think we can safely say we're dealing with just the one body."

"Of course," Archer said, her tone bordering on impatience. Baines knew it was tension but he hoped it didn't antagonise the anthropologist.

"Oh, you'd be surprised," Kennewell said cheerfully. "I've had cases – not in this country – where we appeared to have one body, but it turned out we had bits and bobs from several different ones. But all these bones look related to me. There's a symmetry, an evenness of length."

"Got it," Archer said. "So what can you tell us?"

"Okay, gender first. Definitely male. If it was female, we'd see an open, circular pelvic inlet, plus a broader sciatic notch, a wider angle where the two pubic bones meet in front, and more outwardly flared hip bones."

"Age? Race? Height?"

"Patience, Inspector." The grey eyes danced. "Barbara here calls me a 'bone whisperer'. I have to coax these details from the remains. But height? I had a chance to measure the bones before you arrived. Five feet nine inches? Perhaps five ten? As for race: take a look at the eye orbits. They're shaped a bit like aviator glasses. Now let's have a peek at the nasal area. See how the nasal sill," she pointed, "has a rather pronounced angulation dividing the nasal floor from the anterior surface of the maxilla." Baines wished she would speak English, but he could see what she meant. "High nasal bones with a peaked angle.

Narrow nasal aperture. These are all features of a European skull."

"So, Caucasian," Baines checked.

"Yes. He also has laterally facing cheekbones, although you'd find that in Africans as well. But everything together? Yes, we have a white male, about five ten."

"Thank you," Archer said. "And we know he was an adult, at least Barbara thought so. Any chance you can take a stab at his actual age, Professor?"

"Call me Belinda, please. Well, let's see what we've got." She took a while to examine the bones while they waited. Baines could see Archer's patience thinning once more. She was about to speak when Kennewell turned to face them.

"Now then," she said, "Dr Carlisle's assessment that we're dealing with an adult was based on all the teeth present being adult. And she's right, of course. In particular, the third molars – the wisdom teeth - have clearly emerged, and this happens between the ages of seventeen and twenty one. But we can do a little better than that. For starters, all the epiphyses of the long bones are fused," Kennewell said.

"Epiphyses?" Baines echoed.

"Sorry. The rounded ends, in simple terms. Also, the medial end of the clavicles are fully fused and the junction between the first and second sacral vertebrae is fused."

As she spoke, she indicated the areas she was referring to, so that Baines had a rough understanding of what she was saying, even if the words had limited meaning for him.

"The xiphisternum – the lowermost point of the breastbone, here – has fused to the sternal body, and you can see some calcification in the costal cartilages – here, at the anterior ends of the ribs."

"So how old was he?" Archer pressed her.

"Also," Kennewell moved back to the skull, ignoring the question for now, "see how the sutures of the skull have started to close in some places and are fully closed in others." She looked at Archer. "Just a couple more things, and then I'll give you my assessment."

"All right," Archer said grudgingly. "You make Barbara look hasty."

The woman's eyes danced again. "I'll take that as a compliment. And I'll enjoy drinking your Prosecco. Because..." She turned back to the bones again. "...the pubic symphseal surface indicates that this was a mature adult. There's no ridging and the ventral rampart and the dorsal plateau are complete."

"If you say so."

Kennewell chuckled. "I most certainly do. And there's some evidence of degenerative change, although not extensive. There's some osteophytic lipping – irregular bone formation - around the bodies of the vertebrae and some of the other joints." She turned to face them. "The best I can say is this man was aged between forty and fifty years. Does that help?"

"Wow," Archer said, evidently impressed. "That precise?"

"I'll do some more detailed analyses, of course, and they might throw up something that can help you narrow down the victim's profile. Don't hold your breath, though."

"Well, you've earned those bottles," Archer admitted. "A ten-year age range will allow us to eliminate a lot of missing persons from our enquiries. And you'll let us know if you come up with anything more?"

"Of course."

"As for the damage," Carlisle added, "I don't think it was just fists and boots that inflicted it. Look closely at the skull." They followed her moving finger as she pointed out one indentation across the face and another across the dome. "Those are lengthy compressions, made, I think, by a hard, round instrument."

"Baseball bat?" suggested Baines.

"I don't think so. Shape and thickness is wrong. I'll have to see if I can narrow it down. But they didn't just use the weapon. I'd say he was punched and kicked also. This is looking like a very personal attack."

"Blimey," Archer said as they emerged into the sunshine. "That was better than I expected."

"Me too," Baines agreed.

"It could quite significantly narrow down the possibles. And then we've got the teeth. Anyone on Will Tyler's list who fits the lovely Belinda's profile, we can start getting dental records compared."

For every missing person who was a possible match, they would need to establish who his dentist had been and get hold of records for a forensic orthodontist to compare. Where possible, the dentist's details would be obtained from the possible victim's family.

It wasn't a cheery prospect, and Baines knew Archer would tread carefully. The families they approached would have their hopes raised that, at long last, the mystery of what had happened to their loved one was about to be solved. Confirmation that they were dead, however devastating, would at least be some sort of closure.

But, for some, that hope would be raised in vain. And the pain of not knowing would return afresh.

Maybe one day the body of a small boy would be found and the possibility would be raised that it was Baines's son. How would he feel? And, if it turned out to be someone else's child, how would he feel about that? Relieved or disappointed?

He knew he needed to steer clear of such thoughts, if he was to concentrate on doing his job properly.

11

"Okay," Archer said to Tyler, "let's start with your three missing men in the Vale. You said you had descriptions?"

Anyone who didn't know Will Tyler would wonder how he ever found anything amongst the papers that carpeted his desk, but Archer knew better. The DC's hand moved across the papers on his desk, and she wasn't surprised when his fingers plucked up a slim, stapled sheaf of printed papers. His eyes scanned the top sheet.

"Aged 40 to 50, you said? And about five nine?"

"So the Bone Whisperer assured us," she said, "and she seemed to know what she was on about."

His eyes lit up. "Got one here. John Leeson. Born 1960, so roughly in the middle of our age range. 5 feet 10 inches. Reported missing June 2005."

"Leeson?" Baines was standing next to Archer, leaning in to read over Tyler's shoulder. "That's a blast from the past. How could I have forgotten him?"

Archer turned to face him, surprised. "You knew him?"

"Not exactly. But he was part of a nasty little drugs ring that crossed county lines in Thames Valley back then. Lucrative, as I recall, but hardly an empire. There were…" He wrinkled his brow. "… either 3 or 4 other gangs fishing in the same pool around the time. I forget all the details – I didn't work the case – but there were occasional spats when someone felt their turf had been encroached on. You wouldn't exactly have called it a turf war, but people got hurt."

"So what about this Leeson?" Archer probed.

"He just vanished off the face of the earth one day. Opinion amongst those who knew him, and who'd talk to us, was divided between those who thought he'd done a runner for some reason and those who thought one of the inter-gang disagreements had got out of hand. I can't remember who led the investigation. My old boss, DI Britton, was involved, I think, but he can't help us now."

Britton had succumbed to cancer a few years ago, his death creating the vacancy that Archer had filled.

"There's a file," Tyler said. "I've requested it."

"Well done," said Archer, "but let's not get ahead of ourselves. Let's make sure it's him, before we dive down that rabbit hole. Can you get hold of his dental records, soon as you can, and get them to Dr Carlisle?"

Tyler nodded. "Straight away, guv."

Archer took Baines's arm and steered him back to her desk. "I don't see Joan or Jason. I guess they must be still checking out the former occupants of our flat. You and I need to get down to Sussex and see this Dennis Ryan. Will's established he still lives at the address Barry Prince gave us, and he found a phone number."

"I'll give him a call before we traipse down there," Baines said. "Although his name rings no bells. I wonder if he was involved with one of the drug gangs. Or maybe one of their 'clients'."

"Maybe," Archer agreed. "But right now, I just want to meet him and assess whether he's a genuine person of interest, regardless of whether our victim turns out to be Leeson or not. In fact, best we don't mention Leeson to anyone until we can confirm it's him." She chewed her bottom lip. "Get hold of Joan, too. Get her and Jason to go and question Hoppers' Security."

"I think Joan would have liked the Sussex run, actually."

"I'm sure. We'll bring her back a kiss-me-quick hat, if we see one."

As Baines walked away, grinning, Archer's phone rang. It was Gillingham.

"I need you in my office, Lizzie. Bring Dan with you. We've got another body. And this one's considerably fresher than the one at Spencer Court."

* * *

Aylesbury's Northfields Estate had been notorious for years, and the police and the local council had launched numerous initiatives to clean up its act. Every glimmer of hope had proved a false dawn. Graffiti would be cleaned from the walls of the soulless and shabby blocks of flats, to try to give residents a sense of pride in their environment, but it would always creep back again. The same went for the estate's reputation for drug dealing and petty criminals.

Decent families on benefit and meagre incomes lived here too, cheek by jowl with lowlifes, forced into this less-than-salubrious concrete jungle by a local demand for affordable housing that could never be met.

For a time, volunteer litter pickers had been deployed, but their souls had been destroyed by the never-ending tsunami of crisp packets, coke bottles and chocolate wrappers, to say nothing of used needles and condoms and the hassle they got from some of the less pleasant residents. Dead furniture, even deader white goods, and fly-tipped sacks of rubble were occasionally taken away, only to be replaced by more of the same. Dumped cars would sit for weeks or months, wearing 'Police Aware' signs like badges of dishonour, until they were finally removed.

It was one such car, a rusting Honda, that Archer, Baines and Phil Gordon, all in crime scene suits, stood around now, peering into the boot. Even on the Northfields, the stench of a decomposing body would eventually offend local sensibilities. Some enterprising soul had forced the boot open to find out what was causing the stink, and had called the police once they had finished vomiting. The pool of puke on the grass at the back of the vehicle added to the charm of the scene.

The dead man's hands were cable-tied behind him, and there was tape on his mouth. There was blood on his clothing, but the state of his face, and the grotesque angles that his broken fingers made, bore ample testament to the punishment he'd taken before he died. It wasn't the warmest of days, but the chill Baines felt had little to do with the weather.

CSIs were processing the scene already, taking photographs, scanning the ground for evidence, dusting the car's interior for prints.

"We found a wallet on him," Gordon said. "Credit cards and driving licence. He was Christopher Meredith. 29 years old, from Reading."

"Reading?" Baines looked from the body to Gordon and back again. "He's a bit far from home." Reading, Berkshire's county town, was about 40 miles away.

"Cash in the wallet," Gordon added. "Couple of hundred pounds, so I can't imagine robbery was the motive. No phone, mind."

Archer had been a little closer to the boot than Baines fancied getting, bending over to examine it and its unfortunate occupant. "Not a lot of blood in the boot. That suggests he was killed some time before he was put in there. Then driven here, presumably."

"I'd assume attempts are being made to trace the car's owner," Gordon replied, "but actually, it's been here a lot longer than the body. The police aware sticker is dated ten days ago – the twenty fourth of February. This body would be in a much worse state than it is and, frankly, smell a damn sight worse, if he'd been here as long as the car has. No one noticed the smell before today. Barbara will doubtless give you a considered time and date of death but, for my money, he's been in there three days tops."

"Let's get this straight," Archer said. "You think he was killed elsewhere, then brought here and dumped in this abandoned car?"

"That's how I read the scene, yes," the crime scene manager agreed.

"Then we might just have the most bone-headed killers in history," Baines said. "If the boot had to be forced by whoever called it in, then maybe the killer had a key."

"You think he dumped the body in his own car?" Gordon shrugged. "Well, there are some ninnies about, but honestly? It probably wouldn't take much knowhow to spring the boot without resorting to crowbars, especially on an older model like this. A more interesting question is, who knew this car was here?"

"Someone from the estate is the most obvious possibility," said Archer. "We'll need to find out all about the victim and his contacts. Who called it in, by the way?"

"Your guess is as good as mine," Gordon said. "They didn't leave a name, and we know half the people on the Northfields are dodgy. More than half of those probably have several cheap, unregistered pay-as-you-go phones. The one that was used to report this is probably in a skip or at the bottom of the canal by now. My guess? Whoever made the call wanted the stench dealt with, but had no desire to get involved."

"I guess you could check the puke for DNA," Baines mused, "but unless we think the caller was also the killer…"

"We'll collect samples, just in case," Gordon said. He glanced over Baines's shoulder at the road. "Here comes Barbara."

They watched as Barbara Carlisle's car drew up. The pathologist got out and suited up before coming over to join them, carrying her bag. She looked first at Archer, then Baines.

"We have to stop meeting like this." She peered into the boot. "Well, this fellow's in rather better nick than the one we examined this morning. If it goes on like this, I'll be being called out to live people next."

12

"Okay," Will Tyler said, "so I've spoken to the Reading station and managed to get passed on to a really helpful DC by the name of Derek Pollard. Your Mr Christopher Meredith was known to our guys there. Went by the name of Kit and was one of two brothers running a tight little gang with big ambitions: a bit of drug dealing here, a dodgy massage parlour there. Their influence has been growing and they've had a few what you might call turf scuffles, rather than turf wars, with other miscreants over the past few years. Derek reckons their outfit seems to be top dog at the moment."

Archer, Baines, Collins and Bell were crowded around Tyler's desk. Baines was standing at his elbow. "So how does Meredith end up dead in the boot of a car on the Northfields?"

"That's the thing. DC Pollard reckons the dynamic has shifted locally of late. There are hints that there's a new player on the block, muscling in on the Reading boys' territory. Pollard thinks they might be from out of town."

"From here?" Archer pursed her lips. "Have Reading been talking to us about this?" Baines caught the annoyance in her voice.

"I don't think they know specifically where out of town."

"All right," she said. "So is it possible that Mr Meredith's come over our way to ruffle feathers and taken on more than he could handle? Does your guy Pollard have a clue who these new players actually are?"

"Seems not."

"I don't like it," she said. "We had a lot of that sort of crap at the Met. A full scale gang war can be messy and bloody."

"We've come close to something kicking off here a few times, but we've been lucky," Baines said.

"I'd like to keep it that way." She looked at Tyler again. "What else do we know about Kit Meredith?"

"Married, two kids. Lives on a middling housing development, so vice can't be paying too badly. Derek said he'd be happy to do the death knock, if we didn't want to traipse over there."

Breaking bad news to families was never a pleasant job, but Archer sighed and shook her head. "Someone from here should go with him, ask some questions. It sounds like we're going to be liaising with Reading until we've got a proper handle on this murder."

"Do you think the boss, or Ashby, might have come across Meredith?" Baines wondered. Both Gillingham and Ashby had been at Reading before they came to the Vale.

"I briefed the boss," Archer said. "If the name rang any bells with him, he didn't let on. But he's been here, what? Eight, nine years now? Meredith would have been maybe 21, so I wonder if this gang even existed in those days. We'll ask Ashby when we see him. He's the networks man, and he didn't come across to us until a bit later. No, I think we're going to have to lean on the Reading force for local knowledge."

She made a face. "One thing the boss did say. Our team has to run with this case *and* the Spencer Court case. There was a nasty burglary last night – two pensioners in their eighties tortured and left for dead. Lara Moseley's handling that investigation, so the quiet spell's well and truly over."

"Are we getting any extra resources?" Baines asked.

"Yeah, that'd be nice. Gillingham says he'll see what he can do, but he didn't say it with much conviction."

Baines groaned. "Oh, terrific. So we've got two murder cases to juggle."

"About the size of it."

It wasn't the first time it had been like this, and Baines doubted it would be the last. "Karen was saying only last night that leave would be cancelled and we'd have to call off the wedding and the honeymoon. Perhaps she was right."

"Sod that," Archer retorted. "After all the work I've put into my speech? And I've spent a fortune on an outfit. We'll just have to manage. Solve them both before the big day." She turned to Collins. "How have you and Jason been getting on, Joan? Did you get hold of the previous residents of flat 1C?"

"We did," Collins replied. "We started with the Aylesbury Travelodge, where Thomas Evans and Amber Kane - the current tenants - are staying. They're in their late 20s."

"Still traumatised by the sudden loss of their home and most of their possessions," Bell added. "They both seemed on edge but, to be fair, they were clearly agitated about us making them late for work."

"What did they have to say about the floor?" asked Baines.

"We asked whether they thought the kitchen floor was the original – if they'd done any work on it," Collins said. "They claim they never thought about it. Reckon it's just the same as in neighbours' flats. Although they'd always thought their floor was a bit uneven. They did mention, though, that the guy who lived above them – a bit of a nosy parker – reckoned the original occupant, Richard White, was a real DIY nut. Moved into a brand new flat and, within a week was knocking it about."

"Drove everyone mad," Bell added. "Nice bloke, but always banging something."

"What sort of things did he do?" asked Archer.

"New kitchen, new en suite, new bathroom. Lots of shelves. A fireplace in the lounge with a really nice electric fire…" Collins sighed. "Amber got quite upset just thinking about it. It seems the whole building may have to be demolished now."

"A new kitchen, you say?" Baines repeated. "So isn't it likely he'd have re-laid the floor?"

Collins shook her head. "I asked that, but they said he hadn't gone so far as to rip the whole thing out. It was the original layout, and they reckon he'd kept the original carcasses. Just changed the doors and the worktops. Immaculate, though. They thought, if he had replaced the floor, there was no way it'd be uneven. The upstairs neighbour told them he was a real stickler for accuracy. Always checking everything with a tape measure and spirit level."

"So you went to see this Richard White?" Archer was evidently keen to move on.

"Milton Keynes. Pleasant little cul de sac. I must say," Collins remarked, "I've seen a few DIY nightmares in my time, but White's house isn't one of them. The place looks pretty well maintained for its age. I'd say our Mr White is not only very competent, but he's got pretty good taste, too."

"But is he the sort of guy who could rip up a floor, slip a body in, and relay it without anyone seeing the join?"

"Maybe. He'd doubtless have the self-confidence."

"What makes you say that?"

"Joan thought he came across as a bit of a know-it-all," Bell said.

"What I actually said," Collins amended, "was that he was patronising, superior and smug."

Baines felt a smile tugging at the corners of his mouth. "You warmed to him then?"

"A bit of a mixture, actually. I felt a bit sorry for him, too. His living room's so immaculate that it felt like a show home, as if no one really lived here. And every surface had at least one framed photograph on it with his wife in. Sharon. She died last year. Cancer. Anyhow," she continued, "as soon as we started asking him about his DIY, he got agitated."

"He knew about the explosion, of course," Bell said, "and he was worried we thought he'd done something to cause it. We had to calm him down. Reassure him that we think there might have been a gas leak in a third floor flat."

"So what about the kitchen floor?" Baines asked.

Collins shrugged. "He insisted he'd done nothing to it. Said it was fine when he lived there, if a bit uneven. Apparently not a job he was interested in tackling."

"I did ask him," Bell said, "if he did re-lay that floor, would anyone know? Like anyone who visited regularly who would have seen if he'd done any work like that. He seemed genuinely unsure. He said they tended not to have friends round when they had a project on, but his brother often dropped round."

"Then he started wondering why we were so interested in the floor," Collins said. "Concluded there must have been something underneath it. Like a body."

"Hasn't he seen the local news?"

"I don't even know if they get the same news as us. But he got rattled. Asked us if he needed a lawyer. When we tried to reassure him we were just gathering information, he got all haughty and asked us to leave."

"So, all in all, it went well?" Tyler commented.

"Marvellous," Collins said.

"But do you believe him?" pressed Archer.

Bell shrugged. "No idea. But we've no real reason for suspecting him, have we?"

"Not at the moment," Collins conceded. "But I don't see how we can rule him out yet, either. Someone put that body in there."

"Worth digging into his background," Archer decided, "but we don't want to spend disproportionate time on that at the moment. Usual stuff. Any criminal convictions. We can check for any obvious connection to the victim as and when we have a name."

"How are you going to carve the two cases up, guv?" Tyler asked.

"I need to think about that. What you've told us about Kit Meredith and gangs worries me. If there's any danger that some sort of tit for tat violence is about to kick off, we need to stop it in its tracks. So, for now, that case has to take priority and the most resources."

"And Spencer Court Man?" Baines asked.

"We'll have to do the best we can on that. In fact…" Baines saw a thoughtful look in her eye. "Will, tell your mate at Reading that someone from here will accompany him on the death knock. Dan, come with me."

Baines followed her out of the main office, along the main corridor with its flaking paint, tired carpet and a couple of dead light bulbs. She turned into the briefing room. He followed her in and she shut the door.

"What's on your mind?" he wanted to know.

"How do you think Joan's doing?" she asked. "It's been a while now since we took her off co-ord and started getting her out of the office more."

Breaking off from a discussion about two murders for a staff matter wasn't what he'd expected. He took a moment to collect his thoughts.

"It's just what she needed," he said. "She's getting more confident, using her initiative, thinking on her feet. Why?"

"I was sort of wondering if we could make a case for her being made up to Acting DS for a while. She could maybe work with me on the Meredith case and you could dedicate yourself to Spencer Court."

He felt a lurch in the pit of his stomach and wasn't entirely sure why.

"I go on leave in just over a week," he said, knowing it wasn't a proper answer. His gut reaction was all negative. Why was that?

If Archer detected his mood, she didn't show it. "I know. We'd have to keep the situation under review. The Meredith case is likely to involve a lot of liaison with Reading, so maybe they'd lend us some support, and then you could have a bit of Jason's time."

He realised why he'd been so taken aback by Archer's proposal, and he didn't like himself for it. Collins had already been told she should be thinking about the sergeant's exam. She was ready for it, and what Archer had in mind was a great opportunity.

"It wouldn't do Joan any harm," he said. "We'd have to manage any jealousy from Jason or Will, although I suspect they'll both be fine. Yes," he said, nodding, "it's a good plan."

"I'll speak to Gillingham then," she said. "Keep it under your hat for now."

They walked back to the office, both lost in their own thoughts.

Baines knew that his suggestion, that Bell or Tyler might be resentful if Collins' temporary elevation was approved, was rich, considering what had been at the core of his initial reaction. He had a lot of time for Collins and would be delighted for her. At the same time, it brought home to him his own situation.

When Archer had first arrived in the Vale, Baines had been Acting DI, covering the post of his late boss, DI Britton, and hoping his promotion might become substantive. Being bumped back down to DS by an incomer from the Met had hurt, and had got their working relationship off on the wrong foot. But that hadn't lasted. He loved working with Archer, and she had become a great friend and confidant. Yet, just occasionally, it struck him that he was now marking time.

Just as Collins was ready to move up, Baines had believed himself to be ready for DI for years. But he remained a DS and now Collins was catching him up, albeit temporarily. It made him feel his career was passing him by.

He did his best to shake the feeling off. Now was not the time for it. Once he returned from honeymoon, then he could start to think seriously about the rest of his life.

13

To give Gillingham his due, he had begged, borrowed and stolen some additional uniformed officers to support the team but there was no chance, for the foreseeable future, of extra detectives. He had, however, been amenable to Collins's temporary promotion, and Archer had left it to Baines to break the news to Collins and manage Bell's and Tyler's reactions.

"They're both fine with it," a relieved Baines had told Archer just before the meeting began. "Both genuinely delighted for Joan."

So Archer had called a quick team meeting to explain how they were going to manage their casework in the immediate future.

A second cork board – this one for Kit Meredith - now sat at the end of the room alongside the Spencer Court board. Arguably, each case merited its own room, but Archer preferred it this way, especially as she might have to ask officers to dip in and out of both cases.

"Okay," she said. "So, we're going to have to keep this short. Let's update on Spencer Court first. Joan, how have you and Jason got on?"

Collins reported back on their informal interviews with past and present residents of the block, and Bell confirmed that he had nothing to add.

"Okay." Archer paused for thought. "But I don't like the way you said Richard White reacted."

"I didn't at the time, guv, but he seemed easily rattled. I'm not sure how much I'd read into it."

"You're probably right, Joan, but can you check whether his record is clean?"

"On it, guv."

"Good." Archer turned to Tyler, "Will, any luck with John Leeson's dental records?"

"Shouldn't be too long, guv," he said. "We got them and the comparisons are being done. You'll be the first to know if we've got a confirmed match."

"Do that," she said. "Meanwhile, we've still got Hopper's Security to talk to and that Dennis Ryan character down on the coast to see. And that's before we even start getting stuck into our new case." She felt suddenly overwhelmed. "Dan, can we put Ryan on a back burner for now? At least until we've got a name for our victim. But you and Jason need to hop to Hoppers' and find out what exactly the security arrangements were on the Spencer Court site."

Baines nodded and she turned her attention to the new board.

"Like it or not, this is a live case. Spencer Court Man's been dead so long that, to put it bluntly, there isn't the same urgency about solving his case. That's why I'm giving priority to Mr Meredith here. Will, can you run us through what's known about him?"

Tyler recited what he'd learned about Kit Meredith's criminal background.

"DCI Gillingham," Archer said, "I don't suppose you came across him or his brother when you were at Reading?"

He swivelled his gaze ceilingwards, but evidently didn't find any answers there.

"Not ringing any bells," he decided. "Steve, how about you?"

"Nor me, Paul."

"Well," Archer said, "first we need to break the news to the wife. Had she reported him missing, by the way, Will?" Tyler shook his head. "That's a bit odd, isn't it?" She shrugged. "We can ask her about that. Joan, you're with me. We'll swing by Reading nick and pick up Will's new best friend, DC..."

"Derek Pollard," Tyler supplied.

"When we get out of here, warn him to expect us. And, once we've finished with the wife, I want to interview the brother. If they were at daggers drawn with a rival outfit, he'll know what was going on."

"Let's hope he wants his brother's killers brought to justice by legitimate means," Ashby commented. "He wouldn't be the first to take the law into his own hands"

"A gang war crossing county lines," moaned Gillingham. "The Super's just going to love that."

* * *

Hoppers' offices were in High Wycombe, the second largest town in Buckinghamshire after Milton Keynes. Apart from seeing a few gigs at the Wycombe Swan Theatre, Baines's contact with the town had been sparse, although he vaguely remembered a survey years back that had ranked it one of the dirtiest in South East England. There had been a good deal of redevelopment more recently, but the town was still known to have some pockets of severe deprivation.

High Wycombe had been no stranger to violent crime in recent years, with shootings, a mini-riot between feuding families and gangs, and anti-terrorism raids related to a plot to carry liquid explosives onto airliners and detonate them. The plot had led to restrictions on the amount of liquid that could be taken onto an aircraft, which still held today.

Hopper's building, on the fringe of the town centre, was beige and nondescript. The operations director was a balding man in his mid-fifties by the name of Ken Wadham.

"Christ, you're asking," he said when they filled him in on what they wanted. "Aylesbury, ten years ago? I mean, yeah, we look after building sites all over the place. We could well have provided cover there. I can check, I suppose…"

"That'd be a start," Baines said, sensing that this was going to be one of those conversations. "We'd also like to know if there were any break-ins or other incidents during construction."

Wadham puffed his cheeks. "I don't know how quickly we can put our hands on the files. But leave it with me, and I'll see what we can do."

Baines looked the director in the eye. "I'd rather you did it now."

Ken Wadham looked about to object, then nodded instead. "Of course. Always happy to help." He motioned to seats. "Make yourselves comfy. This could take a little while. I'll send some coffee and bickies in."

He strode out of his dull, modern office. Baines went and looked out the window at a nondescript urban scene. Two men in overcoats came out of an office building opposite, shook hands and walked off in opposite directions. Cars passed by. No doubt people would be coming out of their workplaces for lunch soon, those for whom a lunch break wasn't a luxury.

After a few moments, Bell joined him.

"You reckon he's gone to shred the records?" the Scot asked.

"Are you serious?"

"Probably not. I suppose his reluctance to hurry was more likely laziness than anything to hide."

"I didn't see anything in his expression or body language," Baines said. "Probably just lazy, as you say. If they don't turn anything up, I'll get a warrant and we'll take this place apart."

A few minutes later, a teenager knocked and entered with mugs of coffee, milk and sugar and a plate of assorted biscuits.

Baines helped himself to a custard cream and munched reflectively. The body in the concrete had made the local news, but Ken Wadham didn't even seem aware that Howard and Burns had been a client back in the mid-noughties. He'd have been around his mid-forties back then, Baines fancied. Assuming he'd been at the company then, he ought to remember. Maybe he'd only joined the firm comparatively recently.

In less than ten minutes, Wadham returned clutching a few sheets of paper.

"Easier than I thought," he said. "The guy we attached to night duty for the Spencer Street site was an Eric Yelland. Last known address in Aylesbury – your patch, Sergeant? – but I've no idea if he's still there. He's been retired about nine years."

Aylesbury. Not so surprising if he'd been security for Spencer Street. But, like the site manager, Barry Prince, someone well placed to know if anything suspicious had happened.

"Have you got that address?" Bell asked. "I'm sure we can track him down."

Wadham scribbled it down and handed him the scrap of paper. "I should tell you," he said, "that a couple of people here remember him. He actually retired a few years early."

"Oh?"

"I gather he was pensioned off to avoid a fuss. A few things happened on his watch – machinery going missing, that sort of thing. Nothing was ever proved, but it happened once too often. We even had the police sniffing around a couple of times, although it was a bit half-hearted, to be honest. I suppose they figured the clients were insured, but it was hurting our business."

Baines recalled Barry Prince saying that Hoppers' had lost the Howard and Burns business for this very reason.

"You remember this?" Baines asked.

"Sorry. Before my time."

"What about break-ins at Spencer Street? The site manager couldn't recall anything like that, but just to double check."

Wadham leafed through the file. "A bit of graffiti on the hoardings is all."

Baines thought they'd taken this as far as they could for now. "You've been helpful."

"Come back if we can help further."

"We will," Baines said, handing him a card and asking him to get in touch if anyone remembered anything.

As they returned to the car, Baines couldn't help reflecting on a security guard who might have been complicit in material being removed from sites. Would he also have countenanced something being brought in?

14

The visit to Reading police station was Archer's first sortie into Berkshire's county town. Collins had driven efficiently, and their journey had taken a little over an hour. Collins had opted for the A404, passing through lush landscapes dominated by the Chiltern hills, punctuated by small towns and smaller villages. From feeling like a fish out of water when she'd first transferred from London, Archer now considered herself fortunate to live in this part of the world. She understood why locals considered the Chilterns to be on a par with Britain's national parks for scenic beauty.

As they approached the station, a sprawling brick-built monolith on Castle Street, Archer noted a blend of architectural styles in the locale: elegant old bath stone properties shared the space with more modern, faceless blocks of flats. Collins had told her on the way that one of the town's traditions was an annual public weighing of its mayor, with the town crier announcing whether they had gained or lost weight during their term of office. The crowd was encouraged to cheer weight loss, as an indication of a year's hard toil, but boo any weight gain. Whilst Collins thought it was quaint, Archer thought it was slightly bonkers, and wondered when the politically correct brigade would get the practice stopped on grounds of fat shaming.

They were collected from reception by Will Tyler's contact, DC Derek Pollard, who turned out to be visibly overweight, sporting a slightly scruffy beard, hair that needed a trim, and a well-worn suit at least a size too small for him. Archer had a fleeting image of him in mayoral regalia, being heartily booed as the results of his weighing were announced.

"Our DCI would like to meet you, Ma'am," Pollard told Archer after handshakes and introductions. "Then I'm to accompany you to see Kit Meredith's wife and anyone else you need to see."

DCI Patrick Mahon was slim, medium height, with brushed back sandy hair and silver-rimmed glasses. His elegant suit and coordinated shirt and tie reminded Archer of her old boss at the Met, Nick Gibson, a man who never looked less than dapper.

Mahon's office was hardly palatial, but it was nicely furnished and had a sleek, business-like feel that Paul Gillingham had never managed to pull off in his Aylesbury equivalent. His desk was well organised, with a minimum of paper, by contrast to the rubbish dump that was Gillingham's working area.

"I thought it would be a good idea to have a bit of a chat about the Merediths," he said once they were all seated around his small meeting table. "As far as I'm concerned, the body turned up on your patch, so it's your case for now. But I gather you don't know where he was actually killed?"

"That's right," Archer agreed. "Although my assumption for now is that he was somewhere in or around Aylesbury when he died. Either he'd come to the town voluntarily, or he'd been abducted from elsewhere – maybe right here in Reading – and then brought into Aylesbury."

"Sounds about right," Mahon concurred. "Although I can't imagine why anyone would kill him here and then go to the trouble of dumping him in Aylesbury. He was found in the boot of an abandoned car, is that right?"

"Yes, Sir. We've no idea why they chose to dispose of the body that way. The smell drew attention to it, but even if they hadn't thought of that, it was only a matter of time before it was removed, and someone was bound to open it up. One of our DCs is checking out the last registered owner, but it had been sitting there for quite some time. I doubt the owner had anything to do with it."

"It's an odd one," said Mahon. "I mean, why not bury the body, or, I don't know, weight it and chuck it in the river?"

"Lots of dodgy people on Northfields estate, where the car was abandoned," Collins said. "If Kit Meredith was doing some sort of business there and there was a falling out, maybe that was a handy place to hide the body for a while. Give the killer time to establish an alibi. Or maybe they planned to move it somewhere more permanent, but someone – quite literally – got wind of it first."

Mahon smiled at the faint pun. "Interesting pair, the Meredith brothers. Chalk and cheese. Kit's the people person – the one with the gift of the gab. I can imagine him making deals, intimidating people with words if need be. His brother, Gary, is the hothead. They're still only a few notches above small-time in reality, but I reckon Gary aspires to be the Godfather of Reading, and he's always ready to feel disrespected and take offence. People who get in the Merediths' way, and don't listen to what Kit tells them, get hurt."

"And Gary does the hurting?" Archer asked.

"People get hurt, but no one will talk to us about it. But yes, we think Gary either dishes out punishment personally or supervises it. It's just never seemed like Kit's style."

Archer privately wondered about that. In her time at the Met, she'd encountered some eloquent, soft-spoken and charming criminals for whom, she'd been certain, violence was a last resort. But she'd also been certain that they recognised that violence was sometimes necessary in their line of work, and weren't overly squeamish about doing what was necessary when the need arose.

She remembered one individual who delighted in brandy with his afternoon espresso, and sported a nice line of bespoke suits from London's top tailors. His bottle-thick spectacles somehow enhanced his smooth, mild image, more stockbroker than gangster. But it was blood flecks on a Paul Smith suit that had convicted him of the murder of a rival. The suit had been rescued from his favourite dry cleaner minutes before they'd gone into a machine and the evidence destroyed.

Still, it wasn't unusual for gangs to have enforcers – hard men who used fists, and worse, to make sure they got their way. Maybe it was as Mahon had said, and Gary Meredith was the brawn to Kit's brains.

"Any possibility the brothers fell out?" She asked.

"What, and Gary killed Kit?" Mahon frowned. "Most unlikely. They're a close family. I'd say they put family first."

"Can I ask, Sir?" interjected Collins. "You obviously know a lot about the Merediths, and they're clearly bad people. Why aren't they behind bars?"

"The usual. No one will finger them. Fear for themselves. Fear for their families. We don't actually suspect the brothers of any actual murders, by the way. Strictly beatings and maimings. A couple of arsons, too. Homes and business premises burnt down."

"You said Gary Meredith saw himself as a bit of a Godfather," said Archer, "but you also said their outfit is less than big time. Where do they sit in the local pecking order?"

"That's a moveable feast," Mahon said. "Until recently, I'd have said there was no real top dog. There's as much organised crime here as you'll find in any large town, especially drugs networks, and the gangs can be quite territorial. We know there are firearms around, too. We've worked closely with Thames Valley's serious and organised crime unit in Oxford and also had some input and advice from the National Crime Agency, but it's a constant problem. We make arrests, get convictions, and if a vacuum is created, someone soon fills it."

He took his glasses off, pulled a handkerchief from his trouser pocket, and wiped a lens.

"I'd say on the whole, the Merediths' strategy is to try and do the filling," he continued as he replaced the handkerchief. "I'd also say they had ambitions to be the top dog, inasmuch as anyone will ever be, but incrementally – not by tearing up trees. Meanwhile, though, we have intelligence that a better organised and more ferocious breed of criminal from out of town – maybe outside the county – has its eyes on dominating the crime scene here." He looked at his watch. "Sorry, I'm forgetting my manners. I should have offered you coffee."

"We're fine," Archer assured him. "So, have you any idea who these outsiders are?"

Mahon gave a hollow chuckle. "Whoever they are, they're more frightening than the Merediths. A couple of small gangs have lost their leadership – a hospitalisation here, a suspicious accident there – but the business has persisted, under new management, we think. No one's talking. Even regular sources who probably know something are shitting themselves. Excuse my French," he added sheepishly.

It all sounded eerily familiar to Archer, her memory reaching back a couple of years to something similar kicking off in the Vale.

"Has the name Connolly come up at all?" she wondered.

Not a flicker of recognition. "I'm pretty sure it hasn't. Why? Do you know something?"

"They're a family firm," she said. "Cloaked in respectability. The old man is Murray Connolly. Hails from Glasgow, but came south as a teenager. On the face of it, he's squeaky clean, with lots of legit business and charitable interests. Rubs shoulders with celebrities. But we're sure there's a multitude of nasty sins beneath that veneer. It's just that no one's ever been able to get anything on him or his family."

"Not quite true, guv," Collins reminded her.

"No," Archer amended. "His youngest son, Desmond, did some time for petty drug dealing. Murray was apparently all humility, crocodile tears about his failing as a parent and determination to do better. But he has two other sons – Fraser and Cameron – who do a lot of the management these days. Cameron's based himself in the Vale, and again, it looks on the surface like the family business interests there are on the level. But we're sure they have fingers in a lot of murkier pies. It wouldn't surprise me if they were eyeing up neighbouring counties."

"That could fit," Mahon said. "Although I hear there's a nasty bunch of Eastern Europeans in Oxfordshire that are expanding their territory too."

"That's helpful, Sir," Archer said. "I think now we should break the bad news to Kit Meredith's wife. She still hasn't reported him missing?"

"No. I checked again just before you arrived. But, the line he was in, maybe it was common enough for him to go off the radar for a few days."

"Not even phoning home?" Collins shook her head. "Sounds a bit off."

"We'll ask about that," Archer said. She looked at Mahon. "I'd quite like to speak to the brother, too. Gary?"

"I'll get you contact details."

15

Baines and Bell returned to the station to check in and see how other strands of the Spencer Court investigation were progressing. They found a somewhat glum-faced Will Tyler.

"Identifying our body isn't going to be quite as quick a job as we'd hoped. It's not John Leeson."

Baines sighed. "Dental records don't match?"

"Not even close. I've got three others from the wider Thames Valley region who fit the height and age profile."

"Let's have them, then."

"Okay. I've got photos, too." He spread three images on his desk, burying other paperwork in the process. He tapped the one on the left. Baines took in the face of a man with sunken eyes and long, unkempt hair. "First one: George Hannah. Alcoholic and drug user. Hails from Oxfordshire, but of no fixed abode when he disappeared from the radar, aged forty one."

"He looks older," Baines remarked. "The lifestyle taking its toll, I'd guess."

"He would turn up on his parents' doorstep in Thame about once a month, cadging food, money. They were a soft touch, even though they knew they were feeding his habits. Then he just stopped coming. They started asking his friends if they'd heard from him and then eventually reported him missing."

He pulled a sheet of paper from under the pictures. "A few convictions... possession... one count of affray... indecency - looks like he turned the odd trick to raise money and was caught in the act one time..."

"No sightings or other information after he disappeared?"

"Not recorded here, no." He pointed to the middle image. "This one. Malcolm Gregg, from Henley. Worked as a freelance bookkeeper, but not a very successful one. Three days after he was reported missing, a whole host of financial irregularities started coming to light. It looked as if he'd been doing some less-than-subtle embezzlement from clients to keep his own lifestyle afloat. Suspicion was that either he'd done a runner, or he'd gone off somewhere to end it all. But, either way, neither sight nor sound of him since."

"So why would he end up under Spencer Court?" Bell said.

A faint smile played around Tyler's lips. "Let's just say he had an eclectic mix of clients. Some would have called the police in a heartbeat if they suspected him of fraud. But there were a few who... well, the last thing they'd want is the law nosing into their financial affairs, but maybe they wouldn't take someone stealing from them lying down, either."

"It still begs the question – why all the way from Henley to Spencer Court?" Baines was feeling frustrated. "I suppose, once we finally put a name to our victim, we can look more closely at their connections."

"Six points of contact, Dan," said Bell. He made it sound like a deeply meaningful contribution.

Baines gave him a sharp look. "What does that actually mean, Jason?"

Bell coloured. "Oh, you know. The idea that everyone in the world is no more than six steps away from each other. You can connect them through a chain of, like, 'friends of friends'."

Baines didn't know whether to be irritated or amused. "Yes, I do know. Isn't that more or less what I was just suggesting?"

"Well, yeah." Bell stared at his feet.

Baines decided to leave it at that. Bell was a decent enough DC, but not always the sparkiest. He blushed a lot less than he used to, but lately he was wont to parrot buzz phrases as if they were pearls of wisdom. Perhaps it was a way of managing his insecurities.

Baines turned back to Tyler. "And the third?"

The subject of the final photograph looked handsome and healthy. His dark hair was well-cut, and he had the hint of a tan about his complexion.

"Timothy Philips," he said. "Tim. Disappeared in the right time frame, aged forty five."

Baines found himself frowning. "That name rings a bell."

Tyler looked at him. "Really?"

"Yeah. Let me think. Tim Phillips..."

"Entrepreneur," Tyler read from his notes.

"That's right," Baines said. "Wasn't he a bit of a philanthropist, too?

"He lived in or near Reading, I think. Or maybe it was his business activities that were based there."

"That was it," Baines agreed. "He founded a couple of community charities, as well as creating some employment in the area."

"A bit of a local hero, then," Bell said.

"So the media thought. Just didn't come home one night, is that right, Will?"

"Said he had to go to a meeting in the evening and was never seen again. It's like he vanished into thin air. No trail at all, cold or otherwise."

"The search spilled over the borders," Baines recalled. "So Oxfordshire, Bucks, Herts. Beds and Northants too, I seem to remember. I think it was even on the national news for a couple of days. But there wasn't enough to sustain the media's interest for too long."

Tyler nodded. "It does ring a faint bell now. But wouldn't Gillingham and Ashby have still been based in Reading around that time?"

"Good point. The Super too, I guess. They might even have been part of the investigation. I'll ask them." He frowned. "Our body in the car was from Reading, but I can't see how the cases can be connected, even if this does turn out to be our Mr Phillips. Good work, though, Will. Go ahead and see if we can sort some dental records for these three."

* * *

Collins sat in the front passenger seat of Derek Pollard's elderly VW Passat, en route to Kit Meredith's family home. Archer was in the back, checking emails and text messages on her phone.

Pollard had said nothing since offering round a packet of Maltesers, which now sat in a tray in the centre console of the car. Both Archer and Collins had declined, but Pollard occasionally delved in the bag and popped one in his mouth. Otherwise, he concentrated on his rather pedestrian driving.

Collins was reflecting on what a momentous week this was proving to be for her. First on the scene at the Spencer Street explosion, and praised by her bosses for her handling of the situation. Now she had a temporary promotion, an opportunity she was determined to grasp with both hands and shine at.

And Charlie had moved in with her – in less than ideal circumstances, and sooner in their relationship than either of them would probably have wished for, but it was mostly working out well. When Collins had tried dating men, and been confused as to why it never worked for her, she'd never been close to having a live-in lover. But this felt right, as if a lot of puzzle pieces in her life had fallen into place. Charlie was supposed to be crashing with her just until something else could be sorted out, but maybe she'd end up sticking around. Collins didn't think she'd mind that a bit.

The only slightly dark cloud was Charlie's obvious disappointment that Collins was describing her new flatmate as 'a good friend' to family and colleagues. Charlie had come out as gay in her teens. Collins had only recently admitted to herself that she even was gay. She'd always been aware, she supposed, that her sexuality was less than clear cut, but she came from a family with definite, old-fashioned ideas about such things. Her parents frowned upon gay celebrities – her father believed homosexuality was a lifestyle choice and had apparently gone off Elton John when he'd discovered the singer was gay. The idea of talking to them about her confusion had terrified her.

A self-contained only child, she had never made friends particularly easily, and her best friend had died in a car crash years ago. At work, she was close to Jason Bell, but not so close that she'd confided in him that she was dating a woman. He still imagined the woman from Spencer Court who was staying at her flat was just a friend, but that there was also a guy on the scene, providing her with some long-overdue romance..

Things were, in many ways, much better in the police than they used to be, with coppers who had come out at work mostly receiving support and equitable treatment. But Collins knew that unreconstructed pockets still existed. DI Ashby, for example, may have undergone something of a transformation in the past year, but he was still not above the odd inappropriate comment, and clearly saw anyone who wasn't straight as lesser mortals. He and DCI Gillingham were old pals, so maybe the boss was of the same mindset.

"I get it," Charlie had said to her in bed last night. "I do. It took me a while to get to grips with who I really am, and actually telling people who mattered – I still remember the knots in my tummy. But you and I are either an item or we're not."

"We are," Collins had assured her. "At least, I think we are."

"But you pretending I'm just a pal makes me feel like a dirty little secret." Charlie's gaze had bored into Collins's eyes. "Look, I know you need time, and I'm not pressuring you. But it won't get any easier, and I won't put up with it forever."

The trouble was, just by saying that, Charlie had put pressure on Collins. But she was right. Collins could keep her true self hidden for the rest of her life or, sooner or later, she was going to have to be honest about it. And, deep down, she knew it would only get harder, the longer she put it off.

Kit Meredith's widow lived in a quiet cul de sac on what Collins supposed an estate agent might describe as an 'executive estate'. The houses were 1980s style, not unattractive, and were detached – that was to say there was about a metre between them. They were open plan at the front, with a pocket handkerchief of lawn, a slim strip of bedding, and private driveway – mostly block paved, but Collins spotted one in gravel and a couple more that had been tarmacked.

They all looked more or less the same from the outside. No overgrown front gardens, no rusting bikes, or kiddies' toys littering the lawns. It was as if the close was awaiting some sort of 'best kept street' inspection. Collins tried to imagine Kit Meredith, gangster, out on his drive on a Sunday morning, washing his car alongside all the other menfolk in the road. Perhaps the aroma of baking bread permeated from an open window.

Lisa Meredith, when she opened the door, proved to look nothing like a Stepford wife. Her blonde hair was scraped back into a straggly bun, the tee-shirt she wore looked as if it had never seen an iron, and the rips in the knees of her jeans didn't strike Collins as designer details. She had what Collins's mother would have called a hard face, a look that intensified when she saw the warrant cards.

"Oh, for God's sake," she muttered. "What's he supposed to have done now?"

"Can we come in, Mrs Meredith?" Archer asked.

Lisa looked up and down the street. "You'd better. You might be in plain clothes, but the curtain-twitchers will smell you for coppers from a hundred yards away."

They followed her into a modestly-furnished living room. A vacuum cleaner, plugged in, stood in the middle of the carpet, and there was a duster on the coffee table.

"You caught me cleaning house," Lisa said. "I'd ask you to excuse the mess, but since you weren't invited… Look, what's this all about? Kit's not here, if you wanted him."

"Perhaps we could all sit down," Archer suggested.

She folded her arms. "No. You won't be stopping long."

Archer glanced at Collins. Lisa Meredith wasn't making a horrible job any easier.

"Mrs Meredith," she tried again. "May I call you Lisa?"

"Whatever."

"Lisa, I'm afraid we have some bad news."

Collins was watching the woman's face closely. You had to be sensible of the newly-bereaved's feelings, but at the same time you needed to watch their reaction. See what it told you.

Lisa's reaction made it clear that she'd had no idea that her husband was dead, unless she was the most accomplished of actors. Archer was barely through that first formal sentence when the hostility drained from her face, along with most of the colour. The corners of her mouth turned downwards, her lower lip trembling.

"I'm sorry to say," Archer ploughed on, "that a body was found this morning that we believe to be your husband –"

"N-no," she stammered. "You're lying. What kind of a trick is this?" Tears were already streaming down her face as she stepped towards Archer, hands shaped into fists.

For a moment, Collins thought Lisa was going to attack Archer. Then she was stepping forward to catch the stricken woman as her eyes rolled back and her knees gave way.

16

When Lisa Meredith fainted, Archer's first thoughts had been to call an ambulance. But Derek Pollard had dealt with the crisis calmly and professionally, describing it as a rare opportunity to put his first aid training into practice. With Collins's help, he got the woman lying on her back on a sofa and raised her legs with the aid of some scatter cushions. He'd loosened the belt of Lisa's jeans and asked Archer to see if she could find some fruit juice. By the time Archer returned with some mango juice, the patient was showing signs of reviving, although she was still pale.

"Shouldn't we still get a doctor or something?" she asked Pollard.

"I think she'll be fine," the DC replied, holding the glass for Lisa to drink. When she'd had a few sips, he withdrew the glass and passed it to Collins. "How are we doing, Lisa?"

"I'm okay," she whispered, making to sit up.

Pollard gently pushed her back down. "You need to rest for a while, or you'll most likely pass out again. You've had a shock. We're so sorry for your loss."

Her eyes widened, as if she had only just taken in the bad news they had brought her.

"But Kit... You say he's dead."

"I'm so sorry," Archer said. "The body will need to be formally identified –"

"We can talk about that stuff later," Pollard cut her off. He held Lisa's hand in his pudgy paw. "Yes, Lisa. I'm afraid there's no doubt."

"B-but how? Why?" She shook her head. "I don't get it. Kit doesn't do this. Getting himself killed. That's more his bloody brother's style. Fucking Gary," she spat.

"What do you mean?" Collins prompted gently. "What about Gary?"

The newly-widowed woman seemed to suddenly realise who she was talking to. She closed her eyes..

"Nothing," she said. "It's just that my Kit's the nice brother. Gary's the short fuse."

"When did you last see Kit?" Archer moderated her tone, making it as tender as Pollard's and Collins's. She'd been a bit blunt with Lisa, she realised. Sometimes it was best to get the bad news out as quickly as possible. Maybe this was an occasion that had demanded a softer approach. Gangster's wives had feelings too. Archer had broken this sort of news dozens of times in her career, but still got it wrong sometimes.

"I don't know," Lisa responded, furrowing her brow. "Monday morning?"

"What were his plans?"

"No idea." She looked at Pollard. "I really think I can sit up, now."

"Okay," he said. "Gently does it, though."

He helped her into a sitting position. She held her hand out to Collins for the glass of juice. Archer waited while she took a couple more sips.

"Can I just check, Lisa?" she said. "You haven't seen your husband since Monday morning, and you had no ideas about his plans for the day?"

Lisa sighed. "All right. Let's drop the pretence. Let's just say he didn't tell me anything at all about his work. Where he was going, what he was doing, who he was seeing. If he was going to be staying away, and for how long. He always said, if anyone came here asking questions about him, I'd never have to lie if I didn't know anything. And he had a point." She gave her first, albeit weak, smile since she'd opened the door to the detectives. "I'm a terrible liar."

"But… presumably he phoned home, or you phoned him?"

"Oh, yeah, I rang a couple of times, but it went to voicemail."

"You left a message?"

"No. We don't do that. To be honest, I think he's… he *was*," she amended, "a bit paranoid about what you guys can find out about him. Anyhow, this wasn't unusual. Sometimes he'd be away on God knows what business. He didn't tell me he was going, nor when he'd be back." She pursed her lips. "It made it a bit annoying, not knowing when he would and wouldn't want dinner." She looked Archer in the eye. "But you haven't answered any of my questions. Where did you find him? How did he die?" She was crying again, but didn't look about to pass out.

"I'm afraid he was murdered. I can't give you details right now."

"Oh, Christ," Lisa muttered. "Why couldn't he have been a civil servant or something? He'd have been good at that. Now what am I going to do? Do you know who did it?"

"We don't. Do you have any ideas?"

"No. I told you. There was his home life and his work life. I knew bugger all about his work life. For all I know, he had enemies coming out of his ears, although I never got that impression. He was always so cool, laid back." She sipped some more juice. "Speak to Gary. He'll know a lot more than I do. But he'll go bloody mad when he finds out what happened."

Collins spoke up. "Any friction between the brothers lately?"

Lisa laughed hollowly. "All the time. But Gary would no more kill Kit than kill his own kids. Her face crumpled. "Oh, Christ, I have to collect the kids from school soon. What am I going to tell them?"

"We're going to arrange a family liaison officer for you, Lisa," Pollard said, "so you know what's going on and have someone on the force to talk to and ask questions. Is there anyone we can call who can be with you?"

"I'll call my mum when you're gone. You speak to Gary. He wouldn't harm a hair on Kit's head, but that doesn't mean this isn't his fault. Maybe he ruffled the wrong feathers and Kit paid the price."

Archer looked at her with interest. "Is that what Gary does? Ruffle feathers?"

"As I said, Kit didn't talk about his work. But he did come home looking worried one evening, talking about being out of his depth and Gary trying to punch above his weight. He said, *He'll piss the wrong people off one of these days.* But I don't know who he was talking about."

There didn't seem to be much more information to be gleaned and the detectives left her soon afterwards. Archer promised to make sure Lisa was kept informed on developments.

"I doubt very much that Kit was quite the nice guy his wife just painted him to be," Collins remarked as Pollard started his car.

"No," Archer agreed. "The business he's in, nice guys finish second. Or dead."

"Well," Pollard said, poised to pop a Malteser in his mouth, "he *is* dead."

Archer smiled at the black humour. "If that makes him nice, all the more reason to check out Mr Nasty. Let's get hold of Gary Meredith."

17

They left a message for Gary Meredith on his home number, and he phoned back within ten minutes, saying that, if they were that keen to see him, they could find him in a the pretentiously named Royal Bar on Gun Street.

"Sounds ominous," Archer remarked.

Pollard laughed. "I suppose it does. Apparently the road had a gunsmiths at one time."

The bar was just a short walk from the police station. Gun Street itself had an assortment of older buildings on one side only, including a number of bars and eateries. On the opposite side of the road lay the lush green space of a churchyard, where headstones nestled amongst shady trees.

"There used to be houses both sides," Pollard said as they approached the bar. "Taking them down that side and extending the churchyard was a 19th Century improvement."

The bar was housed in what looked to Archer like a Victorian-vintage building, but inside it was decorated and fitted out in cutting edge, modern style. Archer was told in no uncertain terms that it was closed until 5pm, but her warrant card gained them hasty admission.

They found Gary Meredith upstairs, playing pool with a neckless chunk of muscle whom Archer felt couldn't possibly be as thick as he looked.

Gary Meredith was probably quite good looking, Archer thought, if you liked that sort of thing. Blue-black hair with a widow's peak, eyes that were almost the same colour, and features more delicate than she had expected for a hard man who dealt in crime and pain. He was about Archer's height, a little under six feet, and slimly built, but with a suggestion of toned muscle underneath the cornflower blue shirt he had teamed with a pair of well-fitted jeans. He flashed her a smile, all white teeth and good dentistry, as he saw the three officers approaching.

"DI Archer, I presume?" There was a hint of local accent, a hint of roughness about his voice. He made a show of taking in Collins and Pollard. "This is quite a deputation. To what do I owe the honour?"

Archer couldn't decide whether he really was channelling some sort of Godfather figure, or just taking the piss. She decided to puncture that puffed-up persona, even if she broke all her personal rules about breaking bad news.

"We thought you'd like to know your brother is dead," she said.

She studied his face closely as she delivered that bald statement. Gary's mouth fell open in a silent *O*.

"My brother?" he echoed. "You don't mean Kit?"

"I understood you only had one brother," Archer answered.

Gary stood motionless for perhaps half a minute. Then he turned to his neckless pool opponent. "Leave us, Robbie."

The man called Robbie shrugged, picked up a jacket from a nearby chair, and put it on with a great deal of faff before reaching for a pint perched on the cushion of the table. Before his fingers could close around it, Gary Meredith snatched up a pool ball and flung it with force at the glass, shattering it. A shard embedded itself in Robbie's hand and crimson blood welled.

"I said, fuck off!" Gary bawled, violence in every syllable. "Now!"

Robbie fled, clutching his injured hand.

Archer was shocked by the suddenness of the change in Gary Meredith, and his extreme reaction to the other man's delay in departing. She was also aware that she had just witnessed an assault, but now was not the time to worry about that.

There was glass and beer on the floor, more on the baize of the pool table, beer mingling with drops of blood. More liquid dripped from the cushion to the floor. The table was probably ruined. Archer wondered if Gary Meredith would be paying for it.

Gary himself was breathing heavily, as if he'd just run a half-marathon. Archer could swear his eyes had darkened, and there was something feral about his features. She folded her arms, leaving a silence for him to fill, and was pleased to see her colleagues mirroring the gesture.

Gary seemed to get his breathing under some sort of control. His features smoothed, the beast inside him banished, at least for now. He blinked hard, three times.

"I haven't seen or heard from Kit since Monday," he said finally, and he might as well have been talking about last night's soap operas. "Not that we lived in each other's pockets. But *dead*? Are you sure?"

"We'll need someone to formally identify the body," Archer replied, "but there's no doubt."

"I'll do that," Gary said. "Lisa shouldn't have to go through it." He sighed, anguish still naked on his face. "So what happened?"

Archer gave him the main details, leaving out the facts that the body had been found in a car boot and that Kit had probably suffered before he died. She had no reason to suspect Gary of his brother's murder but, at this stage, no reason not to, either. More than once she'd known suspects to mention details that only a perpetrator would know, forgetting that those facts weren't in the public domain.

He walked over to a chair and sat down, head in hands. He remained that way for a while. When he looked up, Archer could see that the rage he had managed to control a few moments ago was reasserting itself.

"Do you know who did it?" he all but snarled.

"These are early days in the investigation. –"

"But you have suspects?"

"Not yet, no."

"Well, you'd better find them before I do. That's all I can say."

"Mr Meredith," Collins said, "if you think you know anything about your brother's murder, you should tell us. Planning to take the law in your own hands isn't helpful to anyone."

"Is that right, darling?" his tone was sneering. "I just want justice for my brother. One way or another, I'm going to have it."

"If we can cut the macho tough talk for a moment," Archer said, "maybe we can make some progress. So tell us. Who do you think might have wanted your brother dead? And why would his body show up in Aylesbury?"

"How should I know?" He stared at the floor.

She fought down her rising exasperation. Was this whole outraged grief thing just one big act?

"I think you're better placed to come up with some names than we are at this stage," she said. "You and Kit must have made a lot of enemies in your line of business, and doubtless you know who most of them are."

"What line of business is that?" He was suddenly all flippancy, his mood changes mercurial. "Me and Kit are strictly legit."

"Not according to our records," Pollard commented.

Gary plastered on a cheesy grin. "Hi, Derek. What's the calorie count today?" He turned back to Archer, spreading his arms in a gesture of innocence. "Fair enough. We've made mistakes in the past, but our records have been clean for years."

"That's because you've got cleverer," Pollard persisted. "Not because you've gone straight."

The grin vanished, replaced by something uglier. His nostrils flared as he addressed Archer again. "Can you shut your fat monkey up? I don't mind talking to you, love. You're easier on the eye. Apart from that funny mouth."

It was all Archer could do not to recoil. She felt slapped. She heard Collins intake breath sharply.

Archer herself took a mental count of ten. "This is a serious matter," she said calmly, "and we all want justice for your brother. So let's stop all the posturing. I'm interested in this murder, not in any crimes you may or may not be involved in. So, if you know anything that will help us make an arrest, we need to know."

He seemed to consider this, staring at the floor again. Then he looked up at Archer, nodded curtly, and patted the seat beside him. Archer felt herself stiffening inside at the patronising gesture, but swallowed the feeling and went to join him.

Seated a few inches away from him, she fancied she could feel, even smell, something animal and vicious coming off him. She wondered again how much of his posturing was an act. Also wondered how capable Gary would be of controlling himself if even his own brother got under his skin.

"All right," he said. "I'll tell you what I know." He raised a hand to scratch his cheek. "Off the record?"

Archer shook her head. "No such thing."

He shrugged, his smile vaguely genuine for the first time since she'd laid eyes on him.

"I had to try. Fair enough. Well, you talked about my line of work. We do have a bit of competition here in the town – Derek knows who they are – but on the whole, we all rub along okay.

"Only, lately, all the local firms are being hurt by product coming in from outside."

"Drugs?" queried Collins.

He looked at her as if she was a speck of dust on the floor. "Product. And I wasn't talking to you."

If the putdown stung Collins, she didn't show it. Archer let it slide.

"Where outside?" she said. "And who's supplying it?"

He shrugged. "People talk. We heard it was an Oxford or Aylesbury operation – it wasn't really clear which. Some sort of Eastern Europeans, trying to build an empire fast."

"Do you have names?"

"No one's been naming names, either because they don't know them, or because they're scareder of these guys than they are of me." He flashed an arrogant smile. "Huge mistake, by the way."

Archer thought any gang operating on the Connolly family's turf would be making an even bigger mistake. Maybe they were on the Connolly payroll, doubtless without any evidential connections.

"So, is that what Kit was doing in Aylesbury?" she wondered. "Something to do with these Eastern Europeans? Trying to warn them off?"

Gary shook his head. "He's got –" His voice caught. "He *had* some contacts over in Aylesbury, and he had an idea that he could get a meeting with these guys and broker some sort of deal."

"What sort of deal? The sort where he warns them off? Or the sort where you form some sort of alliance?"

"The sort where we leave each other's markets alone and everyone's happy. I told him it was stupid. They knew exactly what they were doing, working our patch. I told him, if they wanted a war, they could have one." He paused abruptly, as if remembering who he was speaking to. "In business terms, obviously. Nothing violent, or illegal."

"Obviously," Archer repeated. "Because you're strictly legit."

"Right."

It didn't quite sit right with her. "So you didn't want Kit meeting these guys. But did you know he was going anyway?"

"No."

"Yet you say you've heard nothing from him since Monday apart from texts. Lisa assumed he was away on business, and she said he never told her anything about his work. But you must have known he'd effectively gone missing?"

"I'm not my brother's keeper, sweetheart."

She sighed. "Let's get one thing clear. I'm not your sweetheart, and I'm not your love. But I'm someone who can probably find an excuse for arresting you, so mind your manners."

"Typical coppers. Always looking to fit you up."

"I can tell you're crying inside. I still don't get it. You and Kit ran your... your *business* together. How could he go off the radar for three days and you don't know where he is, what he's doing?"

"Well, I guessed where he'd gone. It was pretty obvious. He'd do that sometimes. We'd disagree on something and he'd just go off and do what he thought was right, even though he knew he'd piss me off. Half the time I had to admit he'd been right."

"And the other half?"

"We'd have a big row and something would get sorted. So yeah, I was sure he'd gone to Aylesbury. I didn't like it, but I didn't think they'd be stupid enough to hurt him. Start something I'd have to finish. Well, that's two serious mistakes they've made, isn't it?"

"Two?"

"Trying to muscle in on my business. And killing my brother. It's not going to stand."

"I know what that sounds like," Archer said, "and this time you'd be the one making a mistake. Don't come onto our manor starting a war."

"Are we done?" He stood up. "You've got my number. Let me know when I can see my brother."

"I haven't finished."

"No? Well, I have. Sweetheart. You know your way out, right?"

Archer weighed her options, then nodded. "This is just the beginning. I might be back with more questions. Meanwhile, stay out of Aylesbury."

For answer, Gary Meredith stood up, walked over to the pool table, and picked up his cue. He began potting balls, ignoring the state of the table. He didn't look up as Archer got up and gestured for her colleagues to follow her downstairs.

* * *

For Sonia Meredith, it had been a bit of a humdrum day so far. School run, supermarket shopping, a bit of laundry. She'd just sat down with a mug of tea and a Sudoku when her phone rang. Gary.

"Hi, babe," she said. "All okay?" It was rare for him to call during the day.

"It's Kit." He sounded like he was crying. "He's only gone and got himself killed, hasn't he?"

"Killed?"

94

"The police came to the Royal. "They found his body in Aylesbury. Silly sod must have gone there sniffing about. Christ, Sonia, I told him not to."

She felt her stomach turning over. A rival operation fishing in their pool was one thing. But Kit dead? That was off the scale.

"Jesus, Gary. Do you think they'll come after you?"

"Not if I kill them first. I'm going to find out who it was – "

She knew that tone. "Calm down."

"Yeah? You reckoned Kit was the calm one. Look where it got him."

"Look," she said, "come home. I got us one of those lemon cakes you like. Let's talk about it."

"No, I haven't time for that. I told those coppers, I'm not letting this stand."

"Oh, clever," she couldn't keep the irritation out of her voice. "So if one of these Poles, or whatever they are, turns up dead, no prizes for guessing who the police will arrest first."

"He was my brother, Sonia."

"I know, babe. And I'm sorry." She was. She'd liked Kit. If the fact of his murder hadn't scared her so, she'd probably be feeling the grief more. "Please come home. I know you. You'll do something stupid."

"Gotta go. See you tonight."

The phone went dead. Sonia put her head in her hands, myriad emotions swirling around her head.

Gary and Kit had put so much into building up the operation but Sonia had never been happy about the trade that put a roof over her head and food on her table. Gary was, and she couldn't help who she loved, but it scared her. Every time there was a knock at her door, she feared it would be the police, coming to take him away.

Now she would fear a rival gang, come to kill him.

She'd been arguing for some time that the family could get out of illegal activities altogether. The legitimate businesses that had been developed to mask the dodgier stuff they were into – with her encouragement and, she had to admit, Kit's vision – were doing nicely in their own right.

But Gary loved the cut and thrust too much. Really fancied himself as Mr Big, and that was a self-image she'd so far been unable to wean him off. Surely now was the time for another push in that direction. For her money, if someone else wanted to do the drugs and the women, that was fine. It wasn't going to dent her lifestyle.

She reached for her tea. Her first task was to dissuade Gary from doing anything stupid. That in itself could be a tall order.

18

Baines was finding the investigation into the body at Spencer Court frustrating. Until the name of the victim had been established, they couldn't begin to look at possible motives for his death. Meanwhile, he'd already ticked most of the candidates for having buried the body – or at least admitting whoever *had* buried it to the site – off his list.

Apart from Dennis Ryan, the builder with a murky past, and who was over a hundred miles away in Dorset, only one name remained on the list: Eric Yelland, the security guard who'd been allocated to the Spencer Court site.

Yelland's address was in a cul de sac on a 1980s development, and had probably seen better days. Every piece of visible woodwork was desperately begging for a lick of paint, and at least one window ledge looked beyond salvation. The brickwork was a stranger to re-pointing. As for the little patch of ground masquerading as a front garden, it wasn't quite running riot. Evidently someone had made a crude assault upon it with some secateurs. If they hadn't, the house might have been altogether hidden, like Sleeping Beauty's castle.

"Let's hope the people from *House and Garden* aren't expected," Bell said. "It'd be a real shame to drag him away from his photoshoot."

Baines led the way up the cracked, moss-ridden path to the front door and pressed the bell-push. There was no hint of a bell ringing inside, so Baines tried again. Then he pounded on the door with his fist. There was no reply.

"Not at home," Bell commented. "That, or deaf."

"Let's try the neighbours," Baines suggested. "You take the one on the left, I'll take the right. Maybe they'll have an idea when he's due back."

The properties flanking Yelland's down-at-heel home only served to put it to more shame. Both were immaculate. Baines wondered how they took to the eyesore next door.

The bell-push at Baines's chosen neighbour prompted a reassuring *ding-dong*. The front door had frosted glass panels and, moments later, he was rewarded by the sight of a figure coming to open up.

The woman who answered the door was middle aged and slim to the point of skinny. He suspected she had either been ill or had been on a diet, because the dress she wore looked at least two sizes too large.

"Eric?" she snorted when he told her what he wanted. "I don't see much of him. I'm not sure he gets out much. He certainly doesn't get out into the garden. Can't the council make him tidy it up?"

"You'll have to ask the council, madam," Baines said. "When did you last see him?"

"Now you're asking. Hold on, though. Yesterday morning. I saw him bringing his bins in. It was bin day, you see. He takes them down the side – "

"What time was that?" Baines interrupted.

"I don't know. Let me think. It must have been before 12.30, because I have my lunch at 12.30. Just a shake. It's my diet. They taste horrible, and they don't exactly fill you up, but the weight's dropping off me."

"Well done," he said, thinking she'd already taken it a bit far. "So he took the bins in some time – what? Late morning?"

"The bin men normally come middish morning, so yes."

"And you haven't seen him since?"

"No. Come to think of it, his car's not been there. He parks it outside. Some sort of Toyota. Or Honda. I'm useless at cars. Mind you, the number of accidents he's had with it, it doesn't look like much of anything. Dents all over."

"I don't suppose you've got his mobile number?"

"Oh, no. I wouldn't want to give him any ideas. You start swapping phone numbers with a man, and they expect things. That's my experience."

He glanced at the woman's left hand. No wedding ring. Maybe she'd had a racy single life, packed with men expecting things.

"Anyone else live there?"

"Not unless he's got them chained up in the attic." Her smile suggested she found the thought exciting.

"Do you know how and where he spends his time?" Baines asked.

"No idea," she replied. "We might be neighbours, but we barely say hello, much less pass the time of day. He's not especially social and, to be honest, that suits me fine. The state of his house, the state of his car, the state of *him*…"

"State of him?"

"Scruffy. Very scruffy. He can't own a hairbrush or comb, and he doesn't appear to have much of a wardrobe. What he does wear looks like it's never had a wash or a clean."

It was pretty apparent that this woman disapproved of Eric Yelland. Baines gave her a card and asked her to get in touch when Yelland came home.

It was the same story from the house on the other side – a young mother with two pre-school children. Equally outspoken, she'd told Bell she didn't want much to do with Eric Yelland.

"Said, and I quote, 'he always seems a creepy little man'," Bell reported as they sat in Baines's Mondeo. "Not that she's ever really spoken to him. She did see him drive off around 7pm yesterday though. Doesn't think he's been back since. I asked if he ever had visits from family or friends. She said not. She's never seen anyone visiting him."

"Great neighbours," Baines said. "If it wasn't for the missing car, I'd half suspect he's lying in there unconscious or dead. We might have to break in yet. Maybe the car's in for repair and he's on foot. But let's get back to the station and see what more we can find out about him."

"Funny he disappeared soon after the *Echo* helpfully reported our find at Spencer Street."

Baines had been thinking exactly the same. "And it was on the local TV news, remember."

If Yelland had been involved, if not with the Spencer Court victim's murder, at least with his burial – even if his contribution was no more than leaving a padlock unlocked – then maybe that news item had scared him, sent him on the run before the police came looking for him. It wouldn't be the first time Baines had known a guilty conscience to provoke flight at the first hint that chickens might be coming home to roost.

"We need to find him," Baines said. "He must have family of some description. They must know something about him. And his car. Find out what he owns and let's see if any ANPR cameras have picked it up since yesterday evening."

"Of course," Bell said, "this could all be a damp squib. I mean, the neighbours don't actually know a thing about him. So there's nothing to say he hasn't gone to, I don't know, a trainspotting convention, or to visit a rich maiden aunt. Or maybe he's just got into online dating, met someone last night, and got lucky."

"Or maybe he went to see whoever buried that body. Maybe all he did was take a bribe to let them in and never imagined what they were up to. Then he hears that something sinister might have been found and decides to see the killer. Either for reassurance that it was nothing too bad, or maybe to see if he can squeeze some cash in exchange for his silence."

"If he did that…"

Bell left the thought hanging. If a killer who'd thought himself safe for over a decade suddenly felt threatened, he might decide that eliminating Yelland was better than paying him – maybe time and again – for a silence that could never be guaranteed.

Baines started the car. "Let's not rush our fences though. Your scenarios are as likely, if not more so. Chances are, he'll turn up later this evening and one of his caring, sharing neighbours will tip us the wink."

* * *

Baines and Bell arrived back at the station to find that Archer and Collins had not long returned from Reading.

"We can catch up properly later," Archer said, "but where are we with Spencer Court?"

He told her what little was new.

"Talk to Will," she said. "It looks like we might finally have an ID on the victim."

"Seriously? That was quick work with the dental records."

"I think our Will's a bit of a charmer on the quiet."

"So who is it?"

She smiled. "You're leading the case. Talk to Will."

"And what about the late Mr Meredith?" Baines asked. "Any suspects?"

She gave him a quick run down on her day. He didn't like the sound of it.

"Christ almighty, what's Thames Valley turning into? Things are bad enough with the Connollys pretty much running things in the Vale. Now we might have an Eastern European gang stirring things up all over the region?"

"Well, Reading, anyway. Although I think, for the time being, we need to take anything Gary Meredith tells us with a pinch of salt. I wouldn't rule out the possibility that he's simply lying for some reason."

Baines grimaced. "I almost hope so. The Connollys won't countenance competitors on their turf. If Meredith's mob come in here looking for revenge, the Eastern Europeans will be under attack from both sides. And, at the moment, we don't even know who they are."

Archer nodded her agreement. "There's a small part of me that says, let them all fight it out, and then we can go in and nab the last men standing. But it could get messy and bloody, and innocent people could get caught in the crossfire."

"Plus, the chances are, the last men standing will be the Connollys. But they're so damn good at making sure nothing sticks to them…"

"They'll come out of it all the stronger, and we'll be no closer to chopping off the head here."

They both knew that particular head was Cameron Connolly. It was Murray Connolly's youngest son, Desmond, who was thought to have first seen the Vale as a promising new territory, but he was also the least bright of the three brothers and had made rather a mess of things. Cameron had come in, steadied the ship and decided to make his home in the Vale, a tasty property in Great Missenden, just on the edge of the Vale. Like his father, he presented a respectable, philanthropic persona. Like his father, he was brilliant at ensuring no charges could stick to him, and in cultivating impeccable contacts.

"So what are we going to do?" Baines asked.

"We'll cover all that at the briefing. Which will be 6pm, by the way."

"Not 7?"

Archer shook her head. "I've got a date."

Baines found himself grinning, delighted for her. "Really? Not Dominic?"

She grinned back. "No. Don't get too excited. I'm having a bite and a glass of wine with the Super. Something she wants to talk to me about." She shrugged. "Probably means a lot more work for the team, and no more resources, right?"

He scratched his ear. "That can't be it, though. I mean, she'd go through Gillingham, surely, not over his head." He felt a rush of concern. "Be careful, Lizzie. You don't want to get involved in power politics."

She laughed. "Power politics? What's that?"

But the laugh rang hollow to Baines's ears. He sensed she wasn't entirely happy about the dinner date herself.

"Meanwhile," Archer said, dismissing the subject, "I'm hoping Steve Ashby's famous networks will know something about our Balkan friends. Some names would be good. And, I guess, I should interview Cameron Connolly."

He recoiled. "You're joking."

"I don't think so."

He felt his stomach churning. "You know what happened last time we tangled with that mob."

He remembered the pain as the bullet sliced into him. His terror as the gunman had prepared to finish him off. A now-dead gunman who, naturally, had never been connected with the Connollys, even though neither Archer's team, nor the National Crime Agency, doubted who his paymasters had been.

Archer's eyes had softened. "Of course I haven't forgotten what happened. I remember being at the hospital. The relief when they said you'd be all right. But what are you saying? That we should make Cameron Connolly as untouchable as he thinks he is?"

He shook his head vehemently. "Of course that's not what I'm saying. If we can take him and his organisation down, I'll be in the front line. But you're talking, frankly, about a fishing expedition. You'll likely get nothing out of it, and you'll be putting yourself on that man's radar. Do you really want to do that?"

He realised how tensely she was holding herself. She had broken eye contact.

"No," she said, "of course I don't. But it's what we do. One way or another, I suspect that Cameron Connolly knows exactly who these people are. If he was anyone else, we'd question him. I'm not going to treat him any differently."

19

Archer eyed the Spencer Court board. Baines had made a good job of updating it, including all the people either already spoken to, or still to be contacted, who might have had access to the site when the flats were being built. The name of Eric Yelland was underlined twice, with 'Missing?' written underneath.

The one puzzle piece she knew Baines had by now, but which wasn't on the board, was the identity of the man whose bones had been exposed by the gas explosion on Saturday night. Experts were now saying they were ninety nine per cent certain that the explosion was simple misadventure – a leak ignited by the luckless Warren Carter flicking on his light switch. Archer was grateful foul play wasn't suspected. Resources were stretched enough as it was.

She glanced at Baines, already seated in the front row, along with Bell, Collins and Tyler. She thought she knew exactly why he hadn't put the victim's name up yet. He wanted to produce it, like a rabbit from a hat. She'd have probably done the same.

People drifted into the room in ones and twos. Archer delayed the start by five minutes because people were still coming in. Gillingham had taken his seat at the back a few minutes before six. Ashby scuttled in and joined him just as Archer was starting.

Because it was more current than Spencer Court, she kicked off with an update on the Kit Meredith murder. When she was done, she looked across the room at Ashby.

"Steve, I don't suppose your networking can shed any light on these Eastern European guys?"

He was frowning, possibly a little pink of cheek. Blushing? Well, perhaps. He was the one who insisted he had his finger on the local pulse. How could a bunch of Balkans be making waves in the town and him not know it?

"It's weird," he admitted. "One of the things I've always got my eyes and ears open for is new players on the scene, and people I keep in touch with usually catch a whiff of them pretty quickly. I've heard bugger all about these people. I wonder if your mate Meredith was blowing smoke in your eyes. Maybe he knows more about his brother's death than he's letting on, and he's feeding us bullshit about a non-existent gang so we waste our time on wild goose chases."

"Maybe. Although his reaction when I told him Kit was dead seemed pretty genuine. I'd have said he had no idea."

"Sure," Ashby drawled. "And I recognise that you were there and I wasn't. But Kit's been dead for days. If Gary Meredith was involved, he's had bags of time to rehearse his reaction to the sad news."

She couldn't deny the possibility. "It's a fair point, Steve, and we'll bear it in mind. But, just to humour me, could you keep sniffing around your likely contacts and see if anyone – anyone at all – has heard of these Eastern Europeans?"

He nodded. "Consider it done. I can't promise anything, though."

She floated her intention to confront Cameron Connolly and see what he had to say about either the Meredith Murder or the status of the Balkan gang.

"Good," Gillingham declared. "About time someone rattled his cage. Even if it's a waste of time, at least he'll know we're not ignoring him. Just tread carefully. One of the reasons he and his family manages to keep such a low profile is their influential friends. That and the top dollar lawyers they have on their payrolls."

"Will," she said, "can you do some work on gangs in Thames Valley generally? Speak to the serious and organised crime guys in Oxford. Best talk to Bedfordshire and Hertfordshire too. We're interested in Eastern Europeans who might be trying to expand their turf. DCI Mahon mentioned something in Oxfordshire."

"On it, guv."

"Okay." She paused for a couple of beats. "Right, over to you, Dan. Where are we on Spencer Court?"

* * *

As Baines moved to the front to stand by his board display, Archer stepped away and took his seat. Baines was gratified. It was her way of saying it was his case and he was firmly in the driving seat.

"Okay," he said. "The first thing to say is, thanks to Will, we now have a name for our victim." He turned and pinned a photograph to the board. It was clipped from Will Tyler's printout, and the dark, tanned and good-looking man smiled out, the vitality he exuded a sad comparison with the pile of battered bones now stored at the mortuary.

"Tim Phillips, from Reading," Baines said. "Disappeared third of May 2005, which appears to fit well with the period in which the flats were built. He was the right sort of age and height, and dental records have clinched it."

There were a few murmurs. Baines's gaze strayed to the back of the room and to Gillingham and Ashby. If he'd expected a reaction from the former Reading men, he would have been disappointed. The DCI was staring straight back at him, his mouth a straight line that gave nothing of his thoughts away. Beside him, Ashby wasn't even looking at Baines. He was fiddling with his phone.

Baines continued. "So what do we know about him at this stage? He was a very successful local businessman who also spent a lot of his time supporting local good causes. Well connected, very charming and popular. At the time he went missing, he was married and had a couple of sons still at school. According to what Will has unearthed, he was always on the go, and it wasn't unusual for meetings to crop up at any time of the day, or even the night. The evening in question, he announced that something had come up and he had to go and see someone, but he never came back."

He locked eyes with Gillingham again. "You must remember the case, Sir. It gained quite a profile, with a big search conducted. Were you involved?"

Gillingham gave his head a shake. "Oh, I remember that one all right, but neither I nor Steve were actively involved. We were trying to solve a murder at the same time. But you're right. He was high profile and well-connected. In fact, we found support and resources for our own murder case progressively harder to come by. Tim Phillips was friendly with our Super and the Thames Valley Deputy Chief Constable, you see."

"But you must remember more about the case than we've managed to turn up?"

"Of course. For instance, I know that a lot of scenarios were being pursued. Money troubles, leading to him doing a runner or topping himself was high on the list for a time, but there was no evidence of the business being in trouble, nor of any financial regularities.

"A crazier idea, for my money, was that he'd run off with a woman. Of course, there's always someone wants to tear successful people down and there were occasional hints about him playing away – but they never amounted to much, and they didn't gain much credence. Even so, his lawyers were always quick to make all sorts of threats about unsubstantiated allegations. And I assume the media could never lay a glove on him ultimately, as they rarely printed anything and always retracted it within a day or so. His charities received some nice donations as a result, leaving him smelling all the more of roses."

He shook his head. "I could never see it in any case. If he wanted to change partners, why take off and leave all his wealth behind? The kind of lawyers he could afford would have secured him a pretty good divorce settlement."

"So did the investigation find anything useful at all?" Baines asked.

"Not to my knowledge. I think suicide due to stress or depression were also considered, but he apparently thrived on stress. There was the possibility he'd met with a tragic accident, of course."

"Or been murdered?"

"That too, although it wasn't clear who'd want him dead."

"Turns out someone did." Images of broken bones and a caved in skull flashed through Baines's mind. "And whoever did it wasn't exactly going soft on him." He tipped Gillingham a nod. "Thank you, Sir."

He moved closer to the board. "Jason and I are going over to Reading after this briefing. Coincidentally, we've already established some really useful contacts there through the Meredith case, and I want to be there when the wife gets the news."

Bell spoke up. "Could this be more than a coincidence? Two people from Reading turning up dead in Aylesbury in less than a week?"

"We have to keep an open mind, certainly, Jason," Baines said, "but as I've said to you before, I can't see an obvious connection. They clearly moved in very different circles."

"But what if, despite the investigation finding no evidence, our Mr Phillips had some criminal connections? I mean, we know the Connollys manage to hide their darker activities behind a curtain of respectability."

"That was looked at," Gillingham commented. "At least, I seem to remember it was. Nothing was found, but then I don't know how seriously the possibility was taken. Now I'm wondering."

"Me too," Ashby chimed in. "If this was the Bronx, and not Bucks and Berks, we'd be thinking gangland killing."

Collins put her hand up. Acting DS, and she still acted like a schoolgirl sometimes, seeking permission to speak from teacher. "What if, in his younger days, Kit Meredith was involved with criminal elements that fell out with Mr Phillips? What if he was involved in the killing and, now the remains have turned up, somebody's eliminating witnesses?"

"Whoa," Archer said, standing up. "Look, I agree that we shouldn't rule anything out on either of the cases, but it would be a mistake to rush into connecting them at this stage. If connections are there, there's a good chance they'll emerge naturally as we progress. Do you agree, Dan?"

"I do. I think the connections we need to make here are between the victim and these other names on this board." Baines turned to his display. "We've still got a couple of people we should see: Dennis Ryan in Dorset – he had out of hours access to the site and sounds less than squeaky clean; and, more urgently, Eric Yelland. He was the security guard allocated to the Spencer Court build, but it's possible he's disappeared. We need to find him."

"That could fit well with Joan's scenario, though, couldn't it?" Bell offered. "I mean, if Kit Meredith's been taken out because of a connection with Phillips, maybe this Yelland will be the next corpse to rock up."

Baines didn't rush to close the notion down. It was just about possible, he supposed.

"Remember," Collins added, "the *Echo* stirred up interest in something – they couldn't be sure what – under Spencer Court. Someone out there knew what was there, and now a bad boy from Phillips' town is dead and someone connected to the site is missing." She shrugged. "I'm just saying."

"It's a fair point," Baines acknowledged. "All right. What if my Phillips investigation keeps an eye out for possible links with Meredith and the Meredith investigation looks out for Phillips connections? Lizzie?" He looked Archer's way.

"Makes sense," she agreed.

"As to the other people we've looked at," Baines turned back to his board, "we've spoken to them all. Nothing obvious, but these are early days. Our immediate focus for now will be finding out all we can about Tim Phillips. Something made somebody beat and kick the crap out of him."

"Of course," Ashby remarked, "there is another possibility. Wrong place, wrong time. Or a mugging gone wrong."

"That's always possible," Baines acknowledged. "We'll be checking whether there were any other random violent attacks in and around Reading at the time. A violent mugging, or a random psycho? Either way, this would be unlikely to be a one off." He frowned. "No one seems to know who he went off to meet the night he disappeared. I can't help feeling that's significant. Lots to do."

"Lots for all of us to do." Archer stood up. "Anything else, Dan?" He shook his head. She turned to face the team. "Any other points, or questions, anyone?" No one had any. "Okay. We'll meet again tomorrow to see how we've been getting on. Don't stay here all night, guys."

20

Bell squeezed Collins' elbow as they walked back down the corridor towards the office.

"Thanks for backing me up in there," he said softly, so only she could hear. "About the possibility that our two cases are linked, I mean."

She smiled. "It's a perfectly sensible line of enquiry."

"Yes, but I think they take you more seriously than they do me."

She was touched, but also concerned. He'd seemed genuinely pleased about her temporary promotion. She really hoped that pleasure wasn't tinged with jealousy. She valued his friendship, as well as their professional relationship.

"I'm sure that's not true," she said.

"Oh, but it is." His Glasgow accent was just a little stronger than usual. It often was when he spoke from the heart.

She stopped and pulled him to the side, so people could pass. "Jason, you're a respected member of this team. Has Dan or Lizzie told you you're not?"

"Well, no."

This wasn't really the place for this conversation. Too many people passing on their way from the briefing. She looked across the corridor and spotted a darkened office. "Let's nip in there for five minutes."

They waited for a gap in the human traffic and crossed to the office. Collins put the light on and shut the door.

"Are you really okay with my being Acting DS, Jason? Because I haven't been brown nosing for it, or anything like that."

His eyes widened. "God, no. No, you deserve it. You should have gone for DS ages ago." He shrugged. "It's not about you, not really. It's me. I think they like what I do on the grunt work, like organising a door to door, or chatting up minor witnesses. But I reckon I'm seen as a bit of a lightweight. I mentioned that possible link to Dan earlier today and again at the briefing. You back me up, and suddenly it merits proper attention."

She felt suddenly awkward. If she was honest, the reason Baines had been persuaded by her was that she had probably articulated the argument a little more neatly than Bell had. She wasn't even sure she had swayed Baines that much. He hadn't totally rejected the theory in the first place.

But was it her place to say that to Bell? Would it smack of condescension or arrogance?

"I'm not really the person you should be talking to about this," she said. "Dan's your line manager. Tell him your concerns and ask him for some feedback. He's a decent boss, remember. If he had any major problems with you, I'm sure he'd say."

"Maybe."

The Scot still looked glum. It occurred to her that he often confided in her, on personal as well as work matters. Her own private life was undergoing a seismic upheaval, and he was blissfully unaware. He imagined the 'Charlie' she was seeing was a bloke, and she had made no moves to put him right. It wasn't fair, and it wasn't as though she was flush for people she could talk to.

She swallowed, her mouth dry, as she realised what she was about to do.

"Actually," she said, "there's something I'd welcome your advice on."

He looked a little surprised. "Okay."

She was still tempted to pussyfoot around, but she thought if she didn't come right out with it, she might bottle it. So she told him straight: her lifelong confusion over her sexuality, her feeling – influenced by her family background, and despite that confusion - that being gay was wrong; her attempts and failures to form a meaningful heterosexual relationship; and her stumble into something that felt, for the first time, like coming home. With Charlie.

If she'd thought he had his propensity for blushing under control these days, this was an exception. He tinged pink, then beetroot red as she told him what she had never told anyone before, apart from Charlie herself. It couldn't be helped and, despite his obvious embarrassment at her revelations, at least she hadn't seen in his eyes the disgust she'd been half-dreading.

"Well," he said, when she ran out of words, "it's a surprise, but not a surprise."

That was as clear as mud. "I don't follow."

"What I mean is… Oh, Christ, how can I put this? Look, you're a lovely person. Bright, intelligent, caring. Not bad looking, either." A smile twitched his lips. "I mean, I've gone through a few girlfriends over the years. No one's stuck, and to be fair, the job doesn't help. Not everyone can tolerate dates being blown off at short notice because work intervenes. You know all this, because I've told you."

"What's your point?"

"My point, mate, is that, despite you having so much going for you…" He paused, took a deep breath. "Look, the reason I was so pleased you were dating – even when I assumed Charlie was male – was I've seen precious few signs of anyone in your life. I think you'd have said if there was. Am I wrong?"

"No," she acknowledged.

"So this person must be different. The fact that the difference is that she's a girl? Actually, it makes perfect sense. So what's the problem?"

She exhaled, relieved.

"You're the only person I've told, is the problem. Charlie thinks it's time I came out. Here, and more importantly, to my family. She says we can't be a proper couple if I'm trying to keep her a secret."

Bell regarded her with smiling eyes. "Yeah? Well, I think she's right."

She sighed. "Me too. But I'm terrified. Terrified my family will reject me. Terrified of the prejudice and sniggers behind my back at work. I mean, just because the force has worked hard on equality, and there's every outward sign of it working, doesn't mean everyone's embraced it."

He raised an eyebrow. "You think some folk might have a problem with a black lesbian? Surely not!"

She giggled. "Yeah, okay."

"People will think and feel how they think and feel, Joan. No amount of anti-discrimination policy will change that. What they can't do is go against the policy. So long as they treat you fairly, it's fine. If they privately have a problem with you – well, frankly, stuff 'em. You shouldn't compromise on who you are."

She wasn't hearing anything she didn't already know, deep in her heart. "Okay. So much for this place. I'll think on that. What about my family though?"

"If you tell them and they reject you?"

She nodded, unable to speak.

"Stuff them too," Bell said. "These are the people you should be able to turn to when you've nowhere else to go. If they can't accept you for who you are…" He shook his head, then smiled again. "But you know what? They might surprise you. Your revelation might come as less of a shock than you think."

"Seriously?"

"Seriously. I wasn't shocked, and I can't imagine I know you any better than they do. Pick your time and tell them, is what I'd do. And I wouldn't leave it too long."

She looked at him for a long while, then impulsively leaned over and kissed his cheek.

"I don't know why anyone wouldn't take you seriously, Jason Bell," she said. "You're an awful lot wiser than you know."

21

Archer had felt her phone vibrate in her pocket whilst she and Baines were ensconced with Gillingham, and she'd checked it as soon as she came out of his office. It was 7.10pm.

"Oops," she said.

"What's that?" Baines asked.

"Text from the Super. This sodding dinner date. I'm late. Although, frankly, it's the last thing I could do with right now."

He grinned. "Oh, I don't know. At least you'll get a decent feed, instead of odds and sods from the fridge. With any luck, she'll treat you too."

"I'm not having that," she protested. "I'll pay my share."

"Oh, I don't know." His grin was wicked now. "Maybe her interest is more of a personal kind."

She knew it was a joke, but for some reason it got under her skin. "Grow up, Dan."

"Sorry. Bad taste." He had the grace to look awkward.

"You're forgiven. You okay going off to Reading this evening?"

"Yep. Derek Pollard's going to do the dreaded death knock with me."

"Okay. Keep me posted. Make sure you ask her about Tim's fidelity, but be subtle, yes?"

"Subtlety's my middle name."

She rolled her eyes. "Yeah, right."

* * *

Andrea Lambert had chosen the Broad Leys pub, right next to the station, for their rendezvous. The 16th Century former coaching inn, all exposed brickwork and beams, was fine by Archer, as far as the food went, although there was always the possibility that someone else from the station would come in. Archer felt awkward enough about dining with someone two ranks senior to herself, without everyone at work knowing about it and drawing God knew what conclusions.

Still, she couldn't deny that she liked the way the modernisation of the place had somehow managed to retain its historic character and, on the rare occasions that she had come here, the atmosphere had always felt relaxed, but with a convivial buzz. Tonight's mix of diners appeared to include colleagues like herself and Lambert, families, and one large group of friends who spoke and laughed a little too loud for her liking. Maybe she was getting old and conservative, she berated herself.

Lambert had changed out of her uniform in favour of a charcoal trouser suit and gold shirt. She could have passed as easily for a banker or a lawyer as a senior police officer. Archer had to admit that she looked good. Attractive. Yet, as far as she knew, the woman was single. Maybe she was married to the job, just as many assumed Archer herself was. Maybe Lambert thought Archer preferred it that way and had thought she'd seen somewhat of a kindred spirit in her.

"Before we start," Lambert said after they'd sat down at a corner table, "this is my treat."

Archer raised her hands in protest. "No, Ma'am, I –"

"Andie."

"No, Andie, I can't let you do that. We'll split it."

Lambert flapped a hand. "You can get the next one."

Archer left it at that, deciding that arguing further might come across as churlish. There was to be a next time? She couldn't deny feeling a little flattered that the Super apparently didn't see this as a one-off. Unless it was just something Lambert had said to quell her protests.

"Let's peruse these menus before we get talking," Lambert suggested. "Otherwise they'll be coming to take our order and we'll have to have to send them away."

Lambert chose crispy coconut chicken salad, whilst Archer went for the lamb cutlets.

The Superintendent chose a half-bottle of Californian black Muscat to share, then led some inconsequential small talk about pubs and restaurants while they waited for the drinks to arrive. Lambert asked for an update on the cases, and Archer summarized for her.

"I'll never forget the Phillips case," Lambert said. "Nigh on everything was put on hold to search for him, but it was as if he'd disappeared into the ether. Now we know why."

The wine arrived and Lambert agreed to taste it. Archer watched her swirl the liquid, which was indeed almost black in colour, around her glass before putting her nose in to sniff the bouquet. Finally, she took a sip.

"It's lovely," she said at last.

"Cheers," she said to Archer as they chinked glasses. The wine smelt of roses, and delivered an intense, fruity punch to the palate.

"This is good," Archer said.

"One of my favourites. It's great they stock it here." Lambert took another appreciative sip, then put her glass down.

"So," she said, "here we are."

Archer said nothing, sensing that the reason for this get-together was about to emerge.

"I told you I'd studied your file," Lambert said, "and I've made no secret that I like what I see. Your father was a cop, I believe?"

"He was. A Sergeant. Lung cancer took him too young."

"I'm sorry."

"So am I. I still miss him."

"I know how that feels. My dad wasn't a copper. Just a tradesman, but I adored him. Well, my stepdad, really. My parents split up when I was nine. I never saw my biological father again, and it was good riddance." Archer waited for her to qualify that, but Lambert just shrugged, then smiled. "My stepdad, though. He was great, and he always treated me as if I was his real daughter. He even took me to work with him in the school holidays. But he had a massive heart attack when I was sixteen. My mum died about a year later. Knocked down by a bus on a zebra crossing. The driver had nodded off at the wheel."

"Christ," Archer was shocked. "How awful. I lost my mum too, a few years ago, but to be orphaned so young…" She shook her head. "They'd be very proud of how you turned out."

"We've both been dealt some shitty cards in our lives. Maybe that's why I'd like to see you really fulfil that potential you had before that injury. It's still hard enough for a woman in the force, without a knockback like that."

"It *is* getting better," Archer commented.

"It is. Although don't you pick up those boys' club vibes from time to time?"

Archer could remember back to the days in the Met when there was a bit of a locker room culture amongst some of her male colleagues. Younger times when you either uncomfortably took part in the banter or suspected you'd become the butt of it. She didn't see it here, and she hadn't so much in her latter days in London – possibly, at least in part, down to the leadership of her boss there, DCI Gibson.

"Honestly?" She shook her head. "Not really."

"Fair enough." Lambert smiled. "That's good to hear. What about Gillingham and Ashby though? They seem as close as ever."

"They are," Archer acknowledged. "But then, they go back a long way, as you know."

"That's true. But when I worked with them I always felt like I was on the outside." A shadow fleeted across the other woman's countenance. "It always seemed they talked amongst themselves and only shared with me what they wanted to share. Sometimes I'd need to speak to one of them, and they'd be deep in a conversation that stopped too abruptly when I joined them."

"Did that just apply to the women though?"

It was Lambert's turn to frown. "Actually, no. In fairness, I guess the more junior male officers may well have suffered the same mushroom effect. Of course, Ashby tried it on with me once at a celebration after a collar. I wound up stamping on his foot."

Archer laughed. "He's a reformed character now."

"Really?"

"Saved by the love of a good woman. Seriously. DS Amy Petrescu from Bicester. She was seconded here for a while last year, and it went from there. She seems good for him."

"I always thought he lost his bearings after his marriage broke up. Still, leaving him with a limp didn't exactly help me in being included."

"It didn't blight your career, though."

"Ah, well." Lambert took another sip of her wine. "I was always ambitious. I developed a thick skin, a bloody mind when it came to doing my job, and ears like a bat for overhearing their all-male conversations. But what about your career? I'd say you're way overdue in getting to DCI."

Their food arrived and Archer waited for the waitress to depart before answering.

"It's nice to know you rate me, ma – Andie."

"So would you be interested in Gillingham's post if it became vacant?"

Archer swallowed a mouthful of lamb. "I wasn't aware he was going anywhere."

"Look, keep this to yourself, but things are going to change. The powers that be are looking to realign the CID teams across Thames Valley. There's more and more crime that crosses county borders, and we need to be more co-operative and more agile. They're calling it 'an organic approach to crime detection'. Management speak, but it makes sense."

"I get that," Archer said. "But what's that got to do with –"

"Look, I don't want to put you in an awkward position. But Paul's maybe a bit too hands off for my liking, and certainly for the new regime. And, I suspect, he knows that too. If and when the change happens, chances are he won't be sticking around. He'll either look for a move or decide to take his pension." She sliced off a piece of chicken and speared it with her fork. "I think you'd be great in that role."

Archer *did* feel awkward. But, at the same time, here was someone with influence talking about an important promotion for her. Just how badly did she want it, though?

"I don't want to be party to a plot to push him out," Archer said carefully. "He's not been a bad boss."

Lambert smiled. "Relax. I'm just thinking ahead, doing a bit of succession planning. There's no plot. All I'm saying is, if he did decide to go, the job's yours, if you want it."

Archer's appetite for the food in front of her was drying up. She couldn't deny the prospect of that step up excited her. At the same time, now she was even more fearful that someone else from the station would come in and see her tete a tete with the Super. How would that look if, in a few days, weeks or months, Gillingham was out and she was made up? Would Steve Ashby see it as Archer conspiring to oust his old colleague and friend? How would he react, especially as he'd be passed over in the process?

And yet… she'd fled the Met for this place to rebuild, not only her life, but her career too. She couldn't help feeling flattered, grateful.

Lambert seemed to sense her discomfort. "Let's change the subject, for now," she said. "How's the lamb?"

22

Tim Phillips's former residence was a quietly impressive property in Upper Warren Avenue, in the prestigious area known as Caversham Heights. The Heights stood on high ground in the west of the Caversham district, one of Reading's northern suburbs. According to Derek Pollard, Caversham Heights house prices were among the highest in Reading. Taking in the smart modern property tucked away behind trees and hedges, and the immaculate sweeping gravel driveway, bordered by equally immaculate lawns, Baines had no difficulty believing that. A gleaming blue Mercedes and a red Jaguar stood outside the garage.

That Jackie Phillips, now officially a widow, still lived here was interesting, given that the man Baines assumed had been the family's breadwinner had been missing for over a decade. Certainly, this place couldn't be cheap to maintain.

As they walked towards the house, their feet crunching on gravel, it became clear to Baines that the house backed onto nothing except magnificent country views.

"Very nice," he commented to Bell.

Baines found it difficult to put an age to the woman who answered the door. Her husband would be in his middle fifties of he was still alive, but she could probably have passed for an attractive thirty.

No, he mentally amended, it was all in the colouring and cutting of her dark brown hair, the artful application of just a little makeup, and what he suspected was a gym-toned body. She was, in all probability, not so much younger than Tim Phillips would now have been.

What interested Baines more than her appearance, however, was her expression. This wasn't the first time he'd gone to break bad news to bereaved people, and he doubted it would be the last. It wasn't even the first time he'd broken that news after the deceased had been missing for years.

But most of them *knew,* even before the words were said. They took in the warrant cards, the grave expressions, and you could see the last vestige of hope dying in their eyes. A slump of the shoulders.

Jackie Phillips looked more curious than devastated as Pollard did the introductions.

"Is this about Tim?" she asked.

"Can we come in?" said Baines.

"Of course."

The entrance hall was tastefully tiled, with a smart wooden staircase going up. Baines could see the doorway into a substantial and stylish kitchen/breakfast room ahead. Jackie led them past a formal dining room on the right, before ushering them into the living room, where three tan leather sofas were arranged around a marble-topped coffee table. The overall effect, Baines thought, teetered on the border between stylish, comfortable living and show-home sterility.

A man, probably in his sixties, with salt and pepper hair receding at the temples, rose as they walked in.

"This is Geoff," Jackie said. "My partner."

"Geoff Rice." He shook hands all round. Baines exchanged raised eyebrows with Pollard, who evidently knew nothing of this relationship.

"So," she said, gesturing to the sofas. "It's Tim, isn't it? You've found him?"

"I'm sorry," Archer said as she sat. "There's no doubt."

"He's dead?"

"I'm so sorry for your loss."

She nodded, sitting back down. Whatever she was feeling inside, it wasn't enough to shake her poise. "Well, I can't say I'm surprised, although it's still a bit of a shock. I gave up any real hope he was still alive a long time ago."

Hence the new – or not so new, maybe – partner, Baines supposed.

"Will I have to identify him?" Jackie asked.

"That won't be necessary. I'm afraid, after all this time..." Baines left it at that. "We had access to his dental records, though. From when he was missing."

"Where was he?"

Baines told her and she nodded again. Then she frowned. "How did he wind up there? I mean, why?"

"We don't know. It's possible he was buried there during construction." He wasn't going to say it was highly likely at this stage.

She frowned again. "Some sort of accident? But why would he have been in Aylesbury?"

"I'm afraid an accident's most unlikely."

Jackie shook her head. "So he was murdered then? How?" Her mouth twisted. "I don't know how to react. To tell you the truth, I've finally been giving some thought to getting Tim declared legally dead."

Baines felt this was a surreal remark in the circumstances. It was almost as if the finding of her husband's body had saved her some trouble.

He glanced at the man, Rice. Clearly, she was already trying to move on. Baines could understand that. Wasn't that what he was trying to do by remarrying?

Yet, even though his son had been missing for longer than Tim Phillips had been, he knew he still clung to hope that, against all the odds, Jack might return to him one day. He couldn't imagine himself being so calm if the day ever came when that hope was finally extinguished.

Perhaps, for Jackie Phillips, the grief would hit her later.

"That must sound awful," she said, perhaps reading his expression. "But he's been gone for well over the statutory seven years, and I knew in my heart something bad must have happened to him."

"You thought he was dead, then?"

"Why else would he simply not come home? Disappear off the face of the earth? I've racked my brains. He had no money worries, the business was in good shape, so he had nothing to run away from."

"Did you not think maybe he'd had some sort of breakdown?"

The woman laughed mirthlessly. "There was no sign of his clothes on a beach, or anything like that. We'd been married for over twenty-five years when he went missing. Trust me - Tim wasn't really the breaking down type." She shrugged. "Oh, I wondered for a while if he'd ran off with another woman, but honestly? I can't see him leaving everything he'd worked for behind.

"Don't misunderstand me," she added hastily. "I loved Tim, but he was a winner above all else. He had great lawyers. You had to, when you were thinking on your feet all the time. Tim liked to spot a business opportunity, dive in, and do the deal quickly. He left the legal niceties to Geoff to tie up with the lawyers, and they knew how to make it happen. By the way, you might as well know – your colleagues already do – Geoff was Tim's right hand man. He more or less runs the business for me now."

"Maybe he had money you didn't know about," Baines suggested.

"If that's true, no one has ever found a trace of it. And Geoff would know where to look, believe me. No, Tim wasn't perfect, but he trusted me. All the money was in joint accounts, and I had legal status in the businesses. I guess now he's dead, I can inherit formally and then I really will really own everything." Her face clouded. "I'm going to have to tell the boys."

"How do you think they'll take it?"

"Hard, I think. Growing up without a father, I think they've both clung onto hope that he'd turn out to be alive. They're both grown up now, but..." She tailed off.

Baines gave her a moment before speaking again. "So what *did* you think had happened to him?"

"Honestly? I wondered if he'd been walking beside a river, or the canal, and fallen in. Maybe his body had got snagged on something, so it couldn't come up. Or something equally freakish."

"But you never considered murder?" Baines asked.

"No. For what reason? He didn't do shady business. There was no mafia-type boss about to disappear him. Or so I thought." Her eyes widened. "You think this was something like that?"

"We've really no theories yet. It's early days." Baines glanced Geoff Rice's way. "I have to ask. How long have you two been together?"

Rice looked amused. "You mean had we been having an affair long before Tim disappeared? What, you think we bumped him off?"

"Did you?" Bell spoke for the first time.

"No. The fact is, the night Tim went missing, I was with my sons, finalising the details of my wife's funeral. Cancer. As a family, we were devastated. Tim's disappearance – well, it gave me a sense of purpose at a time when I might have been tempted to give up. Keeping the business going, supporting Jackie…"

"We got close," Jackie said, "and I guess we knew in our hearts how close, long before we did anything about it. Until I finally realised Tim was never coming back, I kept Geoff at arm's length. At the seven-year point, I knew I could make an application to have Tim declared dead, and I finally accepted he must be. I never did do the paperwork, but I finally saw that Geoff and I had a chance of some happiness." She reached over and squeezed his hand.

"And what about Tim?" Baines asked. "Was he always faithful, as far as you know? Again, we have to ask. You did say you wondered if he'd run off with another woman."

She sighed. "I did, didn't I? I also said I couldn't see it, I think."

"You don't have to walk out on your spouse to be having affairs."

"I'm not stupid, Sergeant. They asked me all this when your lot were still looking for Tim, you know. I'm no wiser than I was then. He was very hands on with his work. He'd go off to meetings at odd times. Sometimes he'd phone and say he was going to be in the office all night. And he came into contact with some good looking women. Do I think he was up to something? Maybe. Do I know for sure? No. And I didn't want to know. You probably think I'm a fool."

"No," he said. "I don't think that at all." People had all sorts of ways of protecting themselves, of which looking away was just one.

"What about enemies?" Baines wondered. "He must have made a few on his way up."

"You'd think, wouldn't you?" She smiled. "But honestly? Everyone loved him, even his business rivals. He could be tough and ruthless when he had to, but even then he kept his fist in a velvet glove. I honestly can't imagine anyone wanting to kill him."

Baines rose. "We won't intrude any more for now. Rest assured we're reopening the investigation into your husband's disappearance. Not that it was ever really closed."

"I understand," she said. "Cases go cold."

"We'll be allocating a family liaison officer to support you," Pollard added.

"There's really no need," Jackie assured him. "I'm okay. Honestly."

Baines hoped she would still feel that way when the news had properly sunk in.

Jackie followed them to the door, Rice following. Baines halted and turned to face her. "One last question for now. Have you come across a firm called Howard and Burns?"

"Who are they?"

"They built the block of flats Tim was buried underneath."

"Tim didn't really do property. Not development, anyway. I mean, he might have bought offices that were a better fit for what they needed, after he acquired a new business. Or a factory, or whatever. Maybe Geoff has heard of them?" She turned to her partner.

Rice shook his head. "Can't say I have. Sorry."

Baines nodded, opening the door. "Sorry again for your loss."

As the three police officers walked back down the driveway, they heard the front door close. Even so, Baines waited until he was sure they were out of earshot before he spoke.

126

"Impressions?"

"I don't know, really," Bell said. "She was cool, wasn't she? But if she'd already accepted he was dead, maybe the confirmation was more a relief than anything else."

"Possibly," Baines agreed. He turned to Pollard. "See she gets that FLO. She might not think it's necessary now…"

"Don't worry," the DC said. "I've seen delayed reactions before."

"Good. But it's not just the support side. We need a trusted line of communication who can also be our ears and eyes."

"I've got someone in mind."

"Okay, I'll leave that with you," Baines said. "Meanwhile, Derek, I was wondering if you worked Tim Phillips's missing persons case?"

"Not as such," Pollard replied. "I did a bit of door to door, that sort of thing. You won't find too many people who were at Reading nick in those days who didn't get sucked in. But if you want to talk to someone still there who was hands on, DCI Mahon is your man."

"I'll come over and see him in the morning," Baines said. "We need to clear our lines anyway. Your missing person, our crime scene. How we liaise. And I'll be interested to see if the investigation spoke to Geoff Rice back then. All that stuff about how they got together sounded plausible. But, if he really runs the business now, maybe he was glad to see the back of Tim."

23

Gary Meredith eased himself out of the black BMW and paused to run an eye over the car. He might be grieving, he might be hurting, but appearances mattered. He had a reputation to keep up. It wasn't enough to own a series 7 Beemer. It needed to be immaculate at all times. Robbie, his minder, knew this and kept everything he needed for removing specks and blemishes from the paintwork handy. Meredith was pleased to see everything gleaming in the right places.

So this was Aylesbury's Northfields estate? He looked around at the hulking blocks of flats, looking malevolent in the darkness. It was somewhere around here that his brother's body had been dumped in the back of some shitty old car. Someone was going to pay for that. Leave it to the Filth? No way.

He'd made calls, lots of them. Called in favours. Dared to rattle some pretty dangerous cages. If only Kit had told him what he was doing, who he was talking to, instead of just doing his own thing… well, Gary wouldn't be having to retrace his brother's steps.

These Eastern Europeans. He'd been beginning to wonder if they even existed. Either no one in the business in or around Aylesbury had come across them, or they had instilled a hell of a lot of fear quite quickly for new players on the block. But, in the end, his persistence – and the dangling of a decent wad of cash – might just have got him somewhere.

The person willing to talk to him had been reluctant to say much on the phone. Wanted at least half the money in his hand before he said anything. Gary Meredith got that. He'd have been the same, back before he became a Somebody. But this had better be worth it. He looked at Robbie, standing by the car, waiting to be told what to do. When Gary's wife, Sonia, who didn't like this one bit, had realised she wasn't going to stop him, she'd absolutely insisted on Robbie coming along. Thick as pigshit, but loyal to a fault, and he could handle himself. He and Meredith were both carrying concealed shooters. But they wouldn't be necessary here. If this so called source turned out to be stringing them along, Robbie's fists would inflict sufficient lesson to make him think twice about wasting their time again.

Meredith shoved his hands in the pockets of his long leather coat.

"These blocks all look the bloody same," he said. "Which is the right one?"

Robbie stood looking at him, slack jawed.

"I asked you a question," Meredith said.

"Dunno, boss."

"Well, it's going to be A Block, isn't it? There'll be signs, right?"

"Right."

Christ. "Well, go and look. You *can* read, yeah?"

Robbie winced and strolled off in the direction of the nearest block.

"Get a move on," Meredith bawled after him. Robbie picked up the pace.

Meredith stood alone under a feeble street lamp. Now Robbie wasn't at his side, he felt exposed. Maybe, instead of dispatching his minion to check out the meeting place, he should have gone with him. He patted his coat, confirming that the reassuring bulk of the gun was still there. He'd never used it, and no one in his firm had, apart from one occasion. Generally, gun crime drew a lot of heat, and it wasn't worth it. Still, having the weapon gave him confidence. He was Gary Meredith. No one in their right mind was going to mess with him.

No one should have messed with Kit.

He heard footsteps and turned to see a lean figure in a hoodie approaching, hands in pockets, hunched. Despite his self-assurance, Meredith felt himself tense. Maybe this was his contact. Or maybe it was trouble. He half-hoped it was the latter. He'd been in a mood to hurt someone ever since those two female cops – the one with the weird mouth and the tasty black one – had brought him the bad news.

The hoodie stopped a couple of feet away. In the pale light of the street lamp, facial piercings glinted.

"Nice car," the hoodie rasped.

"I know."

"You're not leaving it here are you? If you're lucky, someone'll have the alloys off it. If you're unlucky, some twat will pour paint stripper over it. That or the whole fucking car will be gone." He chuckled.

"That a threat?" Meredith looked for Robbie. Couldn't see him. A car drove by, something Japanese, bass notes booming out.

The hoodie held up his hands. "Nah. But *are* you going to leave it? I could mind it for you."

Meredith looked him up and down. Just a lowlife out to make a bit of smack money, he reckoned. "How much?"

"Hundred quid?"

"Don't take the piss, son."

"Fifty, then. Anything less, and it's not worth my while."

"We're going to be gone half hour tops. At minimum wage, a fiver's generous. But I'll give you twenty."

"Thirty?"

Meredith sighed. His pride and joy was worth it. "Go on then." He took out a roll of notes and peeled off three tens. "It better be here when I come back, or I *will* find you."

He looked in the direction Robbie had gone. Where had he got to? Irritated, Meredith moved off towards the flats. Up above, clouds obscured the moon.

The opening beneath the first floor walkway was illuminated, but the lighting was as pathetic as the street lamp his car was parked under. He glanced back at the BMW. The hoodie was leaning against it. He'd better not scratch it.

He reached the opening into the block. Rusting metal doors either side led, he assumed, to stairwells. He could see a sign proclaiming that this was A Block. That was all Robbie had been required to check, so why hadn't he returned? Maybe he'd decided to take a piss while he was here. The area stank of urine already, so it wouldn't be like he was offending local sensibilities.

Meredith remembered growing up with Kit in a building not a whole lot better than this one. His dad had worked the same soul-sucking, shit-for-pay job right up until he dropped dead five years short of retirement. By then, his sons were already in the business, some legit, most not, doing jobs for others, but increasingly for themselves. A few years after their dad's death, they'd bought Mum her own nice little house, with the garden she'd always wanted. It hurt that their father hadn't been around to enjoy it too,

This place served to remind Gary Meredith of how far he'd come.

"Robbie?" His voice faintly echoed in the space he stood in. "Where the fuck are you?"

Only silence replied, seeming to mock him. He was just about to turn away when something caught his eye. Some dark substance was running out from under the door to his left, pooling in a hollow where the concrete floor had broken up. In the gloom, it looked black, but his neck hairs prickled as he fancied he detected a coppery tang mingling with the urine stench.

He tried to push the door inwards. It moved halfway and met with resistance. He could have squeezed inside, but he pushed harder and the obstruction yielded.

Robbie lay on his back, his shoulder resting against the bottom of the now open door. Blood was still trickling from a gaping wound, like a second mouth, in his throat, joining the stream that flowed down a slight slope to the doorway and beyond. Meredith's hand flew to his mouth as he stepped backwards, horror and fear combining in a tide of rising panic.

He heard footsteps behind him and started to spin round, but he was already too late. He felt the hair at the front of his head being grabbed, and his head was jerked backwards. Something cold and hard sliced across his throat, leaving a pain that burned like molten metal. He wanted to roar with pain, but the only sound that came was a horrendous gurgling.

He was being lowered to the floor beside Robbie's body. His right hand was still in his pocket, the fingers closed around the butt of his gun. He tried to yank the weapon free, but it seemed far too heavy.

Gary Meredith wondered how he could have walked into such a simple trap. Then all thought left him, fluttering away like petals on a breeze.

24

The best part of the evening had gone again by the time Archer let herself into her home. There were a few bits of post on the mat – bills and junk at first glance – and she carried them into the kitchen. Her footsteps echoed on the bland marble-effect tiling of the floor as she dumped her mail on the worktop and then filled the kettle.

While it bubbled away, she carried the post to her kitchen table. Something warm insinuated itself around her legs, purring softly.

"Hi, Barney," she said, bending to draw her hand through the fat ginger tom's fur. "Nice of you to visit."

Inasmuch as anyone can truly own a cat, she shared this one with her next door neighbour, Dominic. His previous pet, Monty, had been killed by a car, and Barney was in need of a home after his owner's arrest. Archer had agreed to find him a home, and Dominic had accepted him on condition that they adopt him jointly. He knew she'd been toying with getting a cat of her own, but was put off by the crazy hours she often worked, and she had to admit that the odd arrangement worked well. In practice, Dominic did most of the feeding, and Barney probably spent the lion's share of his time with him. But Dominic had installed a cat flap for her, and the feline adoptee came and visited when he felt like it – most likely when he fancied an extra meal.

Archer found his bowls and served him food and water. The kettle had boiled and she made tea, squishing the teabag in the mug, and then carried her drink to the table. She still needed to process her mostly enjoyable evening with Superintendent Lambert, and the tentative offer of promotion if a number of other things came to pass, but she decided to check out her post first.

It seemed mostly as dull as ever: a flyer for a pizza place; a card from an estate agent gagging to sell houses just like hers; a bank statement she'd look at later. But there was also a pale blue envelope, handwritten.

She knew the writing. She put it down in front of her, sipping hot tea. She'd had not a phone call, not so much as a birthday or Christmas card from her brother, Adam, since their mother's funeral. She knew he blamed her, with some justification if she was honest, for not doing her fair share when Mum had become ill, nor after her death, when there was so much to sort out. He'd cut her dead at the funeral and returned cards and presents she'd sent to the children.

So what was this all about?

She ripped open the envelope. The card was jolly on the outside, with cartoon balloons and streamers, and 'Party Invitation' in big funky multi-coloured letters. Inside, her brother had written a short note:

Dear Liz,

It's Nic's 35th birthday on Saturday. I didn't know what to get her, so I asked, and she says what she'd really like is for you and I to make up.

I know it's short notice, and you're probably up to your ears in some murder or other, but maybe we could do lunch or dinner on Saturday? If it helps, we can come over your way. Nic's mum can babysit.

Text me a time and place and I'll book. Bring someone if you like.

Adam

She re-read the note three times. It wasn't much of an olive branch he'd offered her. Adam was plainly only doing it for his wife, who was a fully paid up member of the softie club. Nic was big on family, and she could imagine her hating the idea of her husband being estranged from his only sibling, even if it was by his own choice. She had a nasty feeling that the lunch wouldn't go well but, if she rebuffed him, who knew when there'd be another shot at reconciliation?

She took another swig of tea, found her phone, and composed a hasty text to him, before she got cold feet:

Got ur invite. Thanks. Love to celebrate Nic's b'day. How about the King's Head in Ivinghoe, if you can get a table…

She hesitated. Oh, well – in for a penny, in for a pound.

… for 4? Say 8ish? Otherwise, any pub round here is fine. I'll try not to be waist-deep on bodies.

Should she put a few kisses? Maybe not. He hadn't, and she wasn't feeling very kissy towards him.

"Oh, sod it," she said out loud.

Lxx

She pressed 'send' before she could change her mind.

She checked her watch. Dominic's car had been on the drive when she got home, and he would be nowhere near going to bed yet. Two minutes later, she was standing on his doorstep and he was opening the door.

"Hey!" he said.

His smile always got the corners of her own mouth bending. "Hey yourself."

"Did you want to come in?"

She hesitated. "Not if you're busy."

"Don't be daft. Fancy a drink?"

She'd had only a glass and a bit of wine with Lambert, and she didn't plan to drive again this evening, but she wanted to be sharp in the morning.

"Just tea, please." She stepped into his hall.

"So is this a social call?" he asked as he set about making her drink.

"Sort of." She drew a deep breath. "Are you free Saturday night?"

"Saturday?" He furrowed his brow. "Well, yeah. I've nothing on. What's the plan?"

She told him about Adam's invitation. He already knew much of the history. "I could really use some moral support, but only if you're comfortable with it. It could be excruciating. There could be a row. I just don't know."

"Dinner at the King's Head, and all I have to do at worst is referee a family fight? You're on," he said.

"Great. Thanks, Dominic."

Her phone rang. "Sorry," she muttered as she pulled it out and looked at the screen. "I'd better take this."

Five minutes later, she was in her car and heading back into Aylesbury. It was going to be a long night.

25

Baines couldn't help appreciating the irony that, having agreed to work separate cases, he and Archer had both come to Reading this morning to see the same man. DCI Mahon must be wondering what it was with Aylesbury that the bodies of four Reading residents had turned up there in less than a week.

Archer and Collins both looked shattered. They'd been up half the night after the body of the second of the Meredith brothers had been literally stumbled upon by Ed Studman, a local loser who claimed to have been minding Gary's car for him. The gang boss and one of his henchmen had both been killed in the stairwell of one of the Northfields blocks, their throats efficiently slashed. Unlike with Kit Meredith, there had been no attempt to hide the bodies.

When Archer had briefly filled him in on the murders, Baines had asked if Studman, the person who'd called it in, could be the killer.

"Unlikely," she'd said. "He's got no form, and you'd expect him to have a fair bit of blood on him with the method of killing. There was some on his trainers, where he'd stepped in it, but that was all. He seemed pretty freaked out to me. I reckon he's an okay guy by Northfields standards. He saw a chance to make a few quid minding Gary's motor, eventually looking for him, and found more than he bargained for."

"So what do we think?" Baines wondered. "The mysterious Eastern Europeans, or some other inter-gang rivalry?"

"That or someone in the Meredith outfit who fancies being the boss. Between DCI Mahon and our own digging, we can surely identify any wannabe top dogs. I'm also interested in the Eastern Europeans in Oxfordshire that Mahon mentioned. I hope Will turns something up on them. I'll tell him to prioritise that before we set off."

With Collins, Bell and Derek Pollard, as well as Archer and Baines, six people was a bit of a squeeze for Mahon's office, so he collared a musty meeting room and put in an order for drinks and biscuits. Pollard looked as bleary-eyed as Archer and Collins, having accompanied them to see Sonia Meredith, Gary's freshly widowed wife in the early hours.

"How did she take the news?" Mahon asked.

"Not well," Archer said. "She went crazy, as a matter of fact. Swore a lot, smashed things. I'd imagine it was wise to have a tin hat handy if a row broke out in that house. Became so hysterical when she finally accepted that we were telling the truth that I almost called an ambulance. But Derek and Joan got her calmed down."

"And Robbie Pascoe's dead too?" Mahon shook his head. "He was a dimwit and a thug, but I did admire his loyalty to the Merediths. And you say your CSIs have found nothing useful at the scene?"

"If you believe Ed Studman, Gary was alone by the car when Ed approached him, but headed off for the block soon after. That, and the situation of the bodies, suggests that Robbie had gone ahead and was dead or dying when Gary caught him up. Then Gary was jumped too. They both had pistols in their pockets, but clearly had no chance to use them. There would have been a lot of blood already when Gary got there, but the only shoeprints the CSIs could find are Gary's and Ed's. They were still looking, though."

"But it looks like our killer was either lucky or, more likely, very careful."

"The latter, I'd say. Barbara Carlisle was her usual cautious self, but seems certain both men were taken from behind. It doesn't take a second to slit a throat, if you know what you're doing, so watching your step as you do it probably isn't that hard if you've got surprise on your side." Archer reached for her coffee. "Someone's taken out both the Meredith brothers in short order. Where does that leave their organisation?"

Mahon's laugh was humourless. "Honestly? There for the taking, if anyone wants to. There's no one under them with the brains or the vision to organise themselves. If anyone's likely to take charge, it's Gary's wife, Sonia."

Archer blinked. "I thought the brothers made it a policy that the wives knew nothing."

"Maybe that was the case with Kit and Lisa. Sonia was a different matter. She was active in the overtly legitimate stuff they controlled, and we've suspected she had a role of some sort in their seedier interests. You've seen how fiery she is, but she can be charming too. If anyone can keep the business together, it's her, but I don't know what loyalty she'd command." He gnawed at his lower lip. "If someone's muscling in on Meredith turf, she could be next."

He took a digestive from the biscuit plate, broke it in four, and popped a quarter in his mouth. A few chews, and he swallowed. "But I'm interested in this Northfields Estate of yours. Kit dumped there, Gary killed there. How likely is the killer to live there, or have a connection?"

"Impossible to say, Sir," Archer replied. "Although I'd say probably not. Oh, we've had gangs connected to the estate before, but pretty small time ones. My own hunch is that the killer knew Northfields' reputation and thought that inserting it into the equation would get us looking in the wrong direction."

She'd mentioned this to Baines during their hasty catch-up this morning.

"I've been thinking about that too," Baines ventured. "It could be that the killer – or killers – originally intended just to dump Kit's body on the estate, but spotted the abandoned car and decided to be a bit creative. Then – I'm surmising – Gary comes to Aylesbury looking for answers, gets lured to the estate, and gets himself killed."

"Sounds plausible," Mahon acknowledged. "Reading people and Aylesbury flats. Wouldn't it be great if we could connect Tim Phillips and the Merediths?"

"Is there anything we might be overlooking on that score, Sir?" Collins asked. "Something miniscule that could be the answer?"

"If there is, I'm not seeing it."

Baines mentioned Geoff Rice, Phillips's erstwhile deputy and now his widow's live-in lover. "Did you look at him when you were investigating Tim's disappearance?"

"Of course. He's just a pen pusher though. A clever one. An accountant who's also legally trained too. We got forensic accountants to run the rule over the business and found nothing out of order."

"But if he's as clever as you say, does that necessarily mean there was nothing there to find?"

Mahon sighed. "Who knows? You can't prove a negative. All the right distances were being respected between Tim's commercial work and the charitable side, and his altruism targeted genuine good cause projects. Some quite big ones, too. If there was anything shady going on that Rice knew about, we never looked in the right place."

Derek Pollard spoke, waving a chocolate hob nob for emphasis. "Got to be these Eastern Europeans who offed the Merediths. Probably controlled by some Russian oligarch somewhere in Thames Valley."

Baines saw Archer eyeing the DC with interest. "Are there any?"

"Oligarchs? We had one in Berkshire a few years ago, who died in mysterious circumstances. There was a theory he'd fallen foul of the Russian authorities, but the enquiry ran into the sand."

"There's supposed to be one in Oxfordshire, too," Mahon said. "Also rumoured to have made the wrong enemies, but nothing's happened to him so far. Apparently, he lives on a socking great estate that's guarded like Fort Knox. I only know that because he knew our Berkshire man, but he actually sounds as on the legitimate side as you could hope. Made his fortune from importing high-end cars."

"Money laundering?" Bell asked.

"No idea. Oxford might know. But remember," Mahon added, "we've still only got what Gary told us to suggest that there are Eastern Europeans in play here. There are several small criminal groupings in play in Reading and the surrounding area that might benefit from the collapse of the

Meredith setup. You can't rule any of them out. My biggest fear is that they'll all scent blood and set their sights on Meredith territory, like dogs scrapping over a bone."

"You're worried about a war?" Archer suggested. "So are we."

"I don't know. It's what you expect in big cities, not the Home Counties. But, with criminals increasingly organising themselves everywhere, it's only a matter of time."

Archer's expression was as grim as the DCI's. "Then we need to find the Merediths' killer fast. Can you start questioning the bigger players in your area, Sir? We've got one particular big fish in the Vale that I'm going to start with."

Baines knew who she meant, and he hated it. He knew there would be no arguing with her and, in fairness, it was a logical line of enquiry. He waited while Mahon agreed to the plan of action at his end.

"Are you still happy for us to lead on this?" Archer checked. "As a joint investigation, of course?"

"Makes sense." Mahon agreed. "You've got the two crime scenes."

"Can we move on to the Tim Phillips case?" Baines suggested. He gave Mahon a proper recap.

The DCI looked thoughtful. "So you've got a security guard – who could have let Tim's killer into the site to bury the body – and he's in the wind at around the same time the body turns up. Interesting."

"We're circulating his details nationwide," Bell said.

"And you say there's nothing about Geoff Rice to suspect?" Baines pressed. "Yet his boss's disappearance put him *de facto* in charge of the business and has led to him shacking up with Jackie Phillips. They claim the relationship grew from working together when Tim went missing, but did you maybe see anything to suggest otherwise?"

Mahon was silent for a moment or two, considering the question. "I really didn't." he said finally. "I'll ask colleagues who would have had maybe more contact with Rice and Jackie than I did but, from what I saw, his wife's death devastated him. I think it was pretty grim for the family before she finally passed. I honestly don't believe he'd have been in any fit state to orchestrate a murder and set his sights on Jackie. My take is that Tim's disappearance gave him a reason to throw himself into work. It's a classic coping mechanism, I think."

Baines knew what he meant. When Louise had been murdered and Jack abducted, he'd refused point blank to take any compassionate leave, and wild horses wouldn't have stopped him working the Invisible Man case. Of course, he now knew he'd been storing up emotional problems for the future, but no one could have told him that then.

He was struck too by the parallel between Rice and Jackie and himself and Karen. In each case, tragedy had thrown the couples together, and the bonds that had been forged had deepened.

He knew he should beware of allowing his own experience to influence his thinking on the case, but Rice would have to be a cold, calculating bastard to have hatched a murderous plot before his wife had even breathed her last.

A new thought occurred to him. "What about affairs on Tim's side? When we spoke to Jackie, she wasn't ruling it out, but insisted she hadn't wanted to know."

Mahon smiled. "What the eye doesn't see? Yes, I seem to recall her saying much the same. There were always rumours, but nothing you could pin down. A couple of women he spent a lot of time with, ostensibly on business but, as far as we could ascertain, business was all it was. Some flirting with younger women at events that would have him – rightly – criticised today for inappropriate behaviour, but nothing more that we could find."

Gillingham had said much the same, but Baines decided to press it. "How hard did you push it? I mean, a woman scorned, a jealous spouse or partner..."

Irritation flashed in Mahon's eyes, albeit briefly. "We did our job pretty thoroughly, Dan, believe it or not, and those points actually did occur to us. Although..." He frowned. "To be fair, we were always a bit constrained in those sorts of lines of enquiry."

"Constrained?" Archer echoed.

"It could be a bit of a nightmare, to be honest. Very popular guy, pillar of society, a social conscience he backed with cash, and plenty of connections in high places. You've seen recently what happens when the police and the media are too quick to blacken the name of a high profile figure without any real evidence." Baines knew the kind of case he was referring to: apologies, compensation, and damage to the reputations of agencies that had jumped the gun were often the results.

"Plus," Mahon went on, "Tim had chums amongst the top brass here and at Thames Valley HQ. It was made clear we had to tread carefully. Tim was missing and couldn't answer for himself, was the argument. It didn't mean we didn't look at all the angles. But we had to be discreet. I'm not saying we weren't thorough. But it definitely cramped our style."

"He's dead now," Baines said bluntly. "And you can't libel the dead."

"I agree," Archer said. "No harm in pushing that line of enquiry a bit harder."

"I agree too," Mahon said, "although I'd still be a bit subtle, if I were you. It's your case, but some of Tim's chums still might not appreciate him being cast in a bad light."

"We'll tread lightly," Archer said, "but not too lightly."

"Say there's something in it," Mahon said. "Crime of passion? How does that end with a body under a block of flats?"

She gave him the faintest of smiles. "Serendipity? They had an in to the site? Someone maybe owed them a favour?"

"Maybe." She looked at Baines. "Meanwhile, there's still Eric Yelland, the security guard. We need to find him, Dan. You need to speak to any family and friends he might have. Could be one of them is hiding him, or at least knows where he is. And it's about time you dragged yourself down to Sussex and saw the last of the Spencer Court key holders. This Ryan. How did he suddenly come by enough money to retire to what sounds like a very nice lifestyle?"

"Do you really think we'll solve this one?" Mahon asked. "I promise you, I'm not precious about the job we did back then but, after all this time, with so little to go on? Maybe the case is simply *too* cold. And Jackie Phillips seems to have moved on. Perhaps knowing he's dead is closure enough for her."

"It wouldn't be for me," Baines said with some vehemence. If Jack's body was found tomorrow, that wouldn't stop him wanting to know who the Invisible Man was, and wanting to bring him to justice."

"You sound a bit like Paul – DCI Gillingham."

"In what way?"

"I don't know if he mentioned but, when Tim went missing, they were working a murder case. A teenage prostitute – only 15, I think – strangled and dumped in an alley behind a supermarket. The search for Tim Phillips was given top priority, and the dead girl – Demi was her name, Demi Reeves – was shunted into the sidings. Paul and Steve Ashby were left paying lip service to a young girl's murder. I know they were both furious. It affected them both."

Baines remembered Gillingham mentioning a murder case suddenly starved of resources. "Steve as well?" The Ashby who'd come from Reading to work at the Vale hadn't seemed the type to get emotional about any case.

"Both of them. It changed them in different ways. Paul was just bitter about it. I think, for him, it was one of the cases that haunts you. Steve… well, I don't suppose he's changed much from the officer who left us to join you guys in Aylesbury. But he wasn't always like that. Before the spring of 2005, he had ideals, commitment, a stable enough marriage…" He stopped talking, colouring slightly. "But I'm speaking out of turn. My point is, I remember them both prizing justice above everything. But not everyone's like that. People do lose hope. Maybe Jackie did that a long time ago, and that's why she's managed to get on with her life."

Baines supposed he must be right. Everyone was different.

"Speak to anyone close to Yelland," she said, "and do that interview in Sussex. And, yes, go over the possible affairs again, and push Jackie about it. But don't spend too much time on it. It's just as likely to be gossip."

* * *

Sonia Meredith sat in her living room, daytime TV on but not registering, a large glass of scotch in her hand way too early in the day. She almost wished she'd never given up smoking. For the first time in her life, she craved the relaxation that a nicotine hit could give her.

Gary was dead. She still couldn't believe it. Still kept thinking that, later today, he'd come in through the front door, filling the house with his moody, petulant, excitable, self-centered, loving, never-standing-still presence. He could drive anyone crazy but, God, she had loved him. Now she'd never see him again. The kids would grow up without him.

The pain was beyond unbearable, like a knife being twisted in her guts. She was angry with him for getting himself killed, angry with Robbie for being useless protection, furious at the people responsible for his death. Angry with herself, and guilty too, for having failed to stop him keeping that stupid, risky appointment with these so-called informants.

Yet she knew in her heart of hearts that, sometimes even she simply couldn't get through to her husband. Getting Gary to listen to her was a bit like rolling a dice. Sometimes he did, sometimes he didn't. This had been one of the latter occasions. She got that he was murderously angry about Kit's death, and she also got that, if someone was out to get the Merediths, then the Merediths had better get them first. But he'd had no idea who he was dealing with, nor how dangerous they were.

"They've no fucking idea how dangerous *I* am, either," he'd declared. "Or who *they*'re dealing with. Kit should have stuck to what he knew. I won't make the mistakes he did."

Yet he'd made exactly she same mistakes as his brother. Playing the gumshoe. Asking questions and flashing the cash.

Agreeing to a meeting with Christ knew who. And, doubtless, letting his feelings run away with his brain.

She cringed as she remembered the show she'd put on for the police when they'd come to break the bad news to her. Just for that moment, she'd lost her mind.

She took a sip of scotch. She needed to get her head back on, and fast. The family business, for good or ill, was her livelihood. Her kids' future. She still commanded respect and loyalty, she knew, but she needed to grab the steering wheel, and fast. Otherwise one of the brothers' fuckwit underlings would make a play for power, or whoever had killed Gary and Kit would muscle in, however much blood or death that took.

She took another sip. All she wanted to do was burrow under the duvet, inhale the smell of Gary's favourite tee-shirt, and howl, but that would have to wait. She hadn't been made a widow just so everything she and Gary had worked for could be taken away. If she got a grip now, the underlings would listen to her. Hell, they'd probably be relieved not to have to step up.

She took the glass of scotch into the kitchen and tipped it down the sink, then she picked up her mobile from the worktop. It was time to make some calls. She pulled up her contacts list, and then hesitated, her thumb hovering over the first name in her mind. Did she really want to do this? Gary's killers were still out there. She'd be as good as painting a target on her back.

She could almost hear his voice chuckling in her ear. "They want a fight, babe? Bring it on!"

* * *

Outside the station, Archer asked Baines for a brief word in his car. As they talked, she looked out the window. Collins and Bell stood talking by Collins's Fiesta. They looked relaxed, comfortable. Whether they were talking shop, or just chatting, she couldn't tell.

"Are you okay with this case, Dan?" she ventured. "When Mahon suggested that just knowing Tim was dead might give Jackie closure enough…"

He smiled. It was a sad smile. "I was a bit sharp, wasn't I?"

"Just a bit." She touched his arm. "We've seen what can happen when a case is a little too close to home."

He briefly covered her hand with his own. "Don't worry. That time I nearly spun off turned out to be a good thing. Thank God you got me that counselling. But managing my emotions isn't the same as giving up on Jack. Nor my wanting to see the Invisible Man brought to justice some day."

Archer withdrew her hand and nodded. "I get that, and I'm right there with you, if ever there's a new breakthrough." She didn't voice the possibility that both the serial killer and Baines's son could be dead by now.

"On those rumours of Tim's affairs," he said, "I wonder if any of them had links to Howard and Burns, or the Spencer Court site. I should have checked with Mahon."

"Give him a call. It could all be bollocks, of course, but let's at least see if it takes us anywhere."

"I will." He paused. Took a long breath. "Are you still determined to try and speak to Cameron Connolly about the Meredith murders?"

"You know I am," she said softly. "It's my next call. Don't waste your breath trying to talk me out of it."

"I won't, not if your mind's made up. But you're not going alone."

"I'll take Joan."

He smiled. "No. You'll take me."

She raised an eyebrow. "Who's in charge here?"

"You are, Lizzie. Always. But you and me... we always have each other's backs."

"I thought you were in no hurry to re-acquaint yourself with the Connollys."

"I thought so too," he murmured. "But maybe this is a good time to lay that particular ghost."

26

Cameron Connolly appreciated his house in the village of Great Missenden. It had the security and privacy of its own gates and electronic security system, but wasn't so ostentatious as to draw attention to itself. Set in just under an acre, it stood on swanky Martinsend Lane, where upmarket houses were the norm and the neighbours were at arm's length. If they had any suspicions about where his money came from, it didn't stop them passing the time of day with him when their paths crossed.

The village was one of the richest in Britain, but a bit of generosity never went amiss. Again, he didn't overdo the cash-splashing, but he invested a decent amount in raffle tickets at the village fete, donated prizes, paid a tenner for his British Legion poppy, and generally put his hand in his pocket whenever money was needed, like donations to restoration projects. He also spent money locally, occasionally dropping in at the Nag's Head for a pint, or dining at La Petite Auberge in the High Street.

His father had the right idea. Be a philanthropist and people will be less willing to believe any negative stories. But the old man overdid it a bit. He'd hung out with celebrities. Become something of a celebrity himself. Cameron preferred the low profile. The nice guy not short of a bob or two.

He'd first decided to buy a property in this neck of the woods so he could keep an eye on operations here and make sure his imbecile brother, Des, didn't make any more stuff-ups. This house had seemed perfect for the family, from its parquet-floored reception hall to its six decent-sized bedrooms.

But what had really sold it to him was the brick-built so-called summer house, with its own sitting room, kitchenette and cloakroom. It was useable all year round and perfect for keeping business separate from domestic life, and he'd set the sitting room up as a study with desk, filing cabinets, a comfortable sofa and a small meeting table.

He sat there now, behind his desk, checking his email. There was never much to interest him, in truth. Most serious correspondence was conducted by text between pay as you go burner phones. But he liked to keep on top of the admin. He wasn't as anal as his brother Fraser, who was more or less company secretary to the Connolly family's business interests, but he did see the importance of keeping things tidy.

There was a buzz from the gate. He had the system set up to buzz in the office first and, if he wasn't there, to try the house. He tapped a button on a small desk console and opened an app on his computer screen.

"Can I help you?" If Cameron had ever possessed a Scots accent, it had long since been flattened away by the years down south and the expensive schooling Murray had lavished on his boys.

"Mr Connolly? Mr Cameron Connolly?" A female voice. London vowel sounds. He could see her on his screen now. Blonde. The guy with her was dark haired. They didn't look like Jehovah's Witnesses.

"Who wants to know?"

"It's the police, Mr Connolly. DI Archer and DS Baines. Could we come in and have a word?"

He didn't hesitate. He never hesitated with the police. Hesitant people looked as if they had something to hide. "There's a camera above you. Could you do me a favour and show me some ID? You can't be too careful," he added, smiling to himself.

He watched as they both showed their warrant cards, not bothering to attempt to read them. It was what any cautious resident would have asked. Why have gates if you just let in anyone who claimed to be police?

He gave them directions to the summer house and buzzed them in. He was waiting at the door as they approached.

He studied them carefully without appearing to do so. The man, Baines presumably, was about six feet tall, the woman only an inch or so shorter. There was something funny about her mouth. It drooped on one side. Not a palsy or a stroke, he didn't think, but something. A pity, he thought. She could have been a looker.

The man, now. There was something familiar about him. Baines? Of course. He suppressed a smile. This could be interesting.

That day when Cameron had been with Mad Willie McMurdo. Unseen, they'd held this man's life in their hands, and Cameron had decided to spare him. DS Baines had no idea what he owed Cameron Connolly.

"Come in," he said. "Let me make you a tea or coffee."

"Nothing for me, thanks," the woman said. She glanced at the man. "Dan?"

"No, I'm fine," the man replied. He looked tense.

"Fair enough," he said. "If you're sure. I've got one of those fancy machines here. Does everything but launch a man into space."

Not a flicker back. Miserable sods.

"Well." He kept it genial, gesturing to the sofa. "Take the weight off, at least."

They sat. Cameron perched on the edge of his desk. He hoped that brother Des hadn't had one of his brilliant ideas. His wings had been clipped since Cameron had taken over here, but he *would* keep offering products from the creative side of his brain. A side that had obviously been impaired by too many drugs, before he'd been forced into rehab and warned what would happen if he didn't get clean and stay clean. Blood was thicker than water, and a Connolly was a Connolly, but there were times when discipline had to be instilled.

"So." He lifted his hands, palms up. "How can I help?"

"First up," the woman, Archer, said, "this is all off the record. For now. We need your help, and we think you can help yourself in the process."

"Always ready to help the police."

* * *

150

"Always ready to help the police," Cameron Connolly was saying. There was a curiosity in his eyes, but otherwise he looked as relaxed as they came. A man comfortable in his own space, apparently merely intrigued as to why the forces of the law needed his assistance.

Maybe he was as cool and confident as he appeared. She had to admit the man had charisma. There was nothing of the film star about him, but he exuded the strong masculinity that appealed to her.

She'd noticed him appraising her earlier. Not the mental undressing she occasionally experienced. He'd studied her face. Must have noticed that droop.

She wondered why she cared.

"So how can I help?" he asked, and she realised she'd been distracted for a moment.

She inclined her head. "Thank you. There are a few things we wanted to pick your brains about. I take it you follow the local news?"

"A bit."

"Then you might be aware that we're investigating three murders. Two brothers by the name of Meredith - Christopher, or Kit, and Gary - and a colleague of theirs, a Robbie Pascoe. Does it ring a bell?"

"Not sure. Crime news depresses me, and I try to ignore it."

I bet you do, Archer thought. She let the silence build.

"So…" he finally broke it, "what's it to do with me?"

"No one's suggesting you had anything to do with it as such, Mr Connolly," Baines spoke up. "But we know – how can I put it? – we know you have a wide network of *contacts*, in similar lines of business to theirs."

"I don't know what you mean."

The game plan had been to carefully avoid directly accusing Connolly of being mixed up in anything illegal. Now Archer found she wasn't in the mood for pussyfooting around after all.

"Then we'll make it clear," she said. "Still off the record, we know exactly what your real business interests are in the area. We can't prove it, and at this precise moment we don't care about that. What we do care about – and so should you - is that it's possible that a group, possibly of Eastern European origin, may be looking to expand their horizons into Reading, where the Merediths operated, and also into Aylesbury Vale."

His look was a study in surprise and puzzlement. "You mean gangsters?" His face clouded. "Look, this isn't the first time my family has been accused of being involved in criminal activity."

"As DS Baines said, no one is accusing you –"

"I think maybe I should contact my lawyer."

"That's your right, of course. But all we're doing here is asking you for help. As a good citizen. And in your own interests. If there really is a gang operating in and around the Thames Valley region, and killing off the opposition..." She shrugged again. "That could be dangerous and harmful to all manner of business interests."

He stood up, walked over to a window, and looked out at a well-tended garden. After perhaps a minute, he walked back to his desk and perched again. He smiled, his eyes twinkling.

"Well, I do admire frankness," he said at length. "And as I said, I'm always keen to help the forces of law and order. We need to keep our streets safe, after all. So how do you think I might help?"

"First of all," Baines said, "you're sure you've never encountered the Meredith brothers?"

"I've already made it clear that we're not gangsters."

"But not all their business interests are strictly *il*legal."

"That's as may be. But I don't have much to do with Reading either," Connolly said.

"But you must know a lot of people."

"Given your diverse interests," Archer added.

Connolly smiled again. "Well, I can't deny that. Although I'm sure none of the people I know are criminals either."

"Perish the thought," Archer said.

"Still, people do sometimes hear things," he conceded. "No harm in me asking a few questions, I suppose."

"That would be most helpful."

He grinned. "You know I'm beginning to feel like quite the Sherlock Holmes. Consulting detective. The man the flat-footed bobbies come to when they're baffled."

Archer handed him a card. For an instant, their fingers brushed, and she wondered if he felt the same electric thrill she did. She faltered momentarily, but quickly recovered. "Well, Sherlock, if you have anything for us, call me any time."

"Oh, I will." He stood up again. "Look, officers, despite what you might have heard about me and my family, we're simple businessmen. Yes, we move in wide circles, and I won't deny we might occasionally accidentally rub shoulders with the odd bad lad – "

"Like your brother Desmond?" Baines threw at him.

A flash of annoyance passed over Cameron Connolly's face and was gone. "Des was young and stupid when he got into trouble. He's paid his debt to society, and the family are united in making sure he stays away from prison from now on." Archer believed that. "He's clean. We all are. Which is why, for all the whispers behind our backs, Des's little slip-up is the only stain on any of our reputations." He said that with some disgust. The word was that little love was lost between Cameron and Desmond.

"I hear you," Archer said. "And we really would be grateful for any help. Because, if we have to, we'll leave no stone unturned to solve this case. We might have to make waves in a lot of people's business interests. Illegal and legitimate."

"You know," Baines added. "Shake the trees and see what falls out."

"I'll choose not to take that as a threat," Connolly said. "Well, it's been a pleasure, but I really do need to get on. I'll think about what you said, maybe ask around. Don't hold your breath, though. It's not like I deliberately surround myself with killers."

He was looking at Baines, his smile knowing.

"You'll be in touch?" Archer checked.

"If I hear anything, yes." He locked eyes with her. "Maybe a drink? Just the two of us?"

Was he flirting with her? More games? Why did she feel herself blushing?

"Just call me, okay?"

He still had her card in his hand. He studied it, then placed it carefully on his desk. "Count on it, Lizzie. I've got your number."

He switched his gaze to Baines, pointed his first and middle finger at him like a gun and let his thumb fall like a hammer. "I've got yours too, DS Baines."

27

"So we've actually bearded Cameron Connolly in his den," Baines muttered once they were back in the car.

Archer's look was full of concern. "Are you okay?"

He thought about that. That mock shooting gesture – what was that?

Yet he realised he was calmer than he would have expected. "Actually, yes. I guess the monsters in our minds are always bigger and scarier than they are in the flesh. Not that he isn't a monster." He looked Archer in the eye. "He was flirting with you, didn't you think? Cheeky sod."

Whatever he'd expected, it wasn't the pink flushing around her throat. Nor the way she broke eye contact.

"Maybe he thinks all women are taken in by his charm," she said.

He couldn't resist the tease. "But not you, obviously, DI Archer."

"Oh, piss off." It sounded like banter, but with an edge to it.

"Be careful with him," Baines said, more seriously. "I don't think he's the kind of man you should give encouragement to. Or let inside your head."

"Oh, for God's sake, Dan." A definite edge now. And the blush hadn't subsided. "What do you think I am? He might be easy on the eye, but I know what he is. I'm a big girl, you know. I'm not about to be taken in by –"

"A pretty face? Well," he affected a grin, "I'm pleased to hear it. More to the point, though, do you think we accomplished anything? Other than giving him a laugh?" He shook his head vehemently. "Chances are, word will get out to every villain in the Vale and beyond that we were so desperate we begged him for help."

"Good," she said. "I certainly hope so."

"You hope so?" he echoed.

"Think about it, Dan. Bodies are turning up in the Vale. Obviously, the Connollys could be in it up to their necks. But, if they're not, I doubt Cameron's going to appreciate what he thinks of as his territory being used as a battleground and drawing unwarranted attention from us."

It was, he thought, a fair point. Except...

"Except, last time something like that was happening, we thought he had the problem taken care of himself."

"Sure. But why go to the trouble himself, when he could let us solve the problem?"

Baines wasn't convinced, and it must have showed on his face.

"Look," she said, "I want to find out who killed the Merediths and Robbie Pascoe. But, more important still, we need to avoid further deaths. If the worst that comes of this is Cameron Connolly puts a stop to the killings..."

He was taken aback. "You really think that? That Connolly tackling this gang himself – more murder and bloodshed, with innocent people possibly getting caught in the crossfire – would be a result?"

"No!" she said. "Christ, no. I meant..." She shook her head. "Maybe this wasn't such a good idea, after all. I'm running on empty after last night. I don't know what I meant. But not that."

Maybe she was just too tired to think straight. He'd been there himself. But he couldn't quite leave it at that.

"Well, I hope not," he said. "The ends don't always justify the means."

"Thank you for pointing that out," she snapped. Then she shook her head. "Sorry. Look, can we just drop it? I misspoke, or it came out wrong."

"Okay." He felt sorry now for lecturing her. Whatever she might have said, he knew her better than that. He started the engine.

"So," he said, "Do you really think he'll give up names if it keeps us from stirring the shit?"

"I think there's an even money chance, yes. If he can give us what we want to know and it doesn't inconvenience him, he might see it as a favour banked."

"I don't like the sound of that."

Her smile was fierce, somehow emphasising its lop-sidedness. "Don't worry. He might see it that way, but he'll be disappointed if he ever tries to cash in."

"All right," he conceded, only slightly reassured. "What next?"

"Back to the office. I want to see what the rest of the team have dug up for us."

He laughed. "Let's hope it's not another body."

He selected first gear. As he rolled forwards, the gates swung open and a gleaming blue Mercedes glided in. It drew up alongside them. A bear of a man sat at the wheel. In the passenger seat was a brown-haired man in his 20s. The latter waved as Baines pulled away.

"Desmond Cameron," Archer said, "and that was Willie McMurdo at the wheel, unless I'm mistaken. Do you reckon they've come for afternoon tea?

"I doubt it," Baines said. "Cameron doesn't seem to have much time for his kid brother, does he? Imagine sitting around that table."

* * *

Cameron Connolly sat behind his desk, still thinking about that little visit from the police. Or, specifically, from DI Lizzie Archer. There had been something about her that had appealed to him. Even the weird droop to her mouth. It had made him curious, but it hadn't repelled him. What was the story there? He suspected he could find out.

Co-operating with the police was a new one on him. She'd made a good case for why he might want to. It might be an interesting exercise.

He'd had cops in his pocket before. He didn't think for a moment that would ever happen with this one. And Archer's suggestion that the cops might be crawling all over his business if the body count kept rising? That had happened before. If Archer imagined there was anything to be found, she didn't seem the type to need an excuse.

Still, if he could be seen to be helping the police, they'd owe him one, wouldn't they?

DI Lizzie Archer would owe him one.

He was a family man and, most of the time, a faithful one. The few times he'd strayed, the women in question had been irresistibly desirable, and he'd wanted to scratch an itch. A policewoman with a less than perfect face didn't fit the usual mould.

So why was he even thinking about doing her any favours? Why would he care if she owed him one?

He opened a search engine on his computer. Typed in her name and rank.

This could be interesting.

As the search results came up, the door opened and Desmond bounced in, an all-too-familiar grin on his face.

Cameron's heart sank. He rolled his eyes. "What do you want?"

"Good to see you too, Bro." He took out a handkerchief and wiped his nose. Cameron noted the pinkish tinge of his eyes.

"Have you been snorting coke again? Christ, I hope you haven't been driving under the influence? I've just had the police here."

"I know. I saw them leaving. Pigs written all over them. And no, I haven't been DUI. I got Mad Willie to drive me over."

"He's not your personal chauffer."

"No, he's yours most of the time. Waste of a man like him. You waste me, too."

Cameron sighed. "No, Des, I don't. When you can be trusted with some responsibility, I'll give it to you. Meanwhile, running errands is all you're good for. Laying off the coke might be a start."

"I can handle it." Desmond scowled.

"Yeah, well. Right now, I've got the police coming to me for help, believe it or not. So now's not the time for you to start drawing attention to yourself, okay?"

Desmond moved across to the nearest chair and sat down. "You? Helping the police? What with?"

Cameron grinned and winked, knowing it would enrage his sibling. "Never you mind, baby brother."

28

As Archer and Baines had set off for Cameron Connolly's home, Collins joined Bell in contacting Eric Yelland's next of kin. The missing security guard was divorced, but did have a married daughter, Cassie Osborne, whom Will Tyler had tracked down to Leicester.

Bell had spoken to her on the phone. She'd sounded worried, and had agreed to meet them, so the pair had driven up the motorway to the East Midlands, Bell at the wheel of his Seat.

The journey took a little under 90 minutes. All Collins knew about the city was that the remains of King Richard the Third had been dug up in a car park there, and their football team had unexpectedly won the Premier League last year. Accompanied by a uniformed PC from the local force, they found Cassie Osborne in a small house on a modern estate that could just as easily have been anywhere in the country.

She was not a tall woman, and more than a little plump, with a hair colour that made Jason Bell's ginger seem subdued. She led them into a slightly chaotic sitting room with evidence of school-age children.

"Is there any news?" she blurted. "Has he turned up yet? What's going on?"

"I'm sorry," Bell said. "I'm afraid we still haven't been able to trace him."

"How do you know he's not gone on holiday?"

"We don't. But, if he had, wouldn't you know?"

"Dad's always been a law unto himself. That's the trouble." Her smile didn't touch her eyes.

"Well, wherever he is, we need to speak to him urgently. We've no reason to suppose anything's happened to him, though."

That was only half-true, Collins thought. The best-case scenario was that Yelland had simply chosen now to take a holiday, as Cassie had suggested - although it still struck her as odd that his only daughter wouldn't know. But maybe father and daughter didn't talk much.

Cassie bit her lip. "I hope not. To be honest, I always wondered if he'd come to a sticky end. You tell yourself you're being ridiculous, but…"

"What made you think something like that?"

"Honestly? Dad was always a bit of a fuckup."

Collins spoke. "In what way was he… messed up?"

"Well," she said, "it was gambling mostly. I think he'd been a betting man all his life, and he just kept digging holes for himself."

"What sort of holes?"

"You really don't know? I'd have thought he'd be on your radar."

"Say he isn't," Bell said.

"All right. He was a pretty addictive gambler, and rubbish at it. He used to run out of money, but still think he could win it back."

"So he borrowed money?"

"Yup. And when he couldn't pay that back, he borrowed elsewhere. It got so he owed more and more, increasingly desperately – and recklessly. Some of the people he owed it to sounded pretty dangerous."

This was unexpected. "Loan sharks?" Suggested Collins.

"Sharks is right. He was scared a lot of the time."

"He told you all this?"

"Some. Mum told us some of it, too. They split up, of course. She didn't enjoy coming home to find the furniture or the telly gone, flogged off to feed his habit. Or having thugs turning up on the doorstep with threats to her and to me."

"Such as?"

"Oh, you know. 'Tell Eric we know where your daughter goes to school.' That sort of thing. And then, when I was older and earning, he started coming to me begging for some cash to settle a debt. I helped a bit to start with. But it was like he thought I was a bottomless pit. You'd lend him money and a week later he'd be asking for more. It couldn't go on."

"You stopped paying him?"

"I wasn't exactly flush in the first place, and when I was trying to save up to get married, I started saying no. Telling him to sort himself out. Seek help. I mean, he'd had a job, for God's sake, in security. But, of course, that went out the window."

Collins detected notes of bitterness and sadness mingled in Cassie's tone. "He got fired?"

Cassie gave a twisted smile. "Left by mutual consent. The easy way out for him and the firm. He'd hinted he was risking his job, and I thought he was doing favours for people he owed money to."

Collins sat up on the sofa. "What sort of favours?"

Cassie massaged her temples. "I never asked and he never said anything. It was probably dodgy, though. I love my dad. I remember all the good stuff from when we were little. The seaside. The piggybacks. The doll's house he made me. But he's a weak man who couldn't, or wouldn't, ever get his act together. I can imagine him getting into the wrong sort of thing way over his head."

"Did he say who these loan sharks were?" Bell asked.

"No. I think it was his idea of protecting us. But the reason I think he was doing dodgy jobs is simple. He'd have been homeless by now if he hadn't. Either that or made an example of." She looked Collins in the eye. "That happens, right?"

It would be stupid to deny it. "We have no reason to suppose that's what happened here," said Collins carefully.

"But you're not ruling it out."

"We need to speak to him in relation to a case we're working on. That's all."

Cassie smiled. "So you said. You won't be surprised to find I did an Internet search for Aylesbury news after I agreed to see you. I noticed a body had been found under a block of flats that blew up. I'm guessing it was put there when the block was being built, and dad was one of the security guards there." She arched an eyebrow. "How am I doing?"

She would have made a decent detective, Collins thought. "Did he ever mention the name Tim, or Timothy, Phillips?" The name was being released to the media this morning, so she might as well ask.

Cassie looked pensive, then shook her head. "Sorry."

"Is there anything else you can think of? Anywhere he might have gone?"

"No. I'd tell you if there was. Just find him, please. And let him be okay."

"We're doing all we can," Collins said. "You've been very helpful."

Back in the car, Collins asked Bell what he made of the woman's information.

"It could be something to do with loan sharks," he said, "but my money is still on there being a link to Tim Phillips's murder. Either way, though, I think he's either dead somewhere, or he's gone into hiding."

"Yes, I don't buy the impulsive holiday scenario. Maybe Will's got somewhere with the car." Tyler was requesting any hits on the Automated Number Plate Recognition system for Yelland's Toyota over the past few days.

"Will's a busy boy," Bell said.

"I hope he's coping. I'll ask him, in case he needs more support. Meanwhile, we know who the nastier loan sharks are around the Vale. I suppose we could push them over whether Yelland owed them anything."

"They're unlikely to say, though, are they? Especially if they've done something to him."

"True. But you never know."

They headed back to the M1 in companionable silence. Bell concentrated on his driving. Collins found her thoughts turning to Charlie. Last night, Collins had made her a promise.

As they joined the motorway, Bell spoke, a little tentatively.

"So... Have you given any more thought to what we discussed last night? About coming out, I mean?"

"Yes. I've told Charlie I'm going to tackle both work and the family as soon as I can. The parents are a problem, because I need to make time to sit down with them. It's going to be traumatic, I expect. Doing it over the phone will make it worse, and it feels a little cowardly."

"And work?"

"Well, I don't see why I should stand on my desk and shout, 'Hey, everybody! I'm a lesbian!'"

He chuckled. "Oh, I don't know."

"I'm telling Dan and Lizzie today. I just have to pick my moment to get them together. I think, once I've cleared that hurdle, it will gradually get easier."

"I doubt you'll get anything but support from those two."

She found herself smiling. It was good to be talking openly about this. Her burden felt somehow lighter. "I think you're right."

29

Archer received a call en route back to the station from Cameron Connolly's home, to say that, if she wanted to attend the post mortems on Gary Meredith and Robbie Pascoe, then Barbara Carlisle was ready to start as soon as Archer could get there. Baines agreed to accompany her, and so they drove directly to the mortuary.

They'd held out little hope that the pathologist's examinations would yield anything they didn't already know. It was just as well. Nothing remarkable about the men's physical conditions, apart from the little matter of their throats having been slit, almost certainly by a right handed assailant. Said throat slitting, unsurprisingly, the cause of death. Almost certainly with a razor.

The one thing Carlisle could add that was of interest was that the killing had been extremely efficient.

"One straight, deep slash," she said. No false starts, no sawing motion, no sense of the killer having any hesitation or squeamishness. I'm not saying he or she has had lots of practice, but they definitely knew what they were doing and executed these men with confidence."

Archer absorbed the information. "Does that suggest that the killer might be a psychopath?"

Carlisle smiled. "You know I can't answer that. You need a different kind of doctor. But, if you're asking for my personal opinion, it takes a certain attitude to fellow human beings to dispatch them so coldly and clinically. I don't think you'd find that in the average person. What label you'd pin on it, though, you need a professional to advise you."

"It probably won't help us to identify the killer in any case," Archer said.

"It's not all bad news on the forensic front, though," Carlisle told them. "Have you spoken to Phil Gordon?"

"Not lately."

"I think he was trying to get hold of you. He's found something of interest."

"Oh?" Archer had looked at her curiously.

Carlisle had flashed her best enigmatic smile. "Speak to Phil. I'd hate to steal his thunder."

Archer made the call as they trailed across the car park back to Baines's Mondeo. It had been misty when they'd arrived, but that had burned off. It was still cool outside, but at least glimpses of sun were available through the cloud.

"I gather you've got something for me," she told Gordon. "Why didn't you call?"

"I left you a voicemail."

"Damn. We must have been out of signal range. Sorry."

"Not to worry. We've got something after all, I reckon, but it's hardly a game changer."

Baines had unlocked the car. He held the door for her while she got in, phone still pressed to her ear.

"I'll take any little thing, Phil. What have we got?"

"A partial shoeprint with a trace of blood. We're analysing it, but I'd be surprised if the blood isn't from one of our victims."

"But you said there were no signs that the killer had stepped in any blood. There would have been bloody shoeprints on the concrete floor."

"It's a riddle, isn't it?" There was a chuckle in his voice.

Archer sighed. "Certainly is, Phil. But may we cut to the chase?"

"Sorry, Lizzie. Didn't mean to tease. Well, you'll recall the passage that goes under the first floor walkway, with the stairwell entrances on either side?"

"Yep."

"Well, if you walk through to the rear, there's a spot where the concrete path has crumbled, probably due to age, or frost, or a bit of both. It isn't much – it's roughly an equilateral triangle, about three inches each side, give or take – but it's filled with soft dirt."

"And our killer stepped on it?"

"Someone did. I'm surmising that they'd maybe got a splash of blood on the top of the shoe, and it had trickled down far enough to leave a trace when the shoe sank into the mud."

Archer felt a surge of excitement. "So what can you tell me about it? Presumably it wasn't the only footfall that dirt patch has ever seen?"

"No, but I reckon it was the latest. We should be able to clean it up and maybe even say what make and model shoe it is. Actually, I'd say it's some sort of trainer. Oh, but I'm saving the best till last."

Her pulse quickened. "Go on."

"The shoe came down on the dirt exactly where the size marking is on the sole. Our killer is a size twelve."

She digested this. "That's quite big. Isn't shoe size an indicator of height? Are we looking for a giant?"

"I don't know about that. But he could well be over 6 feet 4 inches in height."

Archer imagined a hulking Russian, Ukrainian or whatever, straight razor in hand. In her mind, he wore a plaid jacket and a black woollen beanie hat. He had a beard.

He was a stereotype from TV and movies. She shook the image out of her head.

"Are there CCTV cameras at the back?"

"In the entryway, covering the front and rear approaches. I take it someone's checking the footage?"

"We've got people going through footage from last night, yes, and we know the rough time that the killings happened. I'll get them to concentrate on the entryway and look out for a big guy at the rear." She felt some of her gloom lighten. Maybe the fog was beginning to lift in more ways than one. "You think it's not a game-changer, Phil? You never know your luck. If our killer's not the brightest light on the Christmas tree, he might just have smiled for the camera."

30

If Phil Gordon's news had offered a ray of hope, Archer's spirits were further lifted as she walked back into the office. There was something different about the atmosphere. She had sensed something like it in the past, when there'd been a hint of a breakthrough. Sometimes the bubble had quickly popped as the hot lead had proved to go nowhere. Occasionally, though, the excitement had been justified, with an arrest soon following.

As Archer took off her coat, she saw Tyler signalling to her. But she was in need of the loo and some coffee.

"Give me five, Will," she said as she took her jar of quality coffee and her mug out of her desk drawer.

When she was back at her desk, a mug steaming in front of her, she had Baines, Collins, Bell and Tyler crowded around her desk. Tyler had loaded some CCTV footage up on his laptop. She recognised the entryway to the flats in which Gary Meredith and Robbie Pascoe had perished, on the night of the murders.

"This is from the camera facing to the rear," Tyler commented. "You'd be surprised how comparatively rarely people enter and exit the back way. It's a long walk round to the front if you want to actually go anywhere. The back is mostly a service area, where bins are kept. There's a chute for normal household waste. Recycling bins have to be used manually, but that's pretty as and when, and you don't see too much evidence of anyone doing it. Besides, who empties their bins after dark?"

Archer didn't say, but with the hours she typically worked, she did so all the time.

"So here's the first interesting bit," Tyler said.

They could see a figure approaching from the left hand side of the screen.

"Is this our man?" Baines asked.

"Watch his behaviour," Tyler said.

The figure reached the entryway, paused, and took a look around him. Tall and heavyset, it had a definite male bearing and, even on the footage, somehow exuded both confidence and menace. Maddeningly, a hood obscured his face. His hands were stuffed in the pockets of a the dark anorak he wore.

For a moment, he seemed to look straight up at the camera, and Archer realised that the hood was irrelevant. The big man wore a black three-hole balaclava, with only the eyes and mouth showing.

"I'd say it was definitely our man," Bell said.

"Anywhere but the Northfields, and I'd agree with you," Collins commented. "I'd guess there are more balaclavas there than you'd think. But the timing... Yeah, it's probably a safe bet."

"You're not wrong," said Tyler. "Keep watching."

The masked man flattened himself against the wall by the entryway. Archer glanced at the time on the screen. It was about 20 minutes before Ed Studman said he'd offered to mind Gary Meredith's car.

"Bear in mind that approaching from the rear reduces the likelihood that he'll be seen," Tyler pointed out.

"Which means he either knows the estate or knows someone who does," Baines added.

Archer thought about that. "Got to be the latter if this is some out of towner. Either that, or the Eastern Europeans already have more of a foothold in the Vale than we knew, and they're already pretty familiar with places like this."

"I'm going to fast forward," Tyler said.

The figure remained in position. Occasionally, he would sneak a quick peek into the entryway and then a man or woman would enter it from the front and open a door into one or other of the stairwells.

"I'm guessing he hears their footsteps," Tyler said. "A quick look to see if it's one of his targets. Okay, this is the next interesting bit..."

The masked man took another peek, then withdrew again. Moments later, a male figure approached. Big and solid, with next to no neck. The two doorways were just about within camera range, and the man paused between them, then turned around, looking from right to left. The entryway was poorly lit, but it was enough.

"Freeze it," Archer said. Tyler obliged. "It's Robbie Pascoe," she said. "For sure."

There was a sense of inevitability about what was to come.

"Can we slow forward it, Will?" she asked.

"Sure." Tyler tapped the screen and the action continued in slow motion. Pascoe made a decision and pushed open the door to his left. As he did so, the masked figure emerged from hiding, moving quickly even on the slow playback.

"Freeze again." Archer's mouth was dry. The big man was advancing on the door Pascoe had just opened. Something in a huge paw of a right hand glinted, even in the bad lighting.

"A razor," Bell said.

"Okay, normal speed, please."

They watched as the drama played out. Robbie Pascoe, in the doorway, turning towards his attacker way too late and being bundled through the stairwell door, the killer's left hand already in his hair, yanking his head back, the right hand bringing the razor up. Archer thought it a small mercy that the actual killing was played out inside the stairwell, out of the range of the camera.

As they continued to watch, the big man pulled the door open from inside, just enough to squeeze through.

"We know Robbie's body was close to the door," Collins commented. "Enough to obstruct it."

Meanwhile, the killer had moved back to his position by the rear entryway. Tyler fast forwarded again. At one point, it looked as if things were going to get messy, as a youngish couple approached. If they stumbled upon Robbie's body, then the killer would have to either abort his mission or add these two to the collateral damage. But they took the door to the right. Archer's gaze kept returning to the left hand door, where something dark was seeping out from underneath and spreading.

The rest of the action played out like some sort of Greek or Shakespearian tragedy. Barely five minutes after the attack on

Robbie Pascoe, the scene they had just witnessed was virtually repeated. They saw Gary Meredith's approach, watched him pause in the entryway and stare at the pool of what Archer knew was blood, oozing out from under the left hand door. Saw him start to push the door inwards, apparently encounter an obstruction, then shove. Saw him step inside the stairwell and out of sight, even as the heavyset masked man, still holding the razor, walked purposely through the entryway and stepped through the door, left hand stretched out, right hand raising the razor.

Less than a minute later, the killer emerged, stepping around the pool of blood, his movements surprisingly nimble for his size. If there was any doubt that he knew about the cameras, he paused and brandished the razor, looking directly into the lens and grinning. Then he turned away and was gone.

"Well, fuck," Baines commented. "Bugger's taunting us. He knows we're watching, but doesn't care. He thinks the mask makes him safe."

Archer badly wanted to wipe the smile off the razor man's face. "So what does this tell us? He's obviously a big guy, but can we work out a decent estimate for his height and build, Will?"

"I spoke to Phil Gordon about that, boss. He'll do some measuring inside the entryway, and then we can get a frame of reference to assess this guy's vital statistics. We're having other footage in the general vicinity checked out too, in the hope we can catch our killer arriving and departing by car."

"Pity there's no camera where Kit Meredith's body was dumped . But let's see if we can spot the same car, the same individual, somewhere in the vicinity."

She touched Tyler's arm. "Brilliant work, Will. One other thing. Where he looks into the camera? Can we take a still from that and maybe blow it up, clean it up, analyse it, whatever the boffins can do? See if we can spot anything at all that might be useful."

Otherwise, what they had was ultimately a bit thin. The killer wouldn't be the only tall, solid man in the Vale that night.

"Okay," she said, "what's next? Will, have you had a chance to interrogate other forces about this mysterious gang?"

"I have. I got a couple of the civilian investigation officers to lend a hand. There's a couple of groups active in Oxfordshire, one centred in Oxford city. Mostly Romanian, but it's thought that there might also be some Bulgarians and Lithuanians in the mix. A lot of drugs, but also human trafficking. It's believed that vulnerable women are snatched off the streets in Balkan countries and forced into sex slavery, working in pop-up brothels. The location keeps changing, so the police are always at least one step behind. No one seems sure who's running the show. There have been a couple of arrests, but small fry who are either too loyal or too scared to finger the bigger fish."

"I'm betting they're no respecters of county boundaries," Baines said.

"You've got that right," Tyler said. "Their activities have almost certainly extended northwards into Northamptonshire and westwards into Gloucestershire, so if they're not operating in Bucks and Berks yet, it's only a matter of time."

"Okay," Archer said, "you need to get me everything there is on that gang. Do we have names?"

"Working on it, guv. There'll be a proper dossier by this evening."

"Great. And get a few stills from the footage circulated to everyone who knows anything about them. See if he rings any bells. I know you can't see his face, but I strongly suspect he's an enforcer. If he's been busy in other counties…"

"Will do."

"Have you got enough help and support, Will?"

He smiled. "Don't worry. A lot of people are helping out. It's just a matter of knowing who to ask."

"I've got a question," Bell said. "Why a razor?"

"Why not?" Collins shrugged. "Quick, quiet…"

"So are other methods. I mean, razor gangs held a reign of terror in my home town back in the 20s and 30s."

"Glasgow?" Archer checked.

"Yep. But by the time I was growing up there, it was knives, machetes, guns…"

"This isn't Glasgow though, is it?" Baines pointed out. "And these guys aren't Glaswegians."

"Fair enough," Bell conceded. "But am I the only one who thinks this is all a bit off? Kit Meredith is tortured and then dumped in an abandoned car, where he isn't found for days. Whereas his brother and his minder are left to lie where they fall. There's lots of blood and it's messy. No consistency."

"Chances are," Collins said, "they wanted to cut the heads off the Meredith's empire, and this was all planned. Kit comes into the Vale asking questions, and they snatch him, torture him and kill him. We were thinking maybe they were going to dump him on the Northfields, maybe to make us think locals are involved. That putting him in the abandoned car was just one extra little flourish, right?"

"And Gary?"

"Okay," Collins continued. "So they guess that Gary will be pretty pissed when his brother finally turns up. They probably have intelligence that tells them he can let his temper cloud his judgement. Not difficult to lure him to the estate with the promise of information. And no need to waste much time in executing him. Maybe they want a lot of mess this time, to frighten people just a little more."

"Not a bad theory, Joan. We badly need a name for at least one of these gang leaders."

She thought about the meeting with Cameron Connolly. It had been a long shot, but him deciding to help the police to take out a potential rival might be their best hope right now.

"Let's keep digging on that, but keep open minds. We don't want to get so fixated on Romanians or whatever that we miss other possibilities. I'll have another chat with Gary's wife, Sonia." She recapped the conversation with DCI Mahon. "Either she'll take the reins or there will be a vacuum that someone else will be eager to fill. Maybe someone inside the gang wants to step up."

"Maybe that somebody is the killer and the Eastern Europe thing is nothing to do with it," Baines suggested

"It's possible. Or maybe, having created this situation, the Eastern Europeans will try to seal their takeover by removing

Sonia, making sure the Meredith operation is headless. DCI Mahon already has an FLO keeping tabs on her and a patrol car driving by every hour or so, but I need to have a proper conversation with her, I think, before she joins the body count."

31

Derek Pollard met Baines and Bell outside Jackie Phillips's home. The Mercedes and Jaguar stood on the drive again, indicating that Geoff Rice, as well as Tim Phillips's widow, was at home. It was Rice who opened the door.

"You've news?" he said.

Baines couldn't help thinking he didn't sound overly enthusiastic. Maybe his partner's missing husband turning up was causing ripples. Perhaps Rice would have preferred Tim to be both gone and forgotten. Despite the loss of his wife shortly before Phillips's disappearance, Baines wondered again if Rice had taken a fancy to Jackie some time before that. Maybe his wife's death, albeit from natural causes – if cancer could be deemed natural – had been the catalyst for him to act on that fancy?

Jackie insisted that Rice go and make some teas and coffees, leaving her alone with the two detectives. Baines asked if she'd like to wait for his return before they started asking questions.

"No, it's fine," she said. "I've nothing to hide."

"Thank you." Baines sat up a little straighter. "We're trying to get a more rounded feel for Tim and his lifestyle. I've got some quite difficult questions, but we have to ask. We asked you before if you ever had occasion to think maybe Tim was seeing other women? You implied that you might have suspected as much, but didn't want to know. We really need you to elaborate. I know it's difficult, but it's important."

She smiled. It was a sad sort of a smile. "Oh, God. I was asked all that when he disappeared. I was probably a bit evasive then, and I suppose it's got to be a habit. The reality is, there was a nasty little unspoken secret in our marriage, and, because I still held out hope that he was still alive, I didn't want anyone else knowing."

"But now?"

She blinked. Tears welled in her eyes and trickled down her cheeks. She brushed them away with the backs of her hands.

"Look, Sergeant. No two marriages are the same. They all involve a few compromises, and it's always ultimately about how far either party is prepared to go with their compromising. In my case, it was quite a long way."

"Can you explain what that means, exactly?"

She sighed. "You have to understand that being married to a man like Tim has a lot going for it. He was a really sweet guy and great company a lot of the time and, of course, his wealth was a definite plus."

"But?" Baines prompted.

She sighed. "Oh, it was a long time ago now, and Tim's dead. It doesn't matter any more if people know. The truth is, our sex life had long since petered out. He wanted – *needed* - something I couldn't – no," she amended, "*wouldn't* – give him."

Jackie covered her face with her hands. Sucked in a long breath. Exhaled slowly, and lowered her hands.

"Tim liked it rough. No, even that's not quite right. The plain fact is…" She looked at her lap. "He once tried to throttle me as we were having sex."

Baines wasn't surprised, but chose to act as if he was. "*Throttle* you?"

"We'd been married about six months when he put his hands on my throat. The sense of panic… I still go cold thinking about it. I had to rip at his face with my nails to make him stop."

"And you say this was just once?"

"Yes. He wouldn't explain where it came from. He said he wanted to choke me until I passed out. That it would make the sex better. Well, maybe for him. But it didn't make it better for me. It was terrifying, and I told him I wasn't having it. He said I ought to try it. Might like it. I told him if he tried that again I would be walking out the door."

"And he left it at that?"

"We carried on making love normally for a few years after that, and had two lovely sons. But I could tell he wasn't really enjoying it much."

"So did you suspect he was getting what he wanted elsewhere?"

"Put it this way. I knew something else was going on. In the end, it got so he couldn't even be bothered to shower when he got home. He'd get into bed with me with their smell on him."

"That's a bit more than not knowing."

"I suppose. You ignore a thing long enough and you can tell yourself it's not there, even when it's right under your nose."

"Did you never confront him?"

"Never. But I wondered. I thought maybe he'd found someone whose appetites matched his own, although I honestly wondered if he could make an actual relationship on the side work. He was very committed – if that's the right word – to his reputation, and I could imagine some sort of kiss and tell story coming out. He wouldn't have risked it. And what if his bit on the side didn't like being strangled any more than I did and started talking?"

She shook her head. "No. It couldn't be an affair. Not a serious one, anyway. Maybe a fling here, a one night stand there. But, when it came to the sex he liked best, I reasoned that he was probably paying for it - and paying enough for it to all be kept discreet. After he disappeared, and Geoff started helping me make sense of our private finances, as well as the business ones, I became certain."

Rice chose that moment to walk in with a tray.

"I'm telling them about Tim's little foibles," Jackie said lightly. "It's time."

He put the tray down, handed out the drinks, then sat beside her on the sofa, holding her hand.

"Tell them about the cash withdrawals," she said.

Rice paused, then shrugged. "Large-ish sums, a couple of times a month."

"Everyone draws cash," Bell commented.

"Not Tim, not normally. Oh, a bit of pocket money, sure, in case he had to pay for a public loo or whatever, but he was a walking credit card economy. He'd put a 70p chocolate bar on a card. At first, neither of us could imagine what he was drawing the money for."

"But when we started really looking at the dates," Jackie said. "I realised they coincided with when I thought he'd been having his filthy throttling sex. And then I *knew*. I felt quite sick."

"Couldn't the cash have been for something else?" Baines pressed, needing to be sure. "Was it possible he was doing drugs, for instance?"

"Not unless he was buying them from a pusher who liked cheap, nasty scent, no."

"When was the last withdrawal before he disappeared? Can you remember?"

"Oh, yes," Rice said. "Twelfth of April 2005 – a couple of weeks before he vanished."

"You seem certain."

"I am. There was a big fundraiser that night."

"There was quite often something major going on when he *indulged* himself," Jackie added. "As if he was giving himself a little reward. Now do you see why it was mostly the money that kept me here?"

"You could have walked away," Baines said. "Took him for half of what he was worth."

"Half? Why should I? Even if I'd got that much, after his lawyers had finished with me. I still had a better life than most, and I had access to *all* that he was worth. Okay, yes, it could be difficult, lonely even, but I had friends, I had interests. And Tim was okay to live with, so long as I knew when to look the other way."

Baines trained his gaze on Rice again. "And you're sure there were no more cash withdrawals after that date?"

"Not that fitted the pattern, no. But there actually was one more, which was a bit odd."

"How so?"

"There was one much larger sum than usual, a couple of days after the Twelfth. Thousands, rather than hundreds. We both racked our brains, but we've no idea what it was for."

"There was one other date," Rice continued, "a couple of days before he went missing, when the normal pattern would have seen him drawing the usual sum. Only he didn't draw any cash that day. And then he was gone."

Baines was absorbing this when another thought came into focus. "The night he disappeared, he went out unexpectedly to a meeting, right?"

"That's right," Jackie agreed. "We have no idea who he was meeting though."

"You see, that's what I don't get," said Baines. "I think you said before that he'd go off to meetings at the drop of a hat. But you didn't ask who with?"

"No, and he rarely said. I think mostly they were business – someone needed to see him urgently, or someone he was keen to see might suddenly have a bit of time open up. I also thought that sometimes the meetings were with women – not prostitutes. But, again, I didn't want to know."

"But we doubt he was seeing a prostitute that night," Rice added, "because he hadn't drawn the cash."

Bell cut in. "I don't get it at all, Mrs Phillips. You couldn't know about those cash withdrawals until much later, when Mr Rice here started going over the personal finances. So, the night Tim didn't come home, you must have thought maybe he was seeing a woman? You even mentioned last time we saw you that you fleetingly entertained the possibility that he'd run off with someone."

"And I also said, Constable, that I immediately dismissed the notion. Tim wasn't one to run away. If he'd wanted someone else on a permanent basis, he'd have wanted her *and* as much of his wealth as he could hang on to."

"But you must also have suspected he might be paying for sex that night."

She was bristling now. "He wasn't though, was he? And, even if I did, it wasn't something I was going to admit. Being taken for a fool is one thing. I wasn't prepared for the whole world to see me as one."

Baines threw up his hands. "But, for heaven's sake, Jackie. Your husband was missing. It was a line of enquiry. And you kept it to yourself."

She looked a little abashed. "I know. I shouldn't have. At first, I thought he'd turn up. That there was no need to mention it unless I had to. Then it had gone on too long and I didn't like to. Because I'd have got the very reaction I'm getting now."

Baines thought he'd never understand people. What a mess. If Jackie had said she thought her husband was using prostitutes, the police would have been bound to make it part of their investigation. Instead, she'd kept it to herself out of some sort of embarrassment.

Meanwhile, Jackie Phillips and Geoff Rice sat side by side, their poses identical – straight backs and folded arms – and their expressions stony.

He sighed. "All right. Let's move away from the prostitutes. You thought he might also be having flings and one night stands?"

"Honestly? I'm not sure. Certainly, he must have been pretty discreet, because no woman came forward, as far as I know, and I never heard a name." She finally had the grace to look worried. "I'm not going to be in any trouble, am I?"

"We'll have to see," Baines said, more harshly than he needed to. He was sick of the games surrounding this case. It wouldn't do any harm for her to stew for a while.

He stood up. "We'll be in touch."

32

Sonia Meredith looked tired when she opened her door to Archer and Collins – a far cry from the woman who'd lost it so spectacularly when she'd learned of Gary's murder. But now the fallout must be pressing down on her like a ten ton weight. Newly widowed, it seemed likely that she was now having to combine handling her grief with trying to hold the family's business interests together.

"I hope you've come to tell me the bastard who killed my husband is in custody," she said when they were all seated in her living room. The room was a bit bland for Archer's taste. Oatmeal carpet, beige walls with ubiquitous prints of Spanish senoritas, brown leather sofas with nondescript floral cushions. The round coffee table was awash with what looked like documents.

Sonia herself was slim, probably gym-toned, with a mane of black hair and pointy features. She wore a long-sleeved tee shirt with designer ripped jeans, the same ensemble she'd been wearing when Archer had seen her earlier.

"I sincerely wish I could," Archer told her. "But no. We're still in the early stages. But you might be able to help us. I didn't ask too many questions earlier on, because you were so upset, but we do need to start asking now."

"Do I need a lawyer?"

"It's your right, but you're not under arrest, and all we're interested in is finding out who killed Gary and Kit. Beyond that, we're not interested in your personal and business affairs. Not today, anyway"

"All right. Ask your questions and we'll see."

Archer thanked her. "First of all, what's going to happen to the family business now Kit and Gary are gone?"

Sonia pinched the ridge between her eyes. Gestured to the paper lake on the coffee table. "Long term? No idea. It wasn't supposed to be like this. For now, I'm trying to get my ducks in a row. Because, if I don't hold the ring now, it'll probably fall apart pretty rapidly."

"Just you? Not Lisa?" Archer thought she knew the answer, but had to ask.

Sonia scoffed. "That little dormouse? Do me a favour. She and I are as chalk and cheese as our two husbands were. I don't know what Lisa and Kit talked about, but it sure as hell wasn't the business. Kit liked keeping her in the dark and, as far as I could make out, she loved it that way."

"But your marriage wasn't like that?"

"No." There was a note of pride in Sonia's voice. "Ours was a proper marriage. We talked about everything, and Gary often asked me what I thought about a decision he had to make." She smiled slyly. "All above board, obviously. If you think he was into anything dodgy, I wouldn't know about that."

"Of course you wouldn't," Archer said. "But did Gary say anything to you about Eastern Europeans – how shall I put it – muscling in on your marketplace?"

"Yes. He thought they'd killed Kit."

"What do you think?"

"He's dead too, isn't he?"

"But would they have other enemies who might want them out of the way?"

Sonia flinched. "I'm sorry to be so blunt," Archer said.

"It's okay. I rather like bluntness. And yeah, I'm sure a lot of people would have liked to be rid of them. But I got the impression that these Romanians, or whatever they are, are a whole new threat level. Kit was stupid to think he could reason with them, and Gary..." Her voice cracked. She gulped, swiped tears away. "Sorry. Gary was always too bloody impulsive. I knew he was determined to find the people who killed Kit, and he wouldn't listen to me when I told him this Aylesbury setup could be a trap."

"I'm assuming he never had any names for these Eastern Europeans?"

"If he did, he never told me. I'm guessing not."

"There's something else I wanted to talk to you about," Archer said. "It sounds very much like you're in charge for the time being. It could make you the next target."

"You think I haven't thought of that?"

"Maybe you should keep a bit of a low profile for a while."

"What sort of a low profile? If I don't show some leadership, those bastards really will walk in and take over. Unless you're closer to arrests than you've said."

"It might not be for long," Collins interjected. "We do have some leads."

Sonia sighed. "We're talking about a diverse portfolio of business interests here – you know and I know what some of them are, but I'm not saying, and Reading police have never had anything on us. It's a portfolio that's headless unless I take charge. Gary liked people who did his bidding without question. You met Robbie Pascoe? If I tell you he was one of our brighter people, you'll see the problem."

"But is it worth endangering your life?" Collins persisted.

"It is to me."

Archer found herself admiring the woman's obstinacy. "We've already arranged for a squad car to pass your house at regular intervals. We can get someone to talk you through safety precautions, although you might not like them. This isn't my patch, but I doubt if there's the budget for a proper surveillance."

"That's okay. I don't especially want the plods sitting outside my house 24/7 anyway. I'll step up my own protection."

"Nothing illegal, I trust?"

"No comment."

Archer wasn't happy. "Sonia, I'd hate you to get yourself killed, and I'd really hate your idea of protection to land you in jail."

"Neither of those things will happen. Trust me."

* * *

"There's got to be more to it than we're seeing," Archer said as Collins started the Fiesta up. "I mean, why is the Northfields estate playing such a big part? I'm not seeing it. If you're after the Meredith's turf, why not fight your battles there? Why dump one body at Northfields and then lure your next victim there as well? I know we've speculated that it's just to sow confusion, but is that all it is?"

"Maybe a warning to organised criminals in the Vale? Putting them on notice?"

"What, like the Connollys? Christ, I hope not. It'll be a bloodbath."

Archer wondered if her gamble on getting some co-operation from Cameron Connolly had been both premature and risky. If he decided there was a gang who posed a threat to him, he might not even wait for them to bring the fight to him.

They drove on in silence for a while. After a few minutes, Collins spoke.

"Guv? This may not be the right time, but then when is?"

"Time for what, Joan?"

"Well..." Collins tailed off.

"Spit it out, Joan."

The younger woman glanced her way. "The fact is... I've got something to tell you."

Archer felt herself tensing. This sounded too much like it was going to be a confession. From *Collins*? The most conscientious officer she knew? It was obviously something she felt uncomfortable raising. Archer hoped it was a lot less serious than it sounded.

"Fire away." She tried to make it sound casual.

"Okay." Collins took a deep breath. "It's about the friend I've got staying with me."

"The one who lived at Spencer Court? One of your girl friends?" Had Collins discovered she'd taken in a drug addict? Or worse?

"Charlie, yes," Collins was saying. "But the thing is, she's not one of my girl friends. She's my girlfriend."

Just for a moment, she thought Collins was telling her she only had one friend. But what about Bell? They were pretty close, weren't they? Or was she saying she only had one female friend. So what? That was actually one more then Archer had these days.

"Say something, guv. Christ, this coming out lark is even harder than I imagined."

"Coming..." The shoe finally dropped. "Oh."

"You disapprove." It was a statement, not a question, Collins sounded stricken.

"Oh, Joan," she said, finding her emotions mingled. A quick stab of pleasure and affection for her colleague, who worked so very hard and deserved joy in her life more than almost anyone she knew. Dismay that her slow wits had given a false impression of displeasure. "You know me better than that. Why would I disapprove? I think it's brilliant."

"Honestly?" Collins's smile was like sunshine.

"Honestly. Sorry, my brain's so full of murder and casework, it's a bit slow on everything else. And I didn't see this coming."

"Nor did I, until I met Charlie. It's all happened so quickly. I told Jason, and he was really cool with it. So supportive, guv. I mightn't have the bottle to tell you, if it wasn't for him. You're really okay about it?"

"I'm thrilled for you. I'd love to meet her."

"You will. Guv, could you tell Dan?"

"Of course. You don't want to do it yourself, though?"

"I'd be amazed if he had a problem but, you know what? Coming out is bloody exhausting. And I've still got my parents to tackle. That'll be fun." Her tone told Archer it would be anything but. Collins sighed. "You're right, though. Dan's my line manager, and we've worked together for years. He deserves to hear it from me. After that, people can find out if it comes up in conversation and like it or not."

"Dead right. It's no one else's business."

"I'll make sure I tell Dan today. Can you do me another favour, then, Lizzie?"

"If I can."

Collins grinned wickedly. "Well... if you're not telling Dan, maybe you could break it to my mum and dad?"

33

Back at the station, Will Tyler had more information about the Meredith murders. CCTV footage had shown a black VW Passat arriving on the Northfields Estate shortly before the masked assassin had appeared at A Block to wait for Gary's arrival. The footage had been interrogated to try to see the driver's face, but the angles and the limited street lighting meant it had proved frustratingly impossible. There was possibly the hint of a moustache, but even that could have been a shadow.

The same car had been picked up on the estate at 3am the morning after Kit Meredith had last been heard from.

"Again, you can't see the driver's face clearly enough and, wherever they actually parked, there can't have been any cameras," Tyler said. "But here's the thing. It isn't registered to anyone resident on the estate."

"Could be a visitor," Collins said. Archer was still taking in her revelation. She didn't care that her colleague was gay, but it had come as a surprise. But then it had apparently come as a surprise to Collins too.

"Ah." Tyler beamed. "It could. But if it is, it's a visitor with bogus number plates who arrives at times that fit in with the two murders, and only at those times."

"ANPR confirms that?" Archer checked.

"Yep."

"And we know the plates are fake because…?"

"Oh, the registration number relates to a black Passat all right. But the owner of that car was definitely elsewhere with it at those times. He travels a lot for work, with stopovers, and CCTV in car parks show he was in Yorkshire and Derbyshire respectively at the times of the murders."

"We need to find that cloned car," Collins said. "This could be our breakthrough."

"I've flagged it as a vehicle of interest on the entire ANPR network," Tyler said. "Although, for all we know, the fake plates go on and come off, depending on what the car's being used for. And there might be more than one set of fake plates in use."

"Still, it's a step forward," Archer acknowledged. "Are we checking out all black Passats registered in Thames Valley?"

"We are, guv. You'll know as soon as I get anything back."

"Did you say you had something on that partial bloody shoeprint left at the Gary Meredith scene, too?" she prompted.

"Yes. Not much help, though. CSI have pinned the tread down to a popular Nike trainer. Of course, if we find the actual shoe, they might be able to match wear and scuff marks in the tread."

"Great. We could go from house to house, like Prince Charming in search of Cinderella."

The evening briefing was approaching. Archer thought she owed herself a coffee. She'd grabbed some chocolate in Reading, and a drink and a snack appealed to her right now. But, as she returned to the office with her drink, Gillingham emerged from his office.

"Blimey," he said, "are you telepathic?"

"Sorry?"

"I was just coming looking for you. Have you got a minute?"

She spared her chocolate bar, in her bag under her desk, a wistful thought and felt her stomach growl in sympathy.

"Of course, boss."

She followed him into his office.

"Shut the door and have a seat," he said. She did so. "Now, then." He steepled his fingers. "I'm wondering if the Tim Phillips case is actually going anywhere?"

She shrugged. "We're making progress slowly, with the Meredith case taking priority. I've only really got Dan and Jason on it, with a bit of support from Will. They're trying to unravel who Tim might have been meeting the night he died, but it's a bit of a dead end, to be honest. Eric Yelland, the Spencer Court security guard, is still missing. We think it's highly relevant, and we're releasing his details asking the public to look out for him, but not approach. There's still one person who had access to the site we haven't interviewed – Dennis Ryan, the one who lives on the coast. If we had more resource, we might have got down there sooner. As it is, Dan's planning on going tomorrow."

Gillingham looked underwhelmed. "The thing is, Lizzie, I've been thinking about this. However Phillips wound up under Spencer Court very likely has nothing to do with why, or when, he was killed. What with his case and the Merediths, your team might as well be working for Pat Mahon in Reading. You're all spending most of your time there."

"They're very co-operative, Paul."

"I'm sure. But no wonder you're all getting nowhere fast, spending half your time up and down the A329."

She felt that some criticism was implied and it irked her. "What would you have us do, Sir?"

"I've given it a lot of thought. I think Reading can investigate Tim's murder more easily than we can." She opened her mouth to protest, and he silenced her with a raised palm. "I'll leave it with Dan until the end of the week but, once he's on leave, that's it. We'll support them from our end, just as they've supported us. And no one's suggesting your team's been doing anything but its usual diligent job. But our priority has to be the murders being committed here and now, and the real possibility that a gang war is about to erupt. I've decided I need everyone on *that* case."

"But –"

"I'm pulling out the stops for extra resources, but that's crazy when members of your team are running with a case that Reading should be leading on, Lizzie. Tim's been gone a long time and, remember, he was their missing person. It's really a cold case, isn't it?"

"That doesn't mean justice doesn't need to be done."

"Of course it doesn't," he agreed. "But it's just an accident of geography that he turned up here at all."

She stared at him. "Accident of geography? We don't know that for sure. Whoever buried Tim at Spencer Court knew about the site and knew the concrete was just being laid. Since we don't know who that was, we don't know what the connection is. What does the Super say about it?"

He shrugged. "I'll clear it with Lambert, just in case Pat has a problem. I know, though, that the Super's concerned about overstretch too."

She felt a frustrated, impotent anger. "But we've done all this work –"

"And it won't go to waste. Leave Lambert to me. Get Dan to speak to Pat Mahon tomorrow about passing the Phillips case over to them at the end of the week, before he goes on leave. Offer all necessary – and, I stress, *necessary* – support."

Archer didn't like it at all. It felt like a job half done. But Gillingham was at least part right, she admitted grudgingly to herself. The Meredith murders, and the chances of a new and lethal gang forcing its way into the Vale, was a more immediate threat that required all the stops to be pulled out – right across Thames Valley, by the sound of things.

"All right," she said with a sigh. "I'll talk to Dan. Can you just let me know the Super's okay with it, though?"

"Very well." He looked irritated, as if she was somehow challenging his authority. "Once we've got shot of that case, we can focus on this potential gang war."

34

The smell of the sea. The sound of waves lapping at the shore. A house, lonely and isolated.
A face at an upstairs window.

Baines jerked awake, gasping. The dream again, somehow more vivid, more real than it had ever been before. Fading fast again, but some broad details he could still hold onto, even if it did feel like grasping a will-o-the-wisp.

There had been a house with a face at the window. What house? He sat up in bed, straining to see them in his mind's eye, but failed to gain any impression of what it had looked like. All he knew was there had been a house and a face. And the sea. Somewhere on the coast.

What coast? He had no idea.

But he knew it had been seeing that face that had awakened him. Whose face? No idea about that, either.

The sea, a house and a face. It meant nothing to him. He had no points of reference. Was it Jack, invading his dreams again, after more than a year's respite? Or was it something symbolic, to do with his impending wedding?

The dream didn't happen every night, but it was the one thing he shared with no one, not even Karen. Not even with Dr Tracey Walsh, the counsellor who had done so much to help him regain his grasp on his sanity.

For the ten years or so after his son, Jack's, disappearance and Louise's murder, he had tried to carry on, suppressing his emotional response to his tragedy. But then, a few years back, he had begun to have vivid dreams, and even waking visions, of a boy about the age Jack would have been, if he was still alive. Dr Walsh had made him see that the dreams and visions were almost certainly an expression of his wish that Jack was still with him, and that he needed to confront his grief – not attempt to bury it, as he had for way too long.

It had taken a while, but those dreams and visions had ceased to trouble him. His relief had been tinged with a sadness that a last vestige of Jack's existence was gone. It that didn't mean he'd given up hoping Jack was still alive somewhere, but his forthcoming marriage was, he knew, hugely symbolic of his acceptance of the need to try to move on.

And yet.

And yet the dreams of Jack had now been replaced by this unremembered, but still disturbing, dream that had started to recur last year. Whatever it was about, whatever its cause, he knew it wasn't good.

He wished he'd told Karen about the dream, although in truth there had been little to tell up until now. This was the first time he'd been able to recall even snatches.

He wondered if he should try to get a short notice appointment with Dr Walsh. Maybe she could help him make sense of it, or maybe even refer him to a hypnotist who could help him remember more.

But no. He couldn't think about it now. Maybe after the wedding. Maybe he'd just save it for next time he saw her. But then he'd resolved to do that before. And that next appointment was a long way off.

He shook himself, peered at the bedside clock. 5.30am. Early for most people, for a Saturday, but not so much so in his line of work. With a killer on the loose, a body count rising, and stakes that could be frighteningly high, every hand would be to the pumps. There was no overtime available, but no one would be taking a break today.

Karen slept on beside him, and he was glad. He knew the hostility of her family was spoiling what should be an exciting, happy time for her, and was costing her sleep. One more reason not to worry her about this dream.

He slipped out of bed, deciding that a relaxing shower and a proper breakfast – instead of the usual snatched slice of toast and mouthful of coffee – would set him up for the day ahead.

Baines had long since got into the habit of using the main bathroom, rather than the en suite, when he rose early, so as not to disturb Karen. Similarly, he kept his work clothes in what had used to be Jack's room. Padding along the landing, he began to play back yesterday's events in his mind, preparing for the day ahead.

Baines wasn't the only one who'd been keeping secrets. Joan Collins had sprung a surprise on him late last night, making him part of a small circle, along with Archer, Bell and Collins's girlfriend, Charlie, who knew that the DC was gay. He wondered what had been worse for her – the years of uncertainty about her true sexual identity, or finally coming to terms with it and plucking up the courage to tell her closest colleagues.

Collins had decided to make time this weekend to introduce her parents to Charlie and break the news to them. She was expecting it to be difficult. He prayed she didn't meet with the hostility that Karen's family had heaped upon their surviving daughter's impending nuptials.

He turned on the shower and began to shave whilst the water decided to come through hot.

Jackie Phillips had also kept secrets, for over a decade. The local darling whose disappearance had sparked a major search, with attendant publicity, had only ever been painted as some sort of local superhero. Apparently there had been rumours of extra-marital affairs, but they hadn't hit the headlines, probably because no one had come forward with kiss and tell stories, eager to make a quick quid or too. If Tim Phillips had been a philandering, whoring hypocrite, he'd apparently chosen his women well.

It still smarted that Gillingham was pulling back from the Phillips case. Standing under the shower, coming more awake, he was determined to make as much progress as possible by the time he went on honeymoon.

Unsolved cases. Baines's own son. Tim Phillips. Also, Demi Reeves, the young prostitute, strangled to death, whose case had stalled because local politics demanded that finding Phillips should be given top priority. Baines thought it ironic that

Phillips's case was now being similarly sidelined, at least by Gillingham. Perhaps it was poetic justice that a man who'd apparently got his rocks off by throttling women was now down the pecking order from dead gangsters, whose activities had doubtless been responsible for considerable human misery.

Demi Reeves had been 15, younger than Jack would be today and already turning tricks, putting her life in danger, and ultimately losing it.

Thoughts swirled in his head. He was curious to know more about Demi's story. Maybe he'd check it out, just out of interest.

He was about to turn the water off when the shower curtain was drawn back. Karen stood there, naked.

"Morning," she said, with a smile he knew well.

"Sorry," he said as he felt himself stirring. "I didn't mean to wake you."

Her gaze swept downwards. "Well, you seem wide awake. And I fancy a shower myself." She stepped in beside him. "You're not in any rush, are you?"

Her hands were already busy, moving upon his body. "No," he managed to say before she kissed him. "I've plenty of time."

35

Archer came off the phone from talking to Patrick Mahon. It seemed that, not only had Gillingham gained ready agreement from Superintendent Lambert to hand the Phillips case off to him, but she had already smoothed the way with her Reading opposite number. Even the ambitious Lambert apparently thought no kudos could gained from this one. So much for her and Gillingham never seeing eye to eye.

Mahon was thus already aware of the change of emphasis. Whether he felt dismay or delight, he was giving nothing away. Pleasant and professional as ever, he said he looked forward to seeing Baines this morning, but stressed that he expected a channel of communication at Aylesbury Vale, just as Derek Pollard had been the conduit when Archer's team had been leading.

"Yes, no problem, Sir," she said. "It'll be Jason Bell. As you know, he's been working the case with Dan."

Meanwhile, the main focus was the murders of Kit and Gary Meredith. To her mind, there was an inconsistency here. As with Tim Phillips, the main claim her team had on the case was that Aylesbury was where the bodies had turned up. The possibility that the brothers had been killed by rivals in Reading – or even in their own organisation – couldn't be ruled out. Although, if Sonia Meredith's assessment of the quality of the foot soldiers in the Meredith army was anything to go on, it sounded improbable that any of them would have either the ability or the ambition to kill their way to the top and make the organisation work.

She wondered if Sonia was safe. She made a mental note to get Baines to check up on the limited surveillance on her house. The arrangement for a car to pass every hour had been stepped up to every half hour. Archer wasn't actually convinced that this was better than nothing. For all she knew, the house was being watched, and the car's pattern noted. Waiting for it to have passed by before making a move would be easy enough.

But, she wondered, what move? Sonia seemed too sharp a cookie to just open the door to any stranger, so where would the attack come from? A bogus pizza delivery? Surely anything like that was too obvious.

She supposed the woman had to go out. Archer couldn't see her settling for being in her own home. It meant that an attack could come anywhere, any time.

Assuming there was any actual threat to Sonia. Archer half-wondered if the deaths of Sonia's husband and brother in law, leaving her effectively in charge, could actually have been something the woman welcomed – had maybe even arranged. Maybe there were no rivals with designs on Meredith turf.

It was true that Tyler had established that there were a couple of Oxfordshire gangs, at least one with Romanian and Bulgarian connections, that seemed to be expanding their reach. But, like the Merediths – and the Connollys – their main players had so far managed to stay a step or two ahead of the law. But Tyler had found no intelligence so far linking those gangs to Reading or the Vale – although she supposed that any such moves had to start somewhere.

It just felt a little soon to be killing off the opposition.

What if there was some other indiscernible purpose in play, and the Northfields connection was something like a magician's sleight of hand - a distraction from what was really going on?

She wondered what progress would be made today. Wondered if Cameron Connolly would call with something for her. Wondered why she hoped he would. She was getting too old for schoolgirl fantasies about fit gangsters. When had she become that pathetic?

Her phone rang and she was surprised to feel heat rising to her face when the caller announced himself, as if, like the Devil himself, just the thought of him was enough to conjure him up.

"And how are you today?" Cameron Connolly enquired.

"I'm fine, thanks." She resented the silly, girlish fluster he had caused, as if it was his fault. He'd better have a good reason for calling.

After a short pause, he said, "I'm not so bad myself, thanks for asking."

"What do you want?"

"I was going to invite you to lunch." Smooth. "But if you're not in the mood – "

His presumptuousness irked her. "I'm not. Call me if and when you have something for me."

"Whoa, whoa, whoa!" he protested. "Who says I don't have anything for you? I just thought it would be nice to discuss it over coffee and cake. You do eat, right?"

"I eat," she retorted, "but I also choose my dining partners. If you've got some information, just give it to me now."

"I don't think so." His voice was low, coaxing. Almost playful. "You see, I'm ever so busy, Lizzie. See what I did there?"

"I'm hanging up," she said. His joke had been rubbish. Well, hadn't it?

"And miss out on what I've got to tell you? Doesn't sound very diligent. And you, DI Archer, come across as committed to your work. Passionate, even."

"Enough games."

"It's not a game. I told you," he murmured, "I'm very busy right now. Doing you this little favour is a distraction. But I have to eat too. So why don't we both deal with our need to eat and I can give you… what you need."

The pause made those last two words into a *double entendre* that caused her to flush again. She should make threats about dragging him down the station to answer her questions, but she didn't want to do that. She didn't want to make it obvious to others she had been talking to him, nor did she want him to simply deny he knew anything.

"Coffee and cake," she said. "No fancy menus or wine, and somewhere very public. Take it or leave it."

"I'll take it," he said. "You choose the venue. So long as they do good cake."

She couldn't help but smile, grateful that he couldn't see it. "Do you know Rumsey's in Wendover?"

"Oh, good choice," he enthused. "Twelve on the dot?"

"Well…" Surely this was a bad idea?

"See you there." He hung up, leaving Archer staring at the phone and wondering what she was getting herself into.

* * *

Baines had introduced Archer to Rumsey's during her first year in the Vale. The business, which also had a branch in Thame, Oxfordshire, specialised in handmade chocolates, of which there were around forty varieties, but also operated charming cafés offering sweet and savoury options that always tempted Archer to forget about her waistline for an hour or so.

Archer occasionally shopped in Wendover when she was looking for something a little different - the town's busy High Street was well-served by independents and small chains. Rumsey's was housed in the Old Bank building on a corner close to the car park. As she entered, its cornflower blue walls and antique furnishings transported Archer to a corner of France. Baines had told her that that the transformation of Rumsey's chocolaterie from what was originally a cottage industry had been inspired by the shop in the film adaptation of Joanne Harris's novel, *Chocolat*.

The shop downstairs was bustling, as ever, the air filled with the clatter of cutlery, the clinking of glasses, and the buzz of conversation. Archer made her way upstairs in search of a table. There she found Cameron Connolly, already seated and reading a newspaper. A waxed jacket hung over the back of his chair and he was casual in a dark blue sweater and tan cords. As she approached, she felt an unfamiliar shyness, as though this was some sort of date. Before she could give herself a good talking to, he looked up and smiled.

"Hi. Did you manage to park okay?"

She had, although only after she'd driven around the small car park once, snapping up a space as a white Range Rover vacated it with impeccable timing. She said so, wondering why she needed to give him the whole story.

"I said we'd order when you got here," he said, putting the paper away. "I've had a look at the menu though. Christ, this place. Are you sure you just want cake? I fancy the smoked salmon salad and at least half the cakes and desserts."

"Just cake," she said. "Maybe a brownie."

"Have a proper early lunch," he urged. "My treat."

She gave him a cool stare. "That, as I'm sure you know, would be entirely inappropriate."

His eyes danced. "And why would that be? I'm not a suspect in your case. There's no conflict of interest. But if you're really not comfortable about it, there can't be anything in the rules that says we can't go Dutch."

"I don't have time, and that isn't what we're here for. We're not friends having lunch together."

"No, we're not," he agreed, still smiling that too-charming smile that she really oughtn't to like. "But we could be."

She sighed and sat down, reaching for a menu. "No, Mr Connolly, we couldn't, and you know it. I shouldn't really be meeting you like this at all."

He shook his head, not exactly angry, but certainly exasperated. "Oh, for God's sake, Lizzie. Like what, exactly? It's not like we're in a hotel and I'm plying you with booze, a room ready-booked. This is just a café. A very nice one, I'll grant you, but I don't have this whole seduction thing going on. You interest me, and I don't think half an hour or so of your time is so much of a trade for the information I have for you. Is it?"

"I don't know yet. But I'm not here to interest you, as you put it."

He stood up, still smiling. "Sod it, then. I'm off."

She felt a twist of panic in her stomach, and for an instant she wasn't sure it was entirely professional in its origins. At the same time, the old 'walking out' routine irritated her.

"Please sit down, Mr Connolly."

He paused, shrugged, replaced his jacket on the chair back, and sat again. "All right. And it's Cameron, please. I meant what I said. I just wanted to have lunch with you. See what I can do to help you, and maybe get to know you a little better. No other agenda." He held his hands up and pushed back the cuffs on his jumper. "See? Nothing up my sleeves."

She found herself unable not to laugh. And she was determined not to like this man. But if having a salad and a dessert with him got her some useful information, she supposed it would be a small enough price to pay. The information had better be good.

"Are you ready to order?" A friendly waitress stood by their table.

"I think it's two smoked salmon salads," Archer said, looking to Cameron for confirmation. He nodded.

"And I'll have an Americano," she added. "Black."

"Same," he said.

As the waitress departed, he gave Archer a conspiratorial smile. "Well, we both have impeccable taste."

"We do," she agreed. "So what do you have for me?"

"Tell you what. Let's do the business bit over dessert. Have a civilised chat over our salads."

"How do you know I'm having a dessert?"

His grin was almost boyish. "Aren't you?"

"We'll see." But she'd spotted a lemon polenta cake on the menu that she fancied. And she wondered if he'd let his guard down if they put the so-called information on a back burner. "All right. Business later."

He looked pleased. "So tell me about yourself. I'm guessing from the accent that you're not originally from around here. I've got a good idea for accents."

"Yeah, a regular Henry Higgins, I bet."

"I think she's got it!" His impression of Rex Harrison was passable.

"Well," she said, "I know you're not from these parts, but there's not much of a Scots burr there, either."

"No, I grew up in London and had the benefit of a very expensive education."

"Courtesy of your father?"

"Of course. What dad doesn't want the best for his kids? Nice deflection of the question, by the way."

She found herself smiling again. "I grew up in London too. I was in the Met before I came here."

He raised an eyebrow. "The Met? What on earth drew you to a backwater like this?"

"I fancied a change."

"Now why do I find that unlikely?" His eyes bored into her. "What's the real reason?"

"None of your business, *Cameron.*" That was too painful to share with many people. Certainly not with him.

"Sorry. I didn't mean to upset you. I'm just curious." He shook his head as if annoyed with himself. "Forget I asked."

For the first time since she met him, he looked lost for what to say next – disarmed and on the back foot. She was surprised to see this vulnerable side.

"It's no big deal," she found herself saying, and then she shrugged. "You'd think I'd have stopped being so sensitive by now."

She told him then: wading into a fracas in a pub, despite being off duty; one of the parties brandishing a broken bottle and transferring his rage to her; making the arrest, but – despite her self-defence skills – not quite coming out unscathed. She skated over the loss of confidence and the slow collapse in her personal life and her career.

"So I transferred here," she said, "precisely because it seemed like a quiet backwater, to give myself a chance to regroup."

"And did it work?"

"For the most part. I'm not sure I had much of a plan for what happened next. I suppose I might have assumed I'd return to London eventually. Instead, I've bought a house and I own half a cat here."

"Half a cat?" He looked intrigued.

As she explained, their food arrived. It broke a spell. She couldn't believe what she'd just shared with a man who might be utterly charming on the outside, but who she knew damn well was part of a family of savage beasts, whose best quality was not getting caught. She knew that and yet she'd allowed herself to be charmed by, and yes, damn it, attracted to him.

He seemed to sense the shift in her mood. "This salad is great, isn't it?" he said half-heartedly.

"It is. But we didn't come here to swap life stories."

"No? *I* did."

"Yes?" She felt a smile tugging at the functional side of her mouth again. "So tell me some of yours. But you have to only tell me things that are true."

"It's a deal."

So, as they ate their salads, he talked about his early days in Glasgow, and the differences he'd noticed in London. He talked a bit about going to an expensive private school, and speculated on whether his father's money had been well spent.

"Did you all go there?" Archer wondered.

"Fraser and I did. Desmond went to something a bit artier – he imagines himself to be 'creative'." He made parenthesis with his fingers. "So did my sister, Grace, actually." His expression softened. "Grace didn't enter the family business. She's back in Scotland, carving out a career as a painter. Dad wanted to rent her a studio, pay to get her exhibited, but she insists on making her own way. Sometimes I wish I'd taken a similar decision." He sounded almost wistful.

"You could have."

"I suppose I could." He didn't enlarge.

"All that education, all those advantages, didn't keep Desmond out of jail," she pointed out.

He swallowed the last mouthful and laid his knife and fork down together, arranging them just so. "No, it didn't. I love all my brothers, but Des has been known to be an arse. He's the young one allowed to get away with all the shit the rest of us weren't." When they'd spoken at Cameron's home, his tone had betrayed his contempt for his youngest sibling. It came through again here. "He's walking the line now though."

"And you're married. With kids." It was a natural point to make, but a loaded one.

"Yeah, and happily so." There was a challenge in his eyes.

"Well, good."

"Anyone in your life? This Dominic, who shares your cat?"

"No," she said, a little too quickly. "There's been no one for a while now."

Her last relationship, three years ago, had ended in disaster, and there had been no one since.

Well, that wasn't quite true, was it? There *was* Dominic. He'd made a sort of advance last year, when his cat, Monty, had died and she was comforting him. She'd pushed him away, scared of losing a good friend and neighbour if things didn't work out. Plus, the idea of seeing your ex when you were putting the bins out just felt too weird and mortifying to her.

Sometimes she wondered if those had been mere excuses – if, by holding back, she was missing out on something good. But that chance, if chance it had been, had gone. He'd made no further attempts to take their friendship to a new level, and she could think of no way of instigating it herself. The only mystery was why there was apparently no other woman in his life.

He was accompanying her to dinner with Adam and Nic tonight. She was still wondering whether to ask him to play the boyfriend, so her brother wouldn't be able to gloat over how alone she was. She was sure Dominic wouldn't mind. It might even be fun.

"That's a shame," Cameron was saying. "And a waste." His hand moved across the table towards hers. It halted halfway. He looked at it in apparent surprise and withdrew it.

"Right," he said briskly, "let's choose desserts and then we can get down to business."

He passed her a menu. When the waitress returned, she ordered the lemon polenta cake she coveted, and he went for the baked blueberry cheesecake. They also asked for more coffee.

"Okay," Cameron said. "I've teased you long enough."

"So you actually do have something for me?"

"Of course. Did you really think I'd got you here under false pretences?"

"It had crossed my mind." She lifted her bag from the floor. "Is it okay by you if I make a few notes?"

"Go ahead. Take down my particulars."

The double entendre was so corny, so obvious, that she burst out laughing. After a moment, he joined in.

"Okay," he said, "so I asked a few people I know. As I said, none of my contacts are criminals."

"Perish the thought."

His eyes danced. "Well, exactly. But people do hear things, if you know what I mean. And what they hear is that there's a gang - mostly Romanian - that's got itself well established in Oxfordshire and is now casting its eyes around neighbouring counties - including this one. If they're not already operating in Aylesbury, it's only a matter of time before they push their luck there."

She was pleased he was giving her something, but at the same time disappointed that, so far, it wasn't news.

"Any names?"

"Yes, actually. It sounds like the main guys fly beneath the radar. I mean," his eyes widened, "what do I know, but I guess that's a skill these people have?" He paused as if for dramatic effect. "Anyhow, the name I've heard - from more than one source - is Lupu."

"Loopy? You're winding me up again."

"No, Lupu. It means wolf or something. Anyhow, there are three brothers. I don't know all the names, but the top man is Dragos."

"Dragos means Dragon, doesn't it? " Was he still yanking her chain? "Dragon Wolf? Are you serious? Because if you're wasting my time..."

He flinched. "I swear I'm not. They sound a bad bunch. The word on the street is drugs, people trafficking, and worse. And they've got an enforcer - I'm not even sure what that means." He was such a picture of innocence that she almost - but not quite - believed him. "It sounds grim though. The person who told me about him said he breaks heads when need be. Maybe worse. They think he's Bulgarian. Built like a brick outhouse. Scar down one side of his face. Sorry," he added, remembering who he was talking to.

She waved it away. "Does he have a name?"

"Must have, but my associate wasn't saying. I reckon he was scareder of the Bulgarian than he is of the Lupus."

"I'm going to have to talk to your associate."

Cameron shook his head.

"No, you're not."

"Cameron, this is a triple murder enquiry."

"So you can't blame my guy for being scared. Look, he told me what he did as a favour. He'll deny the lot, say I was drinking last time we met. He'll give you nothing, I promise you, and I'll lose his trust."

If he wasn't making it up, he'd got her much more than Oxford HQ appeared to know. She wasn't convinced that his source existed; even if he did, he was unlikely to be an honest businessman, any more than Cameron Connolly's protestations cut any ice with her. But it was worth following up. This big Bulgarian sounded like the figure they'd seen on CCTV.

"Any use?" he asked.

"We'll see."

"Better than a no." He checked his watch. "I don't know where the time's gone. I've a meeting."

She looked at her own watch. Colleagues would wonder where she'd swanned off to. "I need to make a move too."

"I'll go down and pay the bill."

"No," she said firmly." I've got this."

"Fair enough. I'll get the next one."

"There isn't going to be a next time," she assured him.

He grinned, his eyes meeting hers in a way that flipped her stomach again. "We'll see."

He waited while she paid at the till.

"We're parked in the same car park," he said. "I'll walk you."

She affected a shrug. "We're going the same way anyhow."

They waited for a gap in the traffic. When it came, he guided her with a hand at the small of her back. Strangely, it didn't feel patronising. They arrived at her Skoda.

"Where are you?" she asked.

He pointed to a black Mercedes in the next row.

"I half-expected a chauffeur to bring the car to the door for you," she said.

He laughed. "Actually, I do sometimes have a driver, but I preferred to drive myself. I gave Willie the afternoon off." He held out a hand. "This has been nice."

"Weird, but nice," she acknowledged, accepting the handshake. He held her hand a fraction too long, his grasp almost burning her.

36

Dragos Lupu enjoyed walking into a club or bar, like this one, where he had a business interest. He liked the attention. He liked being called 'Mr Lupu' – it was a far cry from those early days in England, when he and his brothers had been made to feel like the outsiders their accents and limited command of English marked them out as.

By no means everyone had treated them as inferiors – many in British society were welcoming and friendly to the foreigner. But he had also known patronisation, unspoken looks of scorn and contempt, and downright hostility.

Back then, he had let these things pass, biting down the urge to respond with a fist, or even one of the knives he always had concealed about him – and making sure his kin also kept smiling. If you wanted to make something of yourself in this country, especially in the business field he had chosen, you had to pick your battles, and it didn't do to draw too much attention to yourself. You needed to save the violence for your real enemies. Or for people who stepped too badly out of line to let it go.

These days, his associate, Todor Genkov, took care of most of that stuff.

The brothers had come a remarkably long way in a relatively short time. They'd all worked hard on commanding nigh on flawless English, and on accents with only a trace of Romania about them. He knew he could almost pass for an Oxfordshire native now. Radu and Vladislav still had a little way to go.

They had cultivated a certain charm, too. People liked them, or at least showed them outward respect. It could be out of fear, of course. Charm and a good English accent only got you so far. But who cared, so long as the business thrived?

For Dragos and his brothers, their stake in this bar – one of their more legitimate interests – was something to enjoy. He especially liked being called 'Mr Wolf', an affectionate nod to the literal translation of his surname – although he drew the line at comparative strangers having the temerity to use the name. There was an English idiom he very well understood: 'familiarity breeds contempt'. He was friendly up to a point, but respect was important to him. Familiarity from any Tom, Dick, or Harry who heard his nickname used was the first step on the road to easy contempt.

It wasn't usually difficult to nip such familiarity in the bud without making a scene. It was all in the tone, when he reminded them that his name was Lupu. Few made the mistake twice. None so far had made it three times.

Joe, the barman, was allowed to call him Mr Wolf. He was respectful, and seemed to genuinely like the brothers. His face split into a wide grin as he saw them approaching.

"Mr Wolf!" he said, suddenly ignoring the banknotes and credit cards being waved at him. "Good evening, gentlemen. Usuals all round?"

The brothers had all developed a liking for gin and tonic. It had to be Sipsmith, though, and the bar stocked that brand of London dry gin especially because it was their choice of tipple.

"Yes, please, Joe," Dragos responded. "Family all well?"

"All fine, thank you for asking. And Lucy thanks you for her birthday present."

"The pleasure's all mine." Such touches were important. If you wanted a man's loyalty, you needed to connect with his family, and to show you cared. Asking after them was easy enough. Casually learning their birthdays and making sure you remembered – that made a real impression. And, in Dragos' world, loyalty was important.

The three brothers carried their drinks over to their favourite corner table, which had a permanent 'Reserved' sign on it, so it was always available for them. It was the best spot in the bar for discreet conversation.

Radu and Vladislav sat. Dragos set his glass down carefully on a coaster.

"Toilet," he said. He grinned at them. "I'll know if you touch my drink."

It was an old joke, their mutual chuckles recognising its familiarity and the fact that it was 'their' joke, rather than any real hilarity.

Dragos let himself into the gents', noting with approval that everything was immaculate. He knew such things were important in England, and he insisted upon it.

As he finished urinating, he heard the door open and close behind him. He turned away from the urinal, nodding an acknowledgement to the new arrival as he moved towards the wash basins. He washed his hands fastidiously and headed for the hot air dryer. As he did so, he caught a glimpse of the other man in the mirror, moving behind him.

It all happened so quickly. One moment, he was going to dry his hands and rejoin his brothers, looking forward to that first savouring of his G and T. The next, some sort of cord had been slipped over his head and drawn tight around his throat, abruptly cutting off his air supply. The ligature was swiftly crossed at the back of his neck and pulled even tighter. He clawed ineffectively at his attacker's hands, encountered the leathery feel of gloves.

Dragos was not a small man, but his assailant was having little difficulty in forcing him into a cubicle. He glanced wildly at the toilet door, praying that intervention would come that way. He always had an eye for detail, and picked out the wedge at the bottom of the door that would prevent anyone entering and interrupting this assault. If he was to save himself, it was up to him.

Summoning all his failing strength, he jabbed backwards with his right elbow, encountered something, jabbed again, and heard a satisfying grunt. But there was no surcease in the pressure, no blessed opening of his airway. Already he was seeing spots before his eyes, his head feeling about to burst. His lungs burned with their futile, automatic efforts to draw in a fresh hit of air. He kicked backwards, encountered nothing. Tried again with a different trajectory and hit something. This time there was no answering grunt, and he knew his movements were becoming ever more sluggish and feeble.

He made final, despairing attempts to claw the ligature away from his throat. It had bitten so deeply into the flesh that his scrabbling fingers could not even locate it.

Dragos realised he was about to die just before the eternal darkness claimed him.

The killer locked the cubicle door from inside and arranged Dragos' body on the toilet seat. One final touch and he was done. He heaved himself over the partition, the chipboard groaning under his weight, and into the neighbouring cubicle. He flushed and exited. The corpse would not be found for a while. He removed the wedge from the entrance door and casually let himself out. This was risky. Anyone who might have been trying to get in would see his face. But his baseball cap was pulled down low, and his scarf wrapped around this face. Even if anyone remembered him – and why should they - how much description could they give?

In any case, there was no one there. He moved casually through the bar, through the exit door, and out into the street, his work done.

37

Back at the office, there was no sign of Baines or Bell.

"They've finally gone off to Sussex," Tyler explained. "Jason's been trying to get hold of that dodgy ex-builder, Dennis Ryan, without success, so he got the local force to call round. It seems Ryan and his wife are out of the country – a cruise, the neighbours say. There's a house-sitter there, though – some bloke, apparently, who was out when the officers called by."

"So what's the point of Dan and Jason dragging their arses down to the coast?"

"Dan thought he might as well poke around. Talk to neighbours, the house-sitter. Try and get a picture of this Ryan and how he got so loaded."

She frowned. "Maybe we should have afforded talking to Ryan a bit more urgency before. My fault. Too much going on, Will. Just suppose his wealth really was a payoff for some part in Tim Phillips's murder – maybe even the murder itself – and Eric Yelland was somehow involved? Phillips surfaces, Ryan kills the one person who could implicate him, then he leaves the country?"

Tyler shook his head. "Great theory, boss, but it seems Ryan's pretty chatty with the neighbours. The cruise had been booked for months, and it's a long one. He was gone two days before Spencer Court blew up. He couldn't have been involved in Yelland's disappearance."

"It still works if Ryan didn't dispose of Yelland personally. A phone call from the ship to the right people, with an offer of cash..." It was well worth Baines and Bell making the trip after all. "What else is going on?"

"Oh, yes," Tyler said, "Dan asked me to get him some details on a case in Reading that was going on around the same time as Tim Phillips disappeared. A murder case: Demi Reeves?"

The teenage prostitute whose murder investigation had been hamstrung by the search for Phillips. "Did he say why?"

"No. He said it was probably a waste of time."

Archer groaned internally. The girl had been 15 – just a bit younger than Baines's son, Jack, would be now. It wouldn't be the first time Baines had allowed his own loss to colour his judgement. Why else would he let himself get sidetracked into Gillingham's and Ashby's old case? Waste of time was right.

"Have you got very far with it?"

"I printed a few articles off from the Internet, and Reading are sending me a copy of the file."

She was irritated. "Well, don't do any more. I want you to speak to Oxford. See if the name of Lupu rings any bells in connection with our Eastern Europeans."

He screwed up his forehead. "Actually, remember I said no one in Oxford knew who was running the Romanian gang? That wasn't entirely true. There were a few names that had been bandied about, but our colleagues had nothing concrete on them. Lupu?" He stroked his chin.

"Dragos Lupu?"

"Yeah. I'm almost sure that was one of the names. Sorry, Lizzie. It was so vague."

He looked angry with himself. "No worries," she said. "Can you check them out now?"

"Leave it with me." He was already reaching for the phone.

She returned to her desk. She'd check her emails and then regroup.

So the name that Cameron Connolly had mentioned to her rang a bell with Tyler. She'd supped with the devil, and he might just have given her something. Too easily? What might he hope to gain in return?

She thought of how she'd felt when he'd looked at her. The couple of times he'd touched her. She felt her cheeks burning with the memory. One thing she knew. It had been all about lust on her part. She wasn't so stupid that she could imagine some sort of fairytale romance with such a man.

Relationships. Tonight she was renewing her contact with her only remaining family, and Dominic would be there by her side, supporting her. A good man, and one she'd been attracted to since their first meeting. Their friendship was the easiest she had ever known. With him, she could completely let her guard down, and her troubles always found a ready ear there, any time of the day or night.

She'd imposed phantom taboos about dating a neighbour on herself, and what had that achieved? Two lonely people who could have a shot at something good if they'd allow themselves past the 'just good friends' barrier, while she got the hots for a monster like Cameron Connolly.

Maybe it was time she tore up those taboos and saw where that friendship might lead.

If she could find a way. If it wasn't too late.

"Guv?" Tyler's voice startled her out of her musings. She looked up at him. "Sorry, guv," he said, "but you're not going to believe this."

She shook herself. "Tell me."

"I've just been on the phone to Oxford. Dragos Lupu exists, all right. Or rather, he did."

She wasn't in the mood for cryptic comments. "What are you talking about?"

"Dragos Lupu. He's been murdered."

* * *

The West Sussex village of East Dean lay a few miles north east of Chichester, in a dry valley on the beautiful South Downs. Britain's newest National Park stretched from Winchester to Beachy Head, and Baines and Karen had spent a rare long weekend near here a couple of summers ago, sightseeing and shopping in Chichester, and walking in this stunning countryside.

The journey had been tedious, the best part of three hours, taking in the dreaded M25, barely moving, then the M23, only marginally better.

Baines was struck by the quaintness of the village. He noted a church dedicated to All Saints and a pub called *The Star and Garter*. There was even a large village pond. Ryan's home was a substantial property built – as were the church, the pub and most of the other houses - of flint, with brick quoins and brick window dressings. This one had a slate roof, although he'd spotted a fair smattering of thatch.

"So this is where well-heeled Aylesbury brickies retire to," Bell commented as Baines cut the engine. "Very nice. We're in the wrong job, Dan."

But Baines's eyes were on the battered red Toyota parked on the drive. He nudged Bell and jabbed a finger in the car's direction. "Correct me if I'm wrong, Jason, but does that number plate ring a bell?"

"Must be the house-sitter," Bell said. He squinted as he read the plate. "Shit. Is that what I think it is?"

"We can't both be mistaken," Baines said, throwing the door open. "Let's see if anyone's home."

He led the way to the front door and pressed the bell. He was about to try again when he heard footsteps advancing from within. There was the sound of a key being turned, then the door was opened.

The grey-haired man looked from Baines to Bell. "Yes?" he said suspiciously. "Can I help you?"

The detectives showed their warrant cards and Baines did the introductions.

"And yes," he said. "I think you certainly can help us – Mr Yelland."

* * *

As luck would have it, DS Amy Petrescu, Steve Ashby's girlfriend, was part of the team that had been called to the scene of Dragos Lupu's murder, a bar just outside the city centre. Petrescu was fairly sure the Lupu family had a business interest in the bar, but that had yet to be confirmed.

The Romanian had been garrotted to death and left on a toilet seat in a locked cubicle. The murder had been carried out around lunchtime, when the bar had been busy, and when Dragos and his brothers were known to drop in for a drink. They'd made it easy for anyone looking for a predictable behaviour pattern.

"Bold killer," Archer commented. She and Collins had driven to the bar to meet Petrescu at the scene. "Busy bar, fag end of lunchtime. The guy has to be a gambler and an opportunist."

"With ice water in his veins," Collins added.

"Either that or a little bit crazy," said Petrescu.

"No CCTV cameras in the toilets, I guess?" Archer asked, more in hope than expectation.

"There's a dummy camera, actually. It faces the sinks, not the urinals, but it's incapable of filming. Ironically, it's there to deter drug dealing. The Lupus have been in our sights for a while in the context of drugs, amongst other things, but they've proved pretty slippery."

"Well," Archer said, "one thing's clear enough. Either these really are the guys who've been targeting the Meredith family in Reading, or someone – almost certainly the Merediths – thinks they are and has decided to do something about it."

"Either way, it's not exactly helpful," said Petrescu. "Dragos' brothers - Radu and Vladislav – have gone mental. All the usual bollocks about how we'd better get to the killer before they do. Only you know it's not just bollocks."

Archer nodded. Gary Meredith had given her some similar macho spiel when she'd told him Kit was dead, and look what had happened to him.

It looked as though Cameron Connolly's tip-off had been on the money, but too late to save Dragos Lupu. If this was tit for tat, and now Dragos's brothers were looking for payback, then Sonia Meredith could be in real danger. Danger she'd maybe brought on herself. Maybe she'd known all along who the enemy were. Either that, or she had the same sources as Cameron Connolly.

"You're not wrong, Amy," she told Petrescu. "Whoever's responsible for Dragos' death should have taken out his brothers too."

If Dragos Lupu's blood was on Sonia's hands, all she'd done was stir a hornet's nest. Archer supposed grief, and the urge for revenge, could cloud anyone's judgement, but she would have credited her with more sense. Not that she was at all certain Sonia was responsible.

"I'd like to interview the brothers under caution," she said. "In connection with the Meredith murders."

"I don't know, Lizzie," Petrescu said. "You haven't said who your source is, and you haven't produced any real evidence, either. Is this the time, when their brother is still sitting dead on a toilet seat, just a few yards away?"

Archer glanced over at the lavatory door, propped open while CSIs came and went with cameras, equipment and evidence bags. She knew the local pathologist was also in there.

"You're right, of course," she said. "Maybe I can just have an informal chat to them?"

"I'll have to clear it with my boss, and he's a bit preoccupied at the moment." Petrescu made a face. "I'm really sorry, Lizzie, but I don't want to be the one to stuff up this investigation, even if it is to help yours."

Archer understood. Oxford, Reading, Aylesbury. It was a tangled web. "But you'll be taking witness statements from them?"

"We'll be asking them a few questions, then follow up with the formalities."

"When will you next be talking to them?"

"As soon as they've calmed down. They're in a café across the street. We've asked them to stay there for now."

The words were barely out of her mouth when a rumpus broke out at the bar's entrance. Archer turned to see two dark-haired, leather-jacketed men trying to force their way past uniformed officers guarding the door.

"Oh, Christ," Petrescu murmured. "I wondered how long they'd sit tight."

She headed for the door, Archer and Collins in her wake. Petrescu's boss, DI Ian Ford, arrived at the same time.

"Now come on, gents," Ford said with a hint of a Welsh accent. "You know you can't come in here."

"We want to know who killed our brother," snarled the taller of the pair. "We want to know what you're doing about it."

"And we'll update you as soon as we can," the Oxford DI soothed. For now, let us do our job, and we'll see you in the café for a chat as soon as possible. Or go home, if you prefer, and we'll contact you."

The one who had spoken gave one last push against the unyielding wall of Oxfordshire Constabulary humanity.

"All right," he said. "We wait in café. But we want answers."

"As do we," Ford said. "We'll see you shortly."

The two brothers departed, hands in pockets, shoulders hunched. Archer considered going after them, but thought better of it. Petrescu was right. Things had to be done properly. Plus, if she asked them too unsubtly about the Meredith murders, they might assume – if they didn't already – that the Reading organisation was behind Dragos' death. She didn't want to make things worse.

Still, she ached to ask them about the big Bulgarian Cameron Connolly had alluded to. The man whose description tallied with the CCTV images surrounding the planting of Kit Meredith's body and Gary Meredith's murder. Maybe she could sit in on the formal interviews.

As the four detectives moved away from the door, a CSI approached with a transparent evidence bag and showed the contents to Ford.

"I dunno if this is relevant," he said, "but we found it under the victim's foot."

Archer looked at the bag. It contained a contact card with a business name, address, phone number and web address.

The business was the Royal Bar in Gun Street, Reading.

Where Archer had first met Gary Meredith.

38

Sonia Meredith looked a little better this afternoon – maybe even energised. When Archer had last seen her, she'd been coming round to the realisation that she needed to try to hang onto the family's business interests, or lose them and the livelihood associated with them. Putting aside the fact that a fair chunk of that business was undoubtedly criminal, Archer understood that. The woman had her own future, and that of her children, to consider. Maybe that was enough to give her a focus.

Archer had seen enough of death, from all sorts of angles, to know people dealt with it in different ways. She'd lost both her parents before she turned 40, and both losses had been heartbreaking for her. Yet she'd continued to giver her work priority, telling herself that keeping on catching bad guys would have made her parents proud.

Baines had tried to put his grief in a box, place it high up on a shelf, and simply leave it there. Over the years, bit by bit, that wall had crumbled, and the consequences had almost destroyed him.

Some carried rage around like an eternal flame. Others simply fell apart. For Sonia, keeping things going might be the project that got her through this.

Archer noted a hulking figure behind Sonia in the hallway. Black sweater, jeans. Close-cropped hair. Tattoo of a dagger on one side of his neck. A couple of decent-sized scars on his face and a broken nose. Small eyes. He looked wary and exuded menace.

"It's okay, Josh," Sonia said. "This is DI Archer and DS Collins."

For answer, the man called Josh folded his arms and narrowed his already beady eyes.

"You talked to me about protection," Sonia said, "so Josh is occupying our spare room for a while."

It didn't take the IQ of a nuclear physicist to guess what Josh's role in the organisation was.

"One of your enforcers?" Archer asked casually.

Sonia widened her eyes. Smiled sweetly. "Why, Inspector. Whatever is one of those?" She shrugged. "You'd best come in. I hope you've got news."

She sent Josh to make drinks, which seemed somehow incongruous, like using an industrial buzz saw to cut out paper dollies. The three women sat.

"So is there any news worth a damn?" Sonia demanded. "Or are you just harassing me?"

Archer crossed her legs. "I don't know if you'd call it news, but an Eastern European person of interest – a Romanian by the name of Dragos Lupu – was murdered today in Oxford."

Sonia leaned forward. "You think he was involved in Gary's murder?"

"More to the point, I'm wondering if you or your people were involved in his."

Sonia shook her head, her expression inscrutable. "Never heard of him. Why would you wonder that?"

"Oh," Archer said, "maybe it's to do with a business card found at the crime scene."

"The Royal Bar," Collins added. "Your family has some sort of stake in it, no?"

Sonia didn't blink. "What if we do? It's a completely legitimate business."

"Which is suspected of being a front for criminal activity."

Sonia found a smile. "And yet," she said, "no arrests have been made, no charges pressed. And what's the significance of the card? The Royal has a healthy clientele. Maybe one of them happened near this crime scene. So what? Where was it, by the way?"

Archer hesitated. She and the Oxford team hadn't quite decided yet how much detail of the Lupu killing to make public. Yet she wanted to test the other woman's reaction.

"Dragos Lupu's body was found in a toilet cubicle at a bar," she said as Josh returned with a tray.

Josh snorted at her words. Archer turned in her seat to look at him.

"You think murder's funny, Mr…"

"Kelly," he said, his voice deep, gravelly and nasal. "And if you think this Loopy bloke killed the boss, I think it's fucking hilarious that he cashed in his chips on the bog."

"Josh," protested Sonia, "don't be so rude."

He mumbled something that might have been an apology and dished the drinks out, ham-like paws dwarfing the mugs.

"The card was with the body," Archer said. "Like the killer had dropped it."

"Dropped it or planted it?" Sonia said. "It sounds nice and convenient to me. Too convenient, in fact."

The thought had occurred to Archer, too. The audacity of the killing seemed at odds with the careless dropping of a pretty blatant clue.

"I want a list of everyone on your payroll," she said. "We may want to talk to several of them about their movements today."

"It'll take a few days."

"You've got 24 hours." Archer looked at Josh Kelly, leaning against a wall by the living room door. "How about you, Mr Kelly? Where have you been today?"

He glanced at Sonia.

"It's all right, Josh," she told him. "Answer the inspector."

He straightened up and shoved his hands in his pockets. "Mrs Meredith gave me a call last night and asked me to come and stay here. I've been here ever since."

"Who can vouch for that?" Collins prompted.

"Mrs Meredith."

Collins made a show of scribbling in her notebook. "Anyone else? Mrs Meredith's children?"

"They're at my mother's for now," Sonia said. "I thought that'd be safest."

Archer hoped she was right. The mood of Dragos Lupu's brothers had been ugly, murderous, when she'd spoken to them.

They'd denied having heard of the Merediths, or having anything to do with Reading or Aylesbury. They denied having a big enforcer, or any enforcer, Bulgarian or otherwise, on their payroll, for the little that statement was worth. But they wanted blood for their brother's death, and Archer discerned that a sense of family honour ran deep in them. She couldn't rule out young children being targeted in a blood feud.

"Give me the address and we'll have a squad car keep tabs," she said.

"So what's going on?" Sonia demanded, picking up a pad and pen from the coffee table and writing. "Did this Lupu kill Gary – or have him killed? Have you arrested any of his people? Who do you suppose killed *him*? Because it wasn't us."

Archer thought she'd have followed a similar script in Sonia's shoes. It meant nothing. Only Sonia could vouch for Josh Kelly. Had he been dispatched to Oxford to exact some revenge for the Meredith murders? Or maybe someone else in the outfit?

Or was someone playing the rival gangs, and the police, for fools?

39

"Okay," Archer said, "let's see where we've got to."

It was 6pm and Archer had called the briefing early, ostensibly so the team could get some rest on a Saturday evening before coming back in tomorrow. But Baines knew she had a personal motivation. She and Dominic were dining with her brother and sister-in-law this evening, the first get-together since her mother's funeral. She was nervous about it, but felt that backing out because of work would burn whatever rickety bridges between the siblings remained.

Baines had urged her to keep the appointment, and she had listened.

She opened by running through the latest developments in the Meredith murders, which now appeared to have spilled over into Oxfordshire.

"Not much in the way of forensics so far," she said. "CSIs were still processing the scene last time I spoke to DS Petrescu, but as you can imagine, a toilet in a bar's a total nightmare for them, with the comings and goings. Turns out a couple of people tried to get in before the body was discovered, but the killer must have somehow wedged the entrance door shut. By the time the barman was free and went to check it out, the obstruction had been removed. That was coming up for 2pm. By then the brothers were getting restless as to where Dragos had got to."

"They thought maybe he had food poisoning or something," Collins added. "When they realised he was in a locked cubicle and not responding, they forced the cubicle door."

Archer highlighted the Royal Bar card found at the scene, and her reservations that it might be too obvious a clue.

"Apparently there are also some fibres on Dragos' clothes that could have been left by the killer," she added. "There's the slimmest chance it'll yield some DNA, but more likely there will be a fabric match with the killer's coat."

"The CSIs also thought there might be some cross-transfer of fibres," Collins elaborated. "Something from Dragos' clothing to the killer's."

"If we catch him," Archer said. "And if he still has the coat."

"CCTV?" Ashby asked from his seat at the back behind Gillingham.

"Not in the loos," Archer said, "not that works, anyway. But there are a couple of cameras in the bar." She opened an envelope. "Around the time in question, you see Dragos approaching the toilets. Then this guy," she stuck a blown up picture on the board, "follows him. A few minutes later, he comes back and another camera catches him leaving."

The picture depicted a bulky figure, dressed in black, head down. He wore his baseball cap low, collar up, scarf around the lower half of his face.

"That's the best we've got?" growled Gillingham. "Christ, it could be anyone."

"The build's not dissimilar to Gary Meredith's killer," Bell remarked. "What is it with these gangs that they all have these man mountain enforcers?"

"I don't think a five-foot weed's going to do much enforcing, Jason," laughed Collins. "But the guv and I met a feller at Sonia Meredith's who's apparently there to protect her. He's similar build too. Flimsy alibi, but no evidence so far that he *wasn't* where he said he was at the time of the murder."

"This is all going to kick off, isn't it?" Gillingham said, tension palpable in his voice. "I can just feel it. All it wants now is for one of the Connollys to be taken out..."

"Maybe that was why Cameron was so helpful," Archer said. Baines shot her a sharp glance. *Cameron* now, was it? "Maybe he doesn't want to get involved in this mess any more than we want him to."

"If only you'd gone to him sooner, Lizzie," Gillingham said.

Baines felt his ire rising. Bit it down. He thought the implied criticism was outrageous, but maybe he was a little biased. He acknowledged that he hated the fact that Archer had followed up their meeting at Connolly's home with a one-to-one lunch.

"Yeah, well." Archer was doing her best to shrug it off. "We didn't." She looked Tyler's way. "Will, you've something on the black Passat picked up on CCTV in Northfields at significant times?"

"Yes, guv. Not much use though. It's turned up burned out. The plates we saw on the CCTV were fake, as we surmised, and the engine serial number pins it down to a car reported stolen a fortnight ago. We've tried to get something useful from ANPR, but more dead ends, and CSI aren't super-optimistic about what they can recover."

There wasn't much to add on the Meredith case for now. Baines felt they were sitting on a pressure cooker with no way of turning the heat down.

"Did you want to say anything about Tim Phillips, Dan?" Archer asked. "Although that case is being handed to Reading at the end of the week."

"Unless we solve it first," he said, getting up and coming to the front.

"Not much chance of that." Gillingham's tone was dismissive. Acidic.

Baines didn't rise to it. "At least we can probably rule out Denis Ryan's involvement in Tim's murder," he said. "Maybe Eric Yelland's too. We'll need to verify their stories, but they're plausible, or Ryan's is, anyway."

"Well, don't keep us in suspense," Gillingham said. He seemed to be in one of his grumpier moods this evening. "How did a humble construction worker manage to retire to a posh house in a Sussex idyll?"

"Two words, boss. National. Lottery."

Baines saw Ashby roll his eyes. "Oh, you're joking."

"Jason started making calls on the way home, and they've got all this data protection red tape at Lottery HQ, but Ryan's willing to authorise them to confirm it. He won the jackpot, opted for anonymity, sold his friends, family and colleagues a variety of bullshit about inheritances, football pools, and wins on the horses, and got away with concealing how very loaded he really is. The house is nice, but not too ostentatious, and he says he doesn't get begging letters."

"And Yelland?" prompted Archer.

"Apparently became buddies with Ryan through the building business. Their paths crossed a couple of times when Yelland was guarding sites Ryan worked on and they hit it off. The odd drink turned into a monthly piss-up, and they kept in touch after Ryan moved away. More recently there've been a couple of meet-ups and now Yelland baby-sits Chez Ryan when they do a cruise or whatever, and Ryan pays him something for it. He's been recommended to a few others in the neighbourhood too. Helps with his gambling debts."

"He was upfront about those?"

"Oh, yes. Ashamed, too, I reckon. But he's never proactively tapped Ryan for money. Says they're friends and he doesn't want to abuse that."

"So he was probably desperate for cash when Phillips died," Collins said. "When the killer needed somewhere to conceal a body."

"I know," Baines agreed. "But I'm not sure he was involved. He didn't quite fess up to involvement in thefts from *any* building sites, but he was emphatic that nothing of that sort went on at Spencer Court on his watch."

"He would be, wouldn't he?" Archer said.

"Yes, but on balance I found him credible. Jason?"

The Scot nodded. "A sad little bugger really. I think the bits of house-sitting he does do something to ease his money troubles, and he says he's going to Gamblers Anonymous. At least he's trying."

"That's now," Ashby pointed out. "What about then?"

"I just don't think he'd make a particularly good liar," Baines said. "I reckon, with Eric Yelland, what you see is what you get. I think I believe him."

"So we're nowhere," Gillingham declared. "May as well push the case off to Reading now."

"Hold on, though, Sir," Baines said. "There's just one more angle I'd like to pursue."

"Really?" The DCI could hardly have sounded less impressed. "This had better be good."

"I don't know yet. It's to do with Demi Reeves. The young prostitute who –"

"I know who she is." Gillingham's gaze could have melted a polar icecap. "But I don't see what she has to do with anything."

"No, Sir." Baines chose a submissive approach. "But her case has been mentioned a few times. You were obviously rightly outraged, Sir, that it was sidelined in favour of the search for Tim Phillips. And I got curious."

"Good for you. You're leading a cold case investigation, you're a week from your wedding, and you've got time for curiosity?"

"Sir." There was a warning in Archer's voice. She wouldn't like her colleagues being humiliated in front of everyone. But then she looked Baines in the eye. "What's this all about, Dan?"

He cleared his throat. "Bear with me, Lizzie. Sir. It might well be a waste of time, but it's worth a look, I think."

He recapped on his conversations with Jackie Phillips. How Tim's wife was convinced that there had been, not only other women, but also prostitutes to feed his hunger for his throttling fetish.

"That was his thing. Strangling women to the point of unconsciousness while having sex."

Archer grimaced. "I read up on it online after Dan told me about it. They call it 'breathplay', among other things. Erotic asphyxiation is the technical term. It's meant to enhance the orgasm for the chokee, but it can give a sense of power to the choker too. Sounds like that was what Phillips got out of it."

"Sounds pretty sick to me," Tyler commented.

"And dangerous," Archer said. "People have died."

"Yeah, well. Pretty bloody obvious that strangling someone can lead to death." That got a grim chuckle from the team.

"But so what?" persisted Gillingham.

Baines had been given a sheaf of papers to do with the Reeves case by Tyler on his return to the office. He'd skimmed through them, and curiosity had suddenly turned to something bordering on excitement.

"It could all be a coincidence," he admitted. "But you'll recall that Jackie and her partner, Geoff Rice, had noted large cash withdrawals made by Tim on occasions when Jackie suspected he might have been seeing a prostitute. They concluded they were payments for sex. The last date was the night of a big fundraiser. Twelfth of April 2005."

"And?" Gillingham made a twirling motion with his hand, urging Baines to get on with it.

"And, as you probably remember yourself, Sir, that was also the night Demi Reeves died of strangulation. I don't believe you ever established who her client or clients were that night, did you, Sir?"

"No," the DCI said. "But nor did we have any reason to suppose it was Tim Phillips. It could have been anyone. Assuming it was a client at all."

"Sir, could you humour me and summarise the Demi Reeves case?"

"Later. I'm not wasting everyone's time now."

"But surely, it's worth pursuing, Sir? A man who probably hires prostitutes who let him throttle them is suspected of doing so for the last time precisely when a prostitute is strangled to death. And, if he did kill Demi – probably by accident – then maybe that gives someone a powerful motive to kill him for revenge."

"It's worth a look, Sir," Archer added. Baines sent her glance of silent thanks.

"We'll talk about it after the briefing," Gillingham repeated. "But you're pissing in the wind, Dan. A piddling coincidence doesn't turn a case on its head."

40

Sonia Meredith sat nursing a glass of wine, staring at the TV but not really taking in the words or pictures. Apart from Josh, there was no one else in the house. Only a week ago, the children would have still been up and negotiating to push bedtime back a few more minutes. Gary would have been here, or she would have been looking forward to him coming home and sharing a drink and a chat about their respective days.

Now she was sharing her home with a minder and wondering if tonight was the night someone would come to kill her.

She had always hated Gary's gun, and hated him having it in the house. As far as she was concerned, it was a boy's toy, and she'd always feared that one of the kids might find it. But now she wished it was to hand, instead of in some police evidence locker.

The huge irony was that, these days, the legitimate side of the business, originally a front for the dodgy end stuff, had grown and thrived to the point where the family no longer really needed to be on the wrong side of the law to make a decent living. She'd wanted to get the family out of criminality over time, and she'd thought Kit might have been persuadable about that. But Gary loved being the bad boy, the king pin. He loved the ducking and diving. And this was the result.

But the brothers' deaths had stiffened her sinews. No way was she rolling over now. She would dump the illegal enterprises at a time of her choosing. Meanwhile, she was grimly satisfied that one of the men thought to be responsible for her husband's death was shaking hands with the Devil this evening – maybe rubbing shoulders with Gary, she thought with a smile. But it wasn't over yet.

Two Lupu brothers still standing. And her.

Who would still be on their feet when this was over?

* * *

Baines sat in Gillingham's office. Gillingham himself was seated behind his desk on a bog-standard swivel chair like everyone else's. The fancy executive number he'd managed to blag a few years ago sat in a corner, faux leather worn to the fibres, the seat drooping sadly. The word was that it had collapsed under the DCI a few weeks ago and was beyond repair, with no budget for a replacement.

It had been what Baines's dad called 'top show' – classy on the outside, but ultimately a piece of crap.

"All right," Gillingham said. "You wanted the lowdown on Demi Reeves. I'll make it quick because, frankly, it's a waste of time, and I want to get off home."

"Any background would be useful," Baines said.

"All right," Gillingham said. "Well, Demi Reeves was 15, the daughter of Suzy Reeves, a smackhead prostitute. Suzy was being run by a local pimp, name of Carl Munns. She turned up dead in an alley behind a supermarket. Strangled. It was only in the course of the initial investigation that we learned from some of the other working girls that Demi had been turning some tricks herself." He shook his head, his expression all disgust. "The other girls thought Suzy was making her do it. They reckoned Suzy was putting the kid to work when she was too off her face to do it herself."

"Jesus," Baines felt queasy. It wasn't a unique story, and he'd seen and heard about most shades of human depravity, but this sort of case still turned his stomach.

"Did the mother admit it?" Archer asked.

"She said she'd had no idea. And the pimp denied all knowledge of it. Insisted that, if Suzy *was* sending Demi to work in her place, it was news to him, and something between Suzy and her daughter. We never believed either of them. They'd recklessly endangered a minor and were saving their skins."

"But did you find out who Demi's last client was?

"No."

"So it could have been Tim Phillips?" Baines's pulse quickened. "We should talk again with the mother and the pimp."

"Good luck with that," Gillingham said. "Suzy got an attack of conscience. She wasn't much of a human being – never had been, I suppose - and what we suspected she'd been doing was horrendous, but maybe she did love Demi in her own twisted way. Most probably she couldn't live with herself any more. She took an overdose."

"Suicide? She whores her own kid out and then gets a fit of conscience when it gets her daughter killed?"

"Well, there was a proper inquiry and an inquest. It was either suicide or misadventure. Me, I thought it was suicide. Not that she ever admitted that she knew Demi was working the night she died. Insisted she must have run into some random nutjob."

"Did you take that notion seriously?"

"Not really, no. But maybe she wasn't entirely without a heart."

"Really?" Baines raised a cynical eyebrow.

Gillingham shrugged. "I know what you mean. God knows, I was angry about what she'd done, and so was Steve. We hated Suzy for selling her child, but the scumbags out there who make their living out of creating junkies and then selling them the drugs that destroy their lives made her what she was."

"She had choices," Baines insisted.

Gillingham sighed. "Yes, she did. But that's not what you want to know. Did we suspect Tim Phillips of using prostitutes? No. We thought he probably had affairs, but didn't imagine he'd need to pay for sex. This – what did Lizzie call it? This *breathplay* thing explains why he might do so, but I doubt we'd have made that leap even if we'd known he was into that."

"Even though he'd disappeared within a couple of weeks?"

"What, and someone's going to kill a man like Tim Phillips over one more dead working girl that no one cared that much about? Suzy took her own way out, and Carl Munns almost certainly didn't give a stuff. And Demi literally had no one else."

But Baines had been thinking about that. "What about Demi's father though? Was he on the scene?"

"No one knows who the father was. The name was blank on the kid's birth certificate. It could have been anyone. There's every chance whoever it was didn't even know he had a daughter. The poor kid's life was rubbish and short."

"What about the pimp – Carl?"

"Munns," Gillingham supplied.

"Was it possible that Munns was the father?" asked Archer. "Maybe he did give a damn. Maybe he knew exactly what happened to Demi, or he found out, and he killed Phillips?"

Gillingham shook his head. "Carl Munns was gay. I know a lot of pimps have sex with their girls themselves, but for Munns it was all purely business. He was only interested in what benefitted Carl Munns."

"Worth a word with him, though? After all this time?"

"I doubt it, but even if it was, you're too late on that one too. I heard he died of cancer. I thought good riddance. But look," he said, "this is getting us nowhere. We can't start reopening the Reeves case on the basis of a coincidence of dates."

"And the strangling thing."

"Still too thin, Dan. I stand by what I said before. Our only interest in the Phillips case is that, when he finally surfaced, it was on our patch. Therefore, finding out how that happened could lead us to his killer. My money's still on the actual murder being committed in Reading. So, unless you have any more ideas about how he wound up under Spencer Court, the sooner we hand it back to Pat Mahon, the better."

41

The village of Ivinghoe was a little under ten miles from the office. Archer had been introduced to the King's Head restaurant by Dominic, who'd treated her to lunch there as a surprise for her last birthday. She'd loved the food, the relaxed atmosphere and 'proper' fine dining, and it was the first place that had popped into her head when Adam had asked her to suggest somewhere to meet.

The ivy-clad building sat on a corner of the meandering High Street, opposite both the Norman church and the village green. It was one of an eclectic mix of buildings, in ages and styles. Post-war functionality nestled amongst mock-Tudor facades, and small cottages stood on close proximity to more imposing properties.

She spotted Dominic's Vauxhall Insignia in the small layby outside, the space in front of it big enough for her to squeeze her Skoda into. As she closed the driver's door, he got out of his own car and came to join her.

"Ready for this?"

She realised her stomach was doing cartwheels. "No."

He squeezed her arm. "Come on. You've faced down murderers and God knows what else. You can do this."

She held up the bunch of flowers and card, grabbed at a petrol station on her way here. "I have birthday offerings. I hope they don't get thrown in my face."

He looked around. "Is their car here?"

"I've no idea. Must be around years since I've seen them. They could be driving anything by now."

He led her inside and told the receptionist that they were meeting people, and the table would be booked in the name of Archer.

The fair-haired woman at the desk smiled. "Oh, yes, they're here already. In the room at the end."

The room had a bar, an open fireplace and a selection of antique-looking sofas, chairs and coffee tables. It felt a little like a step back in time, but to a cosier time, before chipboard, plastic and stainless steel took over the world. Adam and Nic sat in the top left-hand corner, and Archer's sister-in-law squealed as they entered,

"Here they are!" Nic exclaimed a little too loudly. She got up and met them halfway across the room, throwing her arms around Archer in an extravagant hug. "So lovely to see you!" She released her grip. "And this hunk is...?"

"Dominic." he supplied.

Nic moved across to him and gave him a quick squeeze and a peck on the cheek. "Lovely to meet you!"

By now, Adam had joined them, looking awkward. He still had their father's dark good looks, although his stomach had maybe spread a little since their last meeting. He leaned toward his sister and barely brushed her cheek with his lips. "Glad you could make it." He nodded to Dominic. "How ya doing?"

"Good," Dominic said. "Good, thanks."

"Well, have a seat and I'll sort some drinks."

He took orders, then moved toward the bar. Archer and Dominic followed Nic back to the table. As they sat, Archer took a proper look at her sister-in-law. Still elegant, her dark hair long but stylishly cut. She wore an indigo jersey dress that hugged her figure. She must still be swimming and seeing her personal trainer.

"I got you these," Archer said, proffering flowers and card.

"Oh," Nic gasped, "they're so beautiful." She made a big deal of sniffing them. If there hadn't always been a touch of the theatrical about her, Archer might have suspected her of irony. "Look, Adam!" She held them up to her returning husband. "Lovely flowers for me."

"Happy birthday." Archer tried to match her for brightness.

"The drinks will be over," Adam said, resuming his seat.

An awkward silence descended.

"Well," Nic said finally. "So, how are we all?"

"Okay," Archer said. "How are the kids?"

"Oh, they're lovely. You don't know what you're missing."

That was so Nic. Some things never changed. The assumption that every woman was as eager to reproduce as she was. Before her injury, when it had looked as if she would be married to Rob, Archer had assumed that children would figure somewhere in her future. But it hadn't been that big a deal. That she'd now turned forty without having a child was not a great regret in her life.

"Got any pictures?"

While Nic scrolled through her phone, showing Archer and Dominic photographs of the children, first the drinks arrived and then menus. By the time the photo gallery was exhausted, they had toasted Nic's birthday and ordered their food. Throughout, Adam had only spoken when spoken to but, in fairness, Nic talked enough for both of them, asking Dominic about his work, then telling them about their latest holiday.

"So where are you two off to this year?" was her next sortie. "Holidays?"

Archer, who hadn't seriously entertained the idea of passing Dominic off as her boyfriend, laughed awkwardly. "We're just friends, Nic."

The smile froze on Nic's face. "Oh. We assumed..." She shrugged. "Oh, but what a waste. So how do you two know each other?"

Archer explained their relationship, with Dominic occasionally chipping in.

"Hold on." Adam spoke unprompted for the first time. "You share a cat?"

So Dominic explained how Barney the fat ginger tom came to be owned by both of them.

"Although, in reality," he concluded, "I always think it's the other way round. He owns us."

Adam shook his head. "All these years, Liz, and I never figured you for a cat person."

"Neither would I have," she admitted.

They were shown to their table. Perhaps at least a little of the ice between her and Adam had melted, because he asked her if work was busy.

"I take it you haven't got much on," he added, "seeing as you're here."

She sipped some wine before answering. "Actually," she said, "I've got two cases on the go, but I can't really talk about them."

"I saw Aylesbury on the national news a few days ago," he said. "That guy who was found under the block of flats – Tim Phillips – that's not one of yours, is it?"

"My Sergeant's leading on it," she said, "but I'm SIO – Senior Investigating Officer," she added for the benefit of a puzzled looking Nic.

The starters arrived then. When the waiter had gone, and the foursome were picking up cutlery, Adam returned to the subject of Tim Phillips.

"I met him once, you know," he said.

"Really?" Archer regarded her brother with unfeigned interest. "When?"

He frowned. "I remember his disappearance being on the news not long after, whenever that was. It was a corporate charity thing. My boss had to cry off and he sent me instead. You came too, Nic."

She screwed up her forehead in thought. "If you say so. You drag me along to so many ghastly dos."

"I probably would have forgotten by now, if he hadn't gone missing. The thing I remember is, it was his event, and he was going round glad handing and being the life and soul, but I saw another side of him. Not once, but twice."

"Another side in what way?" Archer asked. Could this be the same fundraiser Baines had been looking to link to Demi Reeves's murder? She'd supported him at the briefing, but thought he was probably reaching. It would be interesting to hear from someone who'd been there that night.

"The first thing was when I went to the bar. I stood next to him. He was all charm, but then he had to take a call. It was like a mask slipping. I tried not to listen, but he got quite ugly for a moment there."

"I don't suppose you got any impression as to what it was about?"

"It sounded like someone was letting him down. Some plan or other had changed and he didn't like it. I remember he was quite off afterwards. Didn't attempt to resume our conversation. Just paid for his drinks. He was definitely well pissed off."

"It was over ten years ago," Archer said. "I'm amazed you remember."

"Memory like an elephant, my husband," giggled Nic.

"Not really," he said. "It was just all this stuff when he was missing, about how lovely he was. But the phone call was nothing. It was what happened as I was leaving."

"Go on," Archer prompted, wondering if Baines was onto something after all.

"He was outside the entrance to the hotel where it was all happening, having a blazing row with a young woman."

"His wife, perhaps?"

"Definitely not. She was at the event, I remember. This one was younger. She seemed upset. To be honest, it looked like a lovers' tiff."

Archer's mouth was dry. Had her brother unwittingly witnessed something significant?

"Can you remember what this woman looked like?"

He screwed up his forehead. "I'd be lying if I said yes. All I've got is a vague impression. Maybe if I saw her again…"

"I don't suppose you remember the exact date?"

"Unbelievable." Adam cut into his scallop. "How long have we been sat down, and you're grilling me on police matters already." But he was actually smiling. "You think this could be important?"

"I don't know. Probably not. But maybe."

"Well, as it happens, I'm a sad bastard. Still use a paper diary, and I keep every one. I can check when that fundraiser was, if it'll help."

Topic seemingly exhausted, they ate in silence for a few moments.

"You were asking about holidays," Dominic said to Nic. "I'm going walking in the Lake District in the summer, with the Ramblers."

"You never said," Archer remarked, a shade more sharply than she'd intended.

"Didn't I? Well, I know you're not interested in holidays."

"What?" Nic's jaw actually dropped. "Everyone's interested in hols."

"Not Lizzie. Never takes them. She might take a few days off and read in her garden. Even then she keeps in touch with the office."

"Why aren't I surprised?" Adam commented. "Our dad wasn't much better. Never more than a week, and never abroad. The police." He made it sound like an obscenity. "Not a job, but a way of life. Thank Christ one of us managed to steer clear of it."

Archer put a forkful of goat's cheese salad in her mouth, chewed and swallowed.

"Yeah," she said quietly. "Thank Christ."

42

Collins had taken today's early finish as some sort of sign. She'd told herself that, if the opportunity presented itself, she'd take her courage in both hands and introduce Charlie to her parents, making it clear what their relationship was. The part of her that dreaded their reaction, that wanted to funk it, had secretly assumed that the moment wouldn't come. That work would get in the way, and would be the perfect excuse for avoiding what she knew she needed to do.

Since urging Collins to be honest with people who mattered with her, and not to carry on hiding her sexuality, Charlie herself hadn't applied any pressure, allowing her to work out her own time and space. She'd already told the important people at work: Bell, Archer, Baines and. just before going home, Tyler. She'd made it clear it wasn't a secret, and that she didn't care who else they told. Other colleagues could like it or lump it.

But her parents…

The house in High Wycombe had always looked the same to her. Her father put in work every summer to maintain the outside, and even the front door, whenever he repainted it, was always the same shade of blue. It didn't feel like a time warp to her. She liked the comforting familiarity.

Her father looked surprised when he opened the door.

"Well," he said, glancing from Collins to Charlie and back again, "this is an unexpected pleasure."

"I got off work early," she said. "Thought I'd come and see you. This is my friend, Charlie."

Her dad said hello and shook Charlie's hand. "You'd better come in. Mum's watching some rubbish on the telly, so you're saving me from that. Go through, and I'll get the kettle on."

Ten minutes or so later, they were all seated in the living room – which had also changed little over the years – with tea and cake. It was always good to hear the slight Caribbean twang in her parents' voices, an accent she'd never really had. It spoke of home.

Mum had provided a quick run down on family news – hers and Dad's, and Collins' siblings. Normally, she'd move on to uncles, aunts and cousins. Even second and third cousins that Collins had never met and sometimes never heard of. But instead, she turned her attention to Charlie.

"And what is it that you do, Charlie? For a living?"

"I'm a criminal lawyer. It's sort of how we met."

"A lawyer." Collins' mum smiled broadly. "Well, Joanne, you've done well for yourself."

Collins stared at her, wondering if that meant what she thought it did.

"Close your mouth, sweetheart," her mum said. "You'll catch a fly."

Her dad was chuckling. "One thing your mother's always been is quick on the uptake. She's right though, isn't she? Why else would you bring a friend home, out of the blue?"

"Oh, God." Mum's hand flew to her mouth. "Have I got it wrong? You're really just friends?"

Mixed emotions swirled in Collins' very being. Some sort of disappointment that her big announcement had been overtaken by events. Fear of their disapproval. Confusion that they were being so calm. Relief that it was out there.

"You're not wrong," she admitted. "We're a couple. It's very early days yet, but…"

"But we're happy," Charlie added.

"But how did you know?" She looked from one to the other. "Even *I* didn't know for sure until I met Charlie."

"We'd always wondered," Mum said. "I can't explain it. Mother's intuition, maybe."

"But…" She was still confused. "You seem very calm about it. I thought you were both homophobic."

"Why would you say such a thing?" Dad protested.

"You're always having a go at gays on the telly."

238

"Not because they're gay, though. Because they're camp. I don't like all that mincing and prancing and silly clothes, and neither does your mother."

"Elton John?"

"Fabulous music, terrible clothes. Ridiculous glasses. Doesn't mean we're anti-gay."

Mum got up, walked over to the sofa where Collins and Charlie sat, and threw her arms around them both.

"Sweetheart, we don't care what you are. We just want you to be happy. Charlie says you're happy. That's good enough for me."

Collins' eyes swam with tears of relief. Mum stepped back and turned her gaze on Charlie.

"Don't you be hurting my little girl, though, or you answer to me. And it's nothing to do with no phobia."

Charlie took Collins' hand in hers. "I'd better try very hard not to, then."

"Right." Mum gave a satisfied nod. "Who's for more cake?"

* * *

Archer watched the rear indicator on Dominic's car begin to blink as they approached their road. She flicked the stalk on her own steering column to signal the turn.

The evening hadn't gone so very badly. By the time Archer had got in her car for the journey home, she'd been exhausted by the tension of the situation, which had never become entirely comfortable. But there had been a definite thaw in Adam as the dinner had progressed – never quite to the point where she could honestly say everyone was relaxed and enjoying each other's company, but her brother had definitely become engaged in the conversation flow, the initial waves of hostility diminishing. He'd even enjoyed a few jokes with Dominic.

Dominic. As she pulled up on her drive, she stole a glance at him, just opening his car door. He'd charmed them both. Phase two of Nic's reconciliation plan was a Sunday lunch at her home, with the kids present, and she'd included Dominic in the invitation as if, despite what Archer had told her, the neighbours came as a package.

Archer smiled to herself as she got out. Earlier today, she'd allowed Cameron Connolly's charm to set off butterflies in her stomach, whilst loathing herself for allowing him to have that effect. This evening, she'd been out with the best man she knew, one who always supported her without agenda. Following his car home from the restaurant, there had been something comforting about his rear lights, twinkling ahead of her.

He stood on his drive, hands in his pockets. "Coffee?"

"Yes, but I'll make it. Least I can do."

"Great. I prefer your coffee anyway."

In her kitchen, she busied herself getting her coffee machine going, brewing his latte. He leaned against the work surface, watching her.

"So," she said casually, "the Lake District. Are you going with friends?"

"No, just me. The Ramblers have got a country house hotel near Buttermere. It's a good deal – breakfast, dinner, packed lunches, guided walks every day. A lot of singles go. Everyone usually gets along."

"You've been before?"

"Not for a few years. But I love the Lakes, and I thought it was time I got back there."

She poured his coffee, feeling wistful. "We went a couple of times as a family, when Adam and I were in our early teens. I remember great scenery. And rain."

"Oh, yeah." He was grinning. "The rain."

"Still, it sounds great. I wish I was coming."

"I'm sure they'll still have places."

She pressed the button for her own Americano. "Yeah, but you wouldn't want me around, cramping your style."

"Who says I wouldn't?" He put his mug down. "Come on, Archer. When's the last time you took a break? A proper one?"

Images flitted through her mind of her and Rob in Paris, before a jagged bottle had ripped her world apart. It had been such a happy time. She missed that feeling so badly. She felt the beginning of tears – for what, she wasn't sure – and turned her face away from him.

"Too long," she admitted, wondering if he'd hear the tremble in her voice.

"Hey – are you okay?"

She collected her coffee, swallowed hard and turned to face him. "Of course. Just the strain of the evening."

"Went okay, though, I thought. Mind you," he added with a wink, "I reckon a little bit of Nic goes a long way."

"I couldn't have got through it without you. Thank you." Her voice cracked, and the tears came.

He was there in an instant, enveloping her in a hug. "Hey. No need to weep with gratitude. I got a great dinner out of it."

She laughed through the tears, hugging him back.

"You're always there for me, aren't you?"

"That's what best mates do."

Acting on impulse, not daring to think about her response, she turned her teary face up to him. "Is that what we are? Best mates?"

"I hope so."

Had he even heard the challenge in her voice?

"Well, that's great." She started to extricate herself from his embrace.

"We could be more." There was a tentative tremble in his voice. "But I didn't think you wanted that, and I'm never going to push it."

"Maybe you should. How do you know what I want?"

He held her at arm's length. "I don't know. But I know it's been a difficult, emotional evening for you. Do you remember last year, when Monty died? I tried to kiss you, and you said you didn't want that to happen when I was upset. Well, you were right. And I don't want something happening tonight when *you're* maybe not thinking straight."

She thought he might be right. But she also thought it was another missed opportunity.

"So what do we do?" she said. "Hope the right moment'll come along, some time never?"

He gave a half-laugh. "That'd be a pity, wouldn't it? Okay, cards on the table. I value our friendship too much to want to lose it."

"So do I."

"But I'd like to be more than just good friends."

She gave a laugh that sounded like a sob. "So would I."

"So let's just be careful. Take it slowly. Get your cases solved and then maybe we can, I dunno, do some date nights or something. See where it takes us? And be *honest* with each other. Try to make sure, just in case it doesn't work out, there's a way back to being friends again? What do you think?"

She felt the good side of her mouth lift in a real smile. "I think it sounds like a plan. A good one."

He leaned forward and kissed her lightly on the lips. "Solve the cases by the end of the week, and Dan's wedding could be our first official date." He picked up his coffee. "By the way, that date Adam was going to check for you. It's important, am I right?"

The past few minutes had driven work thoughts from her mind. But there had been a ticking at the back of her mind ever since Adam mentioned his meeting with Tim Phillips. If it had indeed been the night Demi Reeves died – *and* the date of the fundraiser when Jackie Phillips believed her husband had last been with a prostitute – then an angry phone call about changed plans looked more significant than Adam could have imagined. And who was the young woman he'd rowed with?

"Important? Yes, it could be," she said. "That'd be ironic, wouldn't it? Adam helping the police?"

He grinned back. "Maybe he missed his vocation after all."

43

The house opposite Sonia Meredith's had been a lucky find. The SOLD sign, the out of control front garden with too much litter blown in not to have been tidied up by someone who cared a damn about appearances had all hinted at emptiness – former occupants moved away and new people not yet in. Checking hadn't been too difficult. A wrongly addressed 'parcel', the address just close enough to look like he was a stupid courier who'd got confused; no reply at the front door, so he'd touted the parcel around neighbours, all too ready to flap their tongues and confirm what he'd suspected. The new owners hadn't yet moved in.

And, the moment they'd closed the door on him, he'd have been forgotten. No one remembers a courier. After that, it had simply been a matter of parking around the corner and slipping in through the side gate under cover of darkness. Getting inside through the rear door had been child's play. He had the house to himself. It was perfectly placed to observe the Meredith house.

After he'd taken out her husband, he'd expected her security to increase more than it appeared to have – maybe even for the police to whisk her away somewhere, or at least a full-time police presence at the house. Either would have made his job harder, especially as the people who paid his wages drew the line at killing coppers, if it could be avoided. The police losing one of their own could raise a shitstorm they simply didn't need. But, whether the woman had refused protection, or whether the police had decided they couldn't afford it, all he'd seen was a marked squad car, cruising past the door roughly every half hour. It was 3.15am and he'd just seen it go by again, slowing down as it passed the house. So obvious.

The timing wasn't so precise you could set your watch by it, but that didn't matter. What mattered was that, once the car had come and gone, he would have ample time to get into the house and do what he needed to do.

Not tonight, though.

Tonight, after the murder of Dragos Lupu, she might expect a swift response. He'd seen the guy she'd moved in, and he looked like he could handle himself. Not well enough to make a difference, obviously, but waiting a little longer would allow the woman and her minder to relax somewhat. That was when you struck – not when they were keyed up and expecting it.

He was glad the children weren't there. They weren't his mission, and he'd have been very sorry to have to harm them, or for them to see something traumatic. He wasn't a monster, after all. More like a soldier obeying orders.

For now, he had plenty of food and drink, and his time was his own. During the day, he'd get some sleep. Meanwhile, he had only to watch and wait.

* * *

When Karen had seduced Baines in the shower yesterday, there'd been a moment when he dared to hope that it signified a lightening of her mood. That maybe she'd come to accept that her parents were never going to come to terms with her relationship with Baines, and had chosen not to be tortured by their rejection any longer. But he'd seen almost immediately that nothing could be further from the truth.

Her lovemaking had had a desperate quality that he'd seen before. It reminded him all too starkly of the first time they'd shared sex, following Louise's murder - Karen turning up on his doorstep drunk and distraught, and looking for the one person who could match her anguish. They'd had no idea that, a decade and a half later, that moment would cumulate in a wedding. At the time, it had been all raw, cathartic sex each of them doing more taking than giving, frantic to lose themselves in a few moments of abandonment.

He'd recognised the same emotions in Karen this time. When it was over, she'd cried. He'd caught her crying several times since, very quietly, but consumed by a misery that was like a knife to his soul.

He guessed the only way she could get her parents to relent would be to call off the wedding. Maybe they'd require her to leave Baines, too. That she was clearly determined, whatever else she felt, not to do that was humbling. He knew how lucky he was too have such unconditional love.

But the situation was eating her up inside. He'd felt powerless. Now he just felt like a wimp, because he'd realised last night, in a restless moment, that he'd stood back, reluctant to interfere in Karen's family troubles. Maybe that wasn't good enough.

It hadn't been the only issue on his mind last night. He couldn't get the possibility that Tim Phillips may have been Demi Reeves' last client out of his mind, especially after a late night text from Archer, saying he might be onto something. Now she sat opposite him in an empty office, having grabbed him for a word before he'd even got his coat off.

He absorbed what she'd just told him, especially the text from her brother that contained a date and nothing more.

"Wow," he said. "So Adam was at Tim's fundraiser the same night Jackie and Geoff Rice believe he saw his last prostitute prior to his disappearance. All those times we've said we don't believe in coincidences, but this is almost *too* perfect. Jackie reckons the event, and his cash withdrawal points to him going whoring again that night. Is it such a stretch to imagine that the phone call Adam overheard might have been Suzy or Carl Munns, telling him Suzy couldn't see him, but they were sending another girl in her place?"

Archer had picked up a paperclip from the desktop and was absently straightening it. "Suppose we're right, then. Do you think he knew or cared that Demi was under age?"

He'd wondered the same himself. "Who knows? Maybe when you've got that sort of a fetish, the urge to scratch the itch is greater than any sense of morality. But if we *are* right, then a couple of other things Jackie and Rice said really would make sense."

"Which are...?"

"Apparently he made one much larger cash withdrawal a couple of days after he would have strangled Demi. Suppose he was paying Suzi and/or Munns off to keep them quiet?"

Archer frowned. "You said Gillingham doubted either of them would have told anyway. They wouldn't have wanted to admit their part in the kid's death."

"But would he know that? He had plenty of money and was used to spending it. He might easily have thought that throwing money at any problem – even this one - was a way to make it go away. Plus, there was one further occasion when they said they'd have expected him to use a prostitute, and he didn't make his usual cash withdrawal."

"Because he was too traumatised by what had happened last time?"

"Maybe simpler than that. He could hardly carry on seeing Suzy for strangling sessions when they both knew he'd killed her daughter that way. Either he was scared of his fetish, or he needed to find someone else to play his games with."

"So what do you think, Dan? Worth another word with Gillingham?"

"I don't know," he admitted. "The boss is pretty weird about this whole theory. He didn't actually tell me point blank not to pursue it, but he clearly isn't interested. He thinks it's a waste of time and resources. We might think Adam's text, and what he told you about that night, adds weight, but it's still all conjecture and circumstance. If we take it to the boss now, I could imagine him getting pissed of and categorically forbidding me from pursuing it further. He really does seem to want to wash his hands of the Phillips case."

"I know." Archer shook her head. "You'd have thought, wouldn't you, that a lead, even a tentative one – and a possible solution to the Demi case – would get his attention."

"I've been puzzling over that too. A chance to finish what he started, with a case that's supposed to have affected him and Ashby so badly. Why kick it into the long grass?"

"Do you think he made mistakes with the case? Missed something, or accidentally compromised some evidence, and now he's afraid his failings could be exposed."

"He'd have had to stuff up quite badly for that to be the reason. But who knows?"

"Why not run through it with DCI Mahon? If you could convince him it was worth pursuing…"

"That makes sense," Baines admitted. "But I've got my teeth into this, Lizzie, and I've got until the end of the week to work the case before I hand over to Mahon. I'd love to crack it myself. Does that sound stupid?"

She started bending the paperclip again, trying to remake its original shape. "No. So what can we do? You said yourself, the notion that Tim may have killed Demi is mostly conjecture. Where does it get us?"

It was a question he'd grappled with during a restless night. "For a start, it gives someone a motive to avenge her. Gillingham ruled out Munns the pimp and Suzy the mother, and he said she had no one else – that no one even knew who Demi's father was. But what if that's not true? Suppose Suzy knew exactly who he was?"

"A rare occasion of unprotected sex for some reason?"

"Something like that. I don't know how old Suzy was when Demi was born, but I'm betting she was quite young. Capable of an accidental pregnancy. Suppose she *did* know, and despite the absence of the father's name on the birth certificate, she told him at some point that he had a child."

"Maybe only after Demi was dead?"

"Maybe. And, just maybe, she told him who she thought the killer was? Just imagine you found that you'd had a daughter you never knew, and now you never would know her because some pervert had throttled her to death in a sex game gone wrong?"

"Of course, he mightn't give a toss." Archer observed.

"Or he might care a lot."

"He might," she agreed. "He might feel cheated. Angry."

"Angry enough to kill?"

She stared at the paperclip for a long moment, then looked at Baines. "Not necessarily. Maybe he only set out to beat the crap out of Tim, but then it just went too far."

"Most likely he lost it once he started. Rage is a terrible thing."

"Okay. But where does that actually get us? We still don't know who the father is, and Suzy's not going to tell us from beyond the grave."

"No, but Reading must have Demi's DNA. We could try for a familial match. You never know your luck. Our killer could be on the database."

Archer frowned. "Probably a long shot, but I've heard of one case in Thames Valley that was solved that way. Mind you, it was backed up by a lot of intelligence and background work. And we know how expensive DNA testing is. We've got nothing here but a hunch. If Gillingham's not interested...."

"Do you think Mahon could be persuaded to source the test, though? If the case is coming back to him anyway?"

"Got to be worth a try. Shall I talk to him, or will you?"

"I'll give it a go," he said. "Come back to you if I need a bigger gun." But talking it through with Archer brought a new thought into his mind. "You know, if we're on the right track with this, it could explain why Phillips had to disappear."

She leaned back in her chair. "Explain."

"All right. Let's go back to the time all this is going on. We're investigating the death of an underage sex worker, and then a high profile local figure goes missing. Has he been abducted? Has he done a Lord Lucan and disappeared for some reason – maybe financial irregularities? Has he been murdered or killed himself and we just haven't found the body yet? One thing's for sure – we're under pressure to find him, far more pressure than we were ever under over Demi's death."

"Yep. I know all that."

"Bear me out. As you also know, we didn't have a body. If we had, then maybe we'd have been totally focused on questions like, who had a motive to kill him. Maybe we'd have dragged the whole thing about his infidelities out of his wife, asked questions around the sex industry and realised then – as we have now – that Phillips was possibly Demi's last client and probably killed her."

She stared at him. "You're right. Make that link, and you start wondering who'd wish to avenge Demi."

"And then you start wondering, just like we are now, if the father is a possible suspect." His mind was racing. "What do you think?"

She didn't answer immediately. She stood up and walked over to the window, looking out on a gunmetal sky over the car park. Abruptly, she turned to face him.

"I'd buy it. Tell all that to Mahon." Her phone began to ring. She checked the screen. "Phil Gordon. I'd best take it."

She answered the call. Listened. Then puffed out her cheeks. "Bloody hell, Phil, are you sure? ... Yes... Yes..." Baines saw her eyes widen. "But this changes everything."

44

"Okay," Gordon said, spreading photographs out on the conference room table. "So this," he tapped a picture showing a partial shoeprint, "was found at the scene of Gary Meredith's murder. There were traces of Gary's blood in the print, so we're fairly confident it was left by the killer. And we've since identified it as a Nike AirMax."

His gaze swept the assembled team: Archer, Baines, Collins, Bell and Tyler. "Now, this," he tapped a second photograph, grainy, with a shoe at the end of a leg, "we got from the CCTV footage at the bar where Dragos Lupu was killed. This guy enters and exits the loos at precisely the time Lupu was in there being strangled. We blew up the section containing the suspect's foot." He tapped that photograph. "See the Nike tick logo? And it looks like an AirMax to me."

He pointed to a separate picture of a shoe with the distinctive Nike logo, obviously printed from a sales website. Everyone looked from one image to the other.

"Could well be," Archer agreed.

"Yeah, but Nike's popular," Bell objected. "I've got a pair of AirMax myself."

"Then you're under arrest, Jason," said Collins, getting a laugh.

"Sure," Gordon said. "It could be coincidence. But, I don't know, it got me thinking. So I looked again at the CCTV footage from Northfields and from Oxford." He clicked the mouse on his laptop and the screen behind him came to life. Moments later, they were watching the dark-clad, balaclava-wearing killer of Gary Meredith.

"Watch closely how he walks," the crime scene manager said. "I'd say he slightly favours his left leg. It's not a pronounced limp, but it's a distinctive gait. I'm guessing he's had a minor problem with his right leg and he corrects it without even knowing he does it."

Archer wanted to be sure. "Show it again, Phil."

Gordon ran the clip again.

"Okay," she conceded. "It's slight, but yes. Distinctive."

"Thanks," he acknowledged. "Now look at our man in Oxford – remember, he wears the same make and model shoe as the other guy."

They watched the bulky figure move across the bar.

"Same gait," said Tyler.

"Similar, at least," Baines said. "Very similar build, too."

"You're thinking this is the same man, Phil?" prompted Archer.

"I'm thinking it's a worthwhile theory. Gait analysis has been used in hundreds of cases now and is a recognised forensic tool. I can get an expert to look at the footage. And you're right about the build, Dan. We'll use known points of reference in both sets of footage to work out fairly accurately both these guys' vital statistics."

"But you're thinking they're one and the same?" Archer knew he was, but she wanted him to say it.

"Balance of probabilities, Lizzie? Yes, I think so."

"So either the Merediths and the Lupus have been hiring the same hit man…" Baines left the thought hanging.

"Or, more likely, some third party is trying to make it look like they're wiping each other out," Archer completed his sentence. "They want to move in on both territories when the dust settles."

Baines looked her in the eye. "I wonder who that could be?"

She felt a sick feeling in her gut. Only yesterday she'd almost been taken in by smooth charm and sexy eyes. She'd woken up pretty quickly, but the thought still made her queasy.

"How long will the analysis take, Phil?"

"It's Sunday, Lizzie. I doubt anything'll happen until tomorrow now. I can pull strings first thing."

"Okay. That'll have to do."

"We're thinking the Connollys though, aren't we?" Baines pushed. "So why not drag smarmy 'Cameron'" - the hint of sarcasm wasn't lost on Archer, and she felt herself reddening – "into the station and grill him until the pips squeak?"

"Because," she said, "- and, no offence, Phil – we've got somewhat of a half-baked theory at the moment. I'd like that analysis done and to present him and his expensive brief with something solid. Plus, we need to show that, not only were Lupu and, in all likelihood, both Merediths, killed by the same man, but there's also a solid link to the Connollys. Otherwise we'll sit down with him and his five-star brief, have no proof of anything, and he'll walk. And he will laugh at us."

"But what's the alternative? He takes out the other Lupu brothers, or Sonia Meredith, while we go through the motions? He'll really be laughing at us then. If we let him know we're onto him, surely he won't take the risk?"

"Risk doesn't seem to bother him, though, does it?" Collins remarked. "Dragos Lupu's murder in a busy bar in broad daylight was pretty audacious, right?"

Archer looked at her thoughtfully. "Yes, Joan, it was. Even as a calculated risk – if it all went wrong, I'd bet the killer, whoever he is, would lead us right back to his paymasters. And some of those theatrical touches – the really obvious Royal Bar card with Lupu's body, trying to incriminate the Merediths; Gary Meredith's killer taunting us on CCTV; and we thought using the Northfields as a body dump and a killing ground was some vague attempt to confuse us. Suppose it was a piece of overthought stupidity?"

Baines looked aghast. "You're right. None of that sounds like the Cameron Connolly we've met. It sounds too amateurish. So don't we think it's the Connollys after all?"

She allowed herself a grim smile. "Oh, I think it's the Connollys all right. Just not Cameron."

45

"No comment," sneered Desmond Connolly. He shot his very expensive solicitor a smug, self-satisfied smirk. It was pretty well all he'd said so far.

They were in Aylesbury's most oppressive interview room, Desmond and his lawyer, Archer and Collins. Archer had already known that Desmond Connolly was nothing like his brother in character but, in the confines of this airless room, she could see little physical resemblance either. Brown scouring-pad hair, pasty complexion, ferret-like features.

"You're a bit of a walking cliché, aren't you, Desmond?" she remarked.

He tried to keep the confident look going, but she read confusion in his eyes.

"I don't even know what that means," he said.

"Oh, you know. I read your file a couple of years ago, when your family had first moved in on the Vale. You're the youngest of a privileged family. Spoilt, used to having your way."

Desmond raised his hand to his mouth, covering an exaggerated mock-yawn.

Archer ignored it. "Before you got caught out running your little drug operation in London, there were also a couple of violent incidents where charges against you were 'inexplicably' dropped."

The lawyer was a middle aged man by the name of Hugh Osborne. Archer knew him by reputation. He rarely lost a case, and probably commanded an hourly rate that would feed an impoverished family for weeks. She suspected his suit had cost more than most people earned in a month.

Now he pushed his spectacles down on his nose and peered at Archer over the rims.

"Inspector, charges that are dropped are not charges at all, and thus not relevant. Now, the clock is ticking, sooner or later, you're going to have to charge my client or release him. I suggest you use the time wisely and don't waste it on cheap jibes and innuendo."

"Of course," Archer continued as if Osborne hadn't spoken, "it was you, Desmond, who first saw the potential of Aylesbury Vale for expanding the family business. But you weren't the right man to run it, were you?"

Desmond blinked and said nothing.

"But your father, Murray, foolishly indulged you until it all went horribly wrong and your brother, Cameron, had to cleaned up your mess. And he's stuck around, hasn't he?" Desmond made no response, but she observed a tightening of his facial muscles. "Cameron's the reason that, just like the London operation, we've never been able to tie any criminal activity back to the family, am I right? The Connollys look after their own, and things happen to anyone thinking of being disloyal."

"More innuendo, Inspector," Osborne said. "And unfounded accusations too. This is clearly a fishing expedition."

"Oh, it's more than that, Mr Osborne," she said. "I'm getting to the point, trust me. I'll get there even quicker, if you stop interrupting."

"So get there, please."

"I've met Cameron," she said to Desmond. "We've talked about you."

A muscle under the suspect's eye twitched.

"I don't get the impression he has a very high regard for you," she said. "I doubt you're being trusted with much responsibility. And I bet you like playing the big man. How does it feel to be treated like the office boy? Especially when you're so 'creative'." She made parenthesis with her fingers, just as Cameron had done in the café.

"Our business is respectable," Desmond began.

"My client has no comment," Osborne interrupted, "and you still haven't asked him a question."

"Here's the thing," she said. "History's repeating itself. When you started trying to build up your business here, it got messy. Bloody. People died. Of course, no blame ever attached to your family. But now people are dying in Reading and Oxford. Top people whose business interests coincide with yours. And, for a while, it looked as if there was a power struggle between them. Tit for tat. We thought they might even be trying to muscle in here."

She took a sip of water. "The trouble is, Desmond, that creativity and practicality aren't always mutually inclusive. I think you were trying to open up new markets in neighbouring counties, to show your brother and your father how they've misjudged you. You got rumours spreading that the Lupus had set their sights on Reading, and that they had this big, scary Bulgarian enforcer." She shook her head. "Does he even exist?"

"How would I know?"

"You might. Because I think you cooked this whole thing up. The trouble is, it's all unravelling now, just like every stunt you pull. Too many theatricals and embellishments."

"That Royal Bar card found with Dragos Lupu's body?" Collins joined in. "Pure Hollywood. Like something out of a cheap crime novel. Way too obvious."

"And Gary Meredith's killer taunting us on CCTV," Archer said. "What was even the point?"

"Kit Meredith's body dumped on the Northfields," said Collins. "We thought it was an attempt to confuse us. Maybe, though, it was a half-arsed attempt to suggest that you guys were targets, too."

"Or maybe," added Archer, "your own brother was lined up as a victim in this phoney gang war. Would you stoop that low?"

"This is bullshit," Desmond protested. But he was staring at the table, and there was a tremor in his voice.

"Is it? Because we've got enough evidence to tell us that the person who actually killed Kit and Gary Meredith also killed Dragos Lupu. And, when we find William John McMurdo – affectionately known as 'Mad Willie' – we'll prove he was the killer. I've seen his file, too. Very enlightening. He walks with the slightest of limps. Did you know every person's gait is distinctive, by the way? I'll bet his limp is identical to that of our killer. And his flat's being searched, even as we speak. We'll find evidence that puts him at two murder scenes at least." Archer was pretty sure Mad Willie still had the trainers he wore when he slashed Gary Meredith's and Robbie Pascoe's throats. Most likely the coat he wore when he strangled Dragos Lupu too, matching the fibres found on the body.

Hugh Osborne raised his hands in protest. "What has any of this to do with my client? Even if any of this is true, you'd just have an employee of my client's family going vigilante for some reason and removing criminals from our streets. Some people would give him a medal. I'd be amazed if he tried to incriminate his employers."

"Oh, me too," said Archer. "Because he's loyal, that much is clear. He'd never lift a finger against any of you. If you did decide to move against Cameron, Desmond, you'd probably have to do your own dirty work, yes? Because Mad Willie wouldn't harm any Connolly, would he?"

"If this 'Mad Willie' is as dim as you imply, Inspector," Osborne said drily, "he's surely not resourceful enough to carry out the daring murders you described."

"Oh, I didn't quite say he was stupid," Archer said. "I think he comes into his own as a man of action. He just needs to be told what to do."

"Like one of those wind-up toys you let go," Collins added.

"What I haven't figured yet," Archer said, "is why Cameron doesn't know. By which I mean, I don't believe for a minute he'd countenance this ham-fisted plan. And I'm surprised Mad Willie hasn't told him."

There was silence in the room for several seconds. Then Hugh Osborne chuckled. He even clapped his hands a couple of times.

"I do love a good fairy story, DI Archer. So are we done? Can my client go?"

Archer looked at Desmond Connolly. His face was even paler, his gaze all over the place. His lower lip was wobbling. How much more did she have to push before the cracks really showed?

"We're nowhere near done," she said. "And I'd like Mr Connolly to start answering for himself."

"No comment." Desmond's voice was shaky. She was surprised how rattled he seemed. She thought her reasoning was right on the money, and that he hadn't expected it. He feared he was going back to jail. Maybe he feared his family's reaction even more.

"All right," she said. "We can play it that way. We'll hold you while we search Willie's gaffe. We'll be bringing him in, too, as soon as we find him. We'll get our evidence, prove he was the killer. Then we'll lean on him to tell us who ordered the hits."

"Willie won't tell you anything," Desmond blurted.

Archer concealed the smile that threatened to break out on her face. Out of the corner of her eye, she saw Collins grin for an instant.

She let the silence play out. Saw the concern in Hugh Osborne's eyes as he regarded his client, willing him not to say any more.

"Oh?" she said lightly, when she thought Desmond had had enough time to reflect on what he'd said. "So there's something for him to tell?" She gave a theatrical sigh. "Look, Desmond, if you're behind these four murders, you're going to be in a lot of trouble, and so is Willie. I do hope he isn't out there, looking to take out a fifth victim. Because you've got a chance to at least stop that. If he's planning to kill someone while you're in here…" She shrugged. "I doubt you'll ever get out of prison, however much you keep your nose clean. These days, a guy like you could have life expectancy to, I don't know, maybe 90. Assuming you don't get on the wrong side of a shiv."

"Imagine that," Collins said. "60-odd years behind bars. Pooing in the corner of your cell. Out in the fresh air for a short time each day. Bloody terrified of inmates a damn sight harder than you, who don't give a monkeys about your family's reputation."

He shrugged, evidently trying not to let it scare him. Archer doubted he was succeeding.

"Or," she continued, "you can stop it now. Tell the truth, and tell us where we can find Willie McMurdo. Do the right thing and make sure no one else gets hurt. You might get at least a little credit."

"Who's next on the list?" Collins urged. "Radu Lupu? Vladislav? Sonia Meredith?"

"Do you even know?" Archer pressed. "Or did you just give him a shopping list?"

"No," Collins said, "there'll be a batting order. What do you call it? A narrative? First the Meredith brothers, then Dragos Lupu, so it looks like revenge. But only you and Willie know what's next in the script, eh, Desmond? Will it be another Lupu, or another Meredith?"

"The smart money's on the Lupus," Archer said. "Leave Sonia the last woman standing, taking the blame. But what do I know?"

"No comment," Desmond said.

"We'll take a short break," Archer said. She eyed Hugh Osborne. "You might want to talk some sense into your client."

***

While Archer and Collins were questioning Desmond Connolly, Baines had left a voicemail on DCI Mahon's mobile and had been waiting on tenterhooks for him to call back.

He accepted the logic of Archer's suggestion that he try to persuade the Reading man to order tests that might identify Demi Reeves's father, rather than take it straight to Gillingham. Gillingham had been eager to wash his hands of the Phillips case, even when Baines had hinted at a connection to the young sex worker's murder. Whether the old case really was simply consuming too much resource, or whether Archer's speculation that something had gone wrong with one or other of the original investigations – something that could be awkward for Gillingham – Baines himself couldn't decide.

He knew, with less than a week to go to his wedding, he should be concentrating on that, and especially comforting Karen. But his professional pride dictated that, if he couldn't wrap up the Phillips case before the end of the week, it wouldn't be for want of trying.

He wondered how Archer was doing. He'd have loved to be doing the interview with her, but he understood why Collins, who'd been working the gangster murders from the start, was the one sitting in.

He would love to see the Connollys nailed for this. To be honest, he'd like them nailed for anything. 30-odd years ago, old-school coppers might have attempted to fit them up, but it was important to him that they be actually guilty. He was toying with calling Mahon again when Archer and Collins entered the office. He waved, and Archer came over.

"Well?" he demanded.

"I don't know," she said. "I've tried to scare him, and now I'm leaving him to stew. My biggest fear is, if we're right, then Willie McMurdo could be out there stalking his next victim even as we speak. I'm hoping Desmond will somehow call him off."

"We confiscated his phone," Baines pointed out.

"Sure. But I bet that snake of a solicitor isn't above lending him his. Or calling Cameron to sort it."

"Do you think Cameron has a clue?"

She shook her head. "Nope. And not just because I had a chocolate brownie with him, either. I still think Desmond is doing all this to prove himself – maybe to Daddy, rather than Cameron. How he suckered Willie into it without Cameron finding out remains to be seen. Meanwhile, I've warned Sonia Meredith to be extra cautious and Amy Petrescu's warning the other Lupu brothers. The bugger is, we can't be sure who's next on the list, nor when the next hit is scheduled for."

46

He was half-dozing when his phone rang. The previous owners of the house he was occupying had thoughtfully left their curtains and carpets behind, and so he was able to keep the house across the road under surveillance from behind next curtains in an upstairs bedroom.

He checked the number on his screen, didn't recognise it, but answered anyway. It wouldn't be the first time one of his bosses called him on an unregistered burner phone.

The voice at the other end announced himself, and he acknowledged the caller.

Then the phone went dead.

He stared at it in disbelief. Thumbed the 'on' button. Nothing.

The battery must have run out. He realised he'd had it on constantly since yesterday without a charge. Worse still, he hadn't brought his emergency charger with him. He was always forgetting the thing.

He brought the knuckle of his right index finger up to his mouth, chewing on it.

A call out of the blue. halfway through a job. What could it have been about? Was the job off? He couldn't see that. This was important stuff, by all accounts. Important to the family, and good for business. But then, why call? Unless it was something urgent.

He knew the value of loyalty. His father had been the same. Please your bosses, and they'd look after you, that had been his motto.

Well, his bosses would not be pleased that he'd failed to charge his phone.

He paced the floor. He had to try to think, even though thinking hurt his head. It wasn't what he was good at. He was good at getting a job done. His old dad had said he had 'low cunning'. But he needed to be told what the job was, and suddenly something had likely changed.

If he wasn't meant to abort his mission, it could only be a change of timing. But sooner or later?

It was broad daylight. Even if he could risk being seen leaving the house to find a phone box, he'd lose sight of the woman's house, and he needed to know exactly what was going on. Who was there. When the police were driving by.

He unstopped his flask and poured himself another tea. This needed some thinking about.

47

As Archer was returning to the interview room to resume questioning Desmond Connolly, Baines tried DCI Mahon's number again. The call was answered almost immediately.

"Sorry, Dan," Mahon said, "I picked up your message and was going to call you back, but I keep getting interrupted. You know what it's like."

"Are you in the office?"

"I might as well be. I'm supposed to be having a Sunday off, but Reading's criminal fraternity seems to have other ideas. Nothing horrendous, but things I need updating on or to approve. Anyway, what can I do for you?"

Baines outlined his theory that Tim Phillips's killer might be Demi Reeves' father.

"We're hoping her DNA might give us a match to someone on the database," he explained. "I know it's a long shot."

"Worth it, though. I'm sure we must have DNA results for Demi already. What does DCI Gillingham think?"

Baines had hoped he wouldn't be asked this question, but it wasn't unreasonable for the Reading DCI to wonder if his Aylesbury opposite number was in agreement.

"He's not convinced, to be honest," Baines said. "But of course, the case is headed back your way, so maybe he wants to save on our budget." The latter wasn't entirely untrue.

"Yeah, fair enough. Maybe I'd be the same in his shoes. Although I'm surprised. Demi's father could have a powerful motive for attacking the person responsible for her death, and now we have enough circumstantial evidence to be looking at Phillips for that crime. If you're right, we could wrap up two long-standing cases from Paul's time. I'd have expected more enthusiasm."

Baines couldn't disagree. He decided the best policy was to say nothing.

"Oh, well," Mahon said. "I'll set something in motion tomorrow. I guess there's no need to fast-track it, after all this time?"

"Well," Baines said, feeling awkward, "the thing is, if we're right, we could make an arrest – maybe even charge someone – before I go on leave. It'd be nice to have it wrapped up. But I know fast-tracking is expensive."

"It is," Mahon agreed. "But leave it with me. I might be able to call in a favour." He chuckled. "I think this is a first."

"What is?"

"Most people want a coffee machine or a set of fish knives as a wedding present. You'd rather have a killer."

* * *

Archer and Collins sat down opposite Desmond Connolly once more. The aroma of stale sweat was now mingling with the already claustrophobic atmosphere. Even Hugh Osborne was looking less pristine.

"So," Archer resumed once Collins had got the recording equipment going again, "what's it to be, Desmond? Are you going to help us?"

He stared fixedly at a spot on the table.

"We've given you a break, and a chance for some discussion with your solicitor," she persisted. She gave Osborne a sharp look. "It's to be hoped he's advised you on what's in your best interests. We will connect four deaths to you, and you're in a lot of trouble. But you can still stop the killing. It'll count in your favour."

He shrugged like a sulky child.

Archer tried again. "We've already got people looking out for Willie McMurdo but, if he's primed to kill again soon, you need to tell us who the target is and where we can pick Willie up."

"Suspect making no attempt to answer the question," Collins said after a moment.

Desmond finally raised his head. "Sorry. Were those questions?" He gave them an insolent grin. "No comment."

48

Sonia was bored to tears, holed up in the house with only Josh Kelly for company. That detective, Archer, had called to say there was still a threat, and to be on her guard. Not to open the door to anyone she didn't know, even if they looked on the level.

She was in the kitchen, making yet another cup of coffee. An open packet of biscuits sat nearby. At this rate, she'd have the caffeine shakes and be as big as a house.

She didn't know how much longer she could put up with this. DI Archer hadn't said who the threat was coming from, but she knew she was suspected of ordering the murder of that Dragos Lupu in Oxford – or at least, she assumed she still was. And she surmised they were responsible for Gary's and Kit's deaths and that she was believed to be next on their list.

But something didn't make sense to her. She hadn't ordered any killings, much as she'd like to have avenged her husband's death. Apart from anything else, the kids had already lost one parent. No way was she going to jail.

But if she hadn't had Dragos Lupu killed, who had?

She knew he had two brothers, also in the family business over in Oxfordshire. Was it possible that one, or both, of them had had their own sibling taken out? A falling out, perhaps, or a desire to share the profits with one less partner? Perhaps that had been the plan all along: kill Kit and Gary, then blame Sonia for their brother's death.

Yet she knew the police didn't have enough so far to even arrest her on, let alone charge her. All they seemed to have found by way of evidence was that stupid Royal Bar card – and even detective Archer hadn't argued with her when she'd suggested it could have been planted to incriminate her.

Josh was catching up on some sleep upstairs. They'd figured that the risk was greatest after dark, so he'd stayed awake all night. It would be a fat lot of good to either of them if the attack came and he was too groggy to do anything.

She hoped the kids and her mum were okay. She'd phoned a couple of times during the day, but it was too upsetting. The children just wanted to know when they could come home.

She finished making the coffee, grabbed a couple more biscuits, and carried them into the living room, where daytime TV was playing softly to itself. Even the mindless pap being served up was better than silence, but she kept the volume low, one ear open for the slightest out of place sound.

She tried to give attention to the TV: 'Midsummer Murders'. As usual, the body count was rising. It was too close to home. She channel-hopped until she found a wildlife documentary. But it quickly became apparent that it was all about animals fighting to the death over territory. Laughing at herself, she kept changing channels until a black and white comedy came on. It was fairly dreadful, but something to watch. She stuffed a biscuit in her mouth, whole.

She wished Gary was here.

49

After an hour of fruitless questioning, consisting principally of Desmond Connolly repeating 'No comment', like a stuck gramophone record, with Hugh Osborne interjecting from time to time, reminding them how long they could hold his client without releasing him, Archer decided on another break.

It wasn't just the legal clock that was ticking. She was convinced more murders were planned. If the youngest Connolly intended to create power vacuums in neighbouring counties that he and his family could exploit, then the job wasn't complete. She supposed it was always possible that the killings had been halted temporarily, waiting for Desmond to give the next order.

Except that there was no sign of Mad Willie McMurdo.

Archer had hoped that Desmond might use a break to borrow Osborne's phone and stand his enforcer down. But if that had happened, wouldn't that have encouraged McMurdo to break cover wherever he was? She was tempted to demand Osborne's phone and have the last call on it triangulated, but that was a legal privilege nightmare.

So this break served two purposes: to leave Desmond to sweat; and to allow herself time to regroup and think of something. So far, her grey cells were letting her down on that score.

Her phone rang and she glanced at it. Butterflies in her stomach. What had prompted her to put Cameron Connolly on speed-dial? The same crush-like stupidity that came over her whenever she saw him or spoke to him.

"Archer," she snapped, annoyed at both him and herself.

"Have you released my brother yet?" No smoothness this time, Straight to the point.

"Who says we're holding him?"

"Don't be damn stupid, Lizzie. Who do you suppose called Hugh Osborne? So what have you arrested him for? There's been no statement yet, has there?"

"I'm not at liberty to discuss operational matters."

"Bollocks." This clearly wasn't a charm offensive day. "I was his one phone call. He said it was about the murders in Reading and Oxford. I thought we were agreed it was a turf war. What's it to do with Desmond?" She heard his breath hiss. "We could have become friends, you know. You'll find I'm a bad enemy to make."

She took a deep breath, ignoring the threat. "Cameron, all I'll confirm is your brother is under arrest pending charges, and we'll be using all the time we need, allowed by the law, to question him. If you want to help, you can contact Willie McMurdo and get him to come to the station for a chat."

"Willie? But..." There was silence on the line. Archer was fearing the signal had been lost when he spoke again. "You think these murders are down to Desmond and that Willie's involved?" He sounded genuinely incredulous.

"We're anxious to speak to Willie. It's in his, and possibly your brother's, interests for him to come forward."

"Thing is," she thought he sounded worried now, "I've tried to phone Willie a few times. Straight to voicemail. The last couple of times, the message has said the phone may be switched off. It could be off, or he could be out of battery."

"Is that unusual?"

"I gave him a portable charger, but he keeps forgetting to take it out with him. But he's been off-grid a while now. With all these murders, I was half-wondering if he'd been targeted. Except you'd think they'd be coming after me or Des, not someone like him." Another pause. "You know, he's been acting funny lately."

She urged herself to stay calm. "In what way?"

"Asking for time off. Being a bit, well, secretive." He chuckled drily. "And Willie's rubbish at secretive. I imagined he'd finally found a girlfriend and was shy about it."

Another pause. "Look," he said, "Willie's father came down to London with my dad from Scotland. We always treated him well, and he was a loyal employee. Same goes for Willie. People often think Willie's slow, but that's not right. He's perfectly capable of independent thought, but doesn't have a strategic bone in his body. Give him a job with parameters and he'll work out how to get it done."

"Like killing someone?"

"I didn't say anything of the sort. We're just talking here."

She tried a different tack. "Say, hypothetically, that Desmond had persuaded him to do a job and not tell you?"

"Willie knows I wouldn't like that. There'd have to be a good reason." He paused again. "No." There was a definite edge to his voice. "That's stupid."

"What is?"

"Nothing."

She didn't believe him.

"Cameron, if Desmond or Willie are involved in these deaths, things will go even worse for them if there's another that we could have prevented. And, if we find out you've been concealing something, it'll go badly for you too."

"Really? Better detectives than you have tried to make cases against my family over the years, and it's always gone badly for them. It's called having a good lawyer. Look," he said, "I'm sure Desmond's not involved in this. But, hypothetically, maybe Willie has got some stupid idea in his head. It's my birthday soon. Hypothetically, maybe it's his idea of a birthday surprise."

"You mean, Desmond told him that?"

"That's not what I said."

"We're wasting time. I'm guessing Willie has an unregistered mobile."

"He might have a cheap pay as you go. You know us frugal Scots."

"Let me have the number and we can try to trace him."

Another dry chuckle. "Why should I give out employees' private information?"

"Stop fucking about, Cameron."

"All right, all right. Just a moment." There was a long pause, then he gave out a string of numbers. Archer noted them down and read them back to him.

"That's it. That's two you owe me."

"Sorry?" She was seriously niggled now. He was still playing games.

"I gave you the Lupus. Not my fault you didn't warn Dragos in time. And now I've given you Willie's number. Although he's probably just with some woman –"

Archer rang off and rushed the number over to Tyler. "I want the last location of this phone, Will, and I want it yesterday."

If she'd been abrupt, he showed no sign of any offence. "On it, guv."

50

Willie McMurdo slipped out the back door of the house opposite Sonia Meredith's. It was still an hour or so to sunset, but there was already a definite chill in the air.

He hated showing himself in the street like this, in the daylight but, after fretting over that missed call from Mr Desmond for a couple of hours, he'd concluded that he must be required to get on with the job.

He really hoped Mr Cameron would appreciate the efforts his younger brother and Willie had put in for his birthday surprise. And that Mr Desmond was right about this being what he wanted: the biggest crime families in Reading and Oxford out of the way so the Connollys could expand their empire.

It was how things had been done when Mr Murray had first come down from Scotland and started carving out his territory in London. Murray Connolly had gone on a charm offensive from day one, using what capital he'd amassed north of the border to kick off some legitimate enterprises and start investing in a small way in his new community. Behind the scenes, men like Willie's dad had set about either subduing or removing obstacles to the more lucrative, but definitely much less legal, trade Mr Murray had set his sights on.

But times had changed. Nowadays, the Connollys mostly acquired new business by talking to, and negotiating with people. Okay, there had been that minor bloodbath in Aylesbury not so long ago.

Willie didn't like to think about that. Mr Cameron and Mr Desmond had fallen out over it. He hoped Mr Desmond was right about this, and that it would make everything all right between the brothers. Willie didn't like discord in the family. It was nice of Mr Desmond to want to do this for his brother, and Willie fully intended to play his part.

But he didn't like having to depart from his plan. He'd always intended to move on the house opposite after dark. The other killings he'd carried out had all carried some risk, but he'd been able to make a plan and minimise the likelihood that he'd be identified afterwards. This was different. Someone could come out of their house, come round the corner in their car, be some Neighbourhood Watch busybody, monitoring the street through net curtains, just as he had been observing the target house.

He hoicked his collar up a little higher, pulled the peak of his cap a little lower. It should be enough. The trick was always to act natural, as if you were just going about the same mundane sort of business as everyone else. People took little notice of you if you did that. Even if they vaguely remembered you, it was unlikely they'd be able to give a description worth a damn.

Willie walked along the side of the house to the corner facing the street, flattened himself against the side wall. Stuck his head out just enough to do a quick sweep. No one in sight.

His right leg twinged slightly as he crossed the road. The trouble with an empty house was, there was no heating. It was bad for his rheumatism.

Like a ghost, he moved up the Meredith driveway and got in close to the entrance. Slim glass panels either side of the door afforded him a convenient view into the empty hall. His lock picks were neat, effective and made little noise. Only the slightest of clicks announced the unlocking of the door. He was inside in less than a second, moving almost silently, more quietly than a man of his bulk was entitled to do.

He could hear the TV playing softly, his keen ears working out where the sound was coming from. Best case was that the woman, maybe her minder too, were in there watching something, guards down. At worst, the man was somewhere else and the woman had gone to make tea or to use the toilet. He stood listening. No tell-tale sounds of a kettle coming to the boil, or a spoon jingling in a cup.

If he was really lucky, the woman would be watching TV alone. The minder might even be upstairs asleep, expecting that, if an attack came at all, it would be under cover of darkness.

Maybe the timing was better than Willie had first thought. He drew the silenced pistol from his pocket. One shot, one muffled pop, and he could be out again without even encountering Sonia Meredith's bodyguard. He wasn't bothered either way, but it would be simpler, quicker and less messy.

He moved towards the sound of the telly and was halfway to the room where the sound was coming from, when a man's voice bellowed from the top of the stairs. Willie turned towards the sound, bringing the gun up, but the big man was already hurtling down, launching himself at Willie from three steps off the bottom. Both men went down with a crash, Willie's hat flying off, the other man on top.

They struggled for a few moments, then Willie managed to slam the gun across the man's face, smashing his nose and causing blood to gush. It gave him just enough advantage to roll them over, so that he was now on top. He levelled the weapon at the man's head, and that was when he felt a sickening, crunching pain across the top of his skull. He looked up, blood already running into his eyes.

* * *

Sonia had found an American rom-com that was at least a little distracting, if obvious. It was pretty obvious that the central couple were the victims of misunderstandings, and it was just a matter of how it would unravel itself. Sonia was betting one or the other, or both, of them would be running to be with the one they lurved in the final five minutes.

If Gary was here, he'd be passing disparaging comments on the whole thing. He'd had his romantic moments, and he'd been soppy as hell over the kids, but he wasn't a fan of girlie movies.

For the umpteenth time, she had to remind herself that he was gone. She wondered when she'd finally get his body back, so she could at least have a funeral. Maybe it would feel more real then. Apparently there were forensic reasons for holding onto him. Whatever that was all about, she hoped it would help the police to catch his killer and remove the threat to herself. This was no way to live.

She gave the film her attention again. It seemed that the heroine had finally woken up to the truth. There was no other woman in the hero's life. The woman she'd seen him with ran a foundation for fluffy animals, and he'd been saving it from closure. Suddenly (here we go) the heroine was running.

She never saw the conclusion, because there was a cry and then a sudden crash in the hall. She paused only for a second before hurrying to investigate. On her way to the hall, she grabbed a china vase from a console unit by the living room door. It wasn't much, but it was the only weapon to hand.

At the bottom of the stairs, Josh was grappling with a big, powerful-looking man and coming off a definite second best. As she rushed towards the fight, the intruder smashed the gun across Josh's nose, breaking it with a sickening crunch, then pointed the weapon at Josh's head. But by then, Sonia was there, bringing the vase crashing down on the gunman's unprotected head.

The vase shattered, but she still held its neck, with jagged shards attached. She jabbed the shards into the man's gun hand, as hard as she could, and he roared with pain, letting the weapon drop. There was a fury in her, fury that this may well be the man who had killed Gary. She went to stab him again, this time in the face, but he grabbed her wrist, ignoring the pain in his hand, and twisted, so that she dropped her own weapon. Blood from his cut head streamed down his face and, through the bloody mask, his eyes blazed with a bestial fury.

Another twist and she was on the floor. But now Josh was back on the move, scrabbling for the gun. The intruder released the woman and punched him in the side of the head. Josh fell on his side and the other man was on him, swinging his fists, hitting him again and again. Blood poured from Josh's nose, and leaked from his mouth, where his lips had mashed against his teeth.

Sonia rejoined the fray, pummelling the would-be assassin ineffectively, but evidently annoying him. He rose to his knees and backhanded her across the face. She recoiled and he punched her in the chest. The gun was still on the carpet. There was blood all over the pile, Josh's and the other man's. But

Sonia and Josh were both down, and the man who had come to kill her had a look in his eyes that was somehow half crazy and half deadly calm. He reached for the gun again.

There was still some fight left in Josh, who grabbed a handful of the man's coat. The man elbowed him in the temple, broke away and grabbed the gun. Panting hard, he got to his feet. And then he giggled, pointing the gun at the Josh, then Sonia, then Josh again.

"Eeny, meeny, miny, moe," he said.

The front door crashed open behind him.

"Armed police," a man's voice bawled. "Put the weapon down!"

The gunman turned towards the sound. Three cops in armour stood just inside the door, training semi-automatic rifles on him. He raised his own pistol.

"Put the weapon down," the cop in front said again.

The man laughed, sweeping the gun upwards. Then the world exploded in a hail of bullets.

51

That Sonia Meredith and Josh Kelly were still alive was the closest of calls.

When triangulation of Willie McMurdo's phone had placed him close to Sonia Meredith's home, Archer had spoken urgently to DCI Mahon, who'd taken the precaution of scrambling an armed response unit. They'd arrived barely in time. It was pure luck that Sonia's front door was flanked by narrow glass panels, through which they'd just been able to see the deadly struggle within.

Mad Willie McMurdo was dead, and Phil Gordon's team, working with Reading CSIs, had already matched his trainers to the shoeprint left at Gary Meredith's murder scene. A black coat found at his home was still being analysed, but Gordon had already compared fibres under a microscope with those transferred to Dragos Lupu's clothing, and was confident that they would be confirmed as a match.

A pay as you go phone had been found on McMurdo's body, and the last number that had dialled it was registered to one Hugh Osborne. The Connollys' solicitor had first claimed that Desmond had begged him to let him make a call, claiming it was to a girlfriend, then insisted that he'd been pressured into loaning him the phone.

Desmond Connolly, on the other hand, had said he knew nothing of any call: that if Hugh Osborne had dialled Willie McMurdo's number, it must have been on behalf of Cameron. In fact, if Mad Willie had killed all those people, it must have been at Cameron's behest – that, Desmond suggested, would explain why both Meredith brothers had been found dead on an Aylesbury estate. Cameron must have wanted it that way.

Cameron had been brought in and interviewed under caution, with another high-priced brief present. If his brother had tried to throw him under a bus, Cameron proved a little more loyal to Desmond. He also displayed what looked like genuine grief for Willie McMurdo.

"What I said to you before," he told Archer. "It was just that I was worried about Desmond. I had no idea that Willie was acting alone, or that he was mixed up in anything criminal. Perhaps some third gang had got to him and was paying him to target the Merediths and the Lupus. As you know, my family are strictly legitimate."

"Really?" Archer sighed. "So how do you explain the call your solicitor, Hugh Osborne's, phone made to Willie a few hours before his assault on Sonia Meredith's home?"

"I can't explain it," he said. "Maybe this third gang were paying him too. You say the call only lasted a second or two? Could have been anything."

But meanwhile, a warrant to search Desmond's flat had been executed. Early results showed he wasn't as creative as he thought he was.

Hugh Osborne had recused himself from further involvement in the case and Murray Connolly himself had sent a top lawyer up from London to represent his youngest son when questioning resumed.

"Okay, Desmond," Archer began. "So we've turned your flat over, and you've not been a clever boy. For starters, the old phone in a plastic bag in a toilet cistern routine is so old it's got whiskers on it. We found your pay as you go, and all the calls are to Willie's."

"So? He works for us." But Desmond was so pale now, he was almost translucent. Archer hoped he wouldn't puke. It looked a possibility. "Of course I'd phone him," he mumbled. "Driving jobs and the like."

"All the calls between that phone and Willie's are clustered around the times of the murders we suspect he committed and you ordered. How do you explain that?"

"He doesn't have to, Inspector," said the solicitor, a handsome middle-aged woman in Armani or some such. Image pure *Vogue*, accent pure East London. "As my client says, he often made work calls to Mr McMurdo. Obviously these timings are coincidence."

"Really?" Archer said for the second time. "And I suppose his browsing history on his laptop is coincidence too. You made it way too easy for us, Desmond. No password? No incognito browsing?" She shook her head and tutted. "We didn't even need expert geeks. Researching the Merediths and the Lupus? Another coincidence?"

"No comment," he mumbled.

"We don't yet know how you persuaded Willie to do those things for you. Maybe we'll work it out, maybe not. It doesn't much matter. You're looking at four counts of conspiracy to murder," she said. "You'd better pray your family has influence inside the prison system, because you're facing serious jail time in a serious jail, where they eat boys like you for elevenses. Still no comment?"

He glanced wildly at his brief. She leaned in close, Armani rustling, to whisper to him.

That was when he did puke. All over his lawyer.

52

Driving home, Baines supposed it had been a good day. Desmond Connolly would be formally charged tomorrow. It was hoped – but no one was counting on it – that smarmy Cameron Connolly could somehow be implicated. Archer was convinced he'd throw his younger brother under the bus before that happened. Either way, Superintendent Lambert was having a press conference set up at which she would praise officers from both Aylesbury Vale and Reading for what she was already calling 'a highly successful joint operation that showed Thames Valley at its best'.

Meanwhile, Baines hoped that DCI Mahon could get some DNA evidence on Demi Reeves' father and that, by some stroke of fortune, he was on the national DNA database. That would at least give him a whole new lead to pursue in the case of Tim Phillips's murder.

He wondered again why he even cared. Phillips was almost certainly a murdering piece of shit in nice guy's clothing, and the lead on the case was heading back to Reading anyway. He could coast his way to the weekend, taking care of Karen, and making sure Saturday's wedding was as happy an occasion as it could be without her parents.

No, he realised. He couldn't accept that. If he wasn't prepared, for reasons of professional pride, to let the Phillips case go, then he shouldn't allow Karen's family to boycott her wedding without a fight.

He stopped the car, let a motorcycle go by, and made a three point turn.

* * *

The look on Karen's father's face when he opened his door and found Baines there couldn't have been more affronted if he'd found a pile of turds on his step.

His in-laws, Robin and Heather, had liked him, maybe even loved him a little, once. When he'd been married to Louise. The father of their grandson. They'd been supportive, despite their own grief, when the Invisible Man had ripped the family apart, and had even approved of his friendship with Karen. They could see how lost their remaining daughter was without her twin, and just how much she needed a good friend to lean on.

All that had changed when Karen had told them they were in love and she was moving in with him. Overnight, his status had changed from something like a son to that of sex pervert.

"Yes?" Robin all but snapped. Then, as an afterthought, "Is Karen all right?"

"She's fine. Can I come in?"

"I'm not sure we've much to say to one another right now, Daniel."

Daniel. Both his in-laws/in-laws-to-be had always insisted on using his full name from day one, and there had been only so many times he could have reminded them that he preferred Dan. He couldn't let it irk him now, or he may as well just walk away.

He held up his hands. "I know what you think, Robin. And I sort of get what you feel. But please. Can I just come in and talk to you both for ten minutes? It's important."

There was an instant when, if he'd been a gambler, Baines would have bet that the door was about to be slammed in his face. Then, with a sigh, the other man stood aside to admit him.

"In the living room," Robin said shortly as he closed the door behind him. Baines walked through. The woman on the sofa, who always looked a little like an older version of Karen and Louise, glanced round. Baines read surprise in her eyes.

"Daniel?"

"Hello, Heather."

"Apparently Daniel has something to say to us." Roger shrugged and nodded towards an armchair. "I suppose you may as well sit."

Baines glanced around the room. It hadn't changed much since he'd last been here, except that they'd rung the changes with the family photographs on show. A picture of the twins as little girls was perhaps a reminder of happier times. The pictures of both girls on their respective wedding days had long gone. There was a picture of Louise, recognisable by a favourite red dress. No other pictures of Karen.

He sat down.

"Is Karen – " Heather began.

"She's apparently fine," Robin said, before turning hard eyes on Baines. "This had better be good."

"She isn't fine," he said. "Not really."

"Is she ill?" Minimal concern in Robin's voice.

"She's desperately miserable."

The older man folded his arms. "Well, I don't know why. She seems to be doing exactly what she wants."

"It's disgusting, what you two are doing," Heather added. "Obscene. When I imagine the two of you…" She shuddered.

Baines really wanted to ask what exactly she was imagining him and her daughter doing, and whether doing that imagining wasn't itself a tiny bit disgusting. It was only for Karen's sake that he let it go.

"Look." He took a deep breath. "We haven't really spoken at all since Karen moved in with me. And I know that, to some people, our relationship must look a bit strange."

"More than strange," Robin confirmed.

"And I can't change that. But you know what happened when Lou died and Jack disappeared. Karen's marriage went on the rocks and both of us were almost insane with grief. It was grief that drove us together, and we started looking out for each other. I don't think either of us was looking for anything more than friendship. I know I wasn't."

He looked from one face to the other. "I certainly wasn't looking to replace Lou. How could anyone? I know what you're thinking. Karen's identical to Lou in looks and in so many other ways. But that isn't why I fell for her. Quite the opposite."

Robin rolled his eyes. "You expect us to believe that?"

This was even harder than he'd expected. Every comment had him clinging to his temper like a man trying to keep a powerful horse from bolting. If he lost control, he'd probably damage whatever was left of Karen's relationship with her family beyond repair.

He kept his voice even. "You think it didn't hurt me, missing Louise so much and seeing her in Karen whenever we met up? Sometimes, it was so like being with Lou that it nigh on broke my heart. Over and over again, I had a living reminder of what I'd lost.

"Except I came to appreciate that they're not interchangeable. Yes, they look and sound exactly alike, and Karen has so many of Lou's mannerisms. But they're very different women. When I finally fell in love with Karen, it was *her* I was falling for – not Lou all over again."

"She's still her sister," Heather pointed out.

"Yes, she is. But, you know, marriage between a widower and his late wife's sister has been legal since 1907. It happens. We can't choose who we fall in love with. I know it's a bit weirder that the sisters are twins in this case. But it just happened."

"It shouldn't have," Robin said. "We should have forbidden the friendship."

Baines couldn't bite his tongue at that. "You're joking, right? This is the Twenty First Century and you're not some Victorian patriarch. Karen will be friends with who she likes, and she'll marry who she likes." He drew a long, steadying breath, reaching for calm, for a more conciliatory tone. "Be that as it may, I do know that, even if she can't have your total approval, or your blessing, she'd desperately like you to be at the wedding. And she'd like you to give her away, Robin."

Robin opened his mouth, but Baines forestalled him with a raised hand. "I once thought my life was destroyed forever. Karen felt the same. Somehow, we've found each other. That's some sort of miracle. She makes me so happy. And I'll do all I possibly can to make her happy too."

"But," Heather was crying, "what about Louise? What would she think?"

"We'll never know," he said softly. "But I hope she'd be pleased for us. Maybe she is."

"Is that all you came to say?" Robin's tone was still surly, tinged with a raw emotion.

Karen's parents were two sad people, and Baines felt sorry for them. But their sadness was in danger of tainting Karen's chance of happiness.

He stood up. "Pretty much, yes. Except to say this. I'm asking – begging – you to come to our wedding on Saturday. You don't have to like it, or approve of it. All I ask is that you try to be glad for whatever happiness she can find. I love her. It will mean the world to her – to us – if you come."

"That was a very pretty speech," Robin said. "I'll give you that. It probably took a bit more than five minutes. Now, if you'll excuse us…"

A sinking sense of hopelessness came upon Baines. It had been a long time since he'd felt quite so unutterably sad.

"Thanks for at least listening," he said. "I'll see myself out."

Heather didn't rise from the sofa, and Robin neither offered a hand to shake, nor moved to see him out. He stepped out into the late afternoon chill, closing the door behind him.

He'd tried. He wouldn't have forgiven himself if he hadn't. But it had been a waste of breath. He knew with a terrible certainly that the wedding – what should be a happy occasion - would be one of the saddest days of her life, and that was how she would always remember it.

53

Archer and Baines arrived at the car park at almost the same time on Monday morning and paused outside the station building, chatting. With them leading different cases, involving each in sorties into different counties, they'd had less chance to talk than usual lately, and Archer realised she'd missed it.

Baines was unusually glum and distracted. At first she thought it was pre-wedding nerves and even teased him that he was terrified about what might be in her best man's speech.

"Don't worry," she laughed. "I'm only going to mortify you a little bit. Your family and old colleagues have been remarkably helpful with my research."

"I wish that was all I had to worry about," he said. "I went to see Karen's mum and dad last night."

The stricken look in his eyes said it all.

"Not good?"

"It was like something out of a Victorian melodrama, Lizzie. Robin didn't quite say, 'Henceforth I have no daughter,' but that sounded like the message."

"Christ, poor Karen."

"It's over 15 years since Lou, died. Neither of us will ever get over it, I don't think, but both of us has sort of come to terms with it, in our way. Jack's a different matter, of course, but…" He held up his hands, as if words were inadequate. "It's different for Karen. Lou was my soulmate, and losing her was bad enough for me, but I know losing a twin is something different again. I've read up on it a lot."

"I'm not surprised."

"Since losing Lou, I always feel like a piece of me is missing. For Karen, I think that literally is the case. To have to choose between marrying me and losing her parents too…"

"But she has chosen, surely? She chose you. She isn't having second thoughts, is she?"

"Not really, no. Oh, the other night she asked if we were doing the right thing, and we talked about it. We both want to get married, no doubt about that. But it's like a big hole in her life has got even bigger. It could blight our chances of happiness forever. I mean, I can say to hell with them, but they're not my parents."

Steve Ashby's glossy Audi slid into the car park and sleeked its way into an available space. They watched him get out and head for the building. He stopped in front of them, blinking.

"Don't tell me you two have taken up smoking and come out here for a crafty one?"

Archer's father had died of smoking-related lung cancer, but she resisted the bite-back. Ashby had in all probability forgotten, the joke popping out of his mouth before he engaged brain.

"Oh, no," he said, before either of them could answer, "don't tell me. You're organising the stag do." He looked at Baines. "You're having one, right? I mean, me and Amy's wedding invite's got lost in the post, but the stag…"

He left it hanging there. Baines looked momentarily awkward. "I'm not really having one, Steve."

"No? Not what I heard."

"I might have mentioned a drink in the pub on Friday night to a couple of the guys." Pause. "You'd be welcome too, obviously."

Ashby beamed. "Great. I'll see if I can order a stripper."

"No!" Baines looked alarmed. "No bloody stripper."

The DI clapped him on the shoulder. "Joke, mate. Christ, you've gone white!"

Baines appeared to relax a little. "Anyway, it depends how work goes, really. This Phillips case…"

"… will be off your plate by then, or so I hear. Well, I'm up for it if it happens. Is Amy welcome too?"

Baines's smile looked forced. "Of course."

"I'll tell her. You might even get a last-night-of-freedom snog, if you play your cards right."

"No need for that." Baines looked a little panicked again.

Archer knew he had some romantic history with Amy Petrescu, from before he'd been emotionally involved with Karen. They remained friends of sorts, but Archer sensed that there was always a bit of a crackle in the air when they were together. When Petrescu had been attached to Archer's team for a few days last year – and formed her attachment to Ashby – Archer had felt that Baines was relieved to see her leave.

"You're easy to wind up today," Ashby grinned. "You want any extra-curricular activity, it's a stripper or nothing."

He strode on into the building. Baines shook his head.

"Forget it," Archer urged.

"Yeah. At least I've got the case to distract me. Although, if we don't get anything from Demi's DNA that tells us who her father might have been…"

"Even if we do, chances are there's no one on the database who comes up as a match."

"I know that," Baines accepted, "and I've no idea where we'd go from there. I reckon there's a big fat key somewhere that would really unlock this mystery, but I don't have a clue where to find it."

"I'd love to know who that woman was that Adam saw arguing with Tim the same night that Demi died. But he can't remember what she looked like, after all this time. Could be nothing anyway."

"We'll see. Meanwhile, how's Sonia Meredith holding up, do you think?"

Archer frowned. "Hard to say. When I last spoke to her, she wasn't interested in any support from us. She's tough. My guess is she'll get through this. The irony is that Desmond's aim was to create a vacuum in the Reading underworld, and he might have succeeded in that after all. Sonia hinted – without admitting her family had ever been involved in anything shady, of course – that she wants to concentrate on legitimate business from now on."

"Someone will step in to run the girls, the drug networks…"

"Yep. Either someone from the current Meredith outfit will go it alone, or either the Lupus or the Connollys will try to exploit the gap."

"Or all three," Baines laughed without humour. "Maybe there'll be a war after all. But it'll be Patrick Mahon's problem, not ours."

"I dunno." She shook her head. "The northern Home Counties gets just a little bit more like London every year. Sometimes I think the bad guys are winning. We really are the thin blue line."

"We can only do what we can. What about Desmond Connolly? You're charging him today?"

"Oh, yes." She couldn't keep the satisfaction out of her voice. "We need to sort a court appearance where he can enter a formal plea."

"If only his whole stinking family were standing alongside him."

"Their turn will come."

* * *

It was midday when Mahon called Baines..

"Can you come over? I've got a familial match on Demi Reeves's DNA."

Her heart skipped a beat. "Tell me."

"I'd rather you came over. You might want DI Archer to come too, if she can spare some time. This really isn't something I want to discuss on the phone."

"What's going on?"

He ignored the question. "Can you come to the office straightaway? And get Lizzie to come. Please."

There was something in his voice that almost scared Baines. "Of course. We'll be as quick as we can."

"Good."

Mahon broke the connection. Baines wondered what had him sounding so spooked. He glanced over at Archer, who was deep in conversation with Collins. He managed to catch her eye.

Less than ten minutes later they were on their way.

* * **

When they walked into Mahon's office, Archer thought the DCI looked somehow older, gaunter than before. Baines said he'd sounded like a very worried man, and it showed. But he'd judged their arrival perfectly. Coffee, the way they liked it, steamed on his meeting table. He waited while they sat.

"Thanks for coming," he said. "Sorry if this meeting feels a bit cloak and dagger. But when I tell you what's in those test results, I think you'll agree it's all a bit delicate."

"All right," Archer said. "You've got our attention. So what do we have?"

He walked over to his desk, opened a drawer, and pulled out a slim sheaf of paperwork, which he spread on the table in front of them Then he indicated a section which he'd marked up with yellow highlighter pen. Archer read it. Read it again.

"Fuck," she said.

She read the highlighted section for a third time, Baines looking at it over her shoulder. The words hadn't miraculously changed.

"Fuck," she repeated.

"Yes," Baines agreed, "that pretty much covers it."

"The question is," Mahon said, "what are we going to do now?"

"Christ, I don't know." She picked up her coffee. Blew on it. Took a cautious sip. Way too hot yet. She'd known it would be, but it gave her a few seconds to think.

"I'm going to have to take this to Gillingham," she decided. "Informally. See what he says. I don't want to make a big deal of it at this stage."

Mahon nodded slowly. "My thinking too. Want me to come with you?"

She thought about it. "I think not, Sir, if that's okay by you."

"You're sure? I mean, you say you don't want to make a big deal of it, but..."

"I know." If she got this wrong, it wasn't going to be exactly career-enhancing. "I think this is best, though. If we need backup, I'll call you."

Outside the Reading station, Baines and Archer sat in the car, talking about Mahon's shock revelation. No matter how many times they went over it, it didn't get any better.

"I won't blame you if you want to keep out of this," Archer said finally. "It's not going to be pretty when I take it to the boss."

Baines wondered if he'd ever admired her so much. "No," he said. The matter had never been in doubt. "No, sod it. I'm in."

54

Gillingham's door was, as usual, ajar. Archer tapped on a door panel as she stepped inside, followed by Baines.

Gillingham looked up from the paperwork he was reading and blinked.

"News?"

Archer turned and closed the door behind them, then faced the DCI again. "News of sorts, yes, boss."

His gaze lingered on the closed door for a moment, then searched both their faces. "Christ, not another death?"

"Not that, no." She gestured to the chairs facing his desk. "May we?"

"Of course." He waved his hand vaguely at the chairs. "Don't tell me you know who killed Tim Phillips?"

"I've got an inkling, Sir, yes. But you're not going to like it."

He held her gaze, but his left eye twitched, then twitched again. "Get on with it, Lizzie. I'm all agog."

He laughed then, but to her ears it sounded false. Had he guessed what was coming?

"First, I owe you an apology, Sir. You told us not to waste any more time on Demi Reeves' case. You implied any suggestion of a link between her and Tim Phillips was a red herring."

He glowered, face darkening. "I did. It was a direct order. You disobeyed me?"

"We had to, Sir. A good detective has to follow through on a hunch. And you've told me more than once that we're very good detectives."

"Yeah, well. You'll be a very good traffic cop if you haven't got anything useful."

She leaned back in her chair, trying to still the butterflies in her stomach, trying to appear more relaxed than she felt.

She reminded him of their earlier conversation, their suspicion that Phillips had been Demi's last client, and that whoever killed Phillips might have taken Demi's death personally.

He barked a laugh. "You're still on that?" He rolled his eyes. "You think this phantom father, who probably doesn't even know Demi existed, killed Tim Phillips in revenge for her death?"

"Something like that, yes."

"What bollocks."

"No, Sir. It isn't."

"And, even if this person knew he was Demi's dad, even if he somehow found out who killed her, why would he take the law into his own hands? Why not just inform the police?"

"I briefly wondered that. But then I thought maybe he had a lot to lose himself if it was known he'd fathered a prostitute's child. Maybe a wife, a family, a career. All three. And, if he knew that Phillips was almost untouchable – that he'd use his local connections to bury any suspicions against him, backed up by high-priced lawyers – then he might just decide to mete out punishment himself."

Gillingham nodded. "Well, it's a good story, I'll give you that. But even if you're on the right track, it's not much use if we don't know the identity of the father."

"That's true," Archer said, "but we can have a go at finding that out. We can test for Demi's familial DNA and see if we have a match."

Gillingham glared at her. "We could, but I'm not authorising it. You know it's very expensive and, even if we do get anything we can use after all these years, then the chances are the father's DNA isn't on any of our databases. On a wild hunch like this?" He slammed his palm on his desktop. "Forget it."

He met her gaze, seemingly daring her to argue.

"Oops," was all she said.

"*Oops?*"

"Already done, Paul."

"What's already done?" But suddenly he was no longer making eye contact.

"Familial DNA. Tested and matched."

"You did what?"

"That's the wrong question. You know what? The Paul Gillingham I know would have a go at me later for disregarding his orders. He might even discipline me. But his first question now would be: who's the father?" She sighed, her heart truly heavy. "But then you already know the answer, don't you, Sir?"

The colour had drained from his face, as if he had seen a ghost or had been taken seriously ill.

"This is a formal interview under caution," she said. "but it's your chance to get it off your chest, just the three of us, here in this room. No recording. That will come later."

As she recited the formal caution, the DCI's shoulders slumped. He looked as though he had aged ten years in less than ten minutes. He passed a hand over his face.

"Does Pat Mahon know?"

"Yes. But he agreed I should talk to you first."

It was Baines who spoke then, shocking Archer with his bluntness. "Sir, we know you were related to Demi. We think you were her father. It's time you told us everything."

* * *

Baines had known Gillingham for longer than Archer. It had been Gillingham who had made him Acting DI when Baines's old boss, DI Britton, had been ill and subsequently lost his battle with cancer. Gillingham who had returned him to DS, against his hopes and expectations, when he'd been offered Archer as a transferee from the Met. It had rankled at the time, but Gillingham had mostly shown him respect and support over the years.

He'd never expected anything like this. Oh, he'd always wondered why the DCI had allowed Steve Ashby such a cushy existence. Mostly he'd thought it was some sort of old pals act, as the pair went back a long way, but he'd occasionally speculated that there was something darker in the background.

Gillingham and Ashby had both worked the Demi Reeves case. Did they both know the truth about her murder? The truth about Tim Phillips's death?

The truth about her parentage?

Archer had been asked the hard question, but Gillingham hadn't answered. Instead, he looked more diminished, more scared with every tick of the clock on his wall.

"We're waiting, Paul," Archer said softly. "Don't make me arrest you on suspicion."

The barest glint of defiance flickered in his eyes. "You wouldn't dare."

"You know I would." The iron in her voice left no doubt that she meant it. "Paul, we've DNA evidence that proves a familial relationship between you and Demi Reeves. Suppose we start there?"

He glanced from face to face. Whatever he might have been seeking, he didn't seem to find it.

"All right," he said finally. "Yes. Yes, I was her father. Oh, Christ." His face crumpled and he had to struggle to master himself. "It was about twenty five years ago, before I'd even met my wife. Suzy Reeves was a nice girl, but hooked on drugs and already turning tricks to feed her habit. I was in uniform – a PC hoping to make Sergeant, hoping to turn detective – and some of my work back then was about trying to clean up the sex trade.

"There was something different about Suzy. I was more idealistic in those days. I wanted to save her – actually thought I *could*, for a while. Somewhere along the line, I fell in love with her, or at least, I thought so. We had a bit of a thing – always in secret, because it was awkward with the job - and I really thought she was turning the corner, getting off the drugs. But all she was really doing was becoming a more accomplished liar."

"So what happened?" Archer asked him. "She got pregnant?"

"Yes, but I swear I didn't know. It must have happened just before I finally washed my hands of her. She never came looking for me to tell me she – *we* - had a daughter. My work changed, I was soon a Detective Sergeant, met my wife. Was married, with our first girl on the way."

He shook his head, as if trying to rid it of a bitter memory.

"For the next fifteen or sixteen years, I was building my career, enjoying my family life. I had no idea there was another girl out there with my blood in her veins. No idea that Suzy's life was in freefall. That she was getting deeper and deeper into drugs, and more and more willing to take risks. In time, she took risks with Demi as well as with her own life. If only I'd known..."

"How could you?" Archer said softly, and Baines agreed. Shit happened. Coppers tried to help people and, just occasionally, they got too involved and crossed a line. Gillingham was hardly to blame for Demi's murder. But what had happened next?

"So anyway," Gillingham continued, "ten, eleven years ago, we get this dead girl – no more than a kid. I was a DI in Reading by then. Well, it upset me, such a young life wasted, but imagine my shock when I realised that Suzy was her mother. Well, something made me do the maths, and the timing... I asked her outright if she was mine. Suzy said she was, but that she'd never told anyone and never would. She said it was the one decent thing she'd managed to do – keep me out of the mess that was her life.

"I couldn't take it in. I felt so guilty, not being there for Demi. I loathed Suzy for what she'd done to our daughter, too. I swore to myself that at least I'd find out who her killer was, if it was the last thing I did."

"So Suzy never told anyone else who Demi's dad was." Baines found himself speaking again, recapping. "Did you?"

Gillingham looked as though he was weighing up his answer. Then he shrugged. "One other person, but I'll come to that."

"It was a conflict of interest, though," said Archer. "You were her biological father and yet you were investigating her murder."

"Who could I tell, Lizzie? The job? What would they have made of that? They'd have done more than take me off the case."

"You don't know that."

"No, I don't. But my immediate reaction was that my behaviour in getting that involved with her wouldn't go down well. And I couldn't see how I could tell the job and my wife, my family, not know. I just felt it was just too sordid for me to make it part of their lives. I wasn't the man my wife thought she'd married, and how do you tell two kids they have an older sister who was on the game and was murdered?"

Baines and Archer let the silence play out.

"No," Gillingham continued. "I decided to keep that to myself. But I still felt a responsibility for the daughter I'd never known. I wanted her killer brought to justice. So I worked on Suzy. Finally got her to tell me who Demi had been with, the night she died. What Suzy's pimp didn't know, because Suzy had been getting paid extra and was keeping the cash from him, was that this particular client had violent tastes."

"Let me guess," Archer said. "He paid extra because he liked the rough stuff, and because discretion was important to him."

"Something like that."

"Tim Phillips?"

"Yes. Obviously. At first, Suzy said she'd deny it all if I tried to get her to make a witness statement. No way was she going to be the woman who'd delivered her daughter into the hands of a man who got his rocks off throttling women."

"She was worried about her reputation?" The irony staggered Baines.

Archer was looking at him with a mixture of pity and disgust. "So... what then? You just decided to take the law into your own hands?"

"No." He was suddenly vehement. "No, of course not. I kept working on her and she finally agreed to come down the station the next day and make a final statement."

"So did you question Phillips?" Baines wanted to know.

"Not immediately, no. I spoke to my DCI, and he didn't like it. On the one hand we had a popular local entrepreneur and philanthropist, a buddy of some of the top brass. On the other, the uncorroborated word of a drug-addicted whore. Plus, if we even attempted to smear Phillips's reputation, he had access to lawyers who'd turn us inside out and back again."

"So what happened?"

"I kept pushing. In the end, the DCI and the Super agreed that, if Suzy made a formal statement as she'd promised, we'd quietly bring Phillips in for questioning on suspicion of Demi's murder. My mistake was in giving her until the morning. She asked for a night's sleep and to compose herself. But overnight, everything changed. Suzy killed herself and Tim Phillips went missing."

"Say we believe you," Archer said. "What did you think had happened to him?"

"We've gone through this. We thought maybe he'd done a runner over money troubles, or gone off with a woman. Had an accident. Been murdered, which turns out to be the case." A shadow passed over his face. "But Demi's a red herring. Phillips must have had enemies…"

"We can't find any. And didn't it cross your mind that maybe someone had tipped him off that he was under suspicion of murder, and he fled?"

"Of course. But only Suzy, me, Steve Ashby, the DCI and the Super knew. We didn't tell the Deputy Chief Constable, another big buddy of Tim's, not initially. And, even if his other mate, the DCI, had warned him, once Suzy was dead we had no statement and no one to corroborate her story. He could have just come back. His lawyers would have driven a coach and horses through our case."

"But surely," Baines said, "you'd have put out that he was wanted by the police."

"No. Once he disappeared, well then the DCC *was* told what I suspected. He was furious. Having none of it. He decreed that nothing more was said on the matter unless and until Tim was found. Something about not blackening a good man's name when he couldn't answer back."

"I'm not sure I'm buying it," Archer said. "Everyone was telling you the case against Tim wouldn't stand up, even with

Suzy's statement. Yes, you'd got agreement to him being questioned, but with kid gloves. I'm betting you knew there and then it wouldn't even get to court."

A shadow passed over his face. "What are you saying?"

Archer threw up her hands. "Paul. Enough. You had motive – the daughter you never knew you had - murdered. And a killer you thought would get off scot free. You had means –"

"Anyone can have a man beaten to death."

"Yes. But it occurs to me that cops investigating those building site thefts might well have sussed out who could provide access to a suitable site for the right price. Maybe Eric Yelland after all, maybe someone else. And let him off in exchange for doing them a favour and then not committing that crime again."

Baines realised she was dead right. It had been under their noses all along

"No," Gillingham protested. "Steve Ashby was leading for us on that. He'd have know who was who."

"Oh, come on, Sir." Baines could restrain himself no longer. "You and Steve were as thick as thieves. So did he aid and abet you?"

"Did you contact Phillips?" Archer pressed. "Tell him you knew what he'd done, insist on him meeting you? Maybe hinted you were bribable. He sounds like he thought money could solve any problem."

"Were you and Steve waiting for him?" Added Baines. "Maybe you only intended to rough him up, but it got out of hand."

"No," Archer said. "They wouldn't want him testifying against them."

The DCI was paler than ever now. There were beads of sweat on his top lip. He seemed to have run out of bluster. Out of excuses?

"Shall I read you your rights, Sir?" Archer pressed. "Make it all formal? And then I'll need to bring DCI Lambert in on it."

"I didn't kill him," Gillingham said. "I swear. But I'll tell you what happened the night he disappeared. The night he died."

"All right, then, Paul, I'll bite." Archer sounded singularly unimpressed. "But you'd better start telling the truth."

Gillingham stared at his desk top. The tension in the room was palpable. When he raised his gaze again, some of the strain seemed to have gone out of him.

"All right," he said. "All right. I've carried this around way too long anyway. It'll maybe take some weight off my soul. But I didn't kill Tim Phillips, I promise you that."

"So you say," Archer said. "With respect, Sir, this had better be good."

55

Eleven years earlier.

"Close the door," Gillingham says as DS Ashby enters his office.

His friend does as he's told and sits down opposite them.

"You told the boss what Suzy told you?"

"Not everything," Gillingham tells him. *"You know what I decided. For now, you and I are still the only ones who know Demi was my daughter, and I'd prefer to keep it that way, if I can."*

"But you told them what she said about Phillips?"

"I did. It wasn't easy, but in the end I got them to agree to questioning him. Provided we've got that statement of Suzy's."

Ashby frowns. "You don't think she'll renege on that?"

"If I have to, I'll bring Suzy in here and drag it out of her. Even then, it might come to nothing. They'll question him all right, but they want it softly, softly. They won't hear of any accusations against Tim bloody Phillips. I mean, I know he's Jesus Christ around here, and I knew he has powerful friends, but for God's sake."

Ashby gapes at him. "You don't think he'll be charged?"

"It wouldn't surprise me." He shakes his head. "What can I do? I know it was Phillips who killed her. But his pals could ruin my career if I push it, and I've got my family to consider."

Ashby looks as mad as Gillingham feels. He has no children of his own, but Demi's murder has angered him almost as much as it had Gillingham, even before he knew the truth about the girl's parentage.

"So we let it go?" His tone is bitter.

"Let's see how it plays out. But you know what? I've a good mind to get Phillips in that alley where Demi's body was

dumped, confront him with it, and look into his eyes. See if he can deny it."

Ashby blinks. "If you're serious, I'm with you. We could use a call box. That way, if he tried to make a complaint, the call couldn't be traced back."

Gillingham shrugs. "Even if he came, most likely he'd just laugh in our faces."

"He might. And then again he might tell the truth. If we're really lucky, maybe his conscience will prick him and he'll come to the station and confess. If Phillips is – apart from a sexual kink that went wrong this time – as decent a man as he's made out to be, then maybe he's carrying a mountain of guilt around with him. Just maybe, if he confesses to us, he will be prepared to face the music after all."

"It's a nice idea, Steve. But let's do it by the book. Suzy's statement, then we can bring him in."

Before Ashby can answer, there is a discreet tap at the door and DS Andrea Lambert walks in without waiting for an answer – something that never fails to irritate Gillingham.

"Can it wait, Andie?"

"Sorry, Paul, no. The DCI and the Super want to see you and Steve right away."

Gillingham sighs. "Come on then, Steve. Hopefully, it won't take too long."

56

"And...?" Archer pressed. "So you're saying you considered confronting Phillips, but you didn't?"

"Exactly." Gillingham said. "It was only probably a pipe dream – at least, it was for me. I don't know. Perhaps we'd have worked ourselves up into doing something silly. But then we were summoned to see the DCI and the Super, and they made it crystal clear we were to go easy on Phillips, and that they didn't think we had much of a case, even with Suzy's statement. Circumstantial evidence, a dubious witnesses versus against a good man, blah blah. Really heavy stuff, and they went on and on. It turned my stomach. By the time we got out of there, I was pretty dispirited and we were both ready to go home. Or, at least, I thought we both were."

"And that was that?"

"Pretty much, as far as I knew then."

"And you're sure you didn't contact Phillips?" Archer demanded. "Maybe he agreed to meet you. You confronted him as you'd discussed, things got out of hand..."

"No."

"What about Ashby? Didn't he ever wonder if you'd met Phillips after all?"

He half-smiled as he shook his head. "You know, he never mentioned it. We never, ever spoke of it again. Sometimes I wondered if he did suspect me, and would just as soon not ask me the direct question. But sometimes I wondered if maybe he'd contacted Phillips himself."

"If Ashby had?"

"As I've said, he was almost as passionate about Demi's murder as I was. That first day after Suzy died and Phillips went missing, I can't deny I half-wondered if Steve had actually carried out our crazy plan, lost control and wound up killing the man."

Archer and Baines exchanged a glance.

"You thought it was Ashby?" Baines was first to speak.

"Honestly? I've thought about it over the years. Not for sure, no. But definitely maybe. It would explain why the body had to be got rid of. The alley where Demi was dumped... our suspicion that Phillips killed her... plus, even if he'd just been dumped elsewhere, we know how good the forensics guys are. Even without any physical evidence, once they started looking for a motive, they might wonder, just like you did, who might seek revenge for Demi. Sooner or later, they might have tested her DNA for familial connections, and found me on their database."

"But that would incriminate you, not Ashby," Baines observed.

"Yes, and he wouldn't want that to happen to me." There it was again: that bond between the two men. "Better that the body was never found. And better for Steve and me that we never mentioned that conversation, not even to each other. It was like an unspoken pact. And with Phillips simply disappeared, there were a host of other, more likely explanations as to what might have become of him."

"But including the strong possibility that he'd been murdered," Archer pointed out.

"Yes, but why suspect a hard-working police officer? The fact that we suspected him of Demi's murder wasn't the same as either of us having killed him."

"It's a good story, Paul," Archer said. "But why should we believe a word of it?"

"Why?" he echoed. "Because it's the truth. Or, at least, *I* didn't kill Phillips. As I said, it was Steve who was investigating the building site thefts. Say, just hypothetically, he did confront Phillips, lost his cool, and he had the idea of burying the body under a building that was going up. Like you suggested, he could have had a suspect for those thefts and agreed to drop the case against him in return for a favour and him keeping a clean nose thereafter. But there's something else you should know."

"Which is?"

"Just this. Whoever buried Tim Phillips would have known how to mix concrete, and make a good enough job of the burial that no one would notice the disturbance."

She closed her eyes. "Possibly." Opened them again. "And your point is?"

"Steve and his wife had extended their house a year or so before. Ashby put some time in at weekends labouring for the builder, to save money. Even learned about bricklaying. And mixing concrete."

The tide of the conversation was turning.

"So all of a sudden, you're shifting the blame onto Steve? Okay, I get that he might have been aggrieved about the injustice of it all. But that's not a motive for a copper to kill, or we'd all be serial killers. Whereas you were the dead girl's father."

"True. He could have done it for me, though. Because he owed me one."

She sat up straight. "You know, I've always wondered. What did he owe you, Paul? And what did you think you owed him?"

"Ask him. That's all I'm saying on the subject. Except this." He also sat up straighter, mirroring Archer's stance. "I did go to that alley, the day Tim was reported missing. No sign of him, Lizzie, but there was blood. Quite a bit of it."

* * *

Even though Archer didn't want to subject Gillingham to the indignity of the cells at this stage in proceedings, she made Baines stay with him while she went to see Ashby, to ensure that the DCI didn't contact him.

"Well," he said, looking up from his phone, "this is an unexpected honour."

"I'm afraid you won't be quite so pleased to see me in a moment," she said.

His smile was puzzled, his tone light. "Oh? Why's that, then?"

She folded her arms. "Let's just say I've been having an interesting conversation with the boss. About Demi Reeves, Tim Phillips, and a meeting in an alleyway in Reading."

"All right," he said. It was an attempt at casual, but he couldn't quite prevent the fear flashing across his eyes.

"I need to interview you under caution, Steve," she told him. "I just did the same with Paul. I hope you're not going to give me any more trouble than he did."

He folded his own arms, mirroring her. "What the fuck are you talking about?"

"I think you know. I've heard the boss's side of the story. Now I'd like to hear yours, before I take it any further."

"What story? I have no idea what you're on about. Is this a windup?"

"I'll tell you after I've cautioned you."

"And what are you going to do if I refuse to be cautioned? Arrest me?"

"That's exactly what I'm going to do, if I have to."

"I'd like to see you try."

"Trust me," she said. "You wouldn't."

"I'm going to see Paul." He stood up.

"Sorry, Steve. I can't allow you two to communicate."

His jaw jutted. "Won't allow?" His voice rose an octave. "Who do you think you are?"

She sighed, wearied by the stress this situation was placing upon her. When she'd got up this morning, she'd had no idea that she would be interviewing two colleagues on suspicion of murder.

"I'm the person who's giving you a chance to explain something that's troubling to me before I take it any further up the chain of command. I'd rather look stupid to you than to Superintendent Lambert, but I'll take that risk if I have to. Your choice."

He stuck his hands in his pockets. "All right. You want to do it here?"

"Interview Room Three is free. It's the nicest."

304

"You being funny?"

"Never so serious. I'll ask Dan to join us."

His eyes widened. "I don't think so. He's junior to me."

"Look," she said, "so far only Dan and I know any of this. I can find Lara Moseley, or take the whole mess to the Super now. Or we can do it my way."

He stood up. "All right," he said again. "So caution me."

She did so. He still looked angry, but she suspected a lot of that anger was bravado.

They walked to the interview room together in awkward silence. Archer was thinking of Amy Petrescu, and what she'd feel about this. Even if Archer concluded he was innocent, she would be devastated that the man she cared for had been treated like a suspect. Would she close ranks with him? Or would she always wonder what the truth was?

Or had he already confided in her?

For herself, Archer knew she was taking an enormous risk. She was just about doing this by the book, but if Gillingham retracted his words and Ashby dismissed the whole thing as fantasy – and then they both complained – what impact would that have on her own future prospects? Cops who grassed up other cops to Professional Standards were rarely popular. This could be much worse, for Baines as well as herself. She would take full responsibility, but she knew mud would stick to him too.

"I'm going to need your phone," she told Ashby inside the room.

"What if I want to call my solicitor?"

"Do you?"

"No. Let's just get on with it." He handed the phone over.

Archer bagged it and then stepped outside and used her own phone to call Baines. "Interview Room Three. Has Gillingham said anything else?"

"Barely a word."

"Is he safe to be left alone?" If Gillingham took it into his head to hang himself with his tie…

"You mean…" He evidently read her thoughts. "I'm sure it'll be fine. He seems calm enough."

"Come down then."

Minutes later they were seated across the table from Ashby.

"This had better be good," he told them.

"Thanks for agreeing to have a chat with us," Archer said, without a trace of irony. "I want to ask you about the night Tim Phillips disappeared – the night he died, as it turned out. Do you need reminding of the date?"

Ashby shrugged. "Let's say I do."

She duly obliged. "Do you recall a conversation with the then DI, Gillingham, about the Demi Reeves case? Specifically one in which he expressed suspicions against Mr Phillips?"

"It was a long time ago."

"Which doesn't answer my question. Did you discuss such suspicions?"

"I really don't remember."

"Really? The murder case you're both supposed to still be bitter about, and a suspect who was about to disappear off the face of the earth, prompting a major search, and you remember nothing?"

He shrugged. "Maybe be did mention it."

Archer nodded. "Maybe he did. All right. Had Paul Gillingham voiced those suspicions elsewhere?"

"He might have."

She stood up. "You know he did, Steve. If you're going to waste my time, I'll terminate this interview and kick it upstairs now."

"Maybe you should."

"Maybe I will. Interview suspended. Come on, DS Baines."

Baines started to rise.

"All right," Ashby said. "All right, stop. Sit down. Please."

They sat.

"Yes, all right. Paul suspected Phillips. Demi's mother, Suzy Reeves, had fingered him as the last client to be with Demi, and she also said he enjoyed throttling women during sex."

"So why hadn't she come forward? Why hadn't she told the police?"

"She told Paul."

"So was she willing to make a statement?"

"Apparently she said she would. But then she killed herself instead."

"You say she told DCI Gillingham. Why him?"

Ashby just looked at her. "He was the investigating officer."

"Would it help if I told you we also have DNA evidence indicating the identity of Demi's father? And that the father has confirmed it?" She took a sip of water from the glass in front of her. "Does that help explain why she confided in DCI Gillingham?"

He sighed. "You obviously already know. She confided in Paul because he's the father. He had no idea until he started investigating Demi's death."

"So what was DCI Gillingham going to do about it?"

"We were going to arrest Phillips as soon as we had Suzy's statement."

"But DCI Gillingham thought Phillips's friends in the chain of command were keen to make it all go away, is that right?"

Ashby made a face, as if a bad smell had wafted into the room. "Put it this way. We had a Super who was mates with Phillips, or at least thought he was. A DCI who was a brown noser and knew the Deputy Chief Constable was a bosom buddy of Phillips. And, by all accounts, they were rubbishing Suzy Reeves' credibility before she even made the statement."

"You must both have been outraged. Enough to take matters into your own hands?"

"What's Paul been saying?"

"Just answer the question, please."

"All right. You obviously know the answer again. Yes, he talked about getting Phillips into the alley where Demi was found and confronting him to see how he reacted. And, just for a moment, I was up for it. But it never happened. The DCI and the Super called us in to make sure we understood that Phillips was to be cut a lot of slack. It was pretty disgusting."

"So what happened next?"

He shrugged. "Paul said he had a few things to finish up, but told me to go home."

"And did you? Remember, we've already got a version of the story from the boss. We want to hear your story."

307

A shifty look flashed across his face and was gone again, but not so quickly that Archer missed it. "What's he been saying?" he asked again.

"You know better than that. We want to hear your version of events." She could see that all the swagger had gone out of him. Whatever the truth was, he was almost ready to face up to it. All he needed was a little push.

"Come on, Steve," she coaxed. "Whatever happened that night, you and the boss have been carrying this about for over a decade. It's time it was all out in the open, whatever the consequences."

It was classic interrogation procedure when you had two suspects. Hint that the other one was saying things that would damage the one being interviewed, unless they told their own truth.

He bit at a hangnail. He wouldn't look at either of them.

"One way or the other, I'll have the truth," Archer said, more softly. "That night. You didn't go home and stay there, did you?"

He looked at her then, and tears were in his eyes, something she'd never, ever expected to see.

"You've got it wrong," he said. "I did go home."

"You didn't lure Phillips to the alley?"

"No. But I did go there the next day."

57

"Why?" Baines asked. "Why go to the alley only after Phillips was reported missing? I'm guessing that was the order of events?"

"Yes. I got to thinking maybe Paul had done something stupid. Carried out his plan and..." He shook his head. "Honestly? I'm not sure what was in my mind, but I decided to take a drive there and see for myself."

"And?"

"And nothing. At least, that's what I thought at first. But, I don't know, I walked right into the alley, back to the far wall, where they could have talked without anyone seeing them. Not that many people would have come by there of an evening, it wasn't that sort of place."

He licked his lips. Took a sip of water. "There's usually a bit of traffic noise during the day, but it was pretty quiet that morning. I remember I could hear my footsteps echoing as I walked back there. It was somehow eerie. I don't really know what made me walk all the way back there. I should have just walked away when I saw Phillips wasn't there. I wish to God I had. But maybe I had an inkling of what I was going to find."

"And what did you find?" Archer prompted.

"I could see what I was pretty sure was blood on the wall and on the ground. Not buckets of it, but enough to know someone had been badly hurt. I suppose I thought it could have been two drunks mixing it, or a smack deal gone wrong. But I didn't take those ideas seriously. Not with Phillips missing." He grimaced. "I didn't know what to do. I didn't know what Paul might have done. But I thought phoning him, before I knew the answers to those questions, was an incredibly bad idea that could come back and bite us both. In the end, I decided all I could really do for now was keep shtum and see what happened. I won't deny I was scared about how bad it could be."

"So what did you say to the boss?"

"Nothing at all. I waited for him to say something to me. When he didn't I thought the less I knew, the better. So, presumably, did he. And we never did talk about it. Ever. Oh, we joined the search for Phillips, and we also made a show of keeping the Demi Reeves case alive. But that was all it felt like – a show."

"Because you thought Phillips had killed Demi and DCI Gillingham had killed him?"

"I didn't want to think anything at all. When Paul moved over here, and asked me to come soon afterwards to fill a vacancy, I was never sure whether it was as a friend, or to keep an eye on me."

"Why did you keep quiet, Steve?" Baines asked. "Why would you make yourself complicit in a thing like that?"

"We were friends."

"It was a bit more than that, wasn't it, though? He said you owed him. Said to ask you what about."

"He said that?" He sipped some more water. "You asked me if I'd lured Tim Phillips to the alley and wound up killing him. Has Paul actually said he thinks that's what happened?"

Baines glanced at Archer. She was just looking at the other DI, her arms folded, her face unreadable. Baines hoped he was being similarly inscrutable, although he knew she was better at it than he was.

Ashby laughed. The sound was somewhere between a laugh and a cough. "Of course, you're not saying, and that speaks volumes. Or does it? I know all the tricks as well as you do."

He sighed and shrugged. "You asked what I owed him for. Fair enough. Back then, we worked closely together. We found ourselves in some tricky situations, like coppers sometimes do, but we always had each other's backs. Literally, on one occasion. We were back to back, fighting off half a dozen thugs until the cavalry arrived."

"And that formed a close bond between you?"

"That's only part of it." He looked her in the eye. "I owe Paul Gillingham my life."

"What happened?" Baines asked.

"It was about a year before this Demi and Phillips stuff all kicked off. We went round to a crackhead's home to ask him a few questions. There was no answer, but the door was unlocked. We took it as an open invitation to see what evidence might be lying in plain sight. Once inside, we split up. Paul took the upstairs, I took the downstairs.

"So I go into the kitchen, and there's the crackhead, pointing a gun and screaming his head off. He orders me to move to the side, and I do it, because you don't argue. But he didn't move. Just pointed that gun right at my head, and there was something in his eyes, like he was working himself up to something. I really thought he was going to pull the trigger."

Baines remembered being in a similar position. He remembered the tightness in his guts, and the tumble of thoughts that had gone through his mind.

"Then Paul comes out of nowhere and just rushes him. The guy turns towards him, still pointing the gun. It all slows down. And then Paul jumps him. The gun goes off, firing into the ceiling, and then Paul's got it off him, I wade in and we get the bastard cuffed." There was an emotion in Ashby's voice that Baines had never heard before. "I asked him why he's taken the risk – him, with a wife he doted on and two daughters – and he just said he had to."

And there it was. On one level, just something cops did all the time. On another level, a sense of deep personal debt.

He shrugged. "So, when Phillips disappeared, and I wondered if he'd done it, I just let it go. But it was like I was carrying this huge weight around. The guilt was massive. I changed. Lost my way, I guess." He shook his head. "I can't believe he's accused me to save himself now."

Archer nodded towards the door. "Dan?"

He followed her outside and she leaned against the wall, arms folded again. She looked grey with stress.

"Well, this is a bloody mess," she said. "What do you make of it?"

He tried to arrange his thoughts. "One of them is lying. Or they both are. Or neither of them are."

"The last of those seems improbable," she said. "Unless the blood they both say they saw was someone else's. You know what seems most likely to me?"

He nodded, knowing the answer. "They killed Phillips together, and now they're blaming each other so we don't know who to accuse."

"Ashby seemed genuinely rattled though."

"And upset. He's either a better actor than I'd have given him credit for, or he really does fear that the boss is setting him up."

A couple of uniforms approached. They fell silent until they had passed, muttering polite greetings.

"Lock him in," she decided. "Then we go back to Gillingham."

The DCI was in his office, assuring them he hadn't moved and complaining that he needed a pee. Baines accompanied him. Back behind his desk, he regarded them curiously.

"So what's the decision? Am I under arrest? Is Steve?"

Archer sat opposite him, drumming her fingers on his desk.

"I've asked you more than once in the past why you cut Steve so much slack," she said. "You once accused me of insubordination. But you do go easy on him. We both know it's true."

"So what did he tell you?"

"He says you once risked taking a bullet for him. That that's what he owed you for. The question is, would he repay you by confronting and killing the murderer of your recently discovered daughter? Or covering up the fact that you did it?"

"I see." He looked wounded. Or cornered. "No prizes for guessing which version he gave you. Look, cards on the table. If it had come out that I'd had an affair with a young prostitute and fathered a child, it would have been awkward, with the job, and with my family. He was the one person I'd trusted with that information. Afterwards, I suspected that the debt he thought he'd owed me made him angrier on my behalf that he should have been. So, when I saw the blood in the very alley where we'd discussed confronting Phillips…"

"You believed he'd killed him for you?"

"Yes. In my heart, I knew Phillips was dead, that Steve was responsible, and that he'd done whatever he'd done out of misplaced loyalty to me."

"And that loyalty bought your silence?"

"And more. His life and career started to crumble afterwards. People thought he'd got too close to the Demi case, but they had no idea *how* close. And then, when I took the job here, and a DI opening came up, I thought I'd bring him across, where I could shield him a bit. He took advantage, no doubt about that, and I let him."

"But there's another scenario, isn't there?" Archer said. "One where Ashby goes to the alley, as you claim you did, sees the blood, assumes you were the murderer, and *that*'s where the misplaced loyalty comes in."

"He said that?"

"And if he did? Is that what really happened?"

"How many more times? I went home. But I doubt my wife can honestly confirm I was in that night, not after all these years. Why would she remember?" He made a sour face. "All these years, and we've never once discussed this. Now he's trying to pin it on me."

Whatever else came out of today, it was doubtful Gillingham's and Ashby's relationship would ever be the same.

Archer puffed out her cheeks. "All right. Dan and I need to confer for a bit. You stay here."

"How long?"

"Until I say otherwise," she snapped. "You're in deep shit, Paul. You and Steve both. Now we have to decide where we go from here."

58

Archer knew she was going out on a huge limb. She couldn't see how Ashby could simply walk away from this, not with what he'd told them, even if keeping quiet about a possible murder scene was all he'd done. A sin of omission, but the blood was evidence. And, if Gillingham was telling the truth, the same applied to him. Plus he should have come clean about his relationship to Demi Reeves. At the very least, there must be disciplinary issues for both of them, maybe even gross misconduct.

She should take it to Lambert now. The longer she delayed, the more she – and Baines – became complicit. Yet it didn't sit right with her. And she didn't know why.

Sure, people who snitched on colleagues weren't always popular, but it wasn't as if this was a trivial matter. Either Ashby nor Gillingham had killed Phillips. She couldn't see any way around that.

So why was she hesitating?

She knew why. The jigsaw was still incomplete at best. She doubted there was enough hard evidence to make a case for murder against either of them, if they stuck to their stories. She needed more.

Yet there was something else. Both men had come at least fairly clean about the conversation they had the night Phillips had disappeared, and their visit to the alley the next morning. What would she have if they hadn't? The DNA proof that Gillingham had been Demi's father, and nothing else.

The DCI had had a long time to think what he'd say if the truth about Demi's parenthood ever did come out. He could have simply feigned surprise when confronted and then made up some yarn or other about Suzy having never told him. But he hadn't. It was as if he – and Ashby – had needed to finally get it out in the open. Maybe they really had been waiting all these years to cleanse their consciences.

Or one of them had.

"One more go at Ashby," she said to Baines. "I suspect we've got about as much out of Gillingham as we're likely to. But Ashby's story is Gillingham saved his life, and he gave him loyalty in return. If he really thinks Gillingham's dropping him in the shit, and if he's got any more to give us…"

"Come on, then," Baines said.

"This is it, though," Archer said. "After this, I'm going to Lambert."

Ashby looked subdued when they returned to the interview room.

"All right," Archer said. "Let's say we understand why the boss has let you take the piss all this time. But he's still adamant that he went straight home the night Phillips died. That his wife will back him up." The lie rolled off her tongue. "That makes your story sound like crap, Steve. Why not go the last few yards and tell us what really happened?"

He stared at the table. "You've never liked me, have you? I thought things had changed, but they really haven't, have they? When it comes down to it, you're ready to think me capable of murder."

He looked up. Looked at Baines. "And you, Dan. Amy told me about your fling. Jealous, are you? Think I'm not good enough for her?" He drew his palms across his face. "She's about all I've got in this world that'll stand by my side. Even Paul…" He brought his fist down on the desk. "Fuck it. You want some evidence? You can have some. But we need to go to my flat. You can cuff me, if you like."

It was tempting. Tempting to throw Gillingham in a cell whilst they went to Ashby's home, too, but things had progressed this far. Somehow, however things turned out, Archer couldn't see Gillingham or Ashby going on the run.

"That won't be necessary," she said. "But we need the whole truth now, Steve. It's time."

* * *

The tension in the mortuary was palpable. Baines could feel the fluttering in his stomach as he obeyed Archer's instructions and, with latex-gloved hands, removed the item he had brought from Ashby's flat from the black bin liner in which the DI had kept it in his loft, and handed it over to Phil Gordon.

It was still wrapped in cling film, but it was clear enough what it was.

Gordon took it from him. Raised an eyebrow. "Where did you get this?"

"One thing at a time," Archer said. "Let's just say it's delicate."

"I'd have to do some measurements," Barbara Carlisle said, "but it looks like it could well have made those indentations in Tim Phillips's skull."

"Phil, I'd like you to get the blood on it tested," Archer said. "I'm as confident as I can be that it'll be Tim's. Apparently there's some bloody fingerprints, too. How soon can you check them against the database?"

"An hour tops. Hopefully less. But whose prints do you think they are?"

"Let's see."

The crime scene manager looked at the so-called evidence in his hands. "This is all feeling more than a little off the books. I hope you two know what you're doing."

"So do I," Archer admitted. "But don't worry. If it all comes back to bite me, I take full responsibility. Call me as soon as you've any information – both of you."

Archer was quiet on the way back to the car. Once inside, she asked Baines to wait before he started the engine.

"You can still step away from this, Dan," she said. "This can turn nasty in more ways than you can imagine."

He laughed. "I'm imagining it already. What do you think I'm going to do? Say I was only obeying orders? One thing Gillingham has said in this sorry day... about him and Ashby having each other's backs. That's you and me, Lizzie. Besides," he added with a certainty he didn't know if he should feel, "it's not going to turn nasty. Not for us, at least. I mean, Ashby has kept that evidence close to him for all that time. I still don't know if I buy that it was all about protecting Gillingham. An insurance policy, more like. That, if this day ever came, he wouldn't be the one taking the fall."

"You don't think Ashby might have fabricated the evidence?"

"Do you?"

"No. He could – should have turned it in then, but he chose to conceal it. He's always thought Gillingham killed Tim, but his loyalty came first. Part of me admires him for that. But he's in serious trouble now, whatever else happens."

"We could have taken what he gave us straight to the Super," he said, not for the first time.

"I know." She sounded exhausted and miserable. "But I want it checked out first, to be sure. For the same reason, I'm not telling Gillingham about it yet. He can stew."

"Like we are," he observed.

"Yeah," she agreed. "Just like we are."

* * *

Archer had decided to talk to Gillingham alone. Meanwhile, something had been nagging her and she'd asked Baines to make some calls. She doubted they would add a single piece to the complicated jigsaw they'd been wrestling, but she wanted to be sure.

"I'm sorry, Paul," she told Gillingham now, seated across his desk from him. "I really am. We've interviewed Steve Ashby on the same basis as we spoke to you, and I can't see anything for it. I've got to tell the Super."

He sighed. "Of course you have. I knew you would. I don't suppose you'd tell me what Steve said."

"You know I can't."

"No." He looked thoroughly miserable. "I guess not. I wish now I'd had the guts to tell my wife at the outset. About Demi, I mean." He looked at her hopefully. "But I promise you I didn't kill anyone. Do you believe me?"

She waggled her hand from side to side. "I really want to. But it's looking as if Philips was definitely killed in that alley, and now I have a piece of evidence that will point pretty strongly to the killer. I'll know pretty soon who that person is."

"What evidence? It can't point to me, because *I wasn't there!*"

The triumph in his tone took her aback. She'd imagined him hoping the incriminating material was never going to surface, and being devastated by the realization that it had done so. It was as if he now thought that evidence would exonerate, rather than damn him.

"I've already told you more than I probably should have."

"From Steve?" Some of his confidence seemed to drain away. "Don't tell me he's managed to fabricate something that incriminates me?" He sounded massively hurt and disappointed. Betrayed.

"'Like I said, I can't say. I'm afraid it's a waiting game."

"I can wait," he said. "I'm fascinated to know what this so-called evidence is."

"We'll talk again when I know more," she said, rising.

"One thing's for sure," he said. "Someone was with Phillips that night, in the very alley where we'd discussed confronting Phillips, and they wound up killing him. We coppers don't trust coincidence, so it had to be me or Steve. And it wasn't me. This so-called evidence? I can only think Steve must have somehow fabricated it." The pain in his eyes was palpable. "In case he needed someone else to blame some day."

She thought about the work Phil Gordon and Barbara Carlisle were doing. If they had Gillingham's prints, on Tim Phillips's blood on a murder weapon, that would be some fabrication. She couldn't see how it could be done. Was Gillingham in denial? Grasping at straws?

The persistent itch that told her they were still missing some vital puzzle pieces returned to trouble her.

Her phone rang and she answered without checking the display, still distracted.

It was a call that changed everything.

59

"I've been looking for you," Andrea Lambert said when Archer finally looked in. "What's going on? Paul Gillingham's door's locked, and there's no sign of him, Steve Ashby, or, until now, you. I thought you were all down the pub or something."

"Sorry," Archer said. "Something came up."

"Something new?"

"The Phillips case."

"Really?" She looked annoyed. "Oh, for pity's sake, Lizzie. This whole thing has Reading written all over it. All we've got our end is a body dump. I agree with your DCI on this one." She sighed. "I've told you. I like to see a woman get on in this job. Don't make me change my mind about you."

"I'm sorry," Archer said again.

"Sort it out. That's your priority. Dump that case back where it belongs. Now, was there anything else?"

"Can I come in?"

The Superintendent looked at her watch. "Not too long, though. I've got another function lined up tonight." She jabbed her thumb in the direction of a red dress hanging behind the door. "And I've got a lot to get through before I leave. You've got all this to look forward to when you make Super."

Archer wasn't at all sure she'd still be a DI when this meeting was over, but she had to play it out now. "Can I sit down?"

Lambert gestured at a chair.

"You know, it's funny, Ma'am," Archer said as she sat down.

"*Andie.*"

"Andie. I almost wish I'd listened to you and DCI Gillingham now. But I kept digging, and now I've got a mess on my hands."

"Go on."

"I couldn't let go of the notion that Tim Phillips was Demi Reeves's killer."

"What?" Lambert looked really annoyed now. "Paul told me about that madcap idea. He specifically ordered you to leave that alone, and quite right too. Why have you continued to waste time on it?"

"I'm afraid I spent more than just time. I spent resources, too."

"What do you mean, spent resources?"

So Archer told her. When she'd finished speaking, Lambert blew out a long breath. "My God. If even half of what you say is true, we need to charge the pair of them with Tim Phillips's murder right away. Get their statements on the record. You should have done it already. They've had time to think. Once they get lawyered up, they'll deny everything, go no comment…"

"I never said the conversations were off the record, Ma'am. And I don't believe they'll retract those statements. Besides, DS Baines sat in with me most of the time. He'll corroborate what was said."

"Yes? Well, that's something. I just hope you're right. If you are, DCI Gillingham's office is all yours. Good work."

"Yes, well. It's not the way I want to make DCI."

"I understand. But we good coppers have to root out the rotten ones, or how can the public have faith in us?"

"You're right, of course."

"What I still don't get, though, is this: you say you interviewed them a couple of hours ago. What have you been doing all this time?"

"Oh, I decided there was just a little more digging I needed to do. You see, at first, I thought they were in it together, deliberately blaming one another in the hope we couldn't make a strong enough case against either. But then Ashby became convinced that Gillingham was stitching him up, and he produced a piece of evidence he claimed to have recovered from the alley where we believe Phillips was killed."

"Evidence?" Lambert's hand strayed to the epaulette on her left shoulder, running her fingers over her Superintendent's crown. "Like an insurance policy?"

"Something like that. He guessed it would incriminate Gillingham. He took it away to protect the boss, but something made him keep it, just in case he ever needed to prove someone else was the killer, and not him."

Lambert's mouth curved upwards, but the smile was nowhere near her eyes. "So we've got Gillingham? Is that what you're saying?"

"We've certainly got the killer." Archer smiled back, even though she felt sick inside. "But you haven't asked me what the evidence is."

"No," Lambert concurred, "but you're about to tell me. Well, don't keep me in suspense."

"Maybe you've already guessed? Or rather, you *know*."

"How on earth could I… what are you playing at, Lizzie?" It sounded like irritation, but there was something else.

"A collapsible police baton. But you already knew that, didn't you?"

Lambert looked her straight in the eye. If she was lying, she was very good at it. "How could I?"

Archer made her tone hard. "Of course, we're waiting for the DNA tests on the blood and hair on it to come back, but the fingerprints on the handle were easy enough to match. Pretty well all coppers' prints are on the national database, as you know. Phil Gordon could have given me the results even more quickly, but he was so worried that he checked and double-checked. Even then, he was reluctant to tell me."

Lambert checked her watch. "I don't know what yarn you're spinning, but I need to be elsewhere." She stood up.

"Sit down, Andie," Archer said sharply. "Please."

The other woman's eyes widened, but she remained on her feet. "You dare use that tone –"

"You told me a few days ago," Archer interrupted her, "what a useful skill it is to listen at doors. Ears like a bat, you said you had."

"So?"

"You were talking about that boys' club thing Paul and Steve had when you all worked together in Reading. How they didn't keep you in the loop. How frustrating that must have been for an ambitious young officer. One with great potential. Look how far you've risen."

"Sorry," Lambert said, her voice brittle now, "is there a point to all this?"

Archer took a long, deep breath. She was really going to do this.

"The night Tim Phillips disappeared," she said. "You had a message for the pair of them. They were to see their bosses. Perhaps for a bollocking. I bet you hoped so. But before you went in, you listened outside, just to hear what the boys' club was talking about. You heard Gillingham admit he was Demi Reeves' father. That Phillips had been Demi's last client, that he liked the rough stuff, and that he was going to be arrested and questioned the next day."

"Did I?"

"You also heard them talking about luring Phillips to the alley where Demi had been dumped, to confront him. Maybe even shame him into confessing."

"I heard no such thing."

"I think you did. And then I think you decided to go out on a limb and go yourself. Because those prints are yours, Andie."

Lambert said nothing. Her shoulders sagged.

"Just before I came in here," Archer continued, "I spoke to Gillingham and Ashby one more time. And guess what? They both remember you being off sick the day after Tim Phillips died, and you coming in the next day with plasters on your knuckles. Something about burning your hands taking something out of the oven. Gillingham remembered because you never normally went sick, and it was all so out of character."

"That baton?" She licked her lips. Staring at the surface of her desk. "You know, I think I did lose one around that time. Maybe Ashby –"

"What? Somehow put your prints on it on top of Phillips's blood? That would be quite a trick. Do me a favour."

Her eyes were wide. "No. I can't explain how, but someone's fitting me up. They can do clever things these days... facsimile fingerprints on latex gloves..."

"You're blustering, Superintendent Lambert. You think I don't know bluster when I hear it?"

"But why me? Why would I have gone so far as to kill him? I mean, if what you say is true, DCI Gillingham, as Demi's father, had a powerful motive. As Paul's friend, and a man immersed in Demi's murder enquiry, so did DI Ashby. What possible motive would I have had?"

"Yes," Archer admitted, "I might have struggled with that myself. Except for a phone call I received a short while ago. You see, the night Demi died, someone at a fundraiser with Tim Phillips witnessed Tim's mask of bonhomie slip, not once but twice. First he took a phone call and got nasty about a change of plan. We think he was being told his usual prostitute, Suzy Reeves, couldn't see him that night, but that a replacement was being sent. We know that was Demi. But that witness also saw Tim in an ugly, passionate, confrontation with a woman, outside the building. Not his wife. Our witness swears it looked like a lovers' quarrel."

"What does any of this have to do with me?"

"You can't guess?" She remembered the nervous excitement in Adam's voice on the phone. His determination to do the right thing. She was proud of him. "Our witness had just seen the same woman on the TV news, making a statement at a press conference about the local gangland killings and the Desmond Connolly arrest."

"Seriously?" Lambert shook her head. "Who is this witness?"

"That will come out in due course. But we will hold a video identification parade, and I've little doubt he'll pick you out." Archer finally allowed herself the faintest smile. "You know, it's funny. He probably would have forgotten the whole thing, if Tim hadn't gone missing, with all the hue and cry. The media were making him out to be the sweetest guy, and he'd seen another side of him. He wasn't even sure he remembered what the woman looked like, and then you jogged his memory on TV."

"Good luck with making that stand up."

"You might be right. But with the baton, I doubt I have to."

"Look," Lambert said. "I don't know who's trying to fit me up, or why, but it won't work. Maybe you're just trying to help your colleagues, but you're really not. And you're certainly not helping your own prospects. So get out of my office now and we'll forget this conversation ever happened."

"I don't think so," she said. "Andie, if you were in my shoes, you'd think you had a strong case. That baton is proof enough that you killed Tim Phillips. It'll be matched to his injuries, his blood. There's your prints. And you think there won't be more evidence? Even after all this time? We'll scrape the murder scene back, layer by layer. Question everyone who might have seen you in the area –"

"Good luck with that too."

"I know. Eleven years ago, who remembers? But we'll nail you in the end. The colleagues you say I'm protecting have come clean. They've owned up to enough to harm their careers, but not to murder. I believe them. Give me a reason to believe *you*."

"You're off the case."

"Really? Tell my line manager."

"Then caution me. If you have the guts."

"Oh," Archer said, "I have the guts. Just a second."

She stood up, realised her legs were wobbly, but did her best to look confident as she crossed to the door. She opened it. Baines leaned against the wall opposite, hands in pockets.

"Could you come in for a second, Dan?" she said, loudly enough for Lambert to hear. "I'm about to caution Superintendent Lambert."

If the prospect scared Baines, he wasn't showing it. He entered the room with a cool Archer admired, and stood witness while she read the senior officer her rights.

"There," Archer said, "it's all official now. We can get you a lawyer. I can place you under arrest now, if you want. But this is your last chance to tell the truth. It's over. Why not make it easier on yourself? Stop defending a hopeless position."

Lambert's eyes were hard and, for a moment, Archer anticipated more bombast. Then a slow smile crossed the woman's lips.

"I was right about you," she said. "You'll go far." She shrugged. "What the hell? I've had a good run. And, if not for that gas explosion, I'd have had a longer one."

"You're ready to talk?" Archer said softly.

"I suppose so. But can you do me one favour? Hear me out and don't interrupt. You'll see none of this is my fault."

60

Eleven years earlier.

DS Andrea Lambert parks the blue VW a few yards from the mouth of the alley and sits behind the wheel for a few moments, wondering if this is such a great idea after all.

This is all because of Gillingham and Ashby's boys' club. She's of equal rank to Steve Ashby, and a damn sight smarter, even if she is new to the rank; but she's the one who gets all the crap jobs, including getting coffee like some sort of tea girl. Is it any wonder she's taken to eavesdropping their conversations? It's the only way she gets to know what the hell's going on half the time. And, frankly, the only way she hears what they really think about her. Ashby apparently wouldn't kick her out of bed, but he's not sure he'd fancy having breakfast with her the next morning. He thinks she's pushy, stuck up and too ready to mouth off about her ideas and opinions.

Not that this has ever stopped Gillingham repackaging those ideas and opinions as his own, taking the credit and not once acknowledging her contributions.

Maybe she is a bit serious, a bit intense. She never really analysed why the police appealed to her as a career, not when she first saw the ad and decided to apply. Only later did she see how much it was about righting wrongs. And the drive to do so has also made her ambitious. Because the higher she climbs the career ladder, the greater the influence she can have on crime rates. Making the world a little safer for people.

Including for teenage sex workers.

So fuck Gillingham and Ashby for resenting a clever woman, and fuck Ashby in particular for his misogyny.

And now, because of all that, because of her eavesdropping, she's heard something that's sickened her. Something she doesn't want to believe. If it's true, then Tim Phillips is a

monster. Yet no one is black and white, she tries to tell herself.
Most people are only shades of grey. She knows about all the
good works Tim has done. But she knows there's a dark side to
him too, beyond the decency. And she knows that everyone is
capable of anything.

She shouldn't be here, she knows she shouldn't, not after the
way Tim treated her. She owes him nothing.

Yet here she is. And it's time to stop procrastinating.

She gets out of the car, locks it, and heads for the alley. It's
dark down there, no street lamps. Only a sliver of moon casts
any light, turning the large bins into hulking shadows, lurking
menacingly. Her footsteps echo as she walks further in. There's
no sign of any other person. Typical. After all her psyching
herself up for this, he hasn't showed.

Wait, though. A movement right at the far end of the alley. It
makes sense that he'd have gone all the way in, discretion the
aim of this meeting. She walk towards the figure. He's wearing
a suit and, as she gets closer, his expression oozes confusion.

He leans in for a kiss and she draws back.

"What's going on?"

She falters then. Once she's said it, it can't be unsaid. So
many lines will have been crossed. With him. With the job.

"Tim, you're going to be arrested tomorrow."

"What?" He looks shocked. But there's something else.
She'd expected what she said would scare him, but she's seen
all sorts of fear in her working life. She's seen the look in his
eyes too many times before.

She knows what Gillingham suspects is true.

"Why wasn't I enough for you, Tim?" she says softly. "How
many women would put up with you throttling them out every
time they go to bed with you? I pretended to like it, but it was
always terrifying. I did it for you. Because I loved you. I still
do."

"We've been through this," he tells her. "You wanted too
much. I'm never going to leave Jackie. But you went on and
on."

"You dumped me by text."

"I thought it was kindest. And I was busy. But you couldn't leave it, could you? You had to turn up at my fundraiser and try and make a scene."

"I wanted to talk to you. You weren't returning my calls. And now I find that, all the time, you wanted rid of me so you could be with your whore. The one you had to pay to play your filthy games. Did paying for it make it even more thrilling?"

The colour drains away from his face. "I don't know what you're talking about."

"But you do, Tim. It's all over your face." She gulps in air. "We know. We know what happened to Demi Reeves. How your regular call girl couldn't make it that night and a much younger model came in her place. You probably didn't mean to kill her. What went wrong?"

The smile that steals over his face tells her he's not about to crumble with remorse.

"I don't know what you're talking about. Demi Reeves? Wasn't that the girl who was murdered? Is that what you're doing? Fitting me up for murder, out of petty spite for me breaking up with you?"

"Susy's already talked. Tomorrow she'll be making a statement, and then you'll be arrested." She shakes her head sadly. "Your friends in high places will probably insist it's handled discreetly, but they won't be able to save you."

"No?" He raises an eyebrow, a familiar and maddeningly patronizing gesture. She feels her annoyance turning to anger, an anger that's been simmering ever since she received that short, cruel text.

"I think you're right," he says. "It'll be handled discreetly and, after a cosy chat, I'll be released. There will be no mention of any of this bullshit to the media, or careers will be destroyed. Because, whatever wild accusations are being bandied about, no one's going to listen. And your career will be the first down the toilet, when the Chief Constable hears about this."

She sees that he's probably right. His lawyers and powerful friends will probably paint Suzy Reeves as a money-grabbing whore, accusing a good man so she can sell her story to the papers and cash in on her daughter's death for some drug money.

This was such a huge mistake.

"I came to warn you," she says.

"You're probably trying to entrap me," he throws back at her. "Wearing a wire. Are you?"

"What? No!"

He steps in closer. "Will you let me check?" He moves in on her, hands slipping over her body, patting her down. Part of her is revolted, with what she now knows, but her body's responses are betraying her. She realises he's between her and the exit. He has her more or less pinned against the alley wall. He's unbuttoning her blouse. There's a faint stab of panic.

"What the fuck are you doing?" She finds some strength, catches his wrists.

"You could have something in your bra."

"This meeting is over." She lets go of him, tries to push past him, but his hands are on her breasts now, inside her half-unbuttoned blouse, inside her bra. He pinches a nipple, and it hurts. It's not the first time he's hurt her, but this time it stirs a rebellion.

"It's only just beginning," he says, and he sounds serious for a moment. He is still cupping her breasts. "No wire," he's saying. "Very good. So I can tell you what you want to know, although I'll deny it if you repeat it. And I will destroy you. Yes, they sent me that slip of a girl. I didn't know she was that young, though. They told me she knew the score, but she didn't. As soon as I laid hands on her neck, she started panicking, struggling. And you know what?"

She hears his heavy breathing. He's close enough that she feels the tip of his erection touching her thigh.

"I said," he says, "do you know what?"

She shakes her head, "No."

"It was the most exciting feeling I've ever had. But I never meant to kill her."

And those words finally cut through any confusion she may have been feeling. How dare this bastard brag about it like *that? As if it doesn't matter. Her anger wins out. And it is rising.*

"So there you are," he says, not letting go, not backing off. "But if you say anything, it'll be your word against mine. My lawyers will take you to the cleaners and your career will be over. In fact, I might just have a word in the right ear anyway. Have you chucked off the force."

The bastard. She's come here out of whatever she thought she still felt for this man-monster, gone out on a limb to give him a chance to prepare for what will happen tomorrow, and how does he repay her? He's assaulting her, and then he's going to take her job away.

Her career is everything to her.

Phillips removes his hands from her breasts. "Or," he says, "you can give me a blowjob, here and now, for old time's sake, and we'll call it quits. What do you say?"

"No." *Her voice comes out as a croak.*

"No? Not to save your career?" *He smiles again, thinking he has her cornered, mentally and emotionally, as well as physically. She's seen such a gleam in his eyes too many times before.*

Anger and indignation, turned down to a slow simmer a few moments ago, flare and explode into rage. The pepper spray is out of her bag before she even realises she's reached for it, and she fires it into his face. He roars, hands going to his eyes, and she yanks out her extendable baton, jerking it open, smashing it across his mouth. He staggers and she hits him over the head with it. He goes down and she uses her feet on him, kicking and stamping. He's pleading with her to stop, but she barely hears it amid all that rage, that fury. She hits him again with the baton, then she casts it aside and uses her fists. He's begging, then merely whimpering as she starts kicking him again.

One last kick and the whimpering ceases.

61

Lambert stopped talking. She looked like a woman who had just run a marathon.

Archer looked at her and felt some compassion. But only some.

"I couldn't help it," Lambert said, her tough façade shattered. "I didn't mean it. He attacked me. I was defending myself. I just lost it."

"But afterwards," Archer said. "You should have called it in. Why didn't you?"

Lambert's mouth twisted into a half-smile-half-grimace. "I shouldn't have even been there. Even if I was believed about him assaulting me, I'd used way more than reasonable force. I stood there in that alley, and I made myself think as rationally as I could. The best I could hope for was my career stalling, always under a cloud, or even a demotion. But dismissal was far more likely, and even that would be a better outcome than some of the alternatives. Criminal charges. Prison, and what that meant for an ex-cop. The shame…"

She shook her head. "No. I couldn't call it in. And I knew, if Phillips's body was found there, Gillingham and Ashby were going to think it too much of a coincidence that he'd been killed at the very spot where Demi had been dumped. They'd probably guess I'd overheard them talking about it. I had grazed knuckles and had left Christ knows what on him – blood, skin and fibres, and that was just for starters."

"So you decided to get rid of the body?"

"Not immediately. I needed time to think what was for the best, but I knew I had to get him out of that alley."

"I'd imagine he was pretty heavy. Did you have help?"

"No. I've always worked out, and I do a lot with weights. So I got home, and I tried to think, and at first I couldn't't."

"The body's still in your boot?"

"Yes. I kept playing what had happened over and over in my mind. And that was when I remembered my baton. I remembered chucking it aside so I could batter him with my fists. It must have rolled under a bin or something, and all I'd been able to think of at the time was getting the hell out of there and getting the body away from the scene. Now I realised I'd never picked it up. It would have my prints and his blood on it. Well, you know that."

"You went back for it?"

"I had to. I drove back there, with Tim's body in my car – like some sort of black comedy – and the baton wasn't there. I was scared at first, but nothing ever came of it. Who had it?

"Later," Archer said. "So why Spencer Street?"

She put the glass down. "I didn't know what to do. I was scared, panicking.. I could have attempted to clean the body, of course, but we know that forensics can sometimes get lucky and find the tiniest trace. I realised it would be ideal if he could just disappear forever. But how?

"And that was when I thought of my stepfather, the person I trusted more than anyone in the world. The one person who'd never let me down. I wasn't thinking of burying him under a building, or anything of the kind, but I needed help from someone – someone strong who I could talk to about the mess I was in. I didn't say what it was about. Just that I was in trouble. That I needed him, and it was best that Mum didn't know.

"He came straight away. He was a keyholder for the flats he was working on, and he made some excuse to Mum about an alarm going off.."

"Spencer Street?" Archer was momentarily confused. "We had a list of keyholders. There was no Lambert." Then the penny dropped. "Of course. It wouldn't have been."

"He could have adopted me, I suppose, but he didn't. I wish he had now." Her face softened for a moment. "His name was Peter Haynes."

Archer remembered that Barry Prince, the Spencer Street site manager, had described him as 'straight as a dye'. Prince had attended the man's funeral.

There was a wistfulness in Lambert's voice now. "Helping me on the worst night of my life was probably the one really bad thing he ever did. He told me not to worry, waited until it was dark. He kept a tarpaulin in the back of his van, and we rolled the body in that. Then he told me not to worry. He was going to make it all go away, but we were never to speak of it. Just pretend it hadn't happened." She gave a hollow laugh. "I didn't even know what site he was working on, and it only occurred to me later that he might have buried Tim's body there. Even then, I kept my pact with him. I never asked. If it hadn't been for that blasted gas leak, the case would have stayed dead and buried."

Archer felt suddenly drained. She'd conducted this whole interview on adrenaline. She glanced at Baines. He looked similarly drawn.

"What did you think when he surfaced again?"

Lambert half-smiled. "First I wanted the investigation centred here, so I could see what was going on and maybe influence it. When it seemed to be running into the sand... well, that was why I supported it going off to Reading, where it would probably go cold again." She chuckled. "Funny thing is, I bet that was Gillingham's thinking too."

It was only after Archer had learned whose prints were on the baton and received that clinching phone call from Adam that she'd seen that rare agreement between her two superiors for what it was. Both had wanted the case gone from here in the hope that it would die. One had done so because she was the killer. Now Archer wondered why it hadn't niggled her more in the first place. She knew she'd worry at it like a loose tooth in the weeks ahead, wondering what else she'd missed.

She sighed. "Is there anything else you'd like to tell us before I charge you with Tim Phillips's murder?"

"No. I think I've said quite enough, don't you?" Lambert's gaze flicked from Archer to Baines and back again. "You think this will be good for your future careers? I've got friends, powerful friends."

"So did Tim Phillips," Archer said.

62

Saturday

The whole office was still suffering shock waves from the week's revelations. Lambert was out on bail. It was too early to say what would happen with Gillingham and Ashby.

Strictly speaking, all Gillingham was guilty of was not reporting his relationship to Demi Reeves and his history with her mother. No actual crime had been committed, and even misconduct was questionable – although the blood in the alley that he and Ashby had failed to mention was an issue. Still, he had decided to make a clean breast of it all to his family, and was taking time off to consider his future. He'd spoken of retirement or looking for a fresh start somewhere else.

Ashby was more problematic. He'd known full well the bloody baton was evidence and had concealed it anyway. That it was out of loyalty to his boss and friend didn't help him, especially as Tim Phillips' and Demi Reeves' murders could have been solved more than a decade ago if he'd turned it in. Demi would have got justice, and even an animal like Phillips probably deserved better. An investigation was underway, and Ashby was suspended for the time being.

In the meantime, Archer was Acting DCI, and the division would know more next week about how the loss of three senior officers in one day was going to be tackled.

Baines had offered to postpone the honeymoon, and Karen was fine with that.

"So long as you don't cancel the wedding," she'd said. "Getting married is the important thing. I can wait for a honeymoon."

But Archer had refused to hear of it. "As your best man and your Acting DCI, I'm ordering you to go," she'd told him. "I want some respite from your ugly mug."

"But that'll leave the team three bodies down."

"Then the bad guys will have to refrain from killing anyone until you're back," she'd insisted. "Just go. Get a break. Just do one thing for me."

"Which is what?"

"For pity's sake tell Karen about that damned dream. And see you book an appointment with your counsellor for when you get back."

The working week had ended on a distressing note for Baines when he'd been coming out of the station to go home on Friday evening. Amy Petrescu was waiting in the car park for him, her hair a mess, her eyes wild. Alcohol wafted off her breath as she flew at him, first slapping him hard across the face, then pummeling his chest.

"You bastard! How could you? How could you?" She was sobbing. "Steve's so scared. He reckons it could be dismissal, maybe even prison." She'd stopped hitting him. Her arms were at her sides, but her hands were still balled into fists. "We were friends. I thought you were even starting to like Steve."

"What can I say, Amy?" He felt wretched, not least that she'd been drinking. Drink had been the source of a lot of problems for Petrescu over the years. "You know I can't say anything about the case, and I've no more idea what's going to happen than you have. You know none of this is my decision."

"Not your decision," she repeated in a childish sing-song voice. "You and fucking Archer. You were told to leave the Demi Reeves case out of it. Why couldn't you do as you were told? You're like some sort of Batwoman and Robin. That Phillips was an utter bastard who deserved all he got. He killed that kid, that Demi. Who gives a shit who killed him?"

"You know it doesn't work like that," he said softly.

"Well, it should." She was quieter now. "Everything that's gone wrong for Steve has been about that case, that time. He was looking out for a friend, a friend who'd saved his life. What was he supposed to do?"

There was nothing he could say, so he said nothing.

"You're getting married tomorrow, right?" Petrescu said finally.

"Yes," he said, wondering why that was suddenly the subject.

"Well, then. I hope you'll be happy, Dan, I really do. God knows, you deserve it. Look," she ploughed on, "I know Steve did wrong, but..."

She seemed to run out of words. She kissed his cheek. Turned on her heel and stalked back to her car.

Now, driving to the register office with Archer, that conversation crossed his mind once more. Ashby had been looking out for Gillingham, and the loyalty had been mutual, almost symbiotic. But it had been ultimately corrosive and destructive.

Baines had also seen the murderous results of Mad Willie McMurdo's blind loyalty to the Connollys, even to a fool like Desmond. He knew what Andrea Lambert's stepfather had done for her out of family loyalty. And it was a sort of misplaced loyalty to a dead daughter that was leading Karen's parents to ruin her wedding day.

He wondered if loyalty was a little overrated.

"You're quiet," Archer said. "Not second thoughts, I trust?"

"Never." He glanced at her. He had to admit that Archer had scrubbed up very well in a pink dress that worked perfectly with her blonde hair. A matching jacket, hat and bag were on the back seat of her Skoda.

"You've definitely got the rings, right?" he checked for the twentieth time as she turned into the police station car park – the register office was only ten minutes' walk away, and at least she was sure of a space.

"No, Dan," she said gravely as she babied the car into a space. "I remember now. I had them in my hand when I used the loo this morning, and I think I dropped them in and flushed them away."

"Not funny."

"Now remember," she lectured as they walked along the Wendover Road towards Walton Street, "no shop talk today."

"Fat chance," he observed. "About a quarter of the party are going to be coppers." He grinned. "What will we do if a body turns up halfway through the ceremony?"

"What? At the register office?"

He laughed. "No. But if we get a call…"

"It'll have to wait, at least until I've done my speech. I haven't put all those hours into planning your humiliation, just for it to be wasted."

"Oh, God," he groaned. "Is it wrong of me to hope for a murder to save the day?"

* * *

Somehow, Baines had managed to put all thought of his first wedding out of his mind until he arrived at the register office. That had been a very different occasion, of course: a church, Louise in white, on her father's arm. Baines's best man a close friend who had long since drifted out of his life.

They'd been so young. In their early twenties, so in love, and with their whole lives in front of them. In his darker days afterwards, he'd often played that day back in his mind, examining it for shadows that might have warned him of what was to come. He'd even wondered if there had always been a darkness in his life, something monstrous that would forever dog his steps.

He had no time to dwell on it further, because music had started to play: 'Ready or Not' by the Fugees. Archer jabbed him with her elbow and they rose together. He turned to watch the approach of his bride.

There were a thousand reasons why this wasn't the usual wedding, but Karen had insisted on two traditions being observed. He would not see her on the morning of the wedding, and he would not see her dress until the ceremony. Now he saw her, all thoughts of darkness evaporated. She was stunning in an ivory lace sheath. But, if her beauty wasn't enough to drop his jaw, the person by her side completed the effect.

Against all the odds, she was walking down the aisle on the arm of her father.

* * *

The wedding breakfast over and the speeches made, Archer could finally relax. Baines and Karen were circulating amongst their select group of guests and she had nothing more to do except announce the cutting of the cake.

Her own speech had seemed to go down well – and Baines had been visibly relieved that the threatened embarrassment hadn't materialised. Karen's father had also made a short, but appropriate speech. Apparently he'd been more affected by Baines's appeal than he'd shown, and Karen's mother had been of the same mood. Archer hoped this could be the start of a reconciliation.

Indeed, reconciliation seemed to be the order of the week. Yesterday, she'd received a text from Adam:

I see your murder is solved. A cop! Wow! Glad I could help.

She knew it was early, maybe fragile, days, but she had hopes that she and her sibling might at least get back on civil terms.

What she hadn't told Baines – wouldn't tell him until he returned from his honeymoon – was that she had arrived home last night to find a black Mercedes parked outside her house. She'd parked on her drive and, as she got out of her own car, Cameron Connolly had emerged from the Merc. He'd marched up to her, quite close, invading her personal space.

"Well," she said, determined not to be intimidated. "This is a surprise. You could have just called if you fancied another coffee. Although," she added before he could utter the retort she saw forming on his lips, "that's probably not going to happen in the circumstances."

He didn't crack a smile. "I just wanted to tell you in person. I gave you Willie's number because you were concerned about him. Not so the police could kill him and arrest my brother. Des is an arsehole, but he's still a Connolly."

"So you've told me. Now, if you'll excuse me…" She stopped talking as an ugly thought crossed her mind. "How do you know where I live?"

He laughed, an ugly sound. "I told you. I'm quite the detective myself. And I haven't finished." He put his face very close to hers. Close enough to kiss her. "I told you. I make a very bad enemy. Maybe one day you'll find out just how bad."

She stared unflinchingly into his eyes. "Ooh," she said. "I'm scared."

"You should be," he said, and he stalked back to his car. She watched him walk away then went indoors. Barney was there and came to wind himself around her legs as she closed the door and leaned against it.

Only then had she started shaking.

Alone for a moment, she surveyed the room. Baines was talking to Joan Collins and the date she'd brought with her. What little she'd seen of Charlie, she'd liked. She mentally wished the couple well. Collins deserved a life outside work, and maybe she finally had a reason to spend just a little less time in the office.

"Nice wedding," a voice murmured in her ear.

She turned to face Dominic. "It is. They deserve to be happy."

"There's only one thing missing," he said.

"Oh?"

He gestured towards a speaker above them. "This pub has decent music, but there's no dancing."

"I don't really think it's a dancing kind of wedding."

"No?" He raised an eyebrow. "Fancy being a rebel?"

Lonestar: 'Amazed' was playing. "You mean…?"

He held out his arms. "Oh, come on, Lizzie. You're looking gorgeous and I love this track."

She looked at him as the music washed over her. Why the hell not? She put her glass down on a nearby table, and then she was in his arms.

"Our first dance together," he murmured.

She snuggled a little closer, laying her head on his shoulder. "Play your cards right, mister, and we might even risk our first kiss before the night's out."

"I might hold you to that."

Change was in the air, and not just at work.

ACKNOWLEDGEMENTS

As usual, it's taken a lot of people to help get this book out of my head, onto the page and into your hands.

I'm indebted to Clare Heron and Professor Sue Black for generously sharing their professional knowledge and helping me get the forensics right. Anything I've made a mess of is all my fault.

Chris Sivers, Debbie Porteous and Vicky Newham have all been involved in reading the manuscript at various stages and making suggestions, and eagle-eyed Sandra Smith has helped with the final polishes needed to make the book as good as it can be. Once again, Jessica Bell has created a magnificent cover.

I've said before that writing can be a lonely business, but the friendship and support of so many in the crime writing community, both online and at the various events I rock up at throughout the year, help keep me motivated. There are far too many to mention here, but I'd like to give special shoutouts to Bob (Robert F) Barker and Janet O'Kane, my partners in crime for over 15 years.

As always, a number of people have lent their names to characters in this book: Lara Moseley, whose namesake appeared early in the Archer and Baines series and has become part of that world; Karen Smart, who I actually only met after I'd already named my character and was delighted to be in the books (sorry, Karen – she's a Baines now); Patrick Mahon; and Belinda Kennewell, who was nominated by Steve Turczyn after he successfully bid for the right to name a character in the 'Authors for Grenfell' auction. As a West London lad, Grenfell is a cause close to my heart, so thanks, Steve.

Thanks, too, to everyone who reads my books, posts reviews and contacts me to ask when the next one is coming out. You're the ones who make the stories live. If you're a new reader, those reviews really do help in this age of algorithms. If you want to keep up with what I'm doing, do sign up for my Subscribers Club, via my website.

And last, but never least, a zillion thanks to my wife, Chris, and my Dad, for all the love, support and encouragement I could ever wish for.

Dave Sivers
Buckinghamshire
2019
www.davesivers.co.uk

Also by Dave Sivers

Archer and Baines
The Scars Beneath the Soul
Dead in Deep Water
Evil Unseen
The Blood That Binds

The Lowmar Dashiel Mysteries
A Sorcerer Slain
Inquisitor Royal

Short Stories
Dark and Deep: Ten Coffee Break Crime Stories

28529339R00208

Printed in Great Britain
by Amazon